PRAIS

"Bardsley launches her Harper Landing series with a touching, chaste romance that sees two struggling people find solace in each other . . . Their shared path from heartache to happiness is sure to inspire."

—*Publishers Weekly*

"Once I started reading it, I could not put it down."

—*Harlequin Junkie*

"Authentic, emotional, and heartwarming, *Sweet Bliss* is the kind of read that you'll want to savor like dessert. With characters you'll cheer for and a romance that will make you swoon, Harper Landing will quickly feel like home."

—Laurie Elizabeth Flynn, bestselling author of *The Girls Are All So Nice Here*

"This sweet, heartwarming love story feels like a breath of fresh air, transporting the reader to a small-town haven where people band together, the bad guy never wins, and you can count on happy endings. A feel-good beach read."

—Kathleen Basi, author of *A Song for the Road*

"As sweet as the title suggests but packing an emotional punch, *Sweet Bliss* is a heartwarming, swoony romance that will sweep you away and stay with you long after you turn the last page. You'll fall in love with Aaron, Julia, baby Jack, and all of Harper Landing, a cozy community where everybody knows your name. Julia and Aaron each have their own challenges and past heartaches to overcome, and watching them not only fall for each other but also bring out the best in each other makes for a beautiful story. Bardsley has written a sweet page-turner, and I can't wait for her next novel, *Good Catch*!"

—Elissa Grossell Dickey, author of *The Speed of Light: A Novel*

"The chemistry between Julia and Aaron is palpable. Their hearts are big and broken and bursting with attraction to each other. I loved watching the two fall in love."

—Casey Dembowski, author of *When We're Thirty*

PRAISE FOR *GOOD CATCH*

"Bardsley returns to small-town Harper Landing (after *Sweet Bliss*) with a charming, uproarious romance . . . As Marlo and Ben navigate knee-slappingly disastrous dates, their walls break down, and they discover what they've been searching for. Their humorous transformation from enemies to lovers is a delight."

—*Publishers Weekly*

"A charming small-town romance . . . fantastic and hilarious."

—*Harlequin Junkie*, Top Pick

"Bardsley is a talented writer with a gift for conveying all the foibles and charms of small-town life. Perfect for those who enjoyed her charming debut, *Sweet Bliss*, Bardsley's standout sophomore effort is a wonderful romance with equal parts humor and heart."

—Elizabeth Everett, author of *A Lady's Formula for Love*

"Finally a novel captures the complex ways that dyslexia continues to inform an adult life."

—Kyle Redford, teacher and education writer at the Yale Center for Dyslexia and Creativity

"With sharp writing and well-defined characters, Jennifer Bardsley takes readers back to the world of Harper Landing. *Good Catch*, the second book in the series, is a sweet enemies-to-lovers romance that is equal parts heartwarming and hilarious."

—Kate Pembrooke, author of *Not the Kind of Earl You Marry*

Praise for *The History Of Us*

"Jennifer's story peels back layer after layer until Dustin and Andrea get down to what really matters—what they feel down deep in their hearts. A lovely story of finding love, healing old hurts, and working together toward a lovely future together."

—Carolyn Brown, *New York Times* bestselling author of *Riverbend Reunion*

"Equal turns thoughtful and sweet, *The History of Us* is a darling read. Dustin and Andrea shine as a couple, and Port Inez is the type of small town that will draw you in like you are a member of the Karlsson family."

—Addie Woolridge, author of *The Checklist*

"Jennifer Bardsley delivers a beautifully written story of love, family, and second chances. You will experience all the feels as the hero and heroine navigate their way toward happily ever after. The characters were written with such authenticity that you will feel as if you know them personally. I enjoyed the love and devotion both main characters showed for their families. Bardsley skillfully handled the delicate subject of Alzheimer's disease with grace and care, weaving it into the story line flawlessly. These two characters truly went on a journey that led them back to each other."

—Joy Avery, author of *Something So Sweet*

"Gripping and emotional, *The History of Us* is a beautiful story of what it truly means to love someone. Bardsley weaves a captivating tale of the complicated but powerful nature of family bonds, taking readers on a journey through the Pacific Northwest with two broken people looking to recover something lost—and along the way, rediscovering their enduring love for each other."

—Elissa Grossell Dickey, author of *The Speed of Light: A Novel*

"Jennifer Bardsley's love stories are exactly what we need right now—books with hope, family, and characters that feel like home!"

—Brooke Burroughs, author of *The Marriage Code*

"With intimate and touching moments set in the breathtakingly beautiful Pacific Northwest, *The History of Us* is a captivating novel that features the challenges and heartache of loving someone with Alzheimer's, the complicated nature of familial bonds, and a satisfying, chaste romance that will leave readers wanting more of Bardsley's compassionate, confident prose."

—Paulette Kennedy, author of *Parting the Veil*

"Jennifer Bardsley's latest is the perfect jaunt through the Pacific Northwest as Dustin and Andrea discover that no amount of time or distance can extinguish the enduring power of a deep connection. *The History of Us* is deeply rooted in hope, family bonds, and taking advantage of second chances."

—Mansi Shah, author of *The Taste of Ginger*

Talk of the Town

ALSO BY JENNIFER BARDSLEY

The History of Us

The Harper Landing Series

Sweet Bliss

Good Catch

Other Titles

Genesis Girl

Damaged Goods

Writing as Louise Cypress

Shifter's Wish

Shifter's Kiss

Shifter's Desire

Bite Me

Hunt Me

Slay Me

Slayer Academy: Secret Shifter

Mermaid Aboard

The Gift of Goodbye

Books, Boys, and Revenge

Narcosis Room

Quick Fix

JENNIFER
BARDSLEY

This is a work of fiction. Names, characters, organizations, places, events, and incidents are either products of the author's imagination or are used fictitiously. Otherwise, any resemblance to actual persons, living or dead, is purely coincidental.

Published by Montlake, Seattle

www.apub.com

ISBN-13: 9781662509193 (paperback)
ISBN-13: 9781662509186 (digital)

Cover design by Elizabeth Turner Stokes
Cover image: © bluefish_ds / Shutterstock; © Checubus / Shutterstock; © feawt / Shutterstock; © Diane Diederich / Shutterstock; © Andriy Lipkan / Shutterstock; © Nataliia K / Shutterstock

Printed in the United States of America

To Penelope Wright,
critique partner and author extraordinaire

SKAGITON MOMS FACEBOOK GROUP

Vanessa Collins
Tuesday, March 1

Wanted: Single moms looking for love! Ladies, I present to you, my brother, Peter Marshal. He's six feet tall, has brown hair and green eyes, owns his own house, is great with kids, and at thirty-three years old, is ready to settle down.

You probably recognize Peter because his face is on the bus stop bench in front of the library and DeBoer's Food Co-op. Yes, he's that Peter Marshal, the number one real estate agent in Skagiton. He can't cook but other than that flaw, my brother is gold.

So here's the thing, ladies, if you want to date my brother, try bumping into him at Carol's Diner, M-F at 8 am. He's there every morning for breakfast. He thinks true love will strike him as he strolls through town. Let's make it happen.

Courtney Nettles
Holy smokes! I don't remember your brother looking like that in high school. Glad I'm single!

Lexie Britt
You and me both, *Courtney Nettles*.

Sabrina Kruger
Your brother sold me and my wife our house. He's the best!

Renee Schroth
8 am? That's right when Skagiton Elementary starts. How am I supposed to be in two places at once?

Alastrina Kelly
I've leaned against his face so many times and not known he was related to you. LOL!

Jessica Luoma
Same, *Alastrina Kelly*.

Courtney Nettles
I hate dating apps. I might just swing over to Carol's tomorrow morning for some pancakes.

Chapter One

Peter loved starting his day at Carol's Diner. He craved the rush of carbohydrates turbocharging his system: the fluffy stack of pancakes, melted butter, and little cups of real maple syrup. Carol served syrup in individual portions since it was so expensive, but she brought out two cups for Peter without asking. Peter appreciated that about her. She took care of him. He would have overtipped even if she hadn't given him extra syrup. Peter always sat at the counter instead of a booth so that it was easier to talk with the older woman while she flew around the diner, tending to customers. He valued their familiar routine. But today when he showed up for breakfast, his normal seat was taped off.

"Sorry," said Carol. "The counter is closed for deep cleaning."

"What?" Peter stared at the blocked-off area in shock. "Where am I supposed to sit?"

Carol put her hands on her voluminous hips. "There's a booth available if you don't mind sharing."

"Sure. If you don't think the other customers will care." Peter's stomach growled. He was desperate for pancakes.

"They won't mind one bit." Carol's eyes twinkled. "Right over there." She waved at a booth by the window where two women were already seated. Peter vaguely recognized one of them from high school. "Here you go," said Carol. "Courtney and Lexie, meet my number one customer, Peter Marshal."

"Oh, we've met," said the woman in the velour tracksuit, fuzzy with cat hair.

"Hi." Peter waved. "Courtney, right? I think you might have been two grades behind me."

"You remembered!" Courtney jumped up and hugged him.

Peter froze before awkwardly patting her shoulder blade. When they separated, he noticed cat fur dusting his sleeve. He attempted to brush it away, since he was allergic to cats, but it stuck to him like glitter.

"Sorry about that," said Courtney. "My cats say hello."

"Cats as in plural?" Peter asked.

"I only have four cats now," said Courtney. "Unless you count the ones in the basement."

"Uh—" Peter struggled with how to respond to that statement.

"I haven't gotten the chance to say hello," said the other woman in the booth, batting her thick eyelashes. "Lexie Britt, nice to meet you." She held out her hand palm down, as if Peter was supposed to kiss it. Lexie wore a tight sweater with a deep V-neck that showed off her cleavage.

"Nice to meet you too." Peter shook Lexie's hand. It felt like holding a dead fish.

"My duty here is done," said Carol. "I take it you want your usual, Peter?"

"That'd be great." Peter nodded. "Thanks." He looked back at the booth, considering his options. Either he sat next to an allergy bomb or the woman with a tilapia handshake. Peter chose the seat next to Lexie and slid onto the bench. "Thanks for sharing. The diner's packed today."

"Our pleasure." Lexie clicked her long fingernails on the table. "So, Peter . . . tell us about yourself."

"There's not much to tell. I've lived in Skagiton all my life, except for college and summers in Alaska when I was younger."

"Alaska?" Courtney twirled a lock of cherry-red hair around her fingertips. "What were you doing up there?"

"Working at a cannery to pay for college." Peter looked away for a second to see if Carol was on her way with a glass of water. He never ordered coffee with breakfast because he drank coffee afterward with his coworker Noelle. They were usually the first two people in the office together, and Peter treasured that alone time with her. It was too bad he wasn't eating breakfast with Noelle instead.

Peter would do anything for Noelle. He had read the same thriller she'd checked out from the library, just so he could talk to her about it. He had taken the blame for her when Rick, the owner of Windswept Realty, had gotten mad that the thermostat had been cranked up to seventy instead of sixty-six. He cut hydrangeas from his yard each summer and brought bouquets for every agent's desk so that he'd have a valid excuse to bring Noelle flowers. Hell, he'd even signed up to coach her son's Little League team. First it had been Tee Ball, and now it was Coach Pitch. He'd been doing it for the past two and a half years since her husband, Jeff, had died. But the one thing Peter wouldn't do was make Noelle feel uncomfortable, which was why he had never told her how he felt.

"You're a real estate agent, right?" Lexie asked, pulling Peter's thoughts away from Noelle. Lexie rested an elbow on the table and gazed at him. "I recognize your face from the bus stop ad."

"You got me." Peter grinned. "What about you two? What do you do for a living?"

Both women began to speak at once, but Lexie spoke louder, edging Courtney out.

"I own my own salon." Lexie arched her back. "You've probably seen the purple sign I had custom made."

"The salon on Second Street?" Peter asked.

"That's right." Lexie beamed. "Beach Blonde." She raked her fingers through his hair. "Have you ever thought of adding babylights? I could bring out the natural gold in your hair."

Peter had no idea what babylights were, but he didn't want to give Lexie another excuse to mess with his hair. "I don't mind the brown," he said, pulling away. "My sister's a brunette too."

"Vanessa?" Courtney asked. "Am I remembering that right?"

Peter nodded. "Vanessa Collins. She's three years older than me."

Lexie's cheeks turned red. "I think I recognize her name from Skagiton Moms, but I'm not sure." She and Courtney exchanged a fleeting glance that made Peter instantly regret mentioning his sister.

Vanessa knew everyone in Skagiton. According to her, she ruled the town. Normally Peter was proud of his sister. Growing up under the shelter of an older sibling like her had been a blessing. Even to this day he benefited from being her brother. Vanessa referred a new client to Peter almost every week. But Vanessa was also opinionated, and occasionally, her passionate views got them both into trouble. Last year she'd spearheaded a campaign to make the school district cancel Grandparents' Day, because it was unfair to students whose grandparents had passed away, lived out of state, or were estranged. *Like their mom.* The level of envy still under his sister's surface surprised him. Debbie, the Windswept Realty office manager and grandmother of two, had blamed Peter for the fiasco, as if *he* were responsible.

"Oh boy," said Peter. "I saw that look between you two. What did my sister do now?"

"Nothing," said Courtney. "Although I think Vanessa is still peeved that Skagiton Elementary held firm on Grandparents' Day."

"I could go my whole life and never hear Grandparents' Day mentioned again, and that would be great," said Peter.

"Order up," said Carol, sliding a plate of pancakes and a glass of water in front of him.

"Thanks, Carol." Peter picked up his fork.

"Why'd Peter get served so fast?" Lexie asked.

"Because he's my favorite." Carol pinched Peter's cheek. "How's this booth doing? Too cozy?"

"Just the right type of cozy." Lexie scooted closer to Peter. "But where's my egg white omelet with spinach and turkey bacon? I ordered it a while ago."

"Turkey bacon," Carol muttered under her breath. Peter hid a smile at her tone. "Weird orders take longer, but I'll check on it." She looked at Courtney. "You're still fine with that coffee and muffin, right?"

"It's delicious." Courtney popped a blueberry in her mouth. When she moved her arm, a bit of cat hair puffed into the air, causing Peter to sneeze.

"Be right back," said Carol.

Peter wiped his nose with the paper napkin. "Excuse me."

"I haven't been sick a day in my life since I started going to CrossFit," said Lexie. "Do you want to see pictures?"

"Oh, ah . . . maybe in a bit." Peter poured syrup over his pancakes, trying to avoid eye contact. "Courtney was going to tell us about herself."

"That's right." Courtney brightened. "It's my turn." She put down her muffin. "I run a cat rescue in my basement. It's a registered nonprofit, and I've placed two hundred and forty-six pets with new owners in the past six years."

"That's amazing," said Peter. "Well done."

"Thanks." Courtney folded her muffin wrapper into thirds. "My daughters help me when they're home. They're in first and fourth grade but spend every other week with my ex."

"They spend equal time with both of you?" Peter asked. He always listened closely when people discussed child-custody arrangements. He'd been eight years old when their mom had run off and never looked back.

"Yes," said Courtney. "I get along great with my ex-husband. He's a wonderful father; we just weren't right for each other."

"What about you?" Lexie asked. "Do you have kids?"

Peter shook his head. "Not unless you count my three nephews or the T. Rexes."

"The T. Rexes?" Courtney asked.

"The Little League team I coach."

"Between coaching and working, you must not have a lot of time for dating." Lexie leaned her elbow on the table. "Are you seeing anyone?"

"No, not at the moment." The only woman Peter wanted to date was Noelle, but she wasn't over Jeff—he could see that. She didn't date, and she still wore her wedding ring. Noelle's desk was like a shrine to her late husband, covered with pictures of their life together. Plus, she lived with her mother-in-law. After Jeff had died, his mom had moved in with Noelle and her young son, Daniel, to help, since day care costs were astronomically high. No, Noelle was definitely not ready to move on. "I was dating a pharmacist from Harper Landing," he said, "but we ended things last year."

"Why'd you break up?" Courtney asked.

Because she wasn't Noelle, Peter thought to himself. "It just didn't work out," he said instead. He might have said more, but an enormous sneeze overtook him. Peter wiped his nose. "I'm not sick," he promised. "It's allergies."

"Something's in the air," said Courtney. "Everywhere I go, people are sneezing."

"I wonder why?" Lexie asked, in a tone that struck Peter as being snide.

"Pollen, I guess," said Courtney. "Someone posted on Skagiton Moms that the maples are supposed to be worse than ever this year."

"If it's on Skagiton Moms, then it must be true." Peter speared his fork into the last morsel of pancakes. "Vanessa talks about Skagiton Moms all the time."

"Enough about Vanessa." Lexie squeezed Peter's biceps. "Let's talk about your muscles. You'd blend right in at CrossFit. Would you like to come with me sometime?"

"Probably not, but thanks for the offer. Real estate keeps me busy."

"I bet." Lexie's hand lingered on Peter's arm a bit too long for his comfort before she glided it away. "How many houses do you sell each month?"

Peter wriggled a couple of inches farther away from her and finished chewing. "It depends on the month. November through February tends to be slow, but usually I clear a few deals a month. Sometimes as many as nine or ten."

"What's your commission?" Lexie asked.

"Three percent." Peter had no issue answering that question because clients asked it all the time, but he could practically see dollar signs spinning around in Lexie's mind as she added up his earnings.

"So on a house that sold for seven hundred and fifty thousand dollars, you take home about twenty thousand?" she asked.

Peter nodded. "But I have to pay taxes on that, plus fees, my health insurance, and retirement savings. It sounds like more money than it is once you take out funds for all of that."

"That's really great," said Courtney. "I remember when . . ." Her eyes became wide, and she didn't finish her sentence.

"When what?" he prompted.

"Um . . . when I used to see you at church when we were younger," she said. "My mom volunteered a lot."

"I didn't go to church," said Peter. Too late, he realized what she meant: the food pantry at Skagiton Methodist, which he and Vanessa had relied on frequently back then. "Yeah," he said. "Times change." He checked his watch. "Speaking of which, I better be off to work." If he lingered, he'd miss the chance to drink coffee with Noelle. Peter opened his wallet and took out two twenty-dollar bills. He laid them on the table right as Carol came to deliver Lexie's egg white omelet.

"Leaving so soon?" Carol asked.

"I've got a coffee date." Peter stood.

"You do?" Lexie asked.

"Not really," he admitted. *I wish.* "But I do need to get to work."

"Always rushing off, this one." Carol picked up the cash. "You want change?"

"Change from you?" Peter shook his head. "Never."

Carol folded the money and put it into her apron pocket. "You spoil me."

Peter grinned. "Because you're worth it."

"And you're a big goofball, but I love you. See you tomorrow?" Carol asked.

"I'll be here." He turned to Courtney and Lexie. "Ladies, it was nice seeing you. Have a great—" Peter sneezed three times in a row. "—day," he finished.

"Nobody gets sick at CrossFit," said Lexie. She wiggled her fingers in a flirty wave. "Think about it."

Peter blew his nose. "Thanks, but no thanks," he said, no longer caring if they noticed how fast he hustled out the door. What was his sister saying in that darn group?

SKAGITON MOMS FACEBOOK GROUP

Sabrina Kruger
Wednesday, March 2

Baseball moms, help me out! First off, what idiot decided white pants were a good idea? How in the world am I supposed to keep these clean? Second of all, any tips for me? Should I just soak them in bleach or what?

Jourdaine Bloomfield
Not bleach, that will ruin the elasticity in the synthetic fibers over time. See if you can find old-school bar laundry soap on Amazon. Rub it into the grass stains and let them sit overnight before you throw it in with Tide.

Carmen Swan
409 spray. I'm not kidding. That stuff works.

Tracey Fukui
A little bit of Dawn dish soap mixed with hydrogen peroxide will keep them white. The washing machine in my rental isn't great, but it does have a heavy setting.

Fern Sharp
So many women are suggesting chemicals. Why not try an organic alternative like baking soda and lemon juice?

Anissa Solas
Have you tried rubbing detergent directly onto the stain?

Vanessa Collins
Baseball mom here, three sons and a combined total of twelve years of baseball drama. Keep a tube of stain stick with you in the car and then on the way home have the kids work on the spots. When you get home, immediately put the pants in the washing machine on the overnight soak setting, and then wash them like normal in the morning. Your snazzy white pants will thank you.

Chapter Two

Noelle stood in front of the washing machine and tried to cool her temper. But darn it, Joyce had ruined an entire load of laundry again. Her mother-in-law was a lot of things—artistic, free spirited, compassionate, and loving—but careful wasn't one of them. From the looks of it, she'd added red dye to the load of whites. Now everything was pink, including Daniel's baseball pants. Noelle squeezed her eyes shut and hoped that when she opened them, the disaster would disappear, but no luck. Fishing through the wet laundry, she found the offending item, a red silk flower in the pocket of Joyce's white sweater. The rose was nothing but frayed polyester and bent wire now, and she tossed it in the trash.

"Mom?" Daniel called from down the hall. "Where are my shoes?"

"Did you check the shoe basket?"

"They're not there."

"Go check the car, then." Noelle pulled out her phone. This was a laundry emergency, and there was one place she knew she'd find answers: Skagiton Moms. She was positive she'd seen a post about baseball pants last night when she had scrolled her feed before bed. Sure enough, there it was. Noelle scanned the suggestions, looking for something that might help prevent Daniel from showing up to his next game looking like a flamingo. "Dish soap and hydrogen peroxide," she muttered. "That might work." She raced to the kitchen for the soap, swung by the medicine cabinet, and hurried back to the laundry room.

"Mom!" Daniel shouted. "I still can't find my shoes!"

"Look harder!" Noelle added what she thought was a safe amount of soap and peroxide to the barrel and set the washing machine to soak until evening. Her smart watch vibrated, signaling that it was time for Daniel to leave for school. If she didn't herd him out the door in two minutes, he'd miss the bus. Their Thursday morning was already off to a rocky start. A couple of days a week, Joyce was there to help facilitate, but on Tuesdays, Thursdays, and Fridays, she did water aerobics at the YMCA.

Noelle raced down the hall toward the front door and opened the shoe basket in the foyer. Digging into the pile, she found Daniel's sneakers in under sixty seconds. "Found them!"

"Those have Velcro. I want my lace-ups."

"But these are perfectly fine, and I know where they are."

"They have dinosaurs on them. I'm not in kindergarten."

"Okay, then." The shoes were perfectly good, but Daniel had always been particular about his wardrobe, and she didn't have time to argue. Noelle glanced around, then on a hunch pulled the shoe basket all the way out. There were the lace-up Nikes. She grabbed them. "Do you have your lunch?"

"What lunch?" Daniel took the shoes from her, sat down, and put them on, tying the laces slowly but carefully.

"The one I made you last night." Noelle had barely been able to keep her eyes open after a long day of work, the baseball game, and helping Daniel with his homework, but she had managed to pack him a nutritious lunch: a SunButter seed sandwich with homemade jam, and carrots that had overwintered in their garden. She hurried to the refrigerator and got it. "Here you go," she said, handing it to Daniel. "We better scoot." They left the house and walked at a brisk pace to the corner where the bus would pick him up.

"Will you be home after school to meet me?" Daniel asked, dragging his feet on the pavement.

"No, but Grandma Joyce will be there. I should be home in time for dinner."

"Okay." He turned as the bus drove up. "See you tonight."

"See you tonight." Those were the same words Jeff had told her as he'd pedaled off to work for the last time. He'd even had the same dreamy grin on his face. Three Novembers ago, when she was twenty-seven and Daniel was four, Jeff had been hit by a car while biking home from his job teaching science at Skagiton Middle School. The Christmas that had followed was a blur. She'd taken four months off of work and returned like a zombie. Jeff hadn't had life insurance, and his pittance from his teacher's pension and child benefits from social security hadn't been enough for her and Daniel to live on. Noelle had been the higher-wage earner in the family, almost since the moment she'd earned her real estate license at her mother-in-law's suggestion. Jeff had agreed. *"You're so innocent,"* he had said. *"Home buyers will love you."*

"I love you, Daniel," Noelle said, despite the lump in her throat. "Have fun at school." She didn't move a muscle until she saw him board the bus and ride away.

On her brisk walk back to the house, her father called. "Hi, Dad," she said, slightly out of breath. "You caught me on my way to work."

"Always a hard worker, just like me."

"Thanks." Hearing her dad's approval felt good, especially since he'd been against her working outside of the home.

Phil had complained bitterly when she'd earned her real estate license, and he had made pointed comments to Jeff about his failure as a provider. *"I don't need my wife to be dependent on me to prove that she loves me,"* Jeff had debated. Nobody argued with Phil. Nobody except for Jeff, that was. That was how come they hadn't seen her parents for two more years until a few weeks after Daniel was born. He had been delivered in the hospital, and that had been another source of conflict between Jeff and her parents, who had thought she should deliver at home. *"My wife deserves medical care,"* Jeff had insisted. *"And my child deserves a birth certificate."*

Noelle had wanted Daniel to have a birth certificate, too, but she had been too timid to admit it to her father. One of the first things she had done after she'd brought him home from the hospital was create a file folder with his important documents: birth certificate, social security card, and pediatrician records. It was similar to the folder she'd made for herself with her delayed birth certificate. Unlike her parents, she would never control Daniel by withholding vital documents from him. Jeff had called it *identification abuse*, but Noelle thought that was a bit harsh. She knew her parents loved her, even if Jeff had disagreed.

"You're probably unaware of this," said Phil, jerking her back into the present, "but there are only forty-seven days until the bloodsuckers come for you."

"Huh?"

"Taxes. Not that the government deserves one cent, but you know how it is. Come up for a visit this weekend, and I'll file them for you."

"What?"

"Just don't bring Joyce. You know I can't stand that woman."

Noelle tensed. "I already filed my taxes, but thanks anyway."

"Maybe it's not too late for me to look them over."

"It *is* too late; they're already submitted. But don't worry—I had Joyce give them a once-over before I filed."

"Joyce looked them over? She's a florist, not an accountant. Better start watching the mailbox for an audit letter. The government will getcha if you let 'em. I should know."

The muscles at the back of Noelle's neck tensed. She was grateful that her father was speaking to her, but conversations like this stressed her out. When her phone buzzed, she was relieved. "Oh gosh, Dad—I'm sorry, but I need to go. A client is calling."

"Always working. Attagirl. Call me later."

"Will do." Noelle clicked to the incoming call and was thrilled to find out it was the retired teachers accepting an offer on their rambler.

"I still can't believe it," said Mrs. Gunderson. "Fifteen thousand dollars above the asking price for our little house."

"Your house has midcentury modern charm that buyers crave right now," said Noelle. Maybe today wasn't going to be a mess after all. She had a price point in her head of what she needed to earn each quarter to pay her bills on time and stash away something extra in the bank. It was only March 3, but she was on target to double her goal. "Housing values are rising all across Western Washington, and Skagiton is no exception."

"I do worry about outsiders buying our home," said Mr. Gunderson, who was on speakerphone with his wife. "I wish we could have picked someone local."

"Spoken like a true Skagitonian," said Noelle with a chuckle. "I've felt like an outsider for the entire ten years I've lived here."

"You're not an outsider," said Mrs. Gunderson. "You're Joyce's daughter-in-law. She brags about you all the time at pickleball."

Noelle flushed with affection for her mother-in-law. "Everyone deserves a Joyce in their life. It's like living with my own personal cheerleader."

"Except Joyce was a drum majorette," said Mrs. Gunderson. "Not a cheerleader."

"Oh," said Noelle. "Right. I was speaking figuratively, but again, that's a mix-up only an outsider would make."

"You can't be an outsider when you're Jeff's wife," said Mr. Gunderson. He cleared his throat. "Er . . . former wife."

"Widow, Daryl. She's his widow."

"That's what I said, Kitty. Jeff always helped me whenever the school district rolled out a new technology program."

"He loved computers." Noelle opened the front door of her house and stepped into the cluttered entryway. She overlooked Daniel's baseball gear on the floor and Joyce's floral-shop mess in the living room to focus on Jeff's picture, smiling at her for eternity from their wedding photo.

"Jeff didn't know a darn thing about changing the light bulb in an overhead projector, though." Mr. Gunderson chuckled. "Burnt his hand the first time he tried!"

"Daryl, be nice."

"I *am* being nice. Can't a man remember his coworker without being nitpicked?"

"Jeff often had his head in the clouds," said Noelle. It pained her to think about Jeff, but she also loved hearing people talk about him. "I can absolutely see him being so wrapped up in his next lesson plan that he touched a hot light bulb without thinking. Thanks for sharing that story about him, and thanks for picking me as your listing agent."

"You did a fine job for us," said Mrs. Gunderson. "Joyce is right to brag about you."

Five minutes later, Noelle was in her Honda Odyssey driving to work, basking in the glow of another sale. Her income came in chunks like this, from the commission fees sellers paid when they sold a house. Some agents, like Peter, made the majority of their income from listings, but Noelle's livelihood was a mixture of representing buyers and sellers. Rick, the owner of Windswept Realty, called her the "queen of condos." But the conversation about being an outsider bothered her. As far as Skagiton was concerned, she was Jeff's widow, Joyce's daughter-in-law, and the woman who, for some reason the Co-op Preschool board of directors still couldn't understand, thought it was acceptable to bring peanut butter cookies to the fall bake sale. That had been such an unforgivable sin that shade had been thrown her way on Skagiton Moms the next morning.

Noelle was mortified every time she thought about the incident. Now that Daniel had a food intolerance, she realized the full gravity of her error. She wished she could go back in time and erase her mistake, but she couldn't. Food allergies hadn't been discussed where she had grown up, so it hadn't occurred to her when she had dropped off the cookies that she might be—how had Vanessa Collins worded it on Skagiton Moms?—"unleashing death bombs on unsuspecting innocents like my son Milo, who is allergic to peanuts." That had been the first—and last—time Noelle had ever commented on Skagiton Moms. "I was the parent who baked the peanut butter cookies," she had written. "I am so sorry for any harm that I caused. I thought that individually wrapping the cookies and clearly labeling them would be sufficient. Again, I am deeply sorry."

The cookies hadn't made anyone sick. As far as Noelle knew, nobody with a food allergy had touched them, including Vanessa's son. If they had, she would have heard about it on Skagiton Moms. But still, in a small town like Skagiton, the stigma remained. Vanessa and her cronies avoided Noelle like the plague, and Noelle returned the favor by avoiding any school sign-ups. She wanted to participate in Daniel's education in a way that her parents hadn't. She wanted her son to be proud of her. But after the cookie incident, Noelle was too skittish to volunteer. She supported Daniel in other ways like helping with his homework and showing up for teacher conferences.

Thinking about Vanessa's cookie shaming made Noelle wonder for the umpteenth time how a man as kind as Peter Marshal could be related to her. There was Peter's Mercedes now, parked in front of Carol's Diner. He always ate there for breakfast. As far as Noelle knew, the man couldn't cook. She glanced out her window for a split second before drawing her eyes back to the road. Skagiton was a former logging town, and the Skagit River ran right by it. A wooden boardwalk lined the street, along with a collection of hundred-year-old buildings, constructed from brick and timber. Noelle drove down Main Street several times a day for years and had never noticed anything strange. But today she saw something peculiar: Peter's car was parked in front of Carol's, but he was walking down the boardwalk as fast as he could without breaking into a run.

She paused at a stop sign—chinos weren't supposed to look so good. Noelle wondered for the millionth time what Peter did to stay in shape. He never mentioned going to the gym. But his toned forearms and trim waistline showed a fitness level that didn't come from selling houses. The car behind her honked, and Noelle lurched forward, embarrassed for ogling.

But then she saw where Peter was headed: the Lumberjane Shack, where, even though the baristas were dressed in flannel, they were known for doing suggestive things with their suspenders.

A few years ago when the coffee stand had opened, Skagiton Moms had talked about it for months. "Did anyone see the full-page ad in the Skagiton Weekly Gazette that Mike Swan put out?" Corine Reeder had originally asked. Of course, that had made all twelve hundred women buy a copy of the newspaper to see the picture of two baristas in tight-fitting flannel long johns stretched out in front of a roaring fire and drinking mochas with the tagline: Stop by for a Hot and Steamy! "I heard that Mike's other coffee stands—the Double D Beans, the Lacey Loggers, and the Cup Overflows—were shut down after an undercover detective from the county's vice department was offered 'a little something extra' with his cappuccino at all three places," Corine added.

Most people thought that the Lumberjane Shack was too risqué for Skagiton, which usually specialized in family-friendly establishments. "If Mike Swan wants to have his skanky coffee stands down in Snohomish, that's fine," Dorothy Caulfield had written. "But keep that smut off of Main Street."

Vanessa Collins, who hated Dorothy with a fiery passion that was evident to everyone on social media, had offered a lukewarm defense of the establishment, mainly because she disliked Dorothy so much. "They're just selling coffee," she had written. "Would I want my husband to stop there? No, but only because it's cheaper to drink at home."

Noelle didn't judge the baristas for what they wore or whom they worked for, but deep down, she was jealous that Peter would drink coffee with the lumberjanes instead of her. It hurt, knowing that. She sped by the espresso stand and kept her eyes on the road.

The fresh air helped, but Peter couldn't stop sneezing. He'd been allergic as long as he could remember. Looking down at his coat, he saw cat hair everywhere. Good grief, had Courtney sat on his coat? Why had she come to Carol's Diner two days in a row? It was bad enough eating breakfast with her and the CrossFit woman yesterday. Courtney had come again today right as he was about to slice into his pancake stack and asked if she could sit next to him. He'd made an excuse about not being hungry and hightailed it out of there. Peter stripped his coat off and shook it hard enough that cat fur flew off into a breeze and across the river. An enormous sneeze engulfed him. As soon as he reached the Lumberjane Shack, he helped himself to napkins and blew his nose while he waited in line under the red-and-white-striped awning. His eyes were so watery he could barely see the purple-and-yellow crocuses growing along the walkway.

Peter usually avoided the Lumberjane Shack because their coffee was no good and their baked goods were just Costco items marked up to ridiculous prices. Plus, it was owned by Mike Swan, who'd tortured him in high school. Mike had been Skagiton High's quarterback, and Peter had been president of the Future Business Leaders of America. Peter had been glad when Mike's other stands had been shut down, because Mike was an asshole. But this was the closest place to his parked car that sold grab-and-go food.

"Hey, handsome, what'll it be?" A buxom lumberjane leaned on the counter and winked at him. Her tip jar was packed. "My name's Wendy."

"Hi, Wendy. I'd like a blueberry muffin, please." Peter was annoyed with himself for patronizing Mike's business, but he was hungry. Not hungry enough for a Courtney-induced allergy attack back at Carol's Diner but hungry enough to overlook his principles.

"Coffee?"

"No thanks. I'll drink it at the office."

Wendy pouted. "But you haven't tried my Hot and Steamy."

"Um . . . I'll pass."

"A Honey Dip? A Steamy Joe? A Big Grinder?"

"I'll stick with the muffin. Thanks."

"Your loss." The young woman shrugged. "That'll be seven dollars and twenty-five cents."

"For a muffin?"

The barista wiggled as she grinned. "Most customers like to round up to ten dollars for the tip."

"Of course they do." Peter reached into his right-side pocket for his wallet but came up empty. "Hang on," he said, checking the left side too. Maybe he had stashed it in his coat. He unzipped each zipper in rapid succession but came up empty handed. "Crap," he muttered. "My wallet's missing."

"Sure it is." Wendy's gaze turned steely. "I don't flirt for free, you know."

"I realize that. I shook out my jacket on the sidewalk. My wallet might have fallen out. Hang on—I'll be right back."

"That's what they all say." Wendy whipped out her phone and snapped his picture. "I'm adding you to our wall of Johns, mister."

Peter didn't know what that meant, and he didn't have the opportunity to ask. Courtney was jogging toward him at breakneck speed in leggings that matched her cherry-red hair. "Peter!" she called, waving her hand in the air. "You left your wallet back at the booth."

"Well, that's a relief." Peter felt his shoulders relax. He smiled as Courtney approached him and forgot about her being covered in cat hair. "Thanks for finding it for me."

"No problem." She trotted to a stop in front of him, her chest rising and falling with her rapid breath. "What are you doing here though? I thought you said you weren't hungry."

"Not hungry for pancakes." Peter's nose tickled. "Muffins are different."

"But Carol's serves muffins too. I don't understand."

"I'm still waiting to be paid over here," said Wendy.

Courtney shot her a look. "Oh. Now I get it." She looked back at Peter and sneered. "You're here for a Hot and Steamy."

"I am not." Peter sneezed. "I'm buying a muffin." After unfolding his wallet, he peeled out a five-dollar bill and three singles. No way was he rounding to ten. He believed in tipping, but he couldn't bring himself to pay a woman to flirt with him. "Here," said Peter as he handed the lumberjane the cash. "I told you I was good for it."

"Why'd you pay her eight bucks for a muffin?" Courtney pointed to the menu board. "They only cost four dollars."

Wendy handed him the bag and then made a big show of stuffing the cash into her bra. "Because he's a handsome charmer."

"You told me they cost just over seven dollars," Peter protested.

The barista winked. "Don't worry, hon; you're safe from our wall of shame."

Courtney whacked him with the back of her hand. "Does your sister know you eat here?"

"What does Vanessa have to do with this?" Peter asked.

"Wait." Wendy's ruby-red mouth opened in an O of understanding. "Are you Vanessa Collins's brother?"

"Oh jeez." Peter helped himself to another napkin and blew his nose.

"I thought I recognized your face from the bus stop." The lumberjane fluttered her lashes. "Has anyone told you that you look like Henry Cavill?"

"That's true," said Courtney. "You do look like Henry Cavill."

"I don't know who that is." Peter grabbed another napkin, just in case.

"Henry Cavill," said Courtney. "The actor?"

Peter shook his head. "Doesn't ring a bell. I better get to work. See you around." He almost made it back to his car before his body shook from three sneezes in a row.

SKAGITON MOMS FACEBOOK GROUP

Carmen Swan
Thursday, March 3

Happy birthday to my brother Mike Swan who owns the best espresso stand around, Lumberjane Shack! If you stop by Friday through Saturday and tell them I sent you, you'll get two dollars off a Big Grinder. That's a double espresso with extra foam.

Vanessa Collins
I'm all for being sex-positive but can we maybe not use Skagiton Moms as a place to advertise a business owner with a past history of solicitation?

Carmen Swan
Nothing was proven, and you know it, *Vanessa Collins*.

Vanessa Collins
Do you want me to grab the police report, *Carmen Swan*? Because it's public record.

Tracey Fukui
I moved here two months ago from California. What am I missing?

Dorothy Caulfield
Mike Swan's a borderline pimp, that's what, *Tracey Fukui*. He used to own three bikini barista stands.

Tracey Fukui
What's a bikini barista stand?

Anissa Solas
A coffee stand where girls showed their tatas for tips, *Tracey Fukui*.

Vanessa Collins
They're banned now, *Tracey Fukui*, but it used to be that some espresso stands in Washington were staffed by women wearing nothing but lace and imagination. A lot of them were hot spots for prostitution.

Carmen Swan
My brother is not a pimp! He had no idea what was going on at My Cup Overflows and was completely innocent!

Vanessa Collins
I've known Mike a long time and he's as innocent as Bill Cosby.

Carmen Swan
Take that back! *Vanessa Collins*, you bitch!

Sabrina Kruger
Attention Moderators. Are you watching this thread?

COMMENTS TURNED OFF.

Chapter Three

The bullpen was quiet since Noelle was the only person in the office besides Debbie at the front desk. Most agents didn't come into the office each morning, preferring to work from home. Some didn't come in at all unless they needed to print color copies or use the conference room. But she came in every weekday because it was the only place she could concentrate. Noelle's desk at Windswept Realty might have been crowded next to half a dozen others, but it was her sanctuary.

But this morning Noelle drank her coffee and fumed. She knew it shouldn't bother her that she'd spotted Peter at the Lumberjane Shack. It wasn't her business what he did in his spare time. But seriously? Why would he go there for coffee when he could drink it here with her? It felt weird drinking coffee alone. Normally she drank it while chatting with Peter in front of the Nespresso machine. He always recycled the pods for her because he knew she hated that part. Nobody else in the office was considerate enough to empty the bin. It was one of the first things Peter did each morning. That was their routine, and Noelle was more miffed than she wanted to be that he'd missed it.

She checked the clock. It was 8:45 a.m. Maybe he wasn't coming in today, or else he was lingering over a second Hot and Steamy. Noelle chewed on a hangnail and tried to focus. After turning on her computer, she pulled up the file on the Gundersons and their rambler. They were the kindest couple, and not only was she happy that she had been able to help them get such a high price for their house, she was also looking forward to announcing the sale. She intended to print postcards and mail them to that particular neighborhood.

Lead generation was an essential part of her business, and Noelle was good, but not great, at attracting new clients. Part of her problem was that she refused to post on Skagiton Moms. Anytime someone mentioned buying or selling a home, Vanessa pounced into the comments. "My brother is the number one selling real estate agent in Skagiton. Give him a call." It was annoying, but there was nothing Noelle could do about it without looking like the second-best choice or, worse, risking Vanessa's wrath.

But Noelle still managed to glean new clients from the group from time to time; she was just less obvious about it. One way was by paying attention to what women talked about. Were they expecting a baby? Maybe they'd need a bigger house. Was their husband cheating on them? Maybe they were headed for divorce. Cold-calling was her least favorite part of the job, but she had turned out to be good at it. She followed a script for different situations and had a higher success rate than other agents in her office. Later today she planned to call Tracey Fukui, whom she knew had recently moved to Skagiton from California and was renting an apartment.

But right now Noelle was focusing on the rambler sale, which was hard to do when Peter's desk was conspicuously empty. There was no way he was still drinking coffee. Maybe the lumberjane was on break, and they were taking a romantic walk by the river. Those baristas were awfully pretty. Noelle forced herself to concentrate and managed to send two emails and create an e-signature form before Peter entered the room.

"Oh," he said, his shoulders sagging. "You already drank your coffee. I was going to see if you wanted some."

"I would have thought you'd be tanked up by now." Noelle took her eyes off of her computer for one second to look at him and then glared back at her screen.

"No, I just got here. I had the weirdest breakfast ever."

"Weird how?" Noelle pretended to continue working, but she was only typing garbled nonsense.

"I'm going to need coffee for this. Can I get you a second cup?"

Noelle handed him her mug. "No milk, please, but the almond creamer would be great."

"I noticed you were avoiding milk. I know dairy's been making Daniel sick, but does it bother you too?"

"Me? The former Dairy Ambassador of Hollenbeck County? No. I can handle dairy just fine, thank you. But I told Daniel that if he gave it up, I'd give it up too."

Peter leaned against her desk. "Daniel's not here, so drinking almond milk seems unnecessary, but I love how you bring up being crowned Dairy Ambassador every chance you get."

"I do not," said Noelle, feeling affronted at his teasing grin. But then she became concerned. "Do I?"

"It must be a pretty big deal. I googled it, and your picture was in the newspaper as well as a bunch of farm journals."

Noelle felt her cheeks flush with embarrassment. Had she mentioned it more times than was strictly necessary? "I made vows," she said. "If my parents knew I drank almond milk, they'd never forgive me." It would be worse than the time they had caught her watching PBS in high school. But not as bad as the day they had found out she was dating Jeff. She had been nineteen years old at the time and had not been prepared to be kicked out of the house. Living in an RV parked in her sister Kerry's yard the next year had helped her grow up fast.

"I promise not to tell your parents. But I also assure you I won't tell Daniel if you go for the real stuff this morning either."

"Now you're making me feel guilty no matter what I drink."

"Would you prefer it black?"

"Do you know me at all?" She couldn't help teasing him back.

"How about I bring you a cup of coffee exactly how you like it?"

"How do you know what that is when I'm no longer sure myself?"

He shrugged. "I have a good guess." Peter grinned again, and the dimple in his right cheek peeked out. It was the same expression he wore on the bus stop advertisement in front of the library, the picture that made him look like Tom Cruise.

Not that Noelle thought Peter looked like Tom Cruise. In fact, she actively focused on *not* thinking he looked like a movie star. He *didn't* smile in a way that turned her knees into jelly. She *never* wondered what it would be like to hop in his Mercedes and cruise along Chuckanut Drive. The very idea would be disloyal to Jeff's memory, the only man she had ever kissed.

Noelle deleted her faux typing and tried not to wonder what Peter was making her. He returned a few minutes later and presented her with a machine-made cappuccino.

"A quarter cup of whole milk steamed, with extra foam." Peter set it on her desk. It was the exact way she'd prepared her coffee before Daniel's diagnosis from the nutritionist.

"Thanks." Feeling a bit guilty, Noelle reached for the mug.

"Not so fast." Peter held up his hand to stop her. "Before you drink that, you need to tell me about Washington State dairy so that you've done your duty as ambassador and can drink this cappuccino with a clear conscience."

"Very funny." Noelle inched her fingers toward the coffee, and Peter pulled it away.

"I'm serious. Tell me something I don't know about the dairy industry."

"Oh." Noelle sat up straight, suddenly realizing that he *was* being serious. "Hollenbeck is two hours away, and I hardly see my brother and sister at all. I don't have that much insider information anymore."

"You still know more about the dairy business than me. Sam's younger than you, and Kerry is older, right?"

"Yup. Middle child here."

"And Kerry's the one with all the kids? That must be expensive."

"They have six now. Hank's a principal at our old high school, and Kerry stays at home."

"She sounds like a saint."

"She'd love to hear you say that too. My brother, Sam, has three kids, all girls. His family lives on our old farm."

"How's that going?"

"The farm's struggling, but my sister-in-law, Shayla, is smart about finances, so she's working hard to turn it around. Last year's hay crop failed because of the drought, fertilizer prices are out of control, and on top of that, our great-great-grandparents' barn is on the verge of collapsing. Sam might have to tear it down if they can't find the money to stabilize it. Hopefully Shayla comes through with something because it would be sad to see the barn bulldozed."

"Couldn't they sell some fields?" Peter asked. "The price of land's skyrocketing up there near Canada."

"They could, but cows still need to eat. People need to eat too. If developers turn farmland into condos, we'll all be screwed. Sam and Shayla get cash offers for their land all the time but always say no."

"There." Peter gave her the cappuccino. "You taught me something new, and your Dairy Ambassador duty is done." He lifted his mug. "To preserving farmland."

"To farmers." Noelle raised her cappuccino.

Peter took a sip. "This hits the spot. I love drinking coffee with you."

Noelle frowned, wondering if Peter used that line with the lumberjanes too. "Careful not to overdo it with the caffeine," she said.

"What do you mean?"

"Those Nespresso pods are potent, and you already visited that coffee stand this morning." She sat down in her chair and ignored her cappuccino.

"What coffee stand?" Peter froze like a deer caught in the headlights. "The Lumberjane Shack? I've never had their coffee." He sat at the desk next to her, even though it wasn't his. "I did buy an emergency blueberry muffin there this morning, and boy was that a mistake. That's what I was going to tell you about—my weird breakfast."

◆ ◆ ◆

She looked at him sideways without turning her head. "Go on."

"You mean leave?"

"No, don't leave." She spun the chair so that she was facing him. "Tell me what happened."

"Oh." He breathed a sigh of relief. "Well, I don't know what's going on at Carol's Diner, but this has been two days in a row now where the counter was closed for deep cleaning when I arrived, and she directed me to a booth. That's how I got stuck sitting with the cat woman again."

"The cat woman? You mean Courtney Nettles?"

"Yes. Did you know she rehomed eighty-three cats last year?"

"She spays and neuters them too. I mean, not personally. She hires a vet. But Courtney holds fundraisers to pay for the bills."

"Well, good for her. I'm sure she has a heart of gold, but I can't sit next to her longer than two minutes without sneezing." Peter dabbed at his still-watering eyes. "I'm allergic to cats. And dogs. And rabbits. And guinea pigs, if you want to be technical about it."

"But not flowers?"

"No, luckily."

"Wow. How did I not know this about you?"

"I never take a listing that mentions cats," Peter confessed. "Dogs, I'm just barely okay with, but not cats. That's why I have prospective clients fill out an intake form. If they mention felines, I pass the referral on to you."

"So that's why you gave me that family moving to Idaho. I thought it was because you had a scheduling conflict."

"I would have squeezed it in if I wanted to, but not with two cats and a litter of kittens."

Noelle took a long sip of her cappuccino. "This is delicious," she said with a line of foam on her upper lip. "Why didn't you tell me about your allergy?"

Peter tugged at his collar. "I don't know. Maybe because it's embarrassing that a teeny-tiny kitten can turn me into a snotty mess?" He looked at her to see how she'd react. The last thing he wanted was for her to think of him as pathetic. Strong, sensitive, and occasionally vulnerable—yes. Snotty mess—no. "By the way." He pointed to her mouth, and his eyes lingered on her lips. "You've got a milk mustache."

"I do?" Noelle retrieved a tissue from the box on her desk and blotted her mouth. "Sorry."

"That would never have happened with almond milk."

"True." She smiled, and her brown eyes sparkled. "So you were at Carol's Diner, and Courtney made you sneeze. Then what happened?"

"Right. Back to my story. In between wheezes, I left money on the table and raced out of there without eating my pancakes. But I was still hungry, and now I was running late. I figured I'd stop at the nearest place for grab-and-go food, and that was—"

"The Lumberjane Shack. I see."

"But never again. I love muffins as much as the next guy, but my sister would kill me if she knew I stopped there. You're not going to tell her, are you?"

"Why would I tell her? Vanessa hates me."

"She doesn't hate you," Peter said, even though he knew that wasn't strictly true. Vanessa rolled her eyes and called Noelle *"the peanut butter bomber"* every time he mentioned her. "She just has strong opinions is all."

"Believe me—I know."

"I'm sure you do. You're in that 'chorus of moms' group with her, right?"

"You mean Skagiton Moms on Facebook?"

"If Vanessa found out I'd stopped at the Lumberjane, I'd never hear the end of it, even though it was strictly for an emergency carb load."

"I can't believe I'm saying this, but on this point I agree with your sister. Why didn't you stop by DeBoer's Co-op instead?"

"Why?"

"Because it would have been cheaper." Noelle frowned. "But I guess the customer service can't compare."

Peter searched her face to try to figure out what she was thinking. Noelle's cheeks had bloomed into a rosy shade of pink, and her brown eyes flashed with intensity. Was she jealous? There was one way to find out. "I'm just glad it wasn't a repeat of yesterday, when I had to fend off the advances of two women simultaneously."

"What?"

"Courtney and this other woman at the diner. I can't remember her name, but she said she could add babylights to my hair to bring out the natural gold." Peter patted his hair. "I told her I'd think about it. What do you think? Would that look good?"

"Yes, and spring for the eyelash extensions too." Noelle picked up her cappuccino with a tight grip. "So . . . the hairstylist . . . did she invite you to CrossFit?"

"How'd you know that?"

"Lucky guess. I bet it was Lexie Britt."

"That's it! Seriously, how'd you know?"

"Well, I'm the queen of condos." Noelle shrugged. "It's not much, but . . ."

"It's a title to be proud of. I see you with your spreadsheets. I watch you circle names that might lead to new clients." He waved his hands around the empty bullpen. "Most of the other agents here work part time. But you've managed to build a successful income from small commissions."

"Thanks, but they're still small. You get the expensive listings with the three-car garages and the mountain views. I get buyers squeaking into whatever hovel they can find or the divorcées like Lexie downsizing into a condo after being screwed by their ex-husband. Do you know how much babylights cost?"

"No. I'm still not entirely sure what they are."

"They're tiny, subtle highlights that are supposed to look natural. Lexie does great work and can charge three hundred dollars."

"For highlights?"

Noelle nodded. "My hair's brown for a reason. I'm too frugal to pay for something like that."

"I like your hair exactly how it is," said Peter. "But you'd be beautiful no matter how you styled it."

Noelle opened her mouth to say something, but no words came out. She gaped at him like an adorable goldfish, which was one of the only pets he could have. The pink in her cheeks had deepened to a dark red. Noelle put on her headset. "If you'll excuse me, I need to make a call about the Gunderson listing."

Have I gone too far with that compliment? Peter wondered. He didn't want to push her. If friendship was all Noelle could offer him right now, he'd take it. But how would he know when Noelle would be ready for more than friendship? Peter decided that it was time to seek advice from the only woman he knew who was both wickedly insightful and willing to analyze every second of his nonexistent love life. As soon as he was done with work, he'd stop by and see Vanessa.

SKAGITON MOMS FACEBOOK GROUP

Melissa James
Thursday, March 3

Who wants to party for a good cause? As many of you know Jourdaine Bloomfield is campaigning for the school district to start sending free menstruation kits home with every student that needs one. Come meet us at Riverwalk Tapas for happy hour on Wednesday, March 9th, at 6 pm before the school board meeting begins at 7.

Jourdaine Bloomfield
Hygiene is a human right. Let's make sure the school board knows that.

Fern Sharp
School board member here. I look forward to hearing your comments. Also, Riverwalk Tapas is a great choice because their salsa is made from organic tomatoes.

Vanessa Collins
Margaritas for everyone! You know I'll be there!

Dorothy Caulfield
Why should taxpayers pay for girls to buy maxi pads?

Corine Reeder
They pay for toilet paper, right, *Dorothy Caulfield*? How is this different?

Dorothy Caulfield
Because we don't send toilet paper home with kids on the weekend, *Corine Reeder*.

Jourdaine Bloomfield
Which is a huge problem in its own right, *Dorothy Caulfield*. EBT cards can't be used on toilet paper, and that's wrong.

Tracey Fukui
What's EBT? *Jourdaine Bloomfield*

Wendy Basi
Food stamps. *Tracey Fukui*

Dorothy Caulfield
It's not my job to pay for people to wipe their butts. If people can't afford to have children they shouldn't have them.

Vanessa Collins
Check your privilege *Dorothy Caulfield.* There are many families in our area who are one paycheck away from disaster.

Dorothy Caulfield
Then maybe they should move someplace cheaper, *Vanessa Collins.*

Vanessa Collins
You're saying people who have lived here their whole life should move? *Dorothy Caulfield,* I've lived here my whole life. I grew up at the food bank. Are you saying I don't belong?

Jourdaine Bloomfield
If anyone doesn't belong it's snotty people like you, *Dorothy Caulfield.*

Corine Reeder
Amen, *Jourdaine Bloomfield.* Love you! *Vanessa Collins.*

Melissa James
You inspire me, *Vanessa Collins, Jourdaine Bloomfield, Corine Reeder.* Let every woman roar.

Olivia Doyle
If you're a mom struggling with food insecurity, please know that the food bank at

Skagiton Methodist Church is here to help. We are open on Wednesdays from 5 to 9 PM. And yes, we have toilet paper as well as diapers, dog food, and sanitary supplies.

Anissa Solas
Our Lady of Hope also has a food pantry open to our parish.

Chapter Four

"Pulled pork and coleslaw?" Peter asked as he walked into his sister's cozy kitchen. "That's my favorite." There were lots of things that Peter appreciated about his sister, but her home-cooked meals were top of the list.

Vanessa rolled her eyes. "You say that about everything I cook." Her dark-brown hair was pulled back into a ponytail. She dished up a plate for her middle son, Greg, who was six years old. Milo, aged twelve, and Waylon, aged four and a half, were already seated at the table next to their father. Even though Vanessa had three boys, a part-time job at Skagiton Elementary School as a paraeducator, and various volunteer commitments, she still managed to get dinner on the table every night at 5:00 p.m. so long as her Crock-Pot worked. Her family rarely ate out due to Milo's severe peanut allergy.

To Peter, Vanessa was part older sister, part mom. When he was little, she was the one that made sure he brushed his teeth before bed and finished his homework before he went outside to play. She watched out for him when they walked home from the bus stop. Vanessa was still like that now, reminding him to make dentist appointments and pointing out when he needed a haircut. Their own mother, Elaine, had run off "to find herself" when Peter was eight and Vanessa was eleven.

One day Elaine had been making him pancakes for breakfast on a Saturday morning and asking for Peter's help planting tulip bulbs in the front yard, and the next day, she had been gone. In the early months of her departure, Elaine would send postcards from the various cities she traveled to, but then her communication went from sparse, to erratic, to nothing at all. The following spring when the tulips bloomed, Peter picked a bouquet on Mother's Day and put it in her favorite vase on the windowsill, certain that she would return. Elaine loved Mother's Day. She always gushed about the cards Peter made for her. He drew her a picture of their family standing in front of the Skagit River and sat waiting for her by the window. But she never came home.

Their father, Jerry, did what he could, but he was a commercial fisherman who worked long hours. He sometimes spent entire months in Alaska, and when he did, his mother would babysit. Grandma Marshal hated children and would chain-smoke in front of the television, watching soap operas and letting her cat, Bernard, rule the house. Peter's allergies kicked into high gear the moment they arrived, and she'd dose him up with Benadryl until he stopped sneezing.

A diabetic, Grandma Marshal would clear the cupboards of anything that threatened to unhinge her glycemic levels. Not even Peter's beloved toaster waffles were safe. She'd cook a big pot of cabbage soup with greasy meat and lima beans and feed that to them for days. It was better than the frozen salmon they normally ate but not nearly as good as the food they got from the food bank when Grandma Marshal wasn't there. Sugary cereal, white bread, canned corn, pasta dinners, and the obligatory "harvest box" of fresh produce that they had to take with the other goodies—Peter would have ignored all the vegetables if Vanessa hadn't made him eat them. Vanessa had always looked out for him, even then. She had been the only person Peter could count on. Vanessa had been his everything.

"Hi, Pete." Ian waved from across the room. He still had on his postal worker uniform. Ian worked at the main USPS office on Third Avenue.

"Hey, Ian." Peter helped himself to a plate from the stack and passed it to Vanessa so she could fix him a plate. "Everything you cook is my favorite because it's always delicious."

"Flattery will get you everywhere." She opened up a kaiser roll.

"I'm surprised to see you here," said Ian. "I thought the T. Rexes had the night off."

"We do." Peter sat down next to Greg.

"And it didn't occur to you to buy your own dinner?" Ian bit into his sandwich.

"And eat by myself?" Peter raised his eyebrows in mock horror. "No, it did not." It wasn't that Peter wasn't responsible, because he definitely was. He paid his bills on time, kept his rain gutters clean, fully funded his Roth IRA, and always remembered to bring reusable bags when he shopped. But he cherished family. "I'm not like most brothers who hate it when their older sister orders them around. Tonight I happen to need expert advice."

"Whatever it is, Uncle Pete, I'm here for you," said Milo. "Music, cars, stock tips . . . I'm your man."

"Do you need help with your Spotify account again?" asked Greg. "Do you still not understand why you can't skip songs?"

"Yes, actually," said Peter, "but that's not why I'm here."

"You need to get a premium Spotify account to skip songs," said Waylon. "It's so worth it."

"And how would you know that?" Vanessa asked, who was finally sitting down to eat. "You're in pre-K. Since when do you have a Spotify account?"

"Um . . ." Waylon shoveled a bite of coleslaw into his mouth.

"I need another subscription like I need a hole in my head," said Peter.

"That's not true," said Greg. "You need Disney Plus so you can give me your password."

"I thought I already gave you my password," said Peter.

"For Netflix," said Greg. "But I want to watch *The Mandalorian*."

"You're not supposed to be watching anything until you master your math facts," said Vanessa. "That was the deal." She pointed at Greg. "At least for addition and subtraction."

"Moooom." Greg rolled his eyes.

"Did you use the flash cards I made you?" Vanessa sliced her sandwich into bites. "Ms. Bricker said that—"

"I know what she said." Greg folded his arms across his chest.

"Don't interrupt your mother," said Ian.

"Ms. Bricker said that you need to practice your math facts twenty minutes every night in addition to your homework." Vanessa blotted her mouth with a napkin.

"Look on the bright side," said Milo. "At least you're not doing long division."

"Speaking of which, how's your homework coming along?" Vanessa asked.

Waylon burped. "I already did my homework."

"Not you," said Vanessa. "Milo. And please cover your mouth when you burp."

"Yeah," said Greg. "Like this." He slapped his hand over his mouth and let out a loud belch.

"I can do better than that," said Milo, letting one rip. Waylon giggled.

"That's nothing," said Peter, enjoying his sister's look of horror. "Wait until you hear your mom burp. Nobody can burp on command as well as my sister. She used to win contests when we spent summers in Alaska." All three boys busted up laughing.

Ian raised one eyebrow. "Is that true, babe?"

"No!" Vanessa glared at Peter. "It isn't."

"Come on," said Peter. "I dare you."

"Only if it will shut you up." Vanessa pounded her chest with her fist a few times and roared out a belch.

"Whoa!" all three boys said at once.

"Told you so," said Peter. "Your mom is amazing. Which is why I need her advice."

"Absolutely, you need my advice," said Vanessa. "What about?"

"Noelle Walters." He tried to say the words in the most neutral way possible so that Vanessa wouldn't detect the depth of his feelings and give him a hard time about it. But it was too late. She was already scowling.

"The peanut butter bomber?" Vanessa ripped off a chunk of bread.

"Don't call her that."

"It's not just the cookies," said Vanessa. "Her mother-in-law was the lead volunteer for Grandparents' Day last year. I'm sure Noelle reveled in my defeat."

"Noelle's too busy to revel," said Peter. "Why do you hate her so much?"

"I don't hate her. I just don't know what you see in her."

"She's my coworker," said Peter, even though it was more than that. His affection for her had begun a few months after Jeff had died when he'd noticed how steady she was in the face of cataclysmic change. Her calm demeanor had called to the part of him that was stuck in chaos. The world shook around her, but Noelle channeled everything she had into providing stability for her son. Plus, unlike his parents, Noelle never missed the chance to say *"I love you"* to her child. Peter heard her say it to Daniel every time she dropped him off at Little League practice.

"What do you want to know about Noelle?" Vanessa asked.

"How do I get her to like me?"

"Like you?" Vanessa tore off another bite of bread. "Why would you want that? I thought you were going to ask me why she dresses like she shops at the Frump Barn."

"Don't be cruel," said Peter. "I mean, is that even a store?"

Vanessa snorted. "No. But if it were, Noelle could be the model."

"She could definitely be a model," said Peter. Another part of Noelle's appeal was her beauty. Her curvy figure and graceful features could make the ugliest of sweaters seem almost attractive. "Noelle is a beautiful woman. If she wants to dress conservatively, that's her choice."

"Or is it?" Vanessa scooted her chair up and rested her elbows on the table. "Wait until you hear what Corine told me about her trip to the Peace Arch."

"What happened?" Peter asked. "Tell me everything." When you needed to drink from the fount of gossip, it was best to come straight to the source.

"Mom, I need to practice catching the ball." Daniel gazed at Noelle over his plate of leftovers with a serious expression. Noelle knew spaghetti three nights in a row wasn't good for her waistline, but that couldn't be helped. It was Joyce's night to cook dinner, but she had a bridal deadline and was buried in a whirlwind of fake hydrangeas.

Noelle had come home after showing a couple three different condos and one townhome and found Daniel in front of the television and Joyce madly tying bows. Her business, Wood You Be Mine?, sold bridal bouquets made out of shaved wood. Noelle couldn't find one clear place in the living room to drop her purse because floral supplies covered every surface. Jeff had been similarly messy, especially when he had run out of his ADHD medicine, and Noelle had learned to live with it. After depositing her belongings in her bedroom, she bit back the words she wanted to say to Joyce about the mess and reheated a container of leftover spaghetti instead. Now all three of them were eating at the kitchen table. The dining room table wasn't an option because that held the finished bouquets.

"You just need to practice catching?" Noelle asked. "Not throwing?"

Daniel spoke with his mouth full of food. "That too. So far all I like about baseball is the outfit."

"Uniform," Noelle corrected.

"That's what I said." Daniel took another bite, his long bangs falling in front of his eyes as he dipped his head. He had the same mop of curly brown hair that his father had.

When Noelle had first met Jeff at a friend's wedding ten years ago, she had thought he was either a surfer or a mad scientist. Later, she had found out it was a bit of both. *"I climb in the summer and snowboard in the winter,"* he'd told her. His infectious smile and easygoing attitude had attracted her from the very start. But now he was gone, and Noelle felt like a wild rose that had lost its support.

"Jeff was a natural sportsman." Joyce's eyes misted like they always did when she mentioned her son. She brushed the tears away. "He played year round, one sport after another." She gazed at Jeff's photo that hung on the wall and kneaded the back of her neck.

"What was his favorite?" Daniel asked before taking a sip of orange juice.

"Whichever sport he was playing at the time." Joyce smiled, and for a moment Noelle caught a glimpse of Jeff. It was the way the corners of Joyce's lips angled upward when she grinned. Daniel shared the same feature. It had been almost two and a half years since Jeff had passed, yet a part of him was sitting with them here at the dinner table.

"I'd be happy to play catch with you after dinner," she told Daniel. "I'll just need to change out of my work clothes."

"I'd help you practice too." Joyce gripped her forehead. "But I'm getting a horrible headache."

Noelle put down her fork. "Oh no. I hope it's not one of your migraines starting."

Joyce opened and closed her eyes a few times. "I don't think so. I'm not seeing spots. Usually my vision craps out fifteen minutes before one comes."

"I'll make you a cup of tea just in case." Noelle stood up and hurried to put a kettle on. She kept a special jar full of dehydrated herbs from her garden for this exact purpose. It was a remedy her mother had taught her. In addition to being a dairy woman and mother, Anika was also a dispenser of home tonics like this one. The only time Noelle had ever visited the doctor as a child was when she had broken her arm in two places falling out of a hayloft. If it had just been broken in one place, Anika might have set it herself, but Noelle's arm had stuck out at such an odd angle that even Phil had agreed they should take her in. Now that she was a mother herself, Noelle took Daniel to the doctor for the slightest sniffle because that's what Jeff would have wanted, but she still sometimes used Anika's remedies, too, because she'd grown up knowing how well they worked.

After Noelle brought Joyce a cup of tea and loaded the dishes into the dishwasher, she hurried to change out of her sweater and skirt and into something more suitable for playing catch. She didn't own any workout gear and had never stepped foot in a gym. The whole idea of group fitness made her nervous because people might stare at her. But she did have a pair of yoga pants from the maternity store that she'd worn when she was pregnant with Daniel. She added the T-shirt that went with it, a shapeless tunic with a butterfly on the front, and headed outside to the front yard while it was still light enough to play catch. Their tiny strip of backyard wasn't an option. Raised garden beds and a hot tub took up the whole space.

"Where's your mitt?" Daniel asked as he pounded his fist into his glove. "It's all about the gear."

"I don't have one." Noelle de-wedgied herself. The yoga pants were generous in the stomach but tight in the back. She already felt uncomfortable but didn't want to let her son down. "Can't I just throw the ball to you, and you can practice catching?"

"Sure. But what happens when I throw the ball back to you?"

"I'll catch it."

"In your hand?"

Noelle, who knew Daniel couldn't throw the ball hard enough to hurt her, nodded. "I'll be careful. If it looks like it's coming in too fast, I'll wait for it to hit the ground."

"Okay." He wound up to pitch. The ball flew in a gentle arc, and Noelle caught it easily.

She felt a nibble of confidence as she tossed it back. Unlike Jeff, she hadn't played sports in high school. Her parents had needed her on the farm. Yet here she was, tossing the ball in the front yard, and she wasn't awful at it—at least not as awful as Daniel. His next few pitches were wildly off kilter, each going in different directions. "That's a lot of power," she said. "Remember what Coach Pete said. 'Look where you want the ball to go as you throw it.'"

"I *am* looking," said Daniel, only his next pitch narrowly missed a parked car and rolled across the street. Noelle ran after it, her breasts bouncing painfully in her underwire bra. She clasped her arm underneath her chest to provide a supportive shelf.

"Got it!" she called, bending down to retrieve the ball. When she stood, she was face to face with the mayor's wife and two others. Noelle dropped her arm and felt her breasts slap against her torso, like inconvenient balloons.

Melissa James jutted out her hip. "Well, hello there, Noelle. Good to see you." Her shiny black leggings and matching tank top had red color blocks that accentuated her generous curves. In addition to her civic duties as the mayor's wife, Melissa was a body-positivity advocate and shared photos of her Rubenesque figure on her Instagram account with over twenty thousand followers.

"Hi, Melissa." Noelle tugged her T-shirt down and wished that she was wearing anything but this old maternity getup. Melissa and her friends were in designer athletic wear.

"Do you know Corine Reeder and Jourdaine Bloomfield?" Melissa asked.

"Not officially. Hang on a sec." Noelle tossed the ball back to Daniel. "I'll be right there," she hollered across the street. Squaring her shoulders, Noelle turned back to the women. "You're the president of the Heritage Tree Committee, right?" she asked Corine.

"That's right." Corine winked. "I speak for the tree canopy." Her hair was styled in an elegant braid that wrapped around her head.

Jourdaine's look was less polished but equally intimidating. Floral tattoos climbed up her arms and accentuated her defined triceps. "Didn't your son go to Co-op Preschool?" she asked. "I remember you from the bake sale."

"Oh." Noelle felt heat rush to her cheeks. Those damn peanut butter cookies would ruin her reputation forever. She'd wanted to do things differently than her parents and be an active participant in Daniel's education, but that experience had scared her off from volunteering ever again. "Yes, he did go to Co-op."

"I was the treasurer for the Co-op board," Jourdaine said, without smiling. "But my main responsibility was making sure we raised funds to cover scholarships."

"A noble mission." Noelle glanced back at Daniel, eager to use him as an excuse to leave this conversation.

"Jourdaine's a CPA," said Melissa. "If you ever need bookkeeping help, she's your woman."

"I'll keep that in mind. Well, it was nice meeting you but—"

"That's so sweet that you're playing catch with your son," said Corine. "I didn't know you were allowed to play sports."

"What?" Noelle asked, surprised by the question.

"Didn't you go to Trivium High School?" Corine pulled out her phone from the hip pocket of her leggings. She tapped on the screen. "I took my Girl Scout troop to Hands Across the Border last year, and we met some girls from Trivium." She flashed a picture of mobs of people standing underneath the Peace Arch that marked the border between the United States and Canada.

"Yes, I did graduate from Trivium, but they let girls play sports."

"But not wear pants, right?" Corine raised her eyebrows.

"You couldn't wear pants?" Jourdaine wrinkled her nose. "What type of sexist nonsense is that?"

"The worst type," Jeff used to say. *"The type that gets into your bones and makes you believe it's true."*

"It wasn't nonsense," Noelle said on instinct. "Trivium is a small private school. They're allowed to make their own rules, and they didn't want the girls to be a distraction."

"By existing?" Jourdaine asked.

"No, I mean they didn't want the girls' wardrobes to be a distraction. To the boys, I mean."

"It's not a teenage girl's responsibility to make teenage boys control themselves." Jourdaine folded her arms.

"I completely agree," said Melissa. "And it's wrong to tell women what they can and cannot wear, as if they should be ashamed of revealing their body."

Noelle felt ganged up on. "Trivium High isn't perfect," she said, "but name me one high school that is." Her alma mater had been her safe place as a teen. Her teachers had liked her. Nobody had yelled at or hit her. She'd followed the rules, blended into the background. She never would have had the courage to enter the Dairy Ambassador competition without her school's support. "Hollenbeck is far away from Seattle, and people are more conservative there."

"So conservative that girls can't wear pants?" Jourdaine asked.

This was why Noelle never felt welcomed by the other women in Skagiton. It didn't matter if she was attending a PTA meeting or reading a post on Skagiton Moms; she preferred staying quiet to avoid attention. It seemed like every mom in Skagiton had a strong opinion and didn't mind broadcasting it to the world—even about something as innocuous as Grandparents' Day! But Noelle hadn't been raised to speak her mind.

"I need to get back to my son," she blurted out. "It was nice meeting you." She darted back across the street as quickly as her legs could carry her. Her heart raced, and sweat dribbled down her back. The underwire from her saggy bra poked tender flesh. She looked back over her shoulder as the women power walked away, deep in conversation.

"Were those your friends?" Daniel asked as he wound up to pitch.

"No, sweetie. They weren't." The ball flew in an arc over her head, and Noelle jumped to catch it. When the ball hit her hand, she felt a sweet smack of satisfaction. But when she returned the ball to Daniel, her smile faded. Did she have friends in Skagiton? Not unless you counted people from work. Jeff had been the one with friends, and some of them still made a halfhearted effort to reach out to her now that he was gone. They'd chat with her at the grocery store or wave to her across the baseball field. But the truth was she lived in a community that she'd never fit in with, so why bother trying?

SKAGITON MOMS FACEBOOK GROUP

Lexie Britt
Thursday, March 3

My ex is a deadbeat and hasn't paid child support in over a year. He's in contempt of court with Skagit Valley but that's not helping at all. He's supposed to be paying $632 a month and at this point he owes me over $7,000. I can't pay the daycare without that money and now I'm two months behind and they're threatening to pull our spots. WHAT AM I GOING TO DO?

Wendy Basi
Girl, I hear you. My kids' dad won't pay support either. Wanna hire a hitman together? LOL! JK (kind of)

Renee Schroth
Have you contacted DSHS? The Department of Social and Health Services? They should be able to help.

Lexie Britt
Yes, *Renee Schroth*, that's how I got him referred to contempt court.

Renee Schroth
See if they can garnish his wages, *Lexie Britt.*

Lexie Britt
He's claiming no income, *Renee Schroth.* He hasn't filed his taxes in two years, even though I know he just bought a brand new truck and went on a fishing trip to Alaska.

Renee Schroth
How'd he do that? *Lexie Britt.*

Lexie Britt
He's a roofer and works for cash, *Renee Schroth.*

Renee Schroth
Maybe sic the IRS on him too? *Lexie Britt.*

Katie Alexander
You need to go through Support Enforcement. It might take time but eventually they'll get that money for you. My daughter's bio dad owed $20,000 before I ever saw a dime.

Courtney Nettles
I am sorry you are going through this. Hang in there, mama.

Carmen Swan
Find a new guy with deep pockets!

Lexie Britt
If only . . . I'm working on it, *Carmen Swan*.

Chapter Five

Friday morning as Peter walked into Carol's Diner, he was still processing the shocking information Vanessa had shared with him at dinner the night before. Noelle had grown up not being allowed to wear pants? Peter had thought of Hollenbeck as a quaint farming town full of the descendants of Dutch settlers, but apparently it was a time machine to a different era. According to the Trivium High School website, the curriculum stressed memorization, critical thinking, and rhetoric. Mathematics didn't advance beyond geometry, but students did study Greek and Latin. Parents were assured that the theory of evolution would not be mentioned and that the school library was "scrupulously curated to be free from illicit material." Peter had spent half the night googling it all. Now he was tired and crabby.

Hopefully a carbohydrate bomb would ease his frustration. When he saw that the counter was available for seating, he breathed a sigh of relief. "I'll have a stack of pancakes, two slices of bacon, and an orange juice," he told Carol.

"Coming right up," she said.

Peter unfolded the *Skagiton Weekly Gazette* and read the letters to the editor. One was a lengthy diatribe against people who didn't pick up their dogs' poop at Riverview Park. Another was a gratitude gush toward the local Rotary Club for building brand-new bookshelves for Skagiton Elementary School's library. Peter had been part of that project, and it felt good knowing that the time he'd spent sanding boards had been appreciated.

"Is this seat taken?" asked a sultry voice.

Peter turned and was surprised to see Lexie Britt. Her cascade of blonde hair was the same light gold as the cigarette pants she wore, and her low-cut black top matched her high-heeled shoes.

"Hi, Lexie." Peter folded his newspaper to make room for her. She slid into the seat next to him, and he caught a deep whiff of her musky perfume. Wrinkling his nose, he hoped fervently that it wouldn't trigger his allergies.

"Here you go," said Carol, setting a plate of pancakes and bacon in front of him, along with his glass of orange juice.

"Thanks." Peter picked up his fork.

Carol pulled a pencil from her gray bun, took a notepad from her apron pocket, and looked at Lexie over the rim of her red glasses. "Still working on that deep-pocket project, I see. When you talked to me about it earlier, I didn't realize you were doing it just for the money. Silly me. I thought love was involved."

"Huh?" Peter asked.

"It's a salon thing," Lexie said quickly. She shot Carol a pleading look and clasped her hands together like she was praying.

Carol sighed heavily and tapped her notepad. "Do you need more time, Lexie? Or do you know what you want? To eat, that is."

Lexie picked the plastic menu up from its spot wedged behind the napkin holder and scanned the offerings. Peter wondered how she was able to see underneath her fake eyelashes, which were so thick that they looked like she'd glued feather dusters to her lids.

"I'll have a piece of whole wheat toast and a glass of water." Lexie put the menu back in its stand.

"That's it?" Carol raised her eyebrows. "No turkey bacon today?"

Lexie shook her head. "It takes too long."

"But just one piece of bread?" Carol asked. "No coffee?"

Lexie shook her head. "No thanks."

Carol pushed her glasses up her nose, scribbled on her notepad, and ripped off a page. She glared first at Lexie and then at Peter. "I don't know what it is with you kids these days and not drinking coffee. This is the Pacific Northwest. Have you no pride?" She stormed off in a huff before either of them could respond.

"I happen to love coffee; I just prefer to drink it at the office," said Peter, feeling like he should explain himself.

"Me too," said Lexie. "Where it's cheaper. I buy the grounds in bulk for the salon." She raked her long fingernails in his hair and grinned. "I still think you'd look cute with babylights."

"I'll keep that in mind." Peter bit into a piece of bacon. "What kind of project did Carol mention again?"

"Oh, uh . . . deep-conditioner training. It's complicated."

"That sounds like a good reason not to have long hair." Peter drizzled syrup over his pancakes. "I hear you know my coworker Noelle. She said she helped you buy your condo."

"That's right." Lexie crossed her leg and dangled her foot so that it almost brushed against Peter's calf. "I should have worked with you, but I didn't know any better."

"What? Did something go wrong?"

"No. Noelle was a fine real estate agent." Lexie rested her elbow on the bar and leaned forward, giving him a view of her chest. "But I'm told you're the best," she said in a breathy voice.

Carol slapped a plate of toast in front of Lexie and let the dish clatter. "Here you go, missy." She pushed a glass of water next to it, and it splashed onto Lexie's sleeve.

"Hey, watch it." Lexie removed her elbow from the counter.

"Oops. Sorry." Carol wiggled her chest like she was at Mardi Gras. Lexie's bustline might have been perfectly formed by plastic surgeons, but Carol's beat her in the volume department. For a sixty-two-year-old grandma, she really knew how to shimmy. "I better see how the other customers are doing," she simpered in a close imitation of Lexie. She rolled her eyes and walked away.

"Well, that was rude." Lexie blotted water off her sleeve with a napkin. "The service here sucks," she said loud enough for Carol to hear.

Carol ignored Lexie but shot Peter a look over the rim of her glasses, like he should know better.

"I'm not sure what put a bee in her bonnet today." Peter offered Lexie more napkins.

"Could you blot me?" Lexie held out her arm. "It's hard for me to twist that way." She contorted her elbow and scooted closer to him.

"Um . . . sure." He patted her firm tricep with the napkin. "Whoa. Those are some impressive CrossFit muscles you have there."

"Thanks." Lexie flexed one way and then another. "Have you ever been?"

"No, I have a home gym in my spare bedroom."

"But working out with a group is more fun."

"For some people, maybe. Not for me, though. I like to lift weights alone with my thoughts and my playlist. Yard work burns calories too."

"What type of music do you like?"

"The classics. Garth Brooks, Reba McEntire, Alan Jackson."

"Country? Yuck. I guess nobody's perfect."

Peter chuckled, rather than argue. He glanced at the clock to check the time—he didn't want to miss out on coffee with Noelle. Thinking about Noelle made him remember what Vanessa had told him about her high school in Hollenbeck, with its antiquated rules for how girls should dress. Lexie had spent time with Noelle while shopping for condos. He wondered what she knew about Noelle's past and if there was a way to delicately ask.

"So how do you like your condo?" Peter loaded another morsel of pancake onto his fork. "Noelle really knows the condo market well, so I'm assuming she steered you toward a good one."

"She did." Lexie peeled back the lid on a third container of jam and spread it onto her toast. "I'm in the Cedar Winds Complex with a great view of the valley. Originally I had wanted to look at a two-bedroom because I thought that was all I could afford, but Noelle helped me create a budget. She found me a new lender who offered a lower interest rate, and I was able to buy a three-bedroom instead. That was four years ago."

"I bet your condo has already gone up in value since then."

"I've made over a hundred thousand dollars. I mean, if I sold now, which I don't plan to do, but if I did, I'd make a profit. Noelle really helped me out a lot." Lexie's posture softened as she slouched forward. "Her husband's accident was so sad."

"Yes, it is. Noelle has a little boy too." Peter set down his fork. "She's originally from Hollenbeck. Did she ever mention that?"

Lexie sat up straight again. "No, she didn't. But enough about Noelle. Tell me more about this home gym setup you have." She squeezed his arm. "Your triceps aren't bad either."

"Oh, it's not much. I've got a treadmill and some free weights. That's about it, really." Peter didn't want to encourage Lexie's flirting. He waved at Carol, signaling for the check. After removing his wallet, he pulled out two twenties for breakfast.

Carol handed him his bill and then delivered Lexie's with a sharp look. "That'll be two bucks for the toast."

Lexie scrambled to unzip her purse. When she opened up her wallet, Peter saw that there was nothing inside besides credit cards and a gum wrapper. Lexie handed Carol a Visa. "I think this one will work."

Carol eyed the Visa suspiciously before plugging it into the credit card reader. When the card reader cleared, she smiled. "There we go—all settled." Carol handed the card back to Lexie and walked away.

"I'd love to see your home gym sometime," said Lexie.

"Oh. Yeah . . . maybe." Peter left the cash next to his plate. "It was nice talking to you. But I need to get to work." Noelle was probably arriving at the office right now, and if he didn't hurry, she'd drink her coffee without him.

Could you call me? said the text from Sam. I need a favor. Her brother rarely texted her, but when he did, it was usually something important, like when Phil had insulted the dairy co-op board of directors and they had threatened to drop Jansen Farms as a partner again, or when Shayla had been T-boned by a berry truck. Noelle sat at her desk and tapped the call button, glad that she was the only one in the office now so she'd have privacy if she freaked out.

"Oh good," said her brother's deep voice. "You called."

"What's the matter?" Noelle asked, her heart pounding.

"Nothing's the matter. I need a favor. I thought I made that clear."

"Oh. Yeah, I guess you did. I'm just—"

"Always on high alert and stressed out, which is why you should move back here."

"We've been over this. I can't just pack up and move back home. My real estate practice is here." Her father might have lingering authority over her, but her brother certainly did not.

"People buy and sell homes in Hollenbeck County too," said Sam.

"But my client list is here, as are all of Daniel's friends."

"What about your friends? You have people here who miss you, and that's what I'm calling about. I need your help."

"With what?" Noelle turned on her computer and crooked the phone between her ear and shoulder as she typed in her password: *Iluvcows4eva.*

"It's about the old barn."

"I love that old place. I have so many great memories of playing hide-and-seek and hanging out there on rainy days."

"So do I. It was the best place to hide when Dad had one of his tempers."

Noelle shuddered, remembering Phil's moods.

Sam continued. "The contractor came out and said it would cost somewhere between three hundred and four hundred fifty dollars per square foot to restore it. That's a quarter of a million dollars. Shayla's applied for a grant to save it, but we need thirty thousand dollars as soon as possible for the contractor to shore it up so he can begin the restoration."

Noelle knew Sam's farm was in distress, but it had to be bad for him to ask his sister for money. "My emergency fund isn't large enough to cover that," she said. "But I have an equity line of credit on my house I could access if I had to."

"What? No, I'm not asking you for money."

"Then what's the favor?"

"In addition to applying for the grant, Shayla has a brilliant idea for how to raise the extra funds. At least *I* think it's brilliant. *Dad* thinks it's crazy."

"What's Shayla's idea?"

"She wants to host a farm-to-table Mother's Day brunch in the equipment barn. We'll clean it out and decorate it so it's—what did she call it?—'farmhouse chic.' She thinks we can fit in thirty tables that each seat eight. If we charge families five hundred dollars a table and have two seatings, we could raise the whole amount in one day."

"Five hundred dollars a table?" Noelle loved her sister-in-law, but she wondered if Shayla had thought this through. "People would pay that in Seattle, but in Hollenbeck?"

"That's what Dad said. But I agree with Shayla. Preserving historic barns is important to people around here. Our neighbors want to help and can go in on tables together."

"I want to help too. What can I do?"

"We were hoping that part of the draw would be you and the other former Dairy Ambassadors serving as waitresses. That would bring media attention to the event as well."

"You got it."

"Thanks. And could you contact them too? Shayla thought there might be a Facebook group or something."

Noelle swiped her mouse and opened her internet browser. "There is. It's mainly filled with posts about kids, cows, and prayer requests. This will really be exciting."

"You're telling me." Sam took a deep breath that was audible over the phone. "Do you think this will work? Because we're all out of options, and Dad entrusted me—"

"Yeah, I know." Noelle spoke more sharply than she intended. Part of her didn't think it was fair that Phil had given the whole farm to Sam and nothing to her and Kerry. But she would never dare voice that opinion aloud.

"Dad thinks saving the old barn is a waste of money and that we should let it fall down completely. But that's an insurance liability. Kids could sneak in there to go exploring and be killed."

"I can imagine. It's an attractive nuisance."

"Shayla thinks that if we fix it up and plant some gardens around it, that it might be a good place for weddings. Lots of farms have side hustles these days. We should have gotten into the pumpkin patch market years ago, but now the competition is too fierce."

"Dad always said harvest fairs were stupid."

"They may be stupid, but they pay the bills. One of the things I've learned since taking over the farm is that a lot of the wisdom Dad taught us is obsolete."

"Your father's the one who's obsolete," Jeff used to say. *"His ideas are not just outdated; they're dangerous."*

"I don't have an ag science degree like you," said Noelle. "If you think restoring the barn can preserve history and make money for our farm—I mean your farm—then I trust you."

"Thanks." Sam cleared his throat. "Dad said he offered to help you with your taxes, but you'd already done them."

"Yup. I did."

"He wouldn't shut up about it. He thinks the government will fleece you. But I reminded him how good you were at math."

"Thanks."

"Shayla says that you and Kerry should have gotten the chance to go to college, too, not just me."

"That would have been too expensive."

"Maybe so, but with your grades, you might have gotten a scholarship. Shayla does almost all of the business side of things for Jansen Farms, and her accounting degree comes in really handy. She does our taxes, too, but I haven't told Dad that."

Noelle laughed. "Coward."

"I'm not a coward. I'm thinking of future revenue streams, aren't I?"

"Pick your battles," said Noelle.

"Spoken like a daughter who got kicked out of the house for dating a public school teacher."

"The horror." Noelle could joke about it now, but the year she'd spent living in a trailer parked in Kerry and Hank's yard had been one of the hardest times of her life. Joyce had suggested therapy a few times, but Noelle couldn't stand the idea of describing her personal history to a stranger. "Email me the details about the fundraiser, and I'll rally the troops."

"Thanks," said Sam. "I'll owe you."

After they hung up, Noelle posted a save the date in the Dairy Ambassadors group. "`Jansen Farms needs your help,`" she wrote, attaching bucolic pictures of cows grazing in front of the old, weathered barn. She followed with an impassioned plea, recounting how much the barn meant to not only her family but the whole community. Within a few minutes of posting, women began leaving messages of support. "`I'll be there,`" said the ambassador from two years ago. "`Can we wear our crowns?`" asked a woman who was two decades Noelle's senior. Watching the support flow through her Facebook feed buoyed her with positivity. These were her people: the women of rural Washington. If she had posted something like that in Skagiton Moms, probably nobody would have stepped up.

SKAGITON MOMS FACEBOOK GROUP

Alastrina Kelly
Saturday, March 5

(Admins, please delete if not allowed.) I am delighted to tell you that Zara Chapman, owner of our local pottery studio Wheel Me Around, has my father's award-winning candles for sale. My dad moved here three months ago from Yakima and in addition to being a yoga instructor, he is also an award-winning candle maker. He incorporates healing crystals that will help you better connect with your chakras.

Jourdaine Bloomfield
Zara is my sister. Her pottery studio is amazing. It's great for birthday parties or girls' nights out.

Melissa James
Speaking of which, we should plan one, *Jourdaine Bloomfield*.

Corine Reeder
Absolutely! *Jourdaine Bloomfield, Melissa James.*

Vanessa Collins
Count me in. I'll call you, *Jourdaine Bloomfield*, after the baseball game, and we'll set it up.

Chapter Six

Spring baseball meant unpredictable weather, but Noelle was dressed for it. Underneath Jeff's old rain poncho, she had on her warmest coat and long pants. But despite those layers, Noelle had been cold as she'd sat next to Joyce on the bleachers, waiting for the Saturday-morning T. Rex game to begin. Now she was retrieving the blanket she kept in the back of her van. Her phone rang, right as she locked the door. "Hi, Dad," she said. "How are you?"

"I'm doing fine," said Phil, "but your mother's having one of her spells."

"Oh no. Is it a migraine or . . . ?" Noelle let the words dangle. Anika's gynecological problems were not something she would ever discuss with her father.

"The other, I think. I sent her to bed to sleep it off. She drank some of her tea, so hopefully that helps."

"Hopefully so."

"This wouldn't be happening if you'd move home and help out."

"Dad, we've been over this before—my job is here in Skagiton."

"Your mother's not as young as she used to be. She needs help. The kale hasn't been planted, and the only reason we have chard is because it overwintered."

"Perhaps you could—"

"Me? Don't you know how much I'm already doing? What are you implying? That I'm not a hard worker? That I'm a lazy SOB?"

"Of course not. I would never say that." Noelle's shoulders tensed up.

"Because I worked myself to the bone my whole life to take care of our family, and what do I have to show for it, huh? Sam married a feminist, Kerry keeps popping out babies like a barn cat, and you've completely abandoned your mother in her time of need."

"I haven't abandoned Mom. I call her a few times a week."

"She doesn't need phone calls. She needs you here at home taking care of things so she can finally get some rest. Daniel should be here, too, pitching in with chores. He could be helping me clean out the gutters today. Boys love climbing ladders."

Noelle shuddered at the thought of her son perched on that mossy roof. "Daniel's baseball game is about to start. I—"

"Could drive up here as soon as it's done and spend the night. Hell, you could spend all week. He's probably learning nothing but propaganda at that school of his."

"I have work here in Skagiton." Noelle clutched her phone with white knuckles. Phone calls with Phil always stressed her out.

"So you won't come? You don't care that your mother is in agony?"

"Of course I care!"

"No, I don't think you do. You've always been a selfish bitch." Phil hung up on her.

Noelle stared at her phone screen, reading the words **CALL ENDED** over and over again. An icy wind blew across the parking lot, causing her to shiver. She quickly texted her mother. How are you feeling? Is now a good time to call?

Thanks for checking on me, Anika replied. My tea is kicking in, and I just took some oil of oregano. After a nap I'll be okay.

I could have a pizza delivered to you tonight so you don't have to cook, Noelle offered.

Thanks but the delivery guy refuses to come to our house anymore after your father reported him for being a communist.

What?

I just want to sleep now. Talk later.

Sorry. I love you Mom.

Love you too, my girl.

As soon as she stopped texting, Noelle hurried to the bleachers. She made it with five minutes to spare before the first pitch. The only awkward thing was scooting past Vanessa and her giant cooler.

"Excuse me." Noelle made herself as small as possible as she climbed past her.

"Glad you could show up," said Vanessa.

Noelle ignored that comment, assuming Vanessa was being rude.

"Is everything all right?" Joyce asked when she reached their spot. "What happened?"

"My dad called. Why don't you stand up for a moment so I can put this blanket down under both of us?"

"Thanks." Joyce helped Noelle spread it out, and then they both sat down. "Next time Phil calls, just don't pick up. That's what I would do."

"Yeah, well, it's not that easy. He's my dad, and my mom's in pain and needs me."

"She needs to see a doctor. There's nothing you can do to help her if she refuses to see one."

"Maybe." Noelle retreated into the cocoon of Jeff's poncho. "Or maybe I'm being a bad daughter by not moving home to take care of them."

"They don't deserve you." Joyce touched her arm. "Do you hear me? Do not for one second think you owe them anything. Jeff wouldn't want that."

"I know."

"Jeff would want you to be happy and out from under your parents' control."

"I realize you're trying to help, but could we please talk about something else?"

Joyce's eyes popped open. It was rare for Noelle to speak so forcefully. "Sure. How about yoga?"

"Huh?"

"Noelle," Peter called, trotting over to her. "Excuse me," he said to the people sitting in the stands. He climbed between them until he reached the center of the bleachers, where Noelle sat. "I need your help. Would you mind monitoring my phone for me? I'm expecting an offer on the Wagner house."

"Sure. No problem."

"Let me unlock it for you." Peter brushed his fingers across the screen.

"Hey, Peter," Vanessa called. "Why are you asking Noelle to do that instead of your own sister?"

Peter handed the phone to Noelle. "Because she's a trained real estate professional and my colleague. Besides, I thought you'd be too busy with snack duty."

Vanessa stiffened. "I can handle snacks and phone calls at the same time."

A whistle blew from the field. "Oops, that's for me," said Peter. "Thanks, Noelle. You're the best."

"She's the best?" Vanessa asked. "Better than your own sister?"

"It's a figure of speech," said Joyce. "I'm sure he didn't mean any harm."

"Please stay out of it, Ms. Walters. I can argue with my brother if I want to."

Joyce wrinkled her nose and sniffed.

Noelle picked up the edge of the blanket and spread it over Joyce to keep her warm. "I forget how you two know each other," Noelle whispered to Joyce as soon as things had cooled down.

"Vanessa's two years younger than Jeff. I used to be in a garden club with their mother, Elaine."

"I didn't know you garden."

"Ha! No, I most certainly don't. I was in that club for about three weeks before I realized it wasn't for me. But Elaine was really into it. Their yard used to look like DeBoer Tulip Farms."

"Wow. I had no idea. Peter does love tulips. He brings bouquets for everyone's desk each spring."

"That seems excessive. Have you suggested wooden arrangements instead? They'd last longer."

"Um . . . it hasn't come up." Noelle floundered for a way to change the subject. "Hey, what was that you were asking about yoga?"

"Oh." Joyce's face brightened. "Yoga, that's right. There's a new instructor at the YMCA that everyone's talking about. His name is Stone, and he's teaching a new class Thursday at nine a.m. that's supposed to be great for beginners. It's right after my water aerobics class gets out, so I could do a double."

"Are you sure that's a good idea?" Noelle didn't want to be rude, but Joyce was no spring chicken.

"It would be fine. Water aerobics is a great workout, but it's not pickleball. I wouldn't try doing a double with pickleball on the same day."

"Whatever makes you happy."

"I was hoping you'd want to come too."

"To water aerobics?"

"No, to yoga. I've never done yoga before, and I'm nervous."

"I've never done it either."

"But you have yoga pants."

Noelle felt her cheeks blush. "Those are old maternity pants. I haven't done a day of yoga in my life."

"Oh. Well, would you think about it?" Joyce asked. "I could really use a friend."

"Sure. I'll be there."

"Thanks." Joyce patted her knee. "That's a huge relief. Back to that phone call with your father . . . have you given any more thought to what I said about seeing a therapist?"

"I don't want to talk about it." Noelle was relieved when a text came through on Peter's phone and then on hers.

"But—"

"Sorry, Joyce. I need to handle this." Noelle tapped on her phone first.

The game began. Noelle kept track as best as she could while also helping the clients. She looked up when it was Daniel's turn to bat, but she wasn't nearly as attentive as Vanessa, who called for every T. Rex by name as they came up to the plate.

"Attaboy, Daniel!" Vanessa called. "Keep your eye on the ball, Greg!"

Noelle didn't understand how Vanessa wasn't hoarse by now, but the boys seemed to appreciate Vanessa's enthusiasm, especially at snack time, when she passed out freshly sliced apples and small bags of potato chips.

But in the middle of the fourth inning, Vanessa's cheer turned fierce. "Get off our field, you big turd!" she shouted.

Noelle looked up from the phones and saw Mike Swan and two buxom lumberjanes strolling down the sidewalk.

"Two dollars off a Hot and Steamy!" The redhead waved coupons in the air, holding on to Mike's arm for support as she balanced on razor-sharp stiletto boots.

"Coupons, get your coupons for the hottest coffee in Skagiton." Mike's chest puffed out like a gorilla. Noelle had never seen him in person before and was surprised at how short he was. He couldn't have been more than five feet three, but he was muscular, had a strongly cut jawline, and would have been handsome if it weren't for the punch-me smirk on his face.

"You've got no business being here, Mike. Now get." Vanessa stood.

"I can be here if I want to, Vanessa." Mike spit on the ground. "You're not the boss of me."

"Vanessa's right," said Joyce. "This is a children's baseball game, not a place to tempt the limits of double-stick tape."

"So glad you noticed." The lumberjane on Mike's left appeared about to spill out of her lacy bra at any moment. The flannel long johns she wore barely concealed her cleavage. "Can I interest you in a coupon for a Honey Dip?"

"No thank you," said Joyce.

One of the T. Rex dads held up his hand. "I'm interested."

His wife elbowed him hard in the ribs, and he lowered his palm.

"Are you sure?" the lumberjane asked, batting her eyelashes. "You look like the type of guy who would enjoy a Big Grinder."

Vanessa glared at all three of them. "Time to go home, Mike."

"You don't own the field," Mike said with a sneer. "You're the type of poor trash that doesn't own anything."

"Take that back!" Vanessa hissed.

"Or what?" Mike laughed and jerked on the lumberjanes' arms. "I can parade my employees wherever I want to." The lumberjane appeared annoyed by Mike's behavior, but kept waving the coupons, as if she had no choice in the matter.

Noelle's gaze went back and forth between Mike and Vanessa as she wondered what would happen next.

Vanessa tilted her head to the side, wearing a look of pure contempt. "Take that back, or I'll give you an Alaskan hello."

"Is that supposed to scare me?" Mike asked. "I don't even know what that is."

Vanessa snorted. "If you don't get off the field in ten seconds, you're going to find out." She flipped open the cooler and dug her hands into the ice.

◆ ◆ ◆

Peter heard Mike scream from clear across the field. It was the same bloodcurdling cry he remembered from his summers working at the salmon cannery in Alaska. His company had had the tradition of welcoming new recruits by dumping snow down the backs of their shirts as soon as they had stepped off the bus.

"Time-out!" Peter blew his whistle and raced across the field.

"What the hell was that?" Mike hollered, hopping from one foot to another. Ice cubes fell down his back and onto the pavement.

"*That* was follow-through." Vanessa climbed back up the bleachers to her cooler and lifted the lid. "Should I get more ice, or are we done here?"

"I'm not going anywhere. Shit, that wasn't follow-through; that was assault."

"She put ice down your back. That was a prank, not assault." Peter spoke as calmly as possible. If he didn't diffuse this situation fast, it could very well come to blows. Mike was an asshole, and Vanessa had spent six summers on Bristol Bay. She could hold her own in any skirmish. But Peter preferred settling disputes with words, not brawn, and he knew the T. Rexes were watching how he handled this. Now was the time to be a good role model, like his coaches had been for him. "Mike, why don't you go find someplace else to pass out coupons?"

"Hi, Peter." The redheaded lumberjane waved at him. It was the same barista who had sold him the blueberry muffin. "Good to see you again."

"Um . . . hi, Wendy." He waved back.

"Sounds like you could use a coupon too, eh?" Mike tried to hand him a slip of paper.

"No thanks." Peter didn't move an inch. "But I do need you to leave the ball fields."

"You can't make me do that," said Mike. "This is a free country. I pay taxes. This park belongs to everyone."

"Actually, it doesn't," said Peter. "The Skagiton Little League Association reserved it. I can show you the paperwork if you want."

"I don't care about paperwork." Mike slapped Wendy on her rear end. "Pass out coupons," he ordered.

"Over my dead body." Vanessa opened the cooler.

Uh-oh . . . Peter's fists clenched reflexively, but he forced them to relax. "Why don't you—"

"Hey, Mike," Joyce called. "How's your fungal infection doing?"

"What the?" Mike looked up at the bleachers.

Joyce smiled mischievously. "Your mom told me all about it at water aerobics the other day. It sounds really nasty. I'm sorry you've been dealing with funk like that."

"Gross." The lumberjane still holding on to Mike's arm let go and stepped away from him. Vanessa cackled, and her laughter was contagious. Half the T. Rex parents joined in.

"I don't have a fungal infection," said Mike.

"Did the third round of antifungal prescriptions finally work, then?" Joyce asked. "That's good news."

"No." Mike shook his head. "I mean I never had an infection to begin with."

"That's not what your mother said." Joyce looked over at Noelle. "That's why you should always wear flip-flops when you shower at the YMCA," she said. "You never know what type of gunk you could pick up."

"What did you say to the woman in the trash bag?" Mike asked.

"That's a rain poncho," Peter said, unable to keep the anger from his voice. "Mike, forget what I said about leaving. Why don't you stick around, and you can explain athlete's foot to the boys later. Or was it jock itch?"

"It was neither." Mike's face was as bright red as a tomato.

"It looks like your face is getting hot there, Mikey." Vanessa scooped up another handful of ice. "Would you like to cool off?"

Ignoring Vanessa's taunt, Mike turned his attention to Peter. "All these years, and you're still a nerd." He rolled his eyes. "You're such a loser."

Mike stomped off.

Peter froze for a half second before looking up into the stands. He gave Joyce a thumbs-up and saw Noelle smiling back at him, clapping. After grinning back at her, Peter blew his whistle. "Time-out's over," he called. "Let's play ball!"

SKAGITON MOMS FACEBOOK GROUP

Tracey Fukui
Sunday, March 6

Where's a good place to buy a bra?

Lexie Britt
Victoria's Secret. It's worth the drive down to Alderwood Mall.

Tracey Fukui
Where's that? *Lexie Britt*, I've only lived here a couple of months and still don't know my way around.

Lexie Britt
Down south, on the way to Seattle. *Tracey Fukui*.

Tracey Fukui
Ah. Gotcha. *Lexie Britt*, I was hoping to not have to drive that far.

Sabrina Kruger
Knockers on Heaven's Door at the outlet mall twenty minutes away. A local mom owns it. Can't remember her name. My wife and I both shop there.

Carol Durango
Seconding the recommendation for Knockers on Heaven's Door. They have all the sizes which is a good thing because the old gals aren't standing at attention like they used to. Hahaha.

Katie Alexander
Have you tried Nordstrom? Unfortunately, that's also a drive.

Melissa James
Tagging *Renee Schroth*, who own's Knockers on Heaven's Door. Renee is such a wonderful body positivity warrior. She will politely and discreetly figure out your measurements and get you into a bra that actually fits.

Renee Schroth
Thanks for the tag, *Melissa James*!

Melissa James
I love what you do, *Renee Schroth*!

Renee Schroth
Knockers on Heaven's Door is my independently owned boutique at the outlet mall. I'm running a buy one, get one fifty percent off sale on all bras, and the spring panty sale starts next week.

Rachel Glass
You sold me my mastectomy bras, *Renee Schroth*. Thank you for making a difficult experience easier.

Renee Schroth
It was my honor, *Rachel Glass*.

Fern Sharp
Have you considered switching to organic food? *Rachel Glass*.

Rachel Glass
I've heard it all before, *Fern Sharp*. But thanks.

Chapter Seven

First thing Sunday morning after Joyce whisked Daniel away to swimming lessons, Noelle hopped in her car and drove to the Goodwill. Mike Swan's nasty comment at the baseball game about her poncho looking like a trash bag had gotten to her. She packed up her maternity yoga pants while she was at it and a bunch of clothes Daniel had outgrown. It burned her to donate sweatpants he had never worn, but Daniel was particular about his wardrobe and refused to wear them. Noelle zipped through the donation line and unloaded all the bags. But at the last moment, she pulled Jeff's poncho out of the pile. It might have looked like a Hefty bag, but it reminded her of Jeff heading off on a hike. After she'd completed her errand, Noelle drove out of town and merged onto the highway. She arrived at the outlet mall five minutes later, before it opened.

Sitting in the car, bundled in her coat, Noelle checked her messages, emails, and social media feed. As a real estate agent, she created her own schedule. But that didn't mean she could ignore her phone. Tracey Fukui had texted her requesting a meeting tomorrow to discuss next steps. She and her husband had recently become clients after Noelle had successfully reached out to Tracey and asked if her family was ready to move out of the apartment they rented and into a property of their own.

Messaging Tracey back took a few minutes. Monitoring the Facebook ads for the condo she was selling took a while longer. "What an amazing kitchen," Peter had commented. "This condo will sell fast." Noelle smiled. That was just like Peter—always trying to boost her sales in whatever way he could. She hearted the comment and reminded herself to thank him in person later. When Noelle was done with her work, she still had ten minutes before stores opened at the mall. That provided just enough time to research the reason she was here today—new bras.

Noelle pulled the saggy elastic strap of her brassiere from where it had slipped off her shoulder. The last time she'd bought bras was when she had finished nursing Daniel five years ago. She wasn't entirely sure which store she should visit today to buy new ones. But thinking back, she remembered a thread about this on Skagiton Moms. Noelle searched on Facebook until she found it and read the suggestions. It seemed like Knockers on Heaven's Door was the place to go.

The idea of a strange woman groping her with measuring tape terrified her almost as much as knowing her actual size, which she guessed would be extreme. But hopefully new bras would help with the back pain she'd been experiencing.

Taking a deep breath, she collected her purse, climbed out of her van, and locked the door behind her. A surprising number of customers were already at the outlets, walking around the outdoor space. The line of people in front of the wine store appeared to be part of a tour group from Canada. Americans drove north for cheap prescriptions, and Canadians headed south for duty-free liquor. Noelle kept walking until she reached Knockers on Heaven's Door, right as the shopkeeper was unlocking the shop.

"Why hello there," said the woman. Her dark-brown hair hung in ringlets that framed her face, like she was a grown-up Shirley Temple. Noelle recognized her from her profile picture as being a frequent poster on Skagiton Moms, but she couldn't remember her name. "You're out bright and early," said the woman as she held open the door.

"Sundays are when I run errands." Noelle stepped inside the boutique and tried not to be overwhelmed, but it was impossible. Lingerie of every type hung on racks around her, from demure nightshirts to lacy corsets. The back wall was completely devoted to bras.

"Can I help you with something, or are you just browsing?"

Noelle was startled. "Um . . ." She'd been gaping at the "Boobs You Can Use" display featuring a mannequin hooked up to a breast pump.

"Do you need a nursing bra?" the woman asked.

"No.'" Noelle shook her head. Years ago, she had owned a pump just like the one on display. *"You can take the girl off the farm,"* Jeff had joked, *"but she'll still find a milking machine."* Thinking about him made the emotions swirling around her churn harder. She was anxious about shopping, nervous from being in a new store, and guilty at the prospect of spending money on herself. But most of all she was sad. Why did it matter what she wore under her clothes? Nobody would see a new bra but her.

Noelle wandered toward the pajamas, since they felt safe. "I need pajamas," she said. While technically true—Noelle did need new pajamas; the ones she owned had holes in them—she knew she had chickened out.

"I have a great section of pajamas on display right now. I'm also running a fifty-percent-off special on bras." The woman extended her hand. "My name's Renee Schroth. Nice to meet you."

Basic pleasantries were something Noelle could do. They were ten times easier than bra shopping. "I'm Noelle Walters. And yes, I could use new bras. While I'm here, that is." She pulled a strand of hair behind her ear. "I'm not actually sure what my size is anymore; it's been a while."

"That's what I'm here for." Renee pointed to the measuring tape that hung around her neck. "Let's size you in the fitting room, and then you can shop."

"Great. Thanks." The tension that clung to her shoulders released ever so slightly. Noelle followed Renee back to the dressing rooms.

"Your name sounds familiar." Renee pulled open a curtain and waited for Noelle to enter the small space. "Have we met before?"

"I'm a real estate agent." Noelle put her purse on the dressing room chair and took off her coat. "Maybe you've seen my name on an open house sign."

"Could be, but I don't think that's it. Your face looks familiar. Are you part of Skagiton Moms?"

"I'm a member, but I never post." If Renee mentioned peanut butter cookies, Noelle was bolting. "Should I take off my shirt?"

"Normally that's not necessary, but your blouse is quite large, so it might be a good idea. Totally your call, though. Whatever you feel comfortable with."

Noelle didn't feel comfortable with any of it, but she wanted to get this over with as soon as possible.

"I guess for the sake of accuracy, I'll go for it." She slipped off her shirt.

"Here we go. Let's give those knockers a proper home, shall we?" Renee raced through the measurements so fast that she was all done sixty seconds later. "You're a 34E."

"What?" Noelle snatched her shirt. "How is that possible? Is that even a real size?"

"Yes, it is a real size. You might also be able to squeeze into a 34DD depending on the brand."

"But that can't be right." Noelle pulled her shirt over her head. "I've been wearing a 38C."

Renee lifted her eyebrows. "I can tell. I bet your back muscles have been talking to you." She slid open the curtain and exited the stall. "Once you wear the proper band size, that'll solve a lot of problems. It all comes down to engineering. You wouldn't sell someone a house that had a weak foundation, would you?"

"No, although condos are my specialty."

"Condos, apartments, houses . . ." Renee waved her hands around. "The same principle applies. We're talking about structure." She pulled bras off the racks one by one. "Unfortunately, expanded sizes usually have increased price tags, but good news for you—I'm running a sale. I mentioned the sale, right?"

Noelle slung her purse over her shoulder. "You did."

"Let me gather a couple of sports bras while I'm at it. Do you need any exercise clothes since you're here?"

"Uh . . . I wasn't intending to buy any today, but I guess I do need at least one outfit. My mother-in-law wants me to try out a yoga class with her at the YMCA."

"I've got magic pants for that. You go pick out some pajamas while I stock your dressing room."

"Pajamas?"

"Like you came in for." Renee chuckled. "Sorry to sidetrack you on that."

An hour later Noelle stood at the register spending more money on clothes for herself in one transaction than she'd spent in the past few years. The dread she had felt a short time ago had been replaced with excitement. Renee and her measuring tape were right. As soon as she got home, Noelle intended to burn every bra she owned because her new ones were so much better. Well, maybe she wouldn't burn them, but she'd definitely toss them in the trash.

"That's it!" Renee handed Noelle two large bags. "I know where I've seen you before. Are you related to a woman named Kerry?"

"Kerry's my sister."

"My ex-boyfriend was friends with her husband, Hank. I drove up there for a baby shower a few years ago."

Noelle grinned. "I was there too." It wasn't often that her Hollenbeck and Skagiton lives overlapped. "I'm sorry I don't remember you. My son was a toddler at the shower, and the whole day was a blur."

"Toddlers are tough. My daughter's in kindergarten, and my apartment is still babyproofed." Renee passed over one more bag. "Don't be a stranger now. Remember that my two-for-one panty sale starts next week."

"I'll keep that in mind." Loaded down with purchases, Noelle left the store right as it began to rain. She ran across the parking lot, trying to dodge drops, and loaded her van as quickly as she could. Thunder cracked, and rain dumped down. Shielding her eyes, Noelle looked back at the mall. The North Face outlet was directly in front of her. Her dad scorned people who wore designer outerwear and said it was a waste of money. But Noelle knew she needed a new raincoat—one that fit properly and didn't make her look like a garbage bag. She locked her van and ran back to the mall.

After receiving six offers on the Wagner Street house in three hours, Peter was ready to declare his Sunday afternoon a success. He sat with the sellers at their kitchen table and laid out their options. "Five of the offers are above listing price, and all six are as is, with no inspection. The highest bid is a contingency offer that's seventy-five thousand above your asking point, but the second highest is sixty thousand above listing and all cash."

Al Glass, a retired ophthalmologist in his early seventies, looked at his wife. "Well, Rachel, what do you think?"

Rachel wiped her glasses on her shirt before putting them back on and studying the chart. Rachel was a dedicated volunteer at the Skagiton Food Bank. She cleared her throat before speaking. "Accepting a contingency offer would make me nervous. How many days left before we need to return the money to our IRA?"

"Fifty-five," said Al. "We have plenty of time."

"It's likely that the buyers with the contingency offer will sell their house fast," said Peter. "But it's definitely a risk. I already spoke to the agent of the second offer, and sixty thousand over is as high as the buyers can go. What would the penalty be if you can't return your IRA funds in time?"

Rachel winced. "A lot more than that. Using our retirement nest egg to buy our house in Harper Landing seemed like a good idea at the time, but now I'm nervous."

"It *was* a good idea." Al patted her hand. "Otherwise we would keep being turned down."

"You're right, especially since you didn't want to do the bridge loan." Rachel squeezed her eyes shut. When she opened them, her expression was clearer.

"Buying in a hot market is challenging, but you persevered," said Peter. "My advice would be to go out to dinner and think about it."

"Great idea." Al rapped his knuckles on the table. "We don't need to decide this very second."

"That's right." Peter nodded.

Two hours later Peter was playing a game of *Pac-Man* on the arcade game he'd bought for his nephews when Al and Rachel called him to say they accepted the second offer.

"I'm glad to hear it," said Peter. "You'll have your funds to return to your IRA, and Harper Landing will have a wonderful new couple to add to their neighborhood."

"I just hope that my dahlias will be in good hands," said Rachel. She and Al were on speakerphone.

"Knowing how temperamental dahlias can be, I agree," said Peter. "I'll stop by the house this summer and offer the new owners some gardening tips."

"They need to be staked properly," said Rachel.

"Especially the dinner plate variety," said Peter. "Otherwise they'll fall over."

"That's right," said Rachel. "Those blooms are heavy."

"So true," Peter agreed. "I'll call you tomorrow to follow up. Enjoy your evening."

"What's left of it," said Al. "It's almost bedtime."

After saying goodbye, Peter worked on the sale for another half hour before taking a break for a late-night bowl of ice cream. It was past eleven, and he knew he should go to bed, but he was too keyed up to sleep. Instead, he scrolled through social media, where a post from Noelle caught his eye. "Save Jansen Farms' Historic Barn! Treat your mom to a Mother's Day Brunch with Hollenbeck County Dairy Ambassadors Past and Present." Peter clicked the post and landed on an event page with more details. Noelle had mentioned that her brother's farm was struggling, but he hadn't realized how serious the issue had become. "Preserve a piece of Ag History," said the page. "Barns Matter." There was a faded picture of Noelle as a child, hand-feeding a calf a bottle, standing in front of the weathered building.

Peter hit the purchase link and sponsored a whole table. His computer autofilled his credit card number and submitted the $500 payment. He felt a thrill of pleasure knowing that he'd been able to help, followed by a wave of anxiety after he realized what he'd done. How was he supposed to fill a table of eight on a holiday weekend two hours away? Sure, he'd paid for the table, but how would it look if it was empty at the fundraiser?

Peter laced his fingers behind his head and stared up at the ceiling, annoyed with himself for being so stupid. He supposed he could contact Noelle's brother and make it a cash donation. That was probably what he should have done in the first place. But then, how would Noelle know that he'd tried to help? A selfish part of him wanted her to know. Maybe it would make her think of him as a friend instead of a coworker—or hopefully something more.

Eight seats to fill . . . Peter chewed that over. Vanessa frequently complained that Ian did a crappy job rallying the boys to pamper her on Mother's Day. Maybe she'd appreciate going out to brunch, even though Noelle was involved? Peter tapped a pencil against the edge of his desk. Vanessa absolutely would love brunch, just not the two-hour drive back and forth. But what if they made a weekend out of it, like a minivacation? That would definitely smooth over the Noelle involvement.

Peter pushed the pencil aside and searched for hotels near Hollenbeck. The fanciest, most luxurious option nearby was the Semiahmoo Resort in Blaine. Vanessa wouldn't be able to say no to that—plus they were running a Mother's Day promotion that included a spa treatment of the recipient's choosing. This was perfect! Vanessa absolutely deserved a weekend of pampering, and Peter, Ian, and the boys would have fun swimming at the pool and exploring the beach. It wasn't a weekend that Ian could afford on a postal worker's salary, but that was what bachelor brothers-in-law were for. Peter booked two rooms and paid extra for ocean views.

This May, he'd support the most important women in his life on Mother's Day, and that felt great. Certainly, it would be better than listening to Vanessa gripe about how Ian and the boys could barely muster a box of chocolates and a store-bought card. He wished he'd thought of treating her to a fun experience on Mother's Day ages ago. Pleased with himself, Peter leaned back in his chair and crossed his arms over his chest. Noelle and Vanessa would be so happy when he surprised them. But then he remembered that he still had two empty seats to fill. Two empty seats was nothing—it wasn't a big deal. What was a big deal, he realized, was that he couldn't offer a seat to his own mother.

Peter turned off his computer and swallowed the sadness rising in his throat. Mother's Day always brought back painful memories. Elaine hadn't contacted him in years. Even if he did want to include his mom in the Mother's Day celebration, he wouldn't even know where to mail the invitation.

SKAGITON MOMS FACEBOOK GROUP

Vanessa Collins
Tuesday, March 8

Attention Single Moms! My brother, Peter Marshal, is still available, which is a mystery to me because he's absolutely the best. He's taking my whole family to Semiahmoo Resort for Mother's Day weekend this May. Can you believe it? Spa treatments too! I'm still in shock.

Anyhow, if anyone deserves happiness, it's Peter, and I would love for him to find a woman who could make his dreams come true. He's on a health kick right now and switching up his breakfast routine. If you want to meet him, swing by the hot breakfast bar at DeBoer's Food Co-op, M–F at 8 am. Don't tell him I sent you!

Courtney Nettles
So that's why he wasn't at Carol's Diner yesterday. Dang it!

Lexie Britt
Has he mentioned me?

Vanessa Collins
No, *Lexie Britt.* Sorry, he hasn't.

Renee Schroth
Mornings are tough for me. Can't you give us some afternoon or evening times to work with?

Vanessa Collins
I'll figure that out and get back to you, *Renee Schroth.*

Jourdaine Bloomfield
You and I both know who would be perfect for your brother . . . *Vanessa Collins.*

Vanessa Collins
Yup. If only, *Jourdaine Bloomfield.*

Chapter Eight

When it came to farm-to-table shopping, DeBoer's Food Co-op could put Whole Foods to shame. Being in the heart of Skagit Valley meant that there was always a wide variety of locally grown goods for sale. Peter had loved coming to DeBoer's ever since he was a little boy. His mom had been friends with the florist. He still remembered standing in front of the bins of fresh daffodils and tulips while Elaine chatted with her friend. Sometimes Elaine would buy him a cookie from the bakery counter to reward him for being patient. He still slowed down every time he walked through the floral section. His mother's memory was as faint as the scent of a hothouse bloom.

Peter sometimes visited the deli for lunch, but this was his first time eating there for breakfast. The hot food and salad bar was a recent addition to DeBoer's Co-op. It was something that Seattleites moving into Skagiton expected, and when the management realized the potential, they cleared away two aisles of farm equipment to make room for a small eating area next to the deli. He stood there, on a rainy Tuesday morning, and examined his choices. Sadly, there weren't any pancakes, which made sense, he supposed, because they might get soggy. The buffet had a multitude of other options, though. Peter loaded his plate with scrambled eggs, fruit salad, roasted potatoes, sautéed spinach, and two strips of bacon. After fumbling his way through the self-checkout kiosk, he grabbed silverware and sat at the communal table in the dining area.

His first bite of eggs was delicious. For the first time in years, Peter wavered in his dedication to pancakes. But the best part about this breakfast was the solitude. Peter unfurled the *Skagiton Weekly Gazette* and popped a grape in his mouth. He was halfway through the letters to the editor—really juicy ones complaining about the new heritage tree laws that prevented homeowners from felling trees over seventy years old—when someone pulled up a chair next to him.

"Is it okay if we join you?" Jourdaine wore a long-sleeved black shirt that covered her tattoos and a skinny pencil skirt that landed below her knees. She looked every inch the successful accountant that Peter knew she was. Jourdaine was practically his older sister. She, Vanessa, and Corine had been extremely close for over three decades. "Sure," said Peter. "Good to see you. But who's *we*?"

"Zara's paying at the register."

"Great," said Peter. "I keep meaning to poke my head into her pottery studio and see what it's like. I've heard great things."

"Yeah. It was her two-year anniversary on Saturday too. I'm incredibly proud of her." Jourdaine left the chair she'd pulled out next to Peter available and sat to the left of it instead. When Zara arrived a minute later, Jourdaine maneuvered her into the empty seat.

"Hi, Peter." Zara cringed. "I'm sorry about crashing your breakfast. Do you want us to move?"

"Of course not. We can catch up." Peter and Jourdaine's sister, Zara, had never been close friends, but they were friendly. Since they were the same age, they'd been thrown together since they were little. Every time Vanessa had gone over to Jourdaine's house in middle school, she had dragged Peter with her so he'd be there, too, when Dr. Helen Bloomfield invited them to dinner. Helen *always* invited them to dinner. She was the type of mom Peter wished he had.

"Jourdaine was just telling me that your pottery studio has been open for two years now," he said. "Congratulations."

"Thanks." Zara smiled. Her hair was the same dark brown as her sister's. Unlike Jourdaine, though, whose hair was cropped into a pixie cut, Zara wore hers shoulder length with pink and green streaks. Today she had on a purple tie-dyed T-shirt underneath a silver sweater that matched her glittery knee-high boots. "I love owning my own business. I thought I would miss teaching more, but I don't."

"That's right. You taught art in middle school—I'd forgotten that." Peter polished off his bacon.

"Yes, but after the last round of budget cuts, it went down to a half-time position." Zara unpeeled the wrapper from her blueberry muffin. "That, combined with my divorce, prompted me to explore other options."

"Which I had been encouraging her to do for years." Jourdaine sliced a wedge of cantaloupe into tiny bites. "Divorce the douchebag and open her own business. She's young, talented, and smart—why not take a risk?"

Peter nodded. "Good point."

Zara blushed. "I'm just lucky that the risk paid off. The community has been really supportive."

"Every time I post about Wheel Me Around on Skagiton Moms, people gush about you," said Jourdaine.

"Your sister pimps for you too?" Peter smiled. "I get half my referrals from Skagiton Moms thanks to Vanessa."

Zara laughed. "Yeah, I'm not in that group obviously, since I'm not a mom, but I feel like I know all about it since Jourdaine tells me everything."

"Almost everything." Jourdaine elbowed her gently, and Peter wondered why.

"So since you worked at Skagiton Middle School, you must have known Jeff Walters," said Peter. Maybe this was an opportunity to find out more about Noelle. His brain was still grappling with what Vanessa had told him about Noelle's conservative upbringing. Peter had known

Jeff only in passing since he had been five years older, but he wondered whether Jeff had agreed with those outdated notions.

Zara sighed. "Jeff was such a great person. I still can't believe he's gone."

"His death is the reason I don't bike in the rain," said Jourdaine.

"Were you friends with him?" Zara asked Peter.

He shook his head. "No, but I work with his wife, Noelle."

"The peanut butter bomber." Jourdaine rolled her eyes.

"The what?" Zara asked.

"Don't call her that," said Peter. "Noelle is a lovely person and an excellent mother."

"What do you mean by *peanut butter bomber*?" Zara asked.

"Don't you remember me telling you about the bake sale from hell?" Jourdaine wrinkled her nose. "The cotton candy machine broke, a four-year-old threw up Rice Krispies Treats all over the front steps, and then Noelle plopped down a tray of peanut butter cookies right in front of the nut-free classroom sign."

"She probably didn't know about the nut-free classroom rule," said Peter.

"How could she not?" Jourdaine asked. "The way the co-op worked, every parent had to volunteer three hours a week. She walked by that sign all the time."

"Maybe she was so focused on Daniel that she didn't notice," said Peter.

"Or maybe Jeff was the one who volunteered," said Zara. "He always came in late. First period was his prep time."

Jourdaine shrugged. "It still seems weird to me."

"So you think Jeff might have volunteered in Daniel's classroom?" Peter asked.

"It's definitely possible." Zara folded her muffin wrapper into thirds. "He was great with kids and a devoted father."

"Strict?" Peter asked.

"No." Zara shook her head. "More like a grown-up goofball. What makes you think he was strict?"

"Oh . . ." Peter scrambled, trying to figure out how to word his concerns. "Nothing, just that Noelle comes from a conservative background, so I wondered."

"Like, politically conservative?" Zara asked.

Peter shrugged. "I have no idea."

"I think you mean chauvinistic," said Jourdaine. "I heard that she never wore pants until she married Jeff."

"Where'd you hear that?" Zara asked. "Jeff never mentioned that to me." Peter was glad she asked the question. If Vanessa had been privy to that piece of gossip, she would have shared it with him. All she had said was that Noelle couldn't wear pants at her high school.

"I can't say." Jourdaine zipped her lips and turned an imaginary key. "Accountant-client privileges."

"One of your bookkeeping clients told you that Noelle didn't wear pants until after her wedding day?" Zara put her silverware on her plate. "Wow."

"Former bookkeeping client," said Jourdaine. "Now she's purchased QuickBooks and thinks she knows everything."

"Wait," said Peter. "Noelle worked on her family's farm in high school. How would she do that in a dress?"

"I don't know. They did it on *Little House on the Prairie* all the time." Jourdaine clicked her long, pointed fingernails on the table. "But enough about Noelle; let's talk about tomorrow night. A bunch of us are getting together for margaritas at Riverwalk Tapas before the school board meeting. You two should come."

"I can't," said Zara. "Sorry. It's fused-glass night at the studio, and I have fourteen people signed up."

"And I don't get involved in local politics," said Peter. "It's bad for business."

"But this is important," said Jourdaine. "It's not political; it's a human rights issue."

"I'm actually not sure what you're talking about," said Peter, ashamed to admit it. He had read the *Skagiton Weekly Gazette* cover to cover this week, but he didn't recall learning anything about human rights violations in the local schools.

"The school district needs to start supplying hygiene products in the bathrooms," said Jourdaine.

"There's no toilet paper?" Peter asked.

"*Of course* there's toilet paper," said Zara. "Jourdaine's talking about sanitary supplies."

"Menstruation is a fact of life, and the school district shouldn't avoid it," said Jourdaine. "Thirty-seven percent of our student population qualifies for free and reduced lunch. This is exactly the demographic who might need help acquiring tampons and pads."

"That makes sense," said Peter, "but it's also a cause outside of my lane. I assume Vanessa is involved, though?"

"You're damn right she is." Jourdaine glared at him. "Are you aware of the humiliation your sister endured when she began menstruating?"

Peter looked to the left and right, desperate for any avenue of escape. "No," he muttered. "I'm not."

"Your dad was in Alaska, your mom had been gone for years, and Vanessa missed a whole week of school because she didn't have any maxi pads. When my mom found out, she made a special trip to Costco and bought her practically a lifetime supply."

"Wow," said Zara. "Go, Mom."

"I had no idea." Peter felt sick to his stomach, and it wasn't from the greasy bacon. He prided himself on his close relationship with Vanessa, but this was a story she had never shared with him. For her not to have mentioned it, even after all these years, meant it was a wound that cut deep. "Okay," he said. "I'll go to the school board meeting."

"Great." Jourdaine turned to Zara. "Are you sure you can't find someone else to cover your fused-glass class? You and Peter could come together."

"Nope, sorry," Zara said, a little too quickly for Peter's taste. He didn't want to go on a quasi date with her either, but his ego was miffed by how fast she shot the notion down.

"Well," he said, standing up. "This conversation has been illuminating. It was wonderful catching up with both of you, but I've got to run."

"See you around," said Zara.

"And I'll see you at the board meeting," said Jourdaine.

"Great." Peter dumped his paper plate into the trash. "See you then." As he walked away from the dining area, he heard Zara chide her sister.

"How could you do that to me?" Zara was saying. "You know I'm not interested in Peter at all."

"Why not? Because he's not a loser like all your past boyfriends?"

"Because he's boring," said Zara. "I could never date someone that dull."

Boring? Peter's pride twisted into knots. *Zara thinks I am dull?* Maybe that was why Noelle still wasn't interested in him. He was a dud. Peter charged out of the grocery store and didn't look back.

Noelle glanced in the restroom mirror one more time. She couldn't believe how different she looked with the new bra. The old gray sweater she wore over it seemed to fit better too. Her shoulders weren't so tense, and it was easier to stand straight. She wondered how she'd look in the waitressing T-shirts the Dairy Ambassadors would be wearing in May. Normally Noelle hated T-shirts because they made her feel lumpy, but perhaps that wouldn't be the case now.

Her visit to the outlet mall had been a success, but Noelle was relieved that Kerry couldn't see her right now, admiring herself in the mirror. Kerry would warn her of the evils of vanity. Her sister rarely spent money on herself. Hank kept control of the cash. When Kerry bought something, she asked Hank for money, and he would give it to her only if he approved of her choices. Hank had had final approval of what Noelle had worn, too, when she had lived in the trailer parked in their yard. It had been humiliating, but Noelle had been used to it since Trivium had been so strict. Noelle had never had stylish clothes. She had been the only Dairy Ambassador contestant in long sleeves.

Noelle thought back to the formal dress she had found for herself at the thrift store. She had felt like a princess from the moment she'd slipped the pale-blue satin over her head and buttoned up the back. But when she'd walked onstage and realized she was the only contestant wearing sleeves, she had wished that she could rip them off.

"Can you believe all of those ridiculous getups?" Anika had criticized afterward. "What true dairy woman wears a strapless dress?"

"This whole thing should have been settled by a ten-minute hand-milking contest," Phil grumbled. "If I'd have known this was a beauty contest, I would never have allowed you to enter."

At the time, Noelle, who had never—not even once—owned new clothes, had felt guilty for being embarrassed of her thrift shop gown. She had been just as vain as those other girls onstage, but she had been too ashamed to admit it.

Noelle sighed and turned away from the mirror. Even after almost a decade of Jeff gently disentangling her from her family's control, their viewpoints were stuck in her brain. Her upbringing had clawed deep roots in her soul. Jeff had chopped down the weeds but had been unable to rip them out completely.

A minute later she was back at her desk, checking emails, when Peter arrived at work. "Ready for coffee?" he asked, his green eyes full of a friendly warmth that instantly lifted Noelle's mood.

"Absolutely."

"So, Miss Dairy Ambassador, will it be cow milk or almond today?"

"I'll go for the real stuff since Daniel isn't here to witness me cheating."

Peter handed her a mug and let her go first with the machine. Neither of them spoke as the coffee brewed. Noelle didn't think anything was wrong at first—her attention was focused on crafting the perfect latte. But when she stepped to the side so that Peter could have a turn, he didn't move. He stared at the wall, lost in thought, wearing a serious expression that she wasn't used to seeing on him. "What's the matter?" she asked. "Is everything okay?"

"Am I boring?" he blurted out.

"What?" Noelle was shocked that Peter would ask such an odd question.

"Am I dull?"

"What? No way. Where did this come from?"

Peter shrugged and popped a pod in the machine. "I don't know. Just . . ."

"Just what?"

Peter's gaze was glued to his partially completed Americano. "I overheard someone say I was boring this morning, and it caught me off guard."

"At breakfast?"

Peter nodded.

"Oh." Noelle frowned. This was Vanessa's fault. She kept offering Peter up on Skagiton Moms like he was an old sofa she was trying to unload. Okay, maybe that was being too harsh, but Noelle didn't like the idea of him walking into one love trap after another. Now, thanks to Vanessa's shenanigans, Peter—the most jovial person Noelle knew—was sad. Irked, Noelle tried to repair the damage. "Anyone who thinks you're boring doesn't know you very well."

"I don't think that's the case." Peter picked his coffee up.

"Well, then, they're dumb. You're not boring; you're stable. That's a good thing."

"Yeah, except for the way you said it just now makes me sound like a horse." The corners of Peter's mouth turned up, like he was attempting to smile, but when his dimples didn't pop out, Noelle knew he was faking it.

"There's nothing wrong with being a horse either," said Noelle, still trying to lighten his mood. "Half the girls in my high school were obsessed with them. We're talking full-fledged cowgirls with pictures of thoroughbreds on their walls and Mane 'n Tail in their showers."

"Mane 'n Tail? Should I know what that is?"

"A horse-to-human crossover shampoo."

"That's a thing?"

Noelle nodded. "I was never a horse girl myself, but I do admire stallions." As soon as the words came out of her mouth, Noelle wished she could clap her hand over her mouth and take them back in. She sounded . . . lewd.

"*Words are just words*," Jeff used to say. "*Don't be embarrassed*."

Blushing, Noelle rushed on, hoping that Peter didn't notice. "You're not boring. You're funny and witty and a great coach. What does this person expect? That you should do cartwheels too?"

"Maybe." Peter leaned against the counter and grinned for real this time. "I didn't know you were so good at pep talks. I should come to you with my bruised ego more often."

"I'm excellent with bruised egos. My mom always told me it was the most sensitive part of a man's body." *Crap!* That sounded lewd too. What was wrong with her this morning? "I mean, um . . . is there Little League practice tomorrow night?"

"No," Peter said, once he'd stopped chuckling. "The school board meeting is tomorrow night. Do you want to come with me? I was planning on attending."

"To the school board meeting? Rick and all that Windswept training material says making friends with politicians was great but that we shouldn't voice political opinions because we might alienate potential clients."

"That's true, and normally I follow his advice, but I thought I might make an exception this time since my sister and her friends are involved."

"You mean the hygiene thing?"

"Yeah."

"I wasn't planning on going." Noelle fiddled with the sleeve of her gray sweater. "It doesn't really impact me since I don't have daughters."

"Vanessa doesn't have daughters either, and I'm not a parent, but I've been the kid that relied on school services before."

"What do you mean?" Noelle asked just as Debbie the receptionist walked in.

"Hi, Peter. Thanks for the flowers at the front desk." Debbie took her mug from the cupboard. "They really perk the place up. Are they from your yard?"

"They sure are. As soon as the forsythia blooms, I know it's time to fertilize the grass."

"Is that what those yellow flowers are?" Noelle asked. "Forsythia?" She'd admired the small bouquets on all the desks in the bullpen and assumed they were from Peter. "I meant to tell you thank you."

"You're welcome. Yes, they're from my forsythia bushes."

"Yellow's my favorite color," said Debbie.

"Peter knows what women like," said Noelle. Debbie snorted and patted herself on the chest. *Dang it!* Noelle squeezed her eyes shut. This new bra she was wearing must be killing her brain cells. "In terms of flowers, I mean," she squeaked out a little too late.

"I love bringing in bouquets. So that's a yes, then? You'll come with me to the school board meeting tomorrow night?"

"What?" Noelle didn't remember agreeing to anything. But she was so embarrassed over her string of accidental innuendos that she agreed. "Sure. Okay."

"Great." Peter gently touched her elbow and led her away from the lunchroom and Debbie's eavesdropping. "I'll pick you up at five forty, and we can stop for dinner at Riverwalk Tapas first with the rest of the attendees."

"Sounds good. Joyce should be home tomorrow night to watch Daniel."

"Perfect." Peter's phone buzzed, and he waved at her before answering it and walking away.

Noelle sat at her desk and updated her calendar. As she typed in the words **Dinner with Peter**, she froze. Had she just agreed to a date?

No, it couldn't be a date. Not with Peter, who was the closest thing she had to a friend in Skagiton. This was two friends attending a political meeting, and that was it. Still . . . Noelle sipped her latte and considered. It wouldn't hurt to circle back to the outlet mall over lunch and pick out a new outfit. Otherwise she wouldn't have anything special to wear.

SKAGITON MOMS FACEBOOK GROUP

Jourdaine Bloomfield
Wednesday, March 9

Tonight's the night! Moms, I hope you show up at the school board meeting this evening to speak up for human rights. Pads and tampons should be as ubiquitous in public bathrooms as soap and paper towels. Other places, like Scotland, have already declared that access to menstrual products is a basic human right. Let's make sure the Skagiton school board agrees. The board meeting starts at 7:30, but show up to Riverwalk Tapas at 6 and I'll buy you a margarita. Hope you can come!

Melissa James
I'm with you, Mama!

Corine Reeder
I'll be there!

Vanessa Collins
Make my margarita a strawberry.

Dorothy Caulfield
This is the most ridiculous waste of taxpayer money I've ever heard about. Government overreach at its finest.

Jourdaine Bloomfield
It's not government overreach, *Dorothy Caulfield*. What's overreach is more than half of the states in our country taxing maxi pads as a "luxury" item, but putting no such tax on erectile dysfunction products.

Corine Reeder
My Girl Scout troop has been sewing reusable menstruation pads to donate for our Silver Award, *Dorothy Caulfield*. Globally, this is a huge issue. In many countries, girls can't go to school when they have their periods. That impacts their education and their future.

Vanessa Collins
Girls here, too, *Corine Reeder*.

Jourdaine Bloomfield
Yes, *Vanessa Collins*.

Tracey Fukui
I'm confused. Does Washington state slap a luxury tax on tampons?

Melissa James
Not anymore but affordability is still an issue, *Tracey Fukui*.

Jessica Luoma
Diva cups. They will change your life!

Sabrina Kruger
I won't be there in person, but I already emailed the board. I agree 100%! Side note: Is this an inappropriate time to brag about having had a hysterectomy?

Carol Durango
Never, *Sabrina Kruger*. Spoken as a fellow sister in the hyster-YES-omy club.

Dorothy Caulfield
You people are nuts. How much control are you willing to give the government? First you want them to educate your kids, then you want them to feed them, and now this? Why have kids at all if you don't want to take care of them?

Angela Grosset
Excuse me, *Dorothy Caulfield*, but I absolutely want to take care of my children. I work forty hours at my first job as a barista, and twenty hours at my second, cleaning houses. If it weren't for my mom watching my toddler, I wouldn't make it. My son's dad

left us when I was six months pregnant and hasn't paid any child support. Don't make assumptions about situations you know nothing about!!!

Olivia Doyle

Sending you love, *Angela Grosset*. You are amazing and are more than welcome to stop by the Food Bank at Skagiton Methodist Church for help. Our doors are open on Wednesdays from 5 to 9 PM.

Angela Grosset

I know. I love you guys, *Olivia Doyle*. I'm not religious but I thank God for the Food Bank every day.

Olivia Doyle

I will see if someone can cover my shift at the Food Bank tonight so I can be there at the school board meeting, *Jourdaine Bloomfield*.

Chapter Nine

His Mercedes E-Class Sedan was always spotless. Peter took it through the car wash each week and wiped off the dashboard with a microfiber cloth every morning. He wasn't a neat freak—driving clients around in his car on a regular basis made maintaining a pristine vehicle essential. But on the ride over to Noelle's house Wednesday night, a crow crapped on his windshield, splattering orangey goo all across the passenger's side, right where Noelle would see it.

"Gah!" Peter turned on his blinker and pulled over. He grabbed a bottle of water and the microfiber cloth and cleaned it off the best he could, and then stashed the dirty rag in his trunk. "This better not be an omen," he muttered as he climbed back into the driver's seat. He took a deep breath and tried to relax.

Tonight was his chance to transform his relationship with Noelle from coworker, to friend, to hopefully something more. It wasn't a date, but it was *almost* a date.

But if it wasn't a date, then why was he so nervous? Peter gripped the steering wheel and bowed his head. With every fiber of his being, he wanted tonight to be perfect. He wanted Noelle to enjoy spending time with him. Maybe she'd even laugh if Peter could be witty enough. Noelle's laughter was a joy he treasured. It would be wonderful to look over in the passenger seat and see her smile. Could he accomplish that?

Maybe . . . or maybe he'd be too dull for her to bother with seeing him again—outside of the office, that was.

Ten minutes later, Peter parked his car in her driveway and took a quick survey of the house. It had been eleven years since he'd sold it to Jeff, and not much about the landscaping had changed. Low maintenance had been Jeff's priority, along with a price point that matched the loan he had secured through the Skagiton Teachers' Credit Union. Jeff had wanted to spend his free time biking, climbing, or snowboarding, not tending to a yard. Grass and a boxwood hedge by the brick had suited him just fine. When he'd seen the hot tub in the back, he'd been sold.

Peter walked up the little path to the front door and knocked. His palms sweated, and when he couldn't figure out how to dry them off, he stuffed them in his pockets.

"Hey, Coach," said Daniel as he opened the door. "Come on in. My mom will be out soon."

"Hi, Daniel," he said as he stepped across the threshold. "Nice to—oh my—" Peter shut his mouth just in time to keep himself from saying something rude. "Wow. That's a lot of . . . um . . . crafting materials in here." Everywhere he looked, Peter saw junk: towers of ribbons, stacks of cardboard boxes, pieces of foam, tables covered in dye, and what appeared to be bags of hamster litter stacked up against the fireplace. He sneezed and pulled out a tissue.

"Are you sick?" Daniel asked.

"No." Peter wiped his nose. "I must be allergic to something here. Do I smell cedar?"

Daniel shrugged. "I don't know what type of wood Grandma Joyce uses to make her flowers." His curly mop of brown hair looked exactly like Jeff's in Noelle's wedding picture hanging on the wall.

"Well, look who's here," said Joyce, walking into the foyer. Her sweatshirt had splotches of orange coloring on the shoulders and a strip of packaging tape stuck to her sleeve. "It's good to see you, Coach Pete. Thanks for getting Noelle out of the house."

"I heard that," said Noelle, walking into the room, holding her purse.

Peter's jaw dropped. He'd never seen her in jeans before—or clothes that actually fit. It wasn't that she was dressed up, because she wasn't, but her V-neck sweater, jeans, and cowboy boots suited her, highlighting her curves. When Noelle put on her black raincoat, she looked stylish enough for Seattle, let alone a sleepy little town like Skagiton.

"What time do you think we'll be home?" she asked.

"I don't know." Peter took his hand out of his pocket and checked his watch. "School board meetings can sometimes run long, and I don't know when the main issue is on the agenda."

"Don't worry about us." Joyce slapped Noelle's back and guided her out the door. "We'll be fine."

"Okay. Well." Noelle bent down and hugged Daniel. "I love you. Be good for Grandma."

"I love you too." After hugging his mom, Daniel looked up at Peter and held up his hand for a high five, like they always did at Little League practice.

"See ya later," said Peter, a big grin on his face.

"So . . . um . . . I guess you've seen what my mother-in-law has done with the place," said Noelle, once they were in the car.

"When you told me it was hard to concentrate at home, I had no idea that's what you meant." He backed out of her driveway and headed toward town.

"Yeah. Her floral business is quite successful. Joyce gets in-person orders as well as online business through her Etsy shop, Wood You Be Mine? But it's taken over our living room for a while now." She pulled a lock of hair behind her ear. "And our dining room."

"Why doesn't she rent commercial space so you can take your living spaces back?"

"She could, but then she wouldn't be there when Daniel came home from school. Usually I'm home to greet him, but not always."

"Oh. That makes sense."

"Sometimes I think it would be better if Daniel was in an after-school program because that might be more enriching."

"Whenever I drive past the YMCA, it seems like they're having fun."

Noelle nodded. "Yeah. Exactly. Originally it was too expensive, but now that the market's changed and I'm earning more money, I could swing it. I just don't know what I'd say to Joyce. She gave up everything to move in with us and take care of Daniel after Jeff died."

"She's a spitfire. My guess is that Joyce could handle whatever you had to tell her."

"Maybe."

"Plus she seems to love her business too. Maybe it would help her to be able to focus on it more."

"That's a good point."

Peter glanced over at her and saw her spin her wedding ring around her finger over and over again. He cleared his throat. "Thanks for coming with me tonight. This is an important issue, but I'd feel weird showing up at a school board meeting alone since I'm not a parent."

"You're a taxpayer. That counts for something."

"Yes, but still."

"I'm happy to come. I think it's an important issue, too, but I'd never go to one of these things alone either."

"Why not?"

"I don't know. My parents . . ."

When she didn't continue her sentence, Peter prompted her. "Your parents what?"

"They don't approve of public education in general."

Shocked that Noelle was finally revealing something about her family that wasn't farming related, Peter sought a way to gently pry more information from her. "What don't they like about it?"

"They think that public schools take control away from parents and teach kids things that aren't true."

"Huh?"

"Like with tonight's issue." Noelle's voice dropped to a borderline whisper as she said it. "Menstrual products. My parents would say that's a subject that parents should deal with at home. My private school, Trivium High, didn't teach anything about that at all."

"No sex ed whatsoever?"

"None. Well, that's not true, exactly. We had a Future Farmers of America club, so . . . we learned some things that way."

They were approaching Main Street now, but Peter slowed the car so the conversation could continue. "Horses and pigs were supposed to teach you about sex ed?"

Noelle nodded. "It sounds stupid when you say it like that, but that's how it was."

"It sounds stupid because it *is* stupid." Peter was unable to keep the judgment out of his tone. "What happened if kids were touched inappropriately? What happened if someone got pregnant and didn't know what to do?"

"That never happened at Trivium."

"Didn't happen, or you didn't know about it because it was swept under the rug?"

Noelle bit her lip for a moment. "I don't know."

"I mean, thinking about life today, something bad probably happened within that community at some point, right?"

"Trivium was so close knit that nobody had secrets."

"You'll never know that for sure, though, will you?" Peter pulled into a parking spot behind Riverwalk Tapas and turned off the car. Now, more than ever, he was glad he was attending the school board meeting tonight. "When I was eight," he said in a quiet voice, "my mom ran off and left Vanessa and me on our own with our father. He was and is a great person, but as a commercial fisherman, he was often gone for long stretches at a time."

"Who took care of you when he was away?"

"Vanessa."

"But she's only a few years older than you."

"Three years. She was eleven when our mom left. At first, our grandmother would come to stay, but then she became too frail to help out. Neighbors would check in on us, too, but for the most part, people minded their own business so that CPS wouldn't take us away. We lived on free breakfast and lunch at school. We'd visit the food bank at the Methodist church each week so we'd have something to eat besides our freezer full of fish."

"I didn't know that about you." Noelle stared up at him with warmth in her brown eyes. "Thanks for telling me."

"I'm telling you because it's why I believe public school and programs like Little League are so important. They provide the safety net that kids like me need. I played baseball. Vanessa was a Girl Scout." Damnit, he was choking up. Peter pulled out a tissue. "Allergies. Sorry." He blew his nose. "Let's go eat."

"Wait." Noelle reached for his hand. She squeezed it for half a second before pulling away. "Did you hear what you said? You said *kids like me*, in the present tense."

"Oh. Sorry, I misspoke."

"No, that's fine. But you're not a kid anymore, right? You're an adult, and look at all you've accomplished. I mean, you're driving a Mercedes." She pointed across the street to DeBoer's Food Co-op. "That's your face on the bench. You don't *need* a safety net anymore. You've *become* the safety net. That's pretty cool."

"Thanks for saying that. But it doesn't matter how much money I save; part of me will always worry that hard times will come again." He looked at the emblem on the steering wheel. "Besides, driving a Mercedes doesn't make a person successful. Mike Swan drives one too."

"You're nothing like Mike Swan."

"Nope. Never have been. Never will be." Popularity and money had nothing to do with it either. It was about choices and treating people with respect. "Mike was a jerk in high school, and he doesn't seem to have grown past that."

"No. He hasn't."

Peter knew that the others were waiting for them with tapas, but he didn't care. Alone time with Noelle was precious. "Did you know anyone like Mike Swan at your high school?" he asked.

"Like Mike Swan?" Noelle raised her eyebrows, and her forehead froze into position like she was paralyzed. "Um . . ." She bent down and picked up her purse.

"You don't have to share. It's okay. I shouldn't pry."

"No. It's not that. It's just . . ." Noelle rubbed the back of her neck, and Peter waited, patiently, for her to continue. As he waited, he marveled about what had just happened. The stars had aligned, and his relationship with Noelle had finally crossed the boundary from coworkers to friends.

"Mike Swan wouldn't have lasted three days at Trivium," Noelle said. She didn't like to talk about this aspect of her schooling because most people didn't understand—not even Jeff when she'd tried to explain it to him. "*That place was garbage*," he used to say. But it wasn't. Trivium was the place that had expanded her thinking beyond the narrow worldview her father had taught her. If it weren't for Trivium, she never would have read the great books, studied ancient history, or learned proper grammar. "Trivium was strict, but only because they were trying to protect us."

"What do you mean?" Peter asked.

"Trivium had a zero-tolerance policy for foul language or sexual innuendo. Mike would have been out on his ear."

"Mike was also a bully. Bullies know how to manipulate situations like that."

"Bullying might have been overlooked—boys will be boys and all—but not swear words. Day one, the principal would have washed Mike's mouth out with soap, day two he would have gotten the paddle, and by day three he would have been expelled."

"Wait. What? I haven't forgotten the 'boys will be boys' part because that's no excuse, but let's go back to the 'washing Mike's mouth out with soap' and him 'getting the paddle' part. That's not legal."

"It *is* legal. Washington State outlawed corporal punishment in public schools a while ago, but it can still happen in private schools. That's one of the reasons my parents chose Trivium. So that the former principal, who also happens to be my sister's father-in-law, could knock some sense into my brother, Sam."

"What the hell?" Peter's horrified expression didn't surprise her.

When she'd told Jeff about Trivium's discipline policy, his reaction had been even worse. As a mandated reporter with the Skagiton School District, Jeff had felt compelled to call CPS. But that hadn't done any good because Trivium's disciplinary program was legal. Hank's dad had never left marks, and he'd had the parents' full permission.

"Look," said Noelle. "I know it sounds rough to someone who grew up in public schools, but private schools are different."

"I have friends from college who went to private school, and none of them got the paddle," said Peter. "There are plenty of great schools out there, secular and religious, that don't use corporal punishment."

"Okay, but Trivium's system works. I never had to deal with a guy like Mike Swan in high school."

"Really? Let's go back to the 'boys will be boys' comment and incidents of bullying."

"Stupid stuff. That's all. Nothing serious."

Peter looked at her sharply. "Did something happen to you or someone you know?"

Noelle looked down at her naked fingernails. She picked at a cuticle. "Not to me, but a few guys gave Sam a hard time. He started out as the shortest boy in his sophomore class and didn't hit his growth spurt until he became a senior. Sam grew six inches in one year."

"*Why'd you let this happen to you?*" her father had asked Sam when he had come home from school with a yardstick glued to his backpack. He should have thrown the backpack away. That's what Noelle would have done.

In fact, the day she'd walked into the ag science classroom and seen a booster seat on Sam's chair, she had thrown her coat over the seat and smuggled it out to the dumpster before her brother could see. That hadn't stopped the whole club from laughing when Sam had arrived. His cheeks had burned red with humiliation when someone had told him what had happened. "*You should have left it, Noelle*," Sam had loudly proclaimed. "*I can take a joke*."

"Bullying someone for what they look like is sick," said Peter. "I'm sorry your brother had to deal with that."

"Me too." She *was* sorry, but being sorry didn't mean there was anything she could do about it. Even now as an adult looking back, she didn't see any way she could have helped. Nobody would have listened to her if she had spoken up, and if she had said something, Phil would have punished Sam for needing his sister to defend him. She would have gotten the belt, too, for making Sam look weak.

"You're not a kid either anymore," said Peter. "Look at you now—about to walk into a public school board meeting and speak up for girls. That's awesome."

"I don't have to speak, do I?" Noelle's heart pounded.

"No, you don't. Being part of the audience will help too." He unclicked his seat belt. "Shall we?"

"Yeah. Of course." She opened her door and stepped into the cold. "You know, women bully each other too. High school isn't the only place that happens."

"I believe it. But don't worry; if anyone calls you the peanut butter bomber tonight, I promise to throw a margarita in their face."

Noelle giggled. "You wouldn't."

"No, probably not. If I threw a drink on one of my sister's friends, she might pelt me with chips."

"Or give you an Alaskan hello." Noelle laughed harder.

"It wouldn't be the first time. What would be worse is if Vanessa refused to feed me dinner. Without her home-cooked meals, I'd starve."

"You could learn to cook," Noelle said as Peter held the door to the restaurant open for her.

"But who would teach me?"

"I could. Or YouTube. I don't know." They were in the restaurant now, and the dim lighting caught her off guard. "I've never been here before." It surprised her that the ambiance was so romantic. "I haven't dined anywhere that didn't include kids' menus in ages."

"They have kids' menus here too." Peter scanned the tables and then looked into the No Minors Allowed section. "But we're sitting in the bar tonight." He breezed past the hostess and kept walking, straight to a tableful of familiar faces.

The first person Noelle recognized was Tracey Fukui, her new client. *Thank goodness for at least one friendly person besides Peter.* Sitting next to her was Corine Reeder from the Heritage Tree Committee and Melissa James, the mayor's wife. On the other side of the table sat Jourdaine Bloomfield, the accountant, and a woman Noelle didn't know. But at the head of the table, holding court, was Vanessa. When she saw Noelle, she bit into a tortilla chip and glared at Peter.

"Hello, everyone." Peter waved. "I know almost all of you here, but do you know my friend Noelle Walters?"

Peter placed a steadying hand on her back for a few seconds before removing it. "Hi," she said, over the sounds of the Spanish guitar. She liked how Peter had called her his friend instead of just his coworker.

"Fancy meeting you here," said Tracey.

Noelle smiled. "Peter, this is my new client, Tracey Fukui. She and her husband moved here two months ago from Central California."

"You're in good hands, Tracey. Noelle is the best."

"Thanks." Tracey traced the rim of her margarita glass with her index finger. "I recognize you from the Little League opening day celebrations. Two of my boys are in Tee Ball."

"That's great," said Peter.

"We're glad you're here tonight, Tracey," said Jourdaine. "You're jumping right in."

Tracey shrugged. "It seemed like a cause that all the cool moms were behind."

"That's why I'm here," said the woman Noelle didn't know. Her gray hair was cut short in a stylish bob, and she wore bright-red lipstick and a leather jacket that was the same brown tone as her skin. "The cool factor." She stood up to shake Noelle's hand. "I'm kidding, of course. I don't know if I've met you before. I'm Olivia Doyle, lead pastor at Skagiton Methodist Church."

"Oh," said Noelle. "My husband's, um . . . his memorial service was held at your church."

Olivia clasped Noelle's hand with both of her own. "My associate pastor usually handles memorials. I hope Vince did a good job for you."

Noelle nodded. Jeff's memorial service was still a bit of a blur. Her brain had blocked most of it out. But she did remember that the overflowing sanctuary had been standing room only and that whatever Pastor Vince had said had helped her get through it. "He did," she affirmed.

Olivia pulled out the chair next to her. "Come take a seat."

"Thanks." Noelle sat next to Olivia, and Peter took the seat beside her.

"I see you kept your jacket on too." Olivia rubbed her arms. "It's chilly in here."

"It is." Noelle scooted her chair up.

"I didn't know you were coming tonight," said Vanessa. "This doesn't seem like your thing."

"Are you talking to me?" Peter reached for the pitcher of margaritas. "Tapas with a table of beautiful ladies is definitely my thing." He poured a glass for Noelle and then another one for himself.

"Always the charmer," Corine said with a laugh. "Some things never change. Remember when you asked to marry me?"

"What?" Noelle blurted out, almost choking on her margarita.

"I was four, Corine." Peter folded his arms. "And you had a full box of Thin Mints."

"You promised to love me forever." Corine blew air-kisses across the table. "But then in high school you borrowed my dad's suit so you could be Jourdaine's backup date to the prom."

"You went to prom together?" Tracey asked.

"No." Jourdaine shook her head. "My date showed up at the last minute. He'd overslept."

"I didn't *want* to go to prom with you," said Peter. "I mean . . . that came out wrong."

"I know what you meant." Jourdaine reached across the table and pinched his cheek. "It was sweet of you to be willing to come to my rescue."

"Why didn't you just go to prom by yourself?" asked Melissa. "Needing male validation seems really unlike you."

Privately, Noelle agreed. Jourdaine was so tough she could probably open pickles without using a jar opener. It was hard to picture her fretting over being stood up.

"I was young and stupid," Jourdaine admitted. "In retrospect I wish I had gone without my boyfriend because he was drunk by the third song and almost got us kicked out after he stood on the table and belted out 'Friends in Low Places.'"

"What was your prom like?" Vanessa asked, looking straight at Noelle.

"Prom?" Noelle's voice squeaked. She gulped a mouthful of margarita before answering. "We didn't have prom at my high school; we had senior dinner instead. It was more of an awards banquet for athletes and service clubs."

"My high school didn't have prom either," said Olivia. "But that's because I went to an all-girls school in Atlanta."

"Atlanta, Georgia?" Tracey asked. "You're not from Washington? I thought I was the only outsider."

"Nope. I'm an outsider too. Born and raised in Georgia. After I was ordained, the United Methodist Church sent me all over. I've served in Colorado, Louisiana, Florida, and now here." Olivia looked up, right as a waiter brought a serving tray full of appetizers.

"Yum," said Corine. "I'm glad we ordered the charcuterie board."

"Anything else I can get you?" the waiter asked after setting down the food.

"Another pitcher of margaritas would be great," said Vanessa. "Thanks."

Noelle, who was only halfway through her first glass, wasn't sure she could handle a second. Tracey was right; this was the cool girls' table—at least Skagiton's version of it. If it were Hollenbeck, they'd be passing bottles of whiskey in the potato fields. She'd never been invited to those gatherings either, but her sister, Kerry, had told her all about them. Kerry used to be pretty wild before she matched up with Hank and discovered religion.

"I'll be right back with those drinks," said the waiter.

"So, Tracey," Olivia asked. "What made you move to Skagiton?"

"My husband works in farm irrigation, and his territory switched." Tracey selected a slice of prosciutto from the platter. "Now his range goes from Skagit Valley, all the way past the Cascades, into Eastern Washington and Alaska."

"That's a lot of driving," said Noelle. "It must be hard to be home alone with three boys."

"It is." Tracey nodded.

Vanessa raised her hand. "Mother of three boys, right here, and I also work a part-time job. Not all of us have constant family help, like *some* people I could mention."

The way Vanessa said it rubbed Noelle the wrong way. It wasn't a competition. "Tracey's husband isn't able to come home each night," she said, loudly enough to be able to be heard over the din of the music. "That's challenging."

Noelle hated confrontation, but she would stand up for her client.

"It *is* hard." Tracey lifted her chin. "As I'm sure you know, Noelle."

"I didn't mean to get in a pissing match with anyone," said Vanessa. "Jeez." As soon as the waiter had set down the new pitcher of margaritas, Vanessa leaned forward to grab it. When she picked it up, the whole pitcher fell forward onto Noelle, and some of the liquid splashed onto her face.

Noelle's brain struggled to make sense of what happened. One minute she was sitting there, munching on a breadstick, and the next she was being doused by a margarita waterfall.

"Oh my gosh!" Vanessa cried. "I'm so sorry. The handle broke."

Noelle didn't know if that was true or not. Her eyes stung from the tequila. "Aah!" she moaned. "I can't see."

"Here you go. I got you." Peter blotted her face with a cloth napkin.

"Dip it in water first," Melissa suggested. "Maybe that will help."

"Waiter!" Vanessa called. "We need more napkins."

Noelle still couldn't see; plus she felt overly warm. She grabbed the zipper on her raincoat and pulled it down, trying to remove the wet garment to no avail.

"I'm so sorry," Vanessa said again. "It was an accident."

Peter's voice was full of worry. "How are your eyes?"

Someone put a damp cloth in her hand. "Here, use this napkin," said Melissa.

Noelle wiped off her face and blinked her eyes open. "Better," she said. "Thanks." But she was still struggling with her raincoat. "I think the zipper's stuck. The harder I pull, the worse it's jammed." Looking down at it, she saw that the zipper foot was caught on fabric. "Oh no."

"Need some help?" Peter asked.

Noelle nodded. "At the risk of sounding like a first grader, yes, I do."

Peter wiggled the zipper back and forth, but it wouldn't budge. "Uh-oh," he said after dozens of tries. "This might be defective."

"It can't be defective; it's North Face," said Vanessa. "That jacket costs more than I earn in a week."

"It was on sale." Noelle sweated like a frozen cocktail. "At the outlet mall."

"Here, let me try it from this angle." Peter knelt in front of her so that he was at eye level with the zipper. "I can't see what I'm doing," he said. "I need more light."

"I got you." Olivia held up her phone and lit the flashlight app.

"There we go." Peter slid the zipper down to the bottom and freed Noelle from her coat.

"Yes! Thank you!" Noelle felt shivers as the cool air washed over her achingly hot neck. "That's so much better."

Peter grinned. "At your service, madam. I aim to please."

"Good thing you were still wearing your raincoat," said Corine. She picked up the broken pitcher and handle. "There's a huge crack. No wonder it broke off."

"Well," said Olivia, "now that you've been baptized, shall we go over our talking points for the meeting tonight?"

"Wait." Vanessa nodded to catch the waiter's attention. "First we need more margaritas since Noelle drank the whole pitcher herself."

"I did not!"

"Relax." Vanessa rolled her eyes. "I'm kidding. Can't you take a joke?"

"Oh," said Noelle, feeling foolish. Spending time with Peter was one thing, but hanging out with the Skagiton moms was another. She couldn't read the room, and that made her feel overwhelmed. Peter, however, seemed to know exactly what everyone was thinking.

"Ha ha, Vanessa. You're hilarious," he said with a sharp edge to his tone.

"Yes, to the talking points," said Jourdaine. "The meeting starts in thirty minutes."

By the time the third pitcher of margaritas arrived, the group had pinpointed what Melissa referred to as their "big ask" and their "compromise ask." Either they wanted free products in every school across the district or, at the very least, in the middle school and high school. But as for Noelle, she didn't finish the rest of her drink, nor did she participate in the lively discussion. Baptism or no baptism, she'd never fit in. There wasn't enough tequila in the world to make her feel comfortable sitting at this table.

SKAGITON MOMS FACEBOOK GROUP

Vanessa Collins
Wednesday, March 9

I know it's almost midnight. But if you're a single mom who's still awake right now, I'd like to remind you that my brother, Peter Marshal, is the most eligible bachelor in town. I want him to date someone who belongs here. Someone who shares similar values. Peter deserves a girlfriend who cares about Skagiton. Is it wrong of me to want a kick-ass sister-in-law who's fun to talk to? I don't think so.

Also, I should have mentioned this earlier, but Peter is smart. Like, really smart. He went to Washington State on a Future Business Leaders of America scholarship. Graduated in three years, too. If you didn't go to college that's not a big deal. I didn't go either. But Peter would probably be happier with someone who did.

Come by the Riverwalk play fields tomorrow night and you'll meet him at Little League practice, or PM me for details.

Lexie Britt
Damn. I'm out, then. I didn't know we needed a bachelor's degree to apply.

Wendy Basi
Same. But just as well. No offense to your brother, *Vanessa Collins*, but I don't date guys who wear polo shirts.

Renee Schroth
What's wrong with polo shirts, *Wendy Basi*?

Wendy Basi
Nothing, if you're forty, *Renee Schroth*.

Vanessa Collins
He's not forty, *Wendy Basi*. Peter's thirty-three.

Renee Schroth
I'm PMing you, *Vanessa Collins*.

Carmen Swan
You sound like you're totally deranged, *Vanessa Collins*. Is anyone else not seeing that?

Alastrina Kelly
I was just thinking that. *Vanessa Collins*, sweetie, are you sure your brother would want you making these posts?

Carmen Swan
LOL! *Alastrina Kelly*, she's not going to answer.

Vanessa Collins
I don't need to respond to every person who says something stupid.

Carmen Swan
And yet you just did, *Vanessa Collins*.

Vanessa Collins
I'm glad we agree that you said something stupid, *Carmen Swan*.

Courtney Nettles
Peter is allergic to cats. You should mention that before you get a woman's hopes up.

Katie Alexander
What about dogs? He sounds perfect for me. I was in FBLA too.

Vanessa Collins
Sadly, Peter's allergic to dogs too, except for poodles, *Katie Alexander*.

Katie Alexander
I own a mobile pet groomer business, so I'm out too then, I guess.

Corine Reeder
The Wagonater? *Katie Alexander*, I love your van! We don't have a dog but I see it all over town.

Katie Alexander
Yup. That's me. *Corine Reeder*, if you're in the market for a pet, I know people.

Chapter Ten

"Why'd you do it?" Peter asked. It was Thursday morning, and he was standing in Vanessa's kitchen, holding a box of special allergen-free doughnuts from DeBoer's Co-op. Although he had no qualms about showing up at her house for dinner uninvited, it didn't seem polite to pop up for breakfast empty handed.

"Why'd I do what?" Vanessa asked as she slapped down slices of bread on a cutting board and slathered them with mustard.

"Why'd you treat Noelle like that?"

"Huh?" Vanessa stacked slices of swiss and turkey on each piece of bread. "The pitcher broke. Splashing her with margarita was an accident."

"I believe you." Peter set the doughnuts on the counter. "But what about afterward? You barely said two words to her all night—and none that were kind."

"That's not true. I told her she had nice penmanship when she wrote her signature on the sign-in sheet at the school board meeting."

"Telling someone their cursive is so nice that they could star in a Victorian horror movie isn't a compliment."

"It is if you like slasher flicks." Vanessa stomped her foot on the wood floor three times. "Boys!" she called, loud enough that they'd hear her in the basement. "Uncle Peter brought doughnuts." Then she went back to making lunches.

"Did they hear you?" Peter asked after nothing happened.

"They heard me," she said, not looking up.

Sure enough, seconds later, Milo, Greg, and Waylon rushed up the steps and into the kitchen.

"Hey, Uncle Pete." Greg grabbed a maple bar in one hand and a chocolate sprinkle in the other.

"Cool," said Milo. "Thanks." He picked a raspberry cream.

Waylon didn't say anything until he'd stuffed half of an old-fashioned in his mouth. "Why are you here?" he asked. "It's not dinnertime."

Peter folded his arms. "I needed to talk to your mother."

"You could have just texted me," Vanessa mumbled. She sealed the lids on the plastic lunch box containers. Three green boxes for the kids and a purple box for her. Ian, whose shift started at 5:00 a.m., had already left for work.

"Some things are too important to text about," said Peter. "Noelle definitely falls into that category."

"Boys," Vanessa said. "Go brush your teeth. We're leaving for school in ten minutes."

"But I'm still eating doughnuts," Waylon said with a mouthful of food.

"Chew faster," Vanessa said, pointing at him.

"I don't get it," said Peter. "Why don't you like Noelle?"

"Who said that I didn't like her?" Vanessa asked.

"Like who?" Greg walked up to the counter and grabbed a napkin.

"This conversation doesn't concern you," said Vanessa.

"So you don't deny it?" Peter asked.

"No. I mean yes. I mean no—I never said I don't like Noelle."

"Daniel's mom?" Greg wiped crumbs off his lips. "What's wrong with her?"

"Nothing," Peter said. "She's wonderful."

"She never brings snacks," said Vanessa. "When you passed the list around at the parents' meeting, she didn't even sign up."

"Perhaps she didn't want to be ridiculed again," said Peter. "I don't blame her."

"It's not just snacks." Vanessa wiped off the tile countertops. "She never signs up for anything. Class parties. Field trips. Nothing. I have never, not once, seen her at a PTA meeting."

"She's a working mom," Peter said, louder than he intended.

Vanessa tossed the microfiber cloth into the sink. "I'm a working mom, too, and I still show up."

"You're not a single parent. How can you be so unfair? Noelle lost her husband, for crying out loud."

"But this was going on before Jeff died," said Vanessa. "Greg, time to brush your teeth." He took one look at his mom's furious expression and rushed out of the kitchen.

"Jeff died when Daniel was in pre-K."

"Yes, and that's tragic. He was a nice guy. I mean, we weren't friends or anything, but he was decent."

"So why can't you cut Noelle some slack instead of expecting her to be superwoman?" Peter brushed hair off his forehead. "I don't get it. You of all people too. You're so big on rooting for women and the disadvantaged and oppressed and then—"

"Disadvantaged?" Vanessa's voice squeaked. "You think Noelle is disadvantaged?"

"Well, yeah. Don't you? She's a widow and a single mom."

"I'm not sure I'd call her a single mom. She's got full-time grandma help."

The way Vanessa channeled her envy into vitriol against Noelle annoyed him. "Are you saying that *you'd* want *your* mother-in-law living with you?" he asked, his voice rising.

Vanessa scowled. "I didn't say that. But at least Joyce showed up to that stupid Grandparents' Day they had last year. She even made wooden flower arrangements for all the tables. Do you know who came with Greg?"

"No." The hurt of their mother leaving them pierced him again. "Should I?"

"Me!" Vanessa slapped her hand across her chest. "I had to be the grandma since Ian's parents live out of town and our parents are . . . you know . . ."

"Okay, Grandparents' Day is triggering; I get that." Peter lowered his voice.

"It's not just triggering. It goes on forever." Tears welled up in Vanessa's eyes. "First Mom leaves, then Dad's gone all the time, and then when I finally think I'm done with that shit, my kids don't have grandparents like everyone else."

"That's hard. I'm sorry. But Noelle—"

"She's a private school grad who owns her own home and makes fistfuls of money selling real estate."

"Real estate is a lot more complicated than that. You make it sound easy, and it isn't. Noelle works hard for her living."

"*I* work hard," Vanessa snapped. "But you don't see me buying a brand-new minivan every two years."

"We *lease* our vehicles. For work. Rick insists that all of the Windswept agents drive late-model cars."

"It's not fair that Noelle makes so much money. She didn't graduate from college like you did."

"How's that any of your business?"

Vanessa picked up her cloth and began vigorously polishing the stove. "I didn't go to college, and you want to know how much money I make as a para?"

"You don't need to tell me that," said Peter.

"Are you sure? You're my landlord, aren't you? You own this house. Don't you think you have the right to know? Or doesn't it matter since you're giving us a charity rate anyway?"

"Your rent has nothing to do with this." How had the conversation veered so far off topic? Peter was here to defend Noelle, not get into a row with his sister over him charging her below-market rent. When Peter had purchased this house as an investment property, leasing it to Vanessa and Ian had seemed like a win-win. Peter still viewed it that way. He had stable tenants, and Vanessa was able to raise her family in a house she otherwise wouldn't have been able to afford.

"Two bucks above minimum wage." Vanessa spat out the words like they were poison. "That's how much I earn at the school district."

"That's . . ." Peter didn't know what to say.

"Ian delivers mail all over this town," she said, "and I'm on the playground and in the lunchroom at the school every day taking care of neighborhood children, and we still wouldn't be able to afford to live in Skagiton without you." She squeezed her eyes shut.

"That's not fair," Peter said. "Skagiton has changed over the past few decades, and it's hard, but—"

"How is it that an ice cream clerk can come here and make a bunch of money and pretend like she's better than everyone, when someone like me, who's the heart and soul of this town, can barely scrape by?"

"What?" Peter stepped back. "Are you mad that Noelle's making a bunch of money or that you're not?"

"Noelle doesn't even comment in Skagiton Moms," Vanessa continued, ignoring Peter's question. "She's a lurker, and I can't stand lurkers."

"And I can't stand judgmental know-it-alls."

"Mom, where's my lunch?" Milo asked, coming into the kitchen wearing his backpack.

"Here you go." Vanessa handed him an insulated bag. "Go get in the car. I'll meet you there."

"What do you mean, *ice cream clerk*?" Peter asked, not that it made any difference to him where Noelle used to work.

"Didn't you hear Pastor Olivia ask Noelle what she did before she sold real estate?"

"No. That must have been when I was in the restroom."

Vanessa blew a puff of bangs off her face. "I flipped burgers when I was younger. I worked in food service too. Still do, if you count the lunchroom. Noelle's no better than me, even though she acts like it."

"She doesn't," Peter said with a surge of anger. "She's shy; that's all."

"Real estate agents aren't shy. That makes no sense. You're just so smitten by Noelle's damsel-in-distress act that you can't see what a horrible person she is."

"No." Peter's blood pounded so hard that he was surprised his heart didn't leap out of his chest. It felt like his throat was constricting. When he spoke, he barely managed to scrape the words out. "You're the horrible person in this scenario—only I've been too stupid to realize it. I don't understand how you can be so cruel."

"That's rich. I dare you to find one person in this town who agrees with you."

"Noelle! Noelle would agree with me!"

"Someone *besides* Noelle."

"You're a snob, Vanessa. You know that? A snob. I just never realized that until now."

"Says the person driving a Mercedes around town. Where'd you get those chinos, Peter? The Brooks Brothers outlet? Is that a sheep I see on your polo shirt?"

"Whoa," said Greg. "What's going on?"

Waylon stood next to him, eating the last doughnut. "Maybe they ate too much sugar."

"There's nothing wrong with my shirt," said Peter. "Or my car." He picked up the empty box of doughnuts and turned toward Greg. "See you at baseball practice tonight."

"And not a moment before," said Vanessa, following Peter to the back door. "Learn to make your own damn dinner."

"Oooooh," said Waylon. "Mom said a bad word."

"Shut up, Waylon," said Greg.

Vanessa swung the door open for Peter. "Good luck with the Dairy Queen."

"Don't call her that," Peter growled.

"What?" Vanessa batted her eyelashes. "I thought you'd be proud of me. Everyone else in town knows her as the peanut butter bomber."

"Because of you," said Peter. "Grow up."

"Maybe you should try that yourself," she said, then slammed the door.

Fuming, Peter jumped in his car and turned the radio on full blast to his second-favorite country station, the one that played music in the morning instead of talk shows. He let Luke Combs's latest hit calm him down on the five-minute drive to work. By the time he arrived at the Windswept Realty parking lot, his blood pressure was back to normal, and he knew what he had to do: walk into the bullpen and apologize to Noelle for Vanessa's rotten behavior. The margarita dumping might have been an accident, but the snide comments clearly hadn't been. Noelle didn't deserve any of it, and Peter was embarrassed to be in this position. The person he had hero-worshipped his whole life, even when she had made him mad, had made the woman he cared about feel like crap. Peter let the song on the radio finish before turning off the car. Then, squaring his shoulders, he walked into the office to face Noelle.

"Hey, Peter." Debbie waved to him from the front desk. "Good morning."

"Hi." Peter smiled. "Happy Thursday."

"Let's hope so." Debbie looked back at her computer.

Peter decided that it *would* be a happy Thursday. He'd make it so. There was nothing that coffee and conversation with Noelle couldn't fix. But when he walked into the bullpen, the lights were off. When he checked the office kitchen, she wasn't there either. Her absence made him ache with loneliness. Peter dropped a pod of coffee into the machine and brewed it in silence. He wished he'd had the foresight to buy an extra doughnut. Not only had he skipped breakfast, but now he was drinking coffee completely alone.

SKAGITON MOMS FACEBOOK GROUP

Alastrina Kelly
Thursday, March 10

Moms, I don't know what to do. My dad has been living with us for three months now after moving here from Yakima. As some of you might remember, my mom died of cervical cancer last year. Yesterday I was cleaning the guest bathroom and found a box of condoms!!! My husband has had a vasectomy so they were definitely not his. What should I do? Should I confront my dad? My husband says I should keep my mouth shut, but I don't think I can.

Lexie Britt
I wouldn't say anything. LOL. This is none of your business.

Dorothy Caulfield
Of course it's her business, *Lexie Britt*. He's living under her roof, isn't he?

Lexie Britt
Yes, but he's a grown adult, *Dorothy Caulfield*. He can have a love life if he wants to.

Dorothy Caulfield
A love life doesn't require a box of condoms. Gross!

Vanessa Collins
You're the one who's gross, *Dorothy Caulfield*. It sounds like *Alastrina Kelly*'s father is a responsible widower who's protecting himself and others against disease.

Alastrina Kelly
But how many others, *Vanessa Collins*? No, wait. I don't want to know! Gah! What am I going to do?

Vanessa Collins
Ask him about it like a mature adult.

Alastrina Kelly
I wouldn't even know what to say, *Vanessa Collins*.

Vanessa Collins
Say: "Hey Dad, I noticed you have a box of condoms underneath the sink. Have you met anyone special that you'd like to invite

over for dinner?" That's what I would do if my dad lived nearby.

Fern Sharp
Do you know if the condoms are organic or not? Personal hygiene products can be riddled with chemicals.

Maggie Swan
Who's your dad and where is he meeting people? I'm just curious.

Alastrina Kelly
I don't know if I should say his name because he'd be so embarrassed, *Maggie Swan*.

Maggie Swan
That's fair. Okay, don't say his name but where does he hang out, *Alastrina Kelly*?

Carmen Swan
Mom. Chill.

Maggie Swan
I was just asking. Jeez!

Alastrina Kelly
The YMCA, *Maggie Swan*. He teaches yoga.

Chapter Eleven

"I don't understand," said Joyce as she reclined on her yoga mat. "You're telling me Vanessa intentionally poured an entire pitcher of margaritas over your new raincoat?"

"Not intentionally, no." Noelle sat cross-legged on her mat and tried to get comfortable. She'd borrowed a mat at the YMCA instead of buying a new one like Joyce had done. In retrospect, that was probably a mistake. The yoga room boasted soft lighting, a wall of mirrors, and relaxing artwork, but the communal mats stunk like old flip-flops.

"Then why'd you say she did it on purpose?" Joyce sipped from her water bottle.

"Who did what on purpose?" asked a woman with short white hair and purple flowers tattooed up her right arm. Her sparkly tanzanite nose ring complemented the petals.

"Nobody did anything on purpose," Noelle reiterated. She didn't know who the stranger was or why the woman thought she could butt into their conversation until Joyce made the introductions.

"Helen, this is my daughter-in-law, Noelle Walters."

Helen reached out her fist for a bump. "Nice to meet you, Noelle. I feel like I already know you since Joyce talks about you so much."

"Er . . . uh . . . nice to meet you too." Noelle fist-bumped her back.

"Helen and I are the only ones from water aerobics who can do rocking horse in deep water," said Joyce.

Helen nodded. "We use the blue weights too."

"That's impressive," said Noelle, even though she didn't know anything regarding the complexities of water aerobics.

Helen rolled out her yoga mat on the other side of Noelle. The studio's lights were low but still bright enough to see well, and instrumental music played in the background. As Helen knelt on her mat, Noelle noticed something about her profile that seemed familiar, but she couldn't quite place it. "Have we met before?" Noelle asked.

Helen smiled sadly. "Probably at Jeff's memorial service."

"Oh. Right." Noelle exhaled, but the stress stuck with her.

"Helen has two daughters," Joyce explained. "The older one went to high school with Jeff."

"Jourdaine was a sophomore when Jeff was a senior," said Helen. "So they had two years together."

"That's it," Noelle blurted out. She covered her mouth with her hand.

"That's what?" Helen asked.

"You're Jourdaine Bloomfield's mom, right? I thought you looked familiar."

"Yup." Helen smiled proudly and sat up straight. "Jourdaine is a CPA."

"She did my books for the first couple of years that Wood You Be Mine? started out," said Joyce. "Jourdaine's smart as a whip."

"Zara's my younger daughter, and she's exceptional in her own way too," said Helen.

Noelle scrambled to remember what she knew about Zara. She thought she'd seen that name on Skagiton Moms, but she wasn't sure. "Zara lives here too, right?"

Helen nodded. "She owns the pottery studio Wheel Me Around. Have you been?"

That was it. "No, not yet. But my son has been asking to go."

"You should," said Helen. "It's fun, and Zara has it set up so that it doesn't matter how big of a mess you make."

Joyce laughed. "That sounds like our living room."

Noelle rolled her eyes. "I'm glad you can laugh about the disappearance of our couch."

"It's either laugh or put up a missing persons sign." Joyce removed her sweatshirt and revealed a tank top and sports bra.

"You're bringing out the guns, I see," said Helen. "I didn't know this was a competition." She flexed, and the flowers encircling her biceps danced. "Zara hates it when I do this." Helen folded her hands in her lap. "Maybe I should wait until she gets here so I can embarrass her."

"Zara's coming?" Joyce clasped her hands together. "Oh, goody. I've been wanting to introduce her to Noelle for a while." She speared Noelle with a look. "It would be good for you to have some friends your age to hang out with. Friends besides me."

"I have friends," said Noelle. "They just happen to live in Hollenbeck." She pulled down her sleeves and popped her thumbs through the built-in hobo mitts. The opportunity to wear her brand-new exercise outfit was the only reason she hadn't chickened out about coming today.

"When did you move here?" Helen asked.

"Ten years ago," said Noelle.

"Oh." Helen lifted her eyebrows. "Well, there's this great Facebook group for moms such as yourself that Jourdaine's always telling me about. Have you heard of it? It's called Skagiton Moms."

"Skagiton Moms . . . yeah, I'm already in it, although I don't comment much." *Or at all,* Noelle thought to herself.

"Really?" Helen raised her perfectly microbladed eyebrows. "Jourdaine claims it's a hoot. She tried to get Zara in, but the moderators wouldn't let her join."

"Why not?" Joyce asked.

"That's what I wanted to know." Helen frowned and stretched out her legs. "Apparently they only let moms join."

"I'm a mom," said Joyce. "Well . . ."

"You're still a mom." Noelle felt Joyce's heartbreak as her own. "To me, and to Jeff." She rubbed her mother-in-law's back.

"Thanks." Joyce reached behind her to squeeze Noelle's hand. "Do you think they'd let me join?"

"Sure," said Helen. "I don't see why not. But I heard it's a drama fest." She looked at Noelle. "Is that true?"

Noelle nodded. "Yeah. Kind of." She felt conflicted admitting that—not out of any loyalty to the group but because she'd been raised not to gossip.

"Jourdaine says that Maggie Swan's daughter is the worst offender," said Helen.

"Ooh!" Joyce's lips formed into an O like she was about to blow out candles on a birthday cake. "Maggie is such a loudmouth that I'm not surprised."

Helen nodded in agreement. "It's true. She won't shut up during water aerobics."

Joyce elbowed Noelle gently in the ribs. "That's how I knew about Mike's athlete's foot."

"He's a toad," Helen sneered.

"And he's maxed out four credit cards and asked Maggie for a loan to make payday," said Joyce.

"Wow," said Noelle. "That's even worse than a fungal infection."

"Yes." Helen grimaced. "He's a toad, and his mother's a skunk. I'll never forget how she knew what Mike was doing to Zara in high school but didn't stop him."

"What happened?" Noelle asked.

"He harassed her," said Helen. "And Maggie let him get away with it because, as she said, 'Boys will be boys.' If it weren't for Jourdaine and her friends Vanessa and Corine, then—"

Suddenly, the lights flickered and then went out completely. When they turned back on, a soft glow lit the room. The instrumental music that had been playing in the background shifted into something with a strong, pounding rhythm mixed with an ethereal flute.

"Welcome, yogis," said a deep voice from the back of the room.

Noelle turned and saw a man with shoulder-length silver hair, skin-tight pants, and an open shirt. The light dancing off the candle he held illuminated his thick patch of gray chest hair as he bowed forward in greeting.

"Yes please," Helen murmured.

"Who's that?" Noelle asked.

"Stone." Joyce waved her hand girlishly.

"Otherwise known as the Silver Fox," said Helen.

Noelle hoped that Stone stood far enough away that he couldn't hear them.

"For today's class you'll need two blocks and a blanket," said Stone as he glided through the classroom. When he reached the stage, he rolled out a teal yoga mat next to a bronze bell and set down the candle.

"Blocks?" Noelle whispered. She had no idea what that meant. Apparently Joyce didn't either because she hopped off her mat and walked up to the front of the classroom to speak with the instructor. No, Noelle realized. *Walked* wasn't the right word; *sashayed* was more like it. She'd never seen her mother-in-law swing her hips like that.

"The props are over in the corner," said Helen.

"Huh?" Noelle asked, still a bit shocked to see Joyce wiggle like a Jell-O mold.

"The yoga blocks and blankets are over there." Helen pointed to a cabinet. "This is my third class. I'm practically a regular."

"Thanks." Noelle stood. "I wonder if I should get some for Joyce too."

"Oh, I wouldn't worry about her." Helen grinned. "Joyce can handle herself. It looks like Stone's giving her a downward dog tutorial right now."

"He is?" Noelle whipped her gaze back to the stage and saw her mother-in-law bent forward, hands flat on the ground, with Stone's palms on her back. Noelle gasped. "Is it normal for yoga instructors to touch people like that?"

"Stone offers adjustments." Helen picked up a square coaster in front of her mat. "If you like adjustments, grab one of these coasters with the props so he knows it's okay to touch you. If not, no problem. He won't offer adjustments unless he sees a coaster."

Passing on the coaster seemed like a good idea to Noelle. In fact, she wished she had passed on this whole class. Sure, she loved her new exercise outfit. The leggings had so much spandex in them that she did a double take every time she walked past a mirror. She'd had no idea her butt could look that good. The short-sleeved top that went with it had a matching jacket. In addition to the thumbholes, there were hidden pockets, reflective striping, and antistink fabric technology. The loop on her zipper could be used as an emergency hair tie. The outfit made her feel like it had magical powers. When she saw her reflection in the mirror, she wanted to exercise. Just maybe not here with Joyce, Helen, and the Silver Fox.

Noelle wandered to the props corner, picked up a blanket and blocks, and came back to her mat, dropping them unceremoniously at her feet. Yoga hadn't even started yet, and she was already stretched past her comfort zone.

"Would it be okay if you moved your yoga mat over a couple of feet?" a woman asked. Pink and green streaks highlighted her hair and matched the bow ties the cats on her leggings were wearing. "I want to squeeze in next to my mom."

"Sure." Noelle pushed her mat over and moved the props along too.

"You're late," said Helen. "But I'm glad you made it. Noelle, this is my younger daughter, Zara."

"From Wheel Me Around," said Noelle. "I've heard great things about your studio."

"Thanks." Zara unfurled her mat and pulled blocks out of her gym bag that she must have brought from home. "I had to wait for the kiln to cool, or I would have been here earlier."

"Don't want to burn down Main Street," said Helen.

Zara shook her head. "Nope. Not today, at least."

Was that a joke? Noelle wasn't sure until Zara grinned, causing her to smile too.

"Well, that was educational," said Joyce as she came back to the mat with flushed cheeks. She held a block under each arm and had a blanket draped over her shoulder. "Stone says that I'm a natural."

"It must be all the water aerobics," said Helen. "You and I have great muscle tone."

"So true," said Joyce, sitting down. "Hi, Zara. Good to see you wearing clothes for once."

"What?" Noelle asked, feeling shocked.

Zara laughed. "She means outside of the sauna. We always seem to run into each other in the locker room."

"Oh," said Noelle, who had never, not once, even considered stepping foot in a sauna. Hang out with naked people? No way.

"Why is the instructor's shirt unbuttoned?" Zara asked.

"I was wondering that too," Noelle admitted. "I thought that it was a yoga thing."

"It's not," said Zara. "At least not for hatha yoga. If this were hot yoga, sure, but . . ."

"Hot yoga. I read about that." Joyce folded her blanket and sat on it. "I think I might pass out if the room were too warm."

"The first time I tried it, I almost died." Zara stretched out her legs. "I had to step out of the studio three times."

"Do they do that here?" Noelle asked. "Hot yoga, I mean."

Zara shook her head. "No, I drove down with a friend to Everett to try it. But the yoga classes the Y offers are great. I usually attend the noon ones. I've been trying to get my mom to come with me for a while now, but she wasn't willing to try until recently."

"Stone came to water aerobics a few weeks ago and explained the benefits," said Helen. "This is a brand-new time slot for yoga."

"I explained the benefits, too, Mom, and you completely ignored me," said Zara.

Helen shrugged. "What can I say? Stone was more convincing."

"The Zumba people are pissed," said Joyce.

"Why?" Noelle asked.

Joyce held her fingertips and stretched her wrist. "Their class had to move to the basketball court."

"Not the pickleball court, though," said Helen. "Nobody messes with pickleball."

Zara shuddered. "The pickleball crowd scares me."

"Don't be ridiculous." Helen wagged her finger. "Half of my friends play pickleball."

"Exactly." Zara leaned back on her hands. "They're a bunch of retirees with too much time on their hands. They won't let you play unless you're a level five expert."

"How many levels are there?" Noelle asked.

"Five and a half," said Helen. "And don't listen to Zara say bad things about my friends. They allow level three and four players to play too."

"Below that, and they make you take the beginners course," said Joyce. "They're a bunch of snobs, if you ask me."

"See?" Zara flicked her mom's shoulder. "Joyce agrees with me. The pickleball crowd is scary."

"*Snobby*," Joyce corrected. "I'm not scared of any of them."

"Well, I am." Zara rolled her ankles around in circles. "That one woman, Dorothy Caulfield, threatened to report me to management and get my membership revoked when she saw my water bottle in the locker room."

Noelle recognized Dorothy's name from Skagiton Moms. If she was remembering correctly, Dorothy was opposed to the hygiene kits and hated Jourdaine's guts.

"What's wrong with your water bottle?" Helen asked. "I gave that to you for your birthday."

Zara held up her Nalgene bottle. "Dorothy objected to the stickers."

"I can't see what they say," said Joyce. "The light's too low. Read 'em for me, will you, Noelle?"

"Um . . ." Noelle glanced up at the clock. Class was due to start in two minutes.

"Here you go." Zara handed her the bottle.

Noelle squinted in the dim light and began to read. "Crush the patriarchy, not the planet. Women carry half the world. Girls just want to have fun-damental human rights. Bitches change the world."

"That's the one that ticked Dorothy off," said Zara. "She said that girls visiting the YMCA shouldn't be exposed to curse words." Zara took her water bottle back and spun it around. "Then I showed her this one, and she went ballistic."

"Ribs don't birth children," Noelle read. "Vaginas do." Her eyes opened wide. Zara's water bottle would have gotten her kicked out of Trivium High School the first day. "Where do you find stickers like that?"

"Amazon. Etsy. Online stores," said Zara. "I'm thinking about selling them in my studio."

A low tone reverberated across the classroom. Noelle looked up and saw Stone ringing the brass bell with a small hammer. "The next forty-five minutes are for you," he said. "Let's begin with a series of deep, cleansing breaths."

Noelle filled her lungs with air.

"Close your eyes, and focus on a thought or saying," said Stone. "Whatever floats into your brain first."

Ribs don't birth children . . . shoot! Anything but that.

"Inhale and exhale, focusing on your phrase," said Stone. "Breathe your mantra in, and let it out slowly."

Ribs don't birth children. Noelle could see it clearly—that sticker on Zara's water bottle—even though her eyes were closed. She tried to push it away, but it was right there in front of her, begging her to think of it: *Ribs don't birth children. Vaginas do.*

"Breathe in," Stone intoned. "Breathe out."

Ribs don't birth children.

Stop. She commanded her brain to pick a different phrase. Something relaxing or about motherhood. But she couldn't think of anything. Her mind wandered across the stickers on Zara's water bottle. *Women carry half the world.*

"Let tension roll off your neck," said Stone.

Women carry half the world. Noelle sucked in oxygen like she was in danger of drowning.

Stone walked past her mat. "Exhale deeply, and let stress melt off your shoulders."

Noelle released a whoosh of air. *Women carry half the world.* She felt that on a deep level. Her arms ached from all she carried. The financial burdens of single parenthood. The challenge of raising Daniel without Jeff. Her loneliness in Skagiton with nobody to confide in except for Joyce. Plus there was the ever-present mental load of daily living. What would she make for dinner? When would she have time to go shopping? Did the oil need to be changed in her car? How many more days until her credit card bill was due?

Women carry half the world. In Noelle's case, it felt like she held up all of it.

"Are you okay?" Zara whispered.

"What?" Noelle opened her eyes. The first thing she saw was Zara's water bottle.

Zara reached into her gym bag. "Here's a tissue," she whispered, placing it gently in Noelle's palm.

Noelle blew her nose. "Thanks," she said, ashamed to have been caught crying.

"Welcome to your first yoga class," Zara whispered. "I'm glad to have a friend with me who's closer to my age."

Noelle stashed the tissue in the side pocket of her leggings. "Me too," she whispered back. "Me too."

SKAGITON MOMS FACEBOOK GROUP

Carmen Swan
Thursday, March 10

Attention all baseball moms! Can anyone pleeeeeease cover my slot at the Snack Shack tonight? My littlest one is puking. Unless you want your hotdogs served with a side of barf germs, I can't work the booth tonight. LOL!

Vanessa Collins
Not it.

Carmen Swan
That's not helpful, *Vanessa Collins*. Can't you keep your big fat mouth shut for once?

Melissa James
There is zero excuse for body shaming, *Carmen Swan*. Don't use fat like it's a curse word.

Carmen Swan
Seriously, *Melissa James*?

Melissa James
Yes, seriously, *Carmen Swan*. Say what you mean without criticizing people for what they look like.

Fern Sharp
Especially since the obesity epidemic, like so many health problems in America, is directly tied to chemicals, *Melissa James*. Do we know if the hot dogs are organic or not?

Tracey Fukui
All three of my boys have practice tonight at the same time. I could probably help.

Carmen Swan
Thank you, *Tracey Fukui*! I'll pm you the details.

Chapter Twelve

The line to the Snack Shack was ten people deep, but Peter had no choice but to wait it out. After his confrontation with Vanessa this morning, he had been forced to find other plans for dinner before Little League practice. The T. Rexes would be here in ten minutes. Hopefully he could wolf down a couple of hot dogs by then. As he waited in line, Peter scanned the fields for any sign of Noelle or Daniel. He hadn't seen her since last night when he'd dropped her off after the school board meeting. She'd seemed tired, and he worried that the evening had been too much for her, especially after Vanessa's mean-spirited comment about her handwriting.

Shoot. Thinking ahead to Mother's Day, Peter realized that inviting Vanessa to Noelle's big event was probably a bad idea. The last thing Noelle would want to do was wait on Vanessa, and it didn't seem like Vanessa would be interested in supporting Noelle either. What an idiot he'd been to think that was a good idea in the first place. No, not an idiot—a foolish younger brother who couldn't see his sister's flaws because he loved her so much.

"Are you Peter Marshal?" asked a woman standing behind him. Her dark-brown hair curled in ringlets around her face, and her Washington State Cougars hoodie fit her snugly.

Peter scanned his memory banks, trying to place her, but came up empty. "Yes," he said. "Have we met before? I'm sorry, I—"

"Oh, we've never been formally introduced." The woman pulled a curl behind her ear. "I recognized you from the bench in front of the library. You're a real estate agent, right?"

"Yup. Are you looking to buy or sell a house?"

"I wish. My daughter and I are crammed into a one-bedroom apartment at the moment. But all of my capital is tied up with my business, so scraping together a down payment is out of the question. They didn't teach me about *that* in FBLA."

"Future Business Leaders of America?" Peter gave her a second look. "*I* was in FBLA. Wait, did you go to Washington State?"

"Nope. I was an Idaho State alum. Sometimes, I wish I was still back in my home state. The music there is better. I can only get two country radio stations here, but other than that, I like it in Washington."

"I love country music. I wish there was more variety on the radio because the two stations we have only play modern stuff."

"Exactly. We need a nineties station. More Garth and less 'hot new thing.'" She held out her hand. "I'm Renee Schroth, by the way. It doesn't seem fair that I should know all about you when you don't even know my name."

"Nice to meet you." Peter shook her hand. "But you're funny. All you know about me is that I'm a real estate agent."

"*And* that you love country music *and* were in FBLA." She bumped him with her hip. "We're practically old friends. Plus, aren't you Vanessa Collins's brother? She talks about you on Skagiton Moms all the time."

Peter stepped forward in line. There were still three people ahead of him. "I get half my clients from Vanessa's word-of-mouth advertising. She's better than a bus stop ad."

"I don't think I've ever heard someone describe their sister that way." Renee chuckled. "Not even my college roommate, who was the youngest of nine. Four brothers and four sisters."

"My college roommate was an only child who didn't do his laundry for three whole months until I showed him how to use the washing machine."

"Eww." Renee wrinkled her nose.

"Next door to us was the current mayor, and his room smelled even worse."

"Ryan James?"

Peter nodded. "Vanessa walked by it when she was visiting me and said it smelled like a truck stop."

"Well, now she has three stinky little boys, right? Karma."

Peter laughed. Talking with Renee was fun. "Spoken like the mother of a daughter."

"You've got a good memory."

"Not really." Peter took out his wallet. "You just mentioned it."

"Yeah, but most people don't pay very good attention."

Embarrassed by praise from a person he'd just met, Peter changed the subject. "Is your daughter at practice?"

Renee nodded. "Softball. At this age it's more playing in mud than anything else, but she loves it. I'm going to surprise her with a pretzel and cheese sauce. It's not much of a dinner, but I was at the shop late and didn't have time to run to the store."

"That's right. You said you had a business. What do you do?"

Renee rolled her shoulders back and lifted her chin with pride. "I own my own clothing boutique at the outlet mall, and it's one of only three stores there that's not a franchise. People come all the way from Canada and Seattle to shop there."

"Cool." Peter scratched the back of his head as he tried to remember the stores at the outlet mall. "Maybe I've been there and didn't know it."

Renee laughed. "I don't think so, unless you like bras."

"I love bras." He grinned. "Just not on me."

"Next," called the woman working at the Snack Shack register.

Peter stepped up to the counter. When he saw who was volunteering tonight, he waved. "Hi, Tracey. How'd they rope you into this?"

"The old-fashioned way: by offering free ice cream." Tracey Fukui adjusted her plastic serving gloves. "But the calculator's broken, and I'm having a heck of a time remembering how to count back change. What'll it be?"

"Two hot dogs and a soda."

"Are you sure you don't want two drinks?" Tracey pointed at Renee. "One for each of you?"

"Oh, we're not together," said Renee. "I'm single."

"Same." Peter's eyes scanned the menu. "But go ahead and put Renee's pretzel and cheese sauce on my receipt so it'll be an even ten bucks."

"You don't have to do that," said Renee.

"I know." Peter picked a bill out of his wallet and gave it to Tracey. "But this way Tracey won't have to make change."

"Thank goodness." Tracey dropped the ten-dollar bill into the cashbox. "That makes it so much easier. I'll be right back."

"What's the name of your clothing store?" Peter asked as they waited for their food.

"Knockers on Heaven's Door."

"Clever."

"Thanks," said Renee. "I always wanted to own my own business, and when the space opened at the mall, it seemed like the right time. That was two years ago. Little did I know that my husband would walk out on our marriage a few months later."

"Yikes."

"Ran off with a coworker." Renee shrugged. "But now my daughter and I are closer than ever."

"Do you think she'll inherit your entrepreneurial spirit?"

"Unfortunately, no. If her ability to sell Camp Fire candy is any indication, we still have a lot of work to do."

"Have her swing by Windswept Realty the next time she sells. I'll be sure to buy a case."

"Wow. You must really love candy."

"And supporting after-school organizations that help kids." Peter stuffed his hands in his pockets. As a boy, he'd sold chocolate bars to fund his Little League fees and popcorn pails for Boy Scouts. Corine Reeder's mom had bought a case of whatever he'd sold. She had been Vanessa's Girl Scout leader and had helped connect Peter with her friend Arlene Davis, whose husband ran Boy Scouts. Social media hadn't existed back then, but those moms had run the town without any Facebook group to help them. Peter knew that he was a lucky beneficiary of their attention.

"Order's up," called Tracey, holding a tray with two hot dogs in one hand and a pretzel in the other. "You can grab a soda from the cooler."

"Thanks." Peter picked up his dogs and dug into the ice chest for a Coke. "It was nice meeting you," he said to Renee as she grabbed napkins for her daughter's pretzel.

"It really was. Thanks again for the pretzel."

At the condiments station, Peter was so focused on the ketchup that he didn't realize Renee was still standing next to him until she spoke up and startled him.

"Would you like to meet for coffee one morning?" she asked.

"What?" Peter jabbed his fist too hard on the dispenser, and ketchup squirted out and splashed his jacket.

"Oh no!" Renee passed him a napkin. "That might stain."

Peter looked down at the T. Rex sweatshirt he was wearing. "It looks like blood. The boys will probably like that."

Renee laughed. "True, but I think I have a stain stick in my purse. Hold this for me." She handed him the pretzel and unsnapped her bag.

"Thanks." Peter wedged the unopened soda under his arm so he could hold three things at once. That was almost as tricky as coming up with a response to her invitation to coffee. She was an attractive woman who seemed like she had a lot going for her, but she wasn't Noelle, whom, out of the corner of his eye, he watched walk onto the field with Daniel. "Thanks for the invitation to coffee, but I'm seeing someone right now." It wasn't a lie so much as a white lie.

"You are?" Renee uncapped the stain stick. "That's a shame." She stepped toward him, so close that a ringlet of her curly hair brushed his face. "Let me get this for you," she said as she scribbled on him with the stain stick.

"Hey," Peter gasped, laughing. "That tickles."

"Laundry is a sensitive matter." Renee capped the stick. "Be sure to wash it in warm water as soon as you get home." She looked up at him through long lashes. "Don't forget."

"I won't," he said, his pulse racing in spite of himself. "Here's your pretzel. I mean, your daughter's pretzel. You never did tell me her name."

"That would be something we could talk about over coffee." Renee winked. "Someday, maybe, if you were ever free." Waving her fingertips, she turned her head and walked away.

"Hey, Uncle Pete," said a voice from behind him.

Peter looked down and saw Greg pounding his fist into a baseball mitt. "Mom says to tell you that practice is supposed to start in two minutes and you better get your butt over there. Only she didn't say butt; she said ass."

"What?"

"She's been cussing all day. What was in those doughnuts you brought us this morning? F-bombs?"

"No. Of course not." Peter shoved a hot dog into his mouth and chewed furiously. Vanessa always lost her cool when she was upset. "Grandpa was a fisherman," he said, with his mouth full of hot dog. "We heard a very colorful vocabulary growing up." He handed the soda to his nephew. "Open this for me. Will ya?"

Greg popped the tab. "Mom also said to tell you that the woman you were talking to right now is a total babe who sells lingerie and that if you don't get her number, you're dumber than she thought. Only she didn't say dumber, she said dumbass. A *bigger* dumbass."

Peter swallowed before speaking this time. "I get the picture."

"What's lingerie?"

"Underwear."

"Yuck!"

Peter dumped the tray into the trash and finished eating the last hot dog as they walked to the practice area. As he approached the T. Rexes, he looked up in the stands and saw Vanessa glaring at him. That didn't surprise him. But what he hadn't expected was seeing the look of pure horror on Noelle's face. There she was, at the opposite end of the bleachers as his sister, staring at him like he was about to burst into flames.

Renee from the bra shop must have seen Vanessa's advertisement on Skagiton Moms and made her play for Peter—that was the only explanation for what she'd just witnessed. Noelle clenched her fists so tightly that her fingernails dug into her skin. How could she have been so stupid? Last night when Peter had taken her out for tapas and to the school board meeting, she should have said something. She could have warned Peter about what his sister was doing, how Vanessa was parading him on Skagiton Moms like a stud bull. How could she be his friend and not warn him about what was happening? Except . . . he didn't look like he needed to be warned. He looked like he really liked Renee and wanted to know her better.

Noelle dropped her gaze to her feet. She stared at the toes of the new brown boots she was wearing, the ones that had a short heel and would be ruined after ten minutes of barn work. She felt foolish for wearing them and the slim black pants that went with them. This whole new outfit was a mistake. Noelle pulled up the hood of her raincoat, even though it wasn't raining, and buried her hands in her pockets so she was fully concealed.

Renee's a nice person, she told herself. *Helpful and considerate. She'd be great for Peter.* That was true—she couldn't deny it—so why were tears forming in her eyes? Her chest tightened, and she felt the strong urge to run home. Noelle blinked rapidly, forcing the tears to disappear. She wasn't crying, and she was certainly not upset. Peter could date whomever he wanted to. Her ankles bobbed up and down, and her boots clicked against the bleachers. When she looked up, Peter and the T. Rexes were encircled around home plate, and Peter seemed to be giving the boys instructions.

Noelle looked over to the Snack Shack, where she'd seen Renee practically nibble Peter's earlobe. But Renee was gone. Taking a deep breath, Noelle tried to steady herself. Peter was her coworker, nothing more. He was allowed to date. He deserved a girlfriend or wife and family of his own someday. Noelle wanted him to be happy. If anyone deserved to be happy, it was Peter, who was always so kind and attentive. She took another deep breath and tapped her toes.

"Would you cut it out with the foot stomping?" Vanessa called. "You're making the bleachers rattle."

Noelle looked at Vanessa's cold expression. "Sorry," she said. Gluing her legs together, she kept her feet still. Hopefully Vanessa didn't notice how on edge she was. Not knowing what to do or how to handle her emotions, she pulled out her phone and texted her sister.

Hey, Noelle typed, uncertain if Kerry would be near her phone.

Hay is for horses.

Yee haw.

What's up Slowpoke? Kerry asked, using her pet name.

Noelle's thumbs hovered over the screen; she was uncertain of what to say. The only time she'd asked her sister for dating advice had been about Jeff.

"Dad said he'll kick me out of the house if I keep seeing Jeff, and I'm not sure what to do," she had told her.

"Do you love him?" Kerry had asked. *"Because if so, you can live in our camping trailer as long as you want."* With a two-bedroom house and so many kids, there hadn't been extra room in Kerry's house. Plus, Hank had objected, saying that Noelle was breaking the fifth commandment.

I'm sad, Noelle typed. That was hard to admit but easier to write than the other things that were on her heart.

Why are you sad? Is this about Jeff?

Yes. I'm always sad about Jeff. But no, it's not.

Which is it, yes or no? Do you want me to call you?

I can't talk now. I'm at Little League practice.

What can I do to help?

Noelle worked a hangnail on her index finger before replying. I think I like someone. As soon as she typed it out, she felt a big whoosh from her soul, like all the truth she'd been holding back blew out in a gust of air.

Who? That's awesome! Why are you sad?

I don't know what to do about it. Or if he likes me back.

Why wouldn't he like you back? You're amazing.

Noelle looked across the field to where Peter was throwing the ball to one T. Rex after another. He's really popular, she typed after looking back down at her phone. The whole town loves him.

So? That doesn't mean he won't like you.

But what should I do? Noelle spun her wedding ring around her finger.

Maybe you could ask him to sit next to you at church, Kerry suggested. That would be my strategy.

Noelle didn't have the energy to explain how she hadn't attended church since moving out of Kerry's trailer. Growing up, her family had never been religious to begin with because Phil had said nasty things about preachers who asked for money. But Kerry and Hank were devout Calvinists. There were three Dutch churches in Hollenbeck. The first two were official Reformed Churches in America, but the third church had splintered off and become exceedingly strict. That was the congregation Kerry and Hank belonged to. It had greeters at the door that would turn congregants away if they weren't dressed modestly and elders who would call you in for counseling if they suspected you of sin.

The pastor of the local Methodist church is nice, Noelle typed, sidestepping the issue of church attendance.

And what about your wedding ring? Kerry asked. Are you still wearing it?

Feeling put on the spot, Noelle looked down at the gold band and small diamond she'd been fiddling with a few moments ago. Yes, she responded tersely.

Kerry didn't reply until a minute later. When she did, it was a complete paragraph. Look, I'm not saying you need to take your wedding ring off, because I can only imagine how painful that would be, but wearing your wedding ring is like advertising to the world that you're unavailable.

So of course the man you like wouldn't have made a move. It looks like you're still married.

Noelle sighed, realizing that her sister was right. So what should I do? she asked, craving her older sister's direction. Making the decision to remove Jeff's ring was too hard on her own.

You could wear it on a gold chain close to your heart, Kerry suggested. Or perhaps move it to your right hand.

Those are good ideas. Noelle swallowed the lump forming in her throat. Kerry giving her permission to move forward helped, but none of this was easy.

Then once you're no longer wearing your wedding ring on your left hand, you could ask your guy to church. But not a Methodist church. Please tell me you're not going to a Methodist church.

I'm not, Noelle answered truthfully. She wasn't attending any church at all.

Well, that's a relief. Methodists let women be pastors.

Women carry half the world. Zara's water bottle sticker flashed across Noelle's mind. But she'd never challenge Kerry by repeating something as silly as a catchy slogan. Instead she typed from the heart. Thank you for always being there for me. Love you.

Love you too Slowpoke!

After she put her phone in her pocket, Noelle sat on the cold bleachers and stared at the field without seeing it for several minutes. She spun her wedding ring around in a circle again and again. *"With this ring,"* Jeff had murmured. *"I thee wed."* It had been the happiest day of her life. Jeff had taken her away from the trailer and the precariousness of her situation. He had taken her away from a town where everyone knew her father as the angry farmer who fought with the dairy co-op over the unfairness of government regulation. As Noelle Jansen, she'd never had a birth certificate, a social security number, or a driver's license, but as Noelle Walters, she did. Noelle Walters had gone to the dentist and had her two back molars replaced. Noelle Walters had received the childhood vaccinations she'd missed as a child. Noelle Walters had a future. Jeff had given her love and a path forward. But now Jeff was gone.

If she took her ring off and moved it to her right hand, could she still be Noelle Walters? She absolutely, positively did not want to be Noelle Jansen again. It was one thing to drive up to Hollenbeck, put on her Dairy Ambassador crown, and help out at a fundraiser, but she could never go back to her old way of living. It was easier to be Jeff's wife than it was to be herself. Kerry was right, though; moving forward meant letting this visible tie to Jeff go.

"I want you to be happy," Jeff had told her the second time they'd met. The first time had been at a friend's wedding. The second, he'd tracked her down to the ice cream parlor where she worked and ordered one scoop after another until her shift had been done. Afterward, they'd sat outside on the metal chairs, talking. *"Let's go somewhere,"* he'd said. *"You don't have to be stuck here. Let me help you be bold."*

Noelle looked out at the field and scanned the horizon until she saw Daniel picking up a fly ball and tossing it back to a friend. A few yards over, Peter was giving a pitching lesson to another kid. That was her future, right there in front of her. Now she just had to be brave enough to claim it. After using her sleeve to wipe tears out of her eyes, Noelle took her wedding ring off and moved it to her right hand, knowing that Jeff would want her to live life to the fullest.

SKAGITON MOMS FACEBOOK GROUP

Olivia Doyle
Friday, March 11

Hello Skagiton Moms! I hope you're staying dry this stormy morning. Skagiton Methodist Church is hosting an interfaith potluck lunch this Sunday, March 13th, to raise money to purchase a walk-in freezer for the food bank. We will also be collecting non-perishable donations. All are welcome and no contribution is necessary to attend. Our focus is on simplifying your life, connecting with friends new and old, and forming community. Please join us at noon in our reception hall.

Corine Reeder
My Girl Scout troop hosted a canned food drive for the food bank last October and was impressed by our community's generosity. If you are able, please donate online to the food bank, even if you can't come to the fundraiser.

Anissa Solas
Father Gabriel mentioned this at Mass. I'll be there!

Jessica Luoma
My family loves Skagiton Methodist. Their kids' program is so much fun. If you're looking for a church home, join us for the 10:30 service before the potluck.

Fern Sharp
I'll be there with a 100% organic fruit salad.

Sabrina Kruger
All are welcome? What exactly do you mean by that? Please be more specific, *Olivia Doyle.*

Olivia Doyle
I mean all are welcome, *Sabrina Kruger.* Our doors are open to every member of our community.

Sabrina Kruger
What about me and my wife??

Olivia Doyle
Absolutely, *Sabrina Kruger.* We have a LGBTQ+ Bible study running on Wednesday nights if you're interested. As an officially recognized Reconciliation church, we are welcoming and affirming. More information can be found on our church website.

Dorothy Caulfield
I'll be praying for you, *Olivia Doyle.*

Jourdaine Bloomfield
What's that supposed to mean, *Dorothy Caulfield*?

Vanessa Collins
Yeah, what the hell, *Dorothy Caulfield*?

Dorothy Caulfield
It means I don't attend churches that teach false doctrine. You shouldn't either, *Jourdaine Bloomfield.*

Jourdaine Bloomfield
I'm Catholic, *Dorothy Caulfield.*

Vanessa Collins
I'm not a church goer, but if I were, Olivia Doyle would be everything I would want in a pastor, *Dorothy Caulfield.*

Alastrina Kelly
Moderators? Help!

Olivia Doyle
Thank you. *Dorothy Caulfield*, I graciously accept your prayers.

COMMENTS TURNED OFF.

Chapter Thirteen

Noelle searched through the recipe file her mom had given her for a wedding present, to no avail. Every dish she had that would be suitable for a potluck had some sort of dairy product. She picked up the phone and called her mom for help. "Hi, Mom, it's me."

"Hello? Who is this?"

"It's Noelle. Are you okay? You sound kind of groggy."

"Oh. Sorry there, chicken; my trouble's bothering me. The new pessary a friend sold me is supposed to help, but I don't think it fits right."

"Are you in pain?" She knew her mom had been dealing with what Noelle suspected was uterine prolapse for over twenty years. Anika refused to see a doctor and insisted on treating her condition with home remedies that didn't seem to work.

"It's not comfortable; that's for sure. But my tea helps. I put a few drops of a new essential oil in the diffuser that is also quite soothing."

"Have you thought any more about what I said about—"

"No. I'm not going to a doctor to be poked and prodded. Women have been dealing with slipping wombs for as long as they've birthed children."

"I understand that, but—"

"No buts." Anika's tone was sharp. "If you called to harass me, I'll go ahead and hang up."

"I didn't call to harass you," said Noelle. "I'm so sorry, Mom. I called because I need your help."

"Yes, you can move back home. I wouldn't be able to manage without your father either."

"No, actually I needed help figuring out what recipe to make for a potluck. I'm, um . . . all out of milk and butter at the moment. I need to go to the store. But my spring garden is going."

"Good for you. Mine's not doing so great. I should weed more."

"Potluck recipes?" Noelle prompted. "Any suggestions?"

"How about a sausage-and-kale casserole? I assume you have frozen shredded cheese. That's what holds it together."

"All out of that, too, unfortunately."

"Chef's salad with fresh spinach?"

"I thought about that, but your recipe's secret ingredient is cherry tomatoes, and they won't be ripe until summer. Right now they're seedlings on my windowsill."

"Good point. Oh, I got it. How about rhubarb pie? You still have the start of Victoria I gave you, right?"

"I do, and it's mammoth. That's a great idea. Thanks, Mom."

"No problem."

"I'd chat more, but I need to get to work. I love you, Mom."

"Love you too."

Noelle hung up and checked the clock. She'd already walked Daniel to the bus stop this morning, but if she didn't leave in the next few minutes, she'd miss coffee with Peter.

"Joyce?" she called. "Have you left for water aerobics yet? I'm leaving for work and wanted to say goodbye."

"I'm here." Joyce walked into the kitchen wearing tight blue yoga pants and a formfitting hoodie. "I'm skipping the pool today and playing pickleball instead." She beamed. "Stone's joining me for a smoothie afterward. That means we'll have seen each other five days in a row."

Noelle's mouth gaped open. "Are those my yoga pants?"

"Yes. Don't they look great on me?" Joyce wiggled. "My butt hasn't looked this good since my forties." She craned her head around to look at her backside. "These must be extra-strength spandex or something."

Noelle scrambled to come up with the words to say. She didn't mind if Joyce borrowed a sweater or jacket, but her brand-new exercise outfit? No way! It wasn't just the hygiene issue of someone else sweating in her clothes. There was also the fact that the outfit was the only expensive thing she had ever bought for herself. Luckily, when Joyce bent over to tie her shoes, Noelle figured out a good excuse for convincing her to change.

"Um . . . Joyce," she said kindly. "Those pants aren't meant to be worn with normal underwear. You've got a horrible panty line showing."

"What?" Joyce stood and raced to the hallway bathroom. "Oh no! You're right. What do I do?"

"Well, unfortunately there are only two options." Noelle slipped on her new brown boots. "One is to wear the special no-show underwear the store sells to go with them. I'd lend you the pair I bought, but that would be gross. The other option is to go commando, but that would be gross, too, since those pants belong to *me*." Putting the extra emphasis on that last word felt good. Noelle picked up her purse and took out her wallet. This would feel good too. As annoying as Joyce could sometimes be—like this very moment, for example—Noelle loved her with all her heart. She plucked out two hundred-dollar bills and gave them to Joyce. "Why don't you stop by the outlet mall and buy your own outfit today? My treat. That way our sweat won't get mixed up."

The frown Joyce wore melted off her face. "Really?" She took the money and stared down at it. "I guess I should have asked you before I borrowed your clothes anyway. I'm sorry."

"What's mine is yours." Noelle put her wallet back in her purse. "If it weren't for you, I'd have never become a real estate agent to begin with. Let's not forget that Jeff originally thought I should get a full-time job at Dairy Queen."

"And there's nothing wrong with that." Joyce put her hand on Noelle's shoulder. "But I knew you'd never be happy serving ice cream for the rest of your life. Plus, you'd spent enough time being ordered around and told what to do. Now look at you, a real career woman."

"Thanks." Hearing Joyce's praise made her feel warm inside, like her heart glowed.

"I better run up and change into my normal clothes." Joyce turned to leave.

"Wait," said Noelle. "I forgot to tell you that I'm going to a community potluck supporting the food bank this Sunday."

"Well, that's something I never thought I'd hear you say. You're not one for large crowds."

Noelle flushed. "It was Kerry's idea. She suggested I invite Peter to come with Daniel and me." Saying the words out loud made them real. Noelle searched Joyce's face to see her reaction. Should she have asked her permission first to date someone that wasn't her son? Maybe.

"I think that's a wonderful idea to invite Peter," Joyce said after waiting a beat. "And a potluck seems like a . . . um . . . a safe choice. If he says no, it could be because he doesn't like casseroles."

"Do you think he'll say no?"

"No. I don't. But I agree with your sister. This is a good way to ask Peter out."

"I'm not asking him out," Noelle said quickly. "I'm only inviting him to a fundraiser."

"Exactly." Joyce nodded. "It's a great step forward."

A step forward. That's exactly what she was trying to accomplish. Noelle took a deep breath and exhaled. "Thanks for your support."

"Don't mention it." Joyce waved the money. "And thanks for the cash. I haven't gone on a shopping spree since forever."

Noelle checked her watch. "Uh-oh. I better get going or I'll be late. Have fun at pickleball."

"Pickleball's just a warm-up." Joyce winked. "The real adventure will be with Stone later."

"I don't need any details," Noelle said, feeling uncomfortable. But Joyce just laughed and buzzed away to change.

Five minutes later Noelle was in her van driving to work, and her thoughts drifted to that long-ago conversation about her employment potential. It had been right after she'd married Jeff and moved to Skagiton with him. The first couple of months had been spent trekking to one appointment after another. She had gone to the Department of Licensing to finally get her driver's license. She'd been driving farm equipment since she was twelve years old but had never gotten her license, since Phil said the government shouldn't tell people whether they were allowed to be behind a wheel. There were also doctor's appointments and visits to the dentist's office. Noelle had never been to the dentist before, and those appointments had been the worst, especially since her two back molars had rotted and needed to be pulled and replaced with implants. Noelle had lived with toothaches for years. Her mother's remedy of packing them with cloves and rubbing her gums with garlic hadn't worked. The surgeon had said she was lucky that the infection hadn't spread yet. A few more months, and it would have gone into her jaw.

But once those ordeals had been over with, Noelle had had very little to do but clean the house, plant her garden, and wait for Jeff to come home each day. She had done some home-repair tasks, too, since

Jeff was horrible at them. She'd replaced the window screens, fixed the backyard sprinkler system, and installed a new garbage disposal. Still, all those tasks had been easy compared to the hard farmwork she was used to. Jeff had suggested she get a job in fast food, perhaps as a manager, but Joyce had intervened.

Her mother-in-law had picked up a course catalog for the local community college and brought it over one day while Jeff was at work. Together, they had looked through every page, highlighting the classes that appealed to Noelle. Originally, Noelle had skipped over the real estate course, until Joyce had pointed out what a good fit she'd be in that field. *"You're a friendly person who's easy to talk to. You know how to fix things, which is helpful when buying or selling homes. This could be a great career path for you."* Noelle had been intrigued with the idea, and when they had told Jeff, he had been supportive. Noelle had earned her license, joined Windswept Realty, and begun selling houses. By her third month she had already made more money than she'd ever thought possible at the ice cream shop. Now, eight years later, she was able to support her son, treat her mother-in-law, and still have income left over to put in the bank. All because of Joyce's counseling.

Noelle parked her Honda next to Peter's Mercedes and turned off the ignition. She stared at her naked left hand. Joyce was right about the church potluck too. This was a safe way to ask Peter out. The worst thing that could happen would be him saying no, and then she could blame it on the Methodists.

Easy peasy. She could totally do this. Noelle spun the ring that was now on her right hand. Her palms sweated, and her heartbeat raced.

Maybe it would be helpful to have a script. When she had first started out in real estate, Noelle had followed a script for almost everything. A script for cold-calling new clients. A script for visiting a seller's house. A script for advising people what their house was worth. That was what she needed—a script.

But she didn't have time to write one. Peter was probably drinking his coffee right now.

Noelle climbed out of her van and shut the door.

Her boots crunched gravel as she walked up to the office. Opening the front door, she was glad to see that Debbie wasn't at the reception desk. If Peter turned her down, there wouldn't be anyone to witness her humiliation.

Noelle marched determinedly toward the break room. The rich scent of brewing espresso filled the air. She squared her shoulders. This was it. The time was now. Noelle was willing to do brave things for love.

◆ ◆ ◆

"Well, look who finally turned up." Peter picked up his coffee and grinned. "Was the school bus late?"

"It was right on time." Noelle unzipped her raincoat. She wore a caramel-colored sweater, which hugged her curves, and formfitting brown slacks. Peter couldn't stop looking at her.

"I need to ask you something," she said, her voice higher pitched than normal. "It's about this Sunday."

"Sure. Ask me anything." Noelle locking eyes with him like that gave him shivers of delight. She'd never looked at him with such intensity before.

"Morning, folks." Debbie bustled into the break room. "Can you believe the roads? I hit a patch of black ice coming down my street. Thank goodness for all-wheel drive."

"Yeah," Noelle murmured, not taking her eyes off of Peter. "Thank goodness."

Peter wished desperately that he knew what Noelle had been about to ask him. Probably it was a question about a Sunday open house or something, but he hoped it was something more.

"Hey, Peter, are you going to stand there blocking the coffee machine or what?" Debbie asked. "Some of us haven't had caffeine yet."

"Oh. Sorry." He stepped aside.

"Sorry I'm cranky, but this morning has been rough. At least Bill warmed up the car for me before I left for work." Debbie popped in a pod and turned on the machine. "He knows how I hate to wait for the windshield to defrost."

"That was nice of him." Peter was still staring at Noelle, but she'd turned away. When she opened the refrigerator, he noticed something sparkle from her right hand—her wedding ring! Peter did a double take and then glanced quickly at her left one. It was as naked as his own.

"You'd think Bill was being nice," Debbie grumbled. "But really it's because he has so much fishing gear stored in the garage that there's no room for me to park my car. I asked him this morning—I said: 'Bill? How many crab pots does one man need?' And instead of answering, he picked up my keys and said he'd warm up my Jeep." Debbie collected her mug and added a hefty amount of powdered creamer. "He hasn't warmed up my Jeep properly in years, and I'm not talking about cars anymore."

"Whoa. What?" Peter snapped his attention over to Debbie.

"Just seeing if you were paying attention." She laughed. "Bill can warm up my Jeep just fine—thank you very much. Thirty-two years of marriage, and he can still keep it humming." She sauntered out of the kitchen area, but before she left, she glanced over her shoulder. "Let that be a lesson to both of you. There's no use hanging around in the cold alone if there's a good person willing to warm up your car."

"I don't understand why she doesn't buy a storage shed for those crab pots." Noelle poured milk into the steamer. "Then she could use the garage too." She hit the foam button.

"Yeah. Um . . ." Peter raked his fingers through his hair and scratched the back of his neck. "You were going to ask me something about Sunday. What was it?"

"Oh." Noelle's shoulders sagged. "Nothing. Never mind. I can't remember." She focused on the coffee machine like it was the most complicated piece of equipment ever.

"Are you sure?" *Damn Bill and his crab pots ruining Noelle's train of thought.* Either she had truly forgotten, or she'd lost her nerve about what she was going to ask him.

"The open house I have this Sunday doesn't start until two," Peter said. Maybe if he kept talking about Sunday, he'd jog her memory.

She wiped off the steam wand and cleaned the milk frother. "For the new construction on the flag lot?"

"That's the one."

"It should sell fast, especially with those quartz countertops." Noelle poured frothed milk into her coffee.

"I think so, too, especially now that the builder put up curtains to block the view of the transmission lines. What's on your docket for Sunday?"

"Oh, um . . . I don't have an open house to run, but I have two buyers who might make an offer. I'll be on standby for their call."

"Smart." Peter thought about asking her out to lunch on Sunday, but he didn't want to freak her out. Sure, she'd moved her wedding ring to her right hand, but maybe her finger was swollen or something. "How'd Daniel seem when he headed off to school this morning? Was he nervous about that math test?"

"You mean the math-facts quiz? How'd you know about that?"

"Several of the T. Rexes were talking about it last night at practice, so we played a game with subtraction facts as we tossed the ball around." Peter shrugged. "I had a coach do that with my team when I was young, and it really helped."

Noelle smiled. "That was really great of you. Thank you."

"No biggie." Peter removed the bin from the coffee machine and added the used pods to the recycle bag. As he rinsed out the container in the sink, he looked at the bulletin board hanging in front of the dish rack. Rick often posted networking opportunities within the community that would help advertise Windswept Realty. Support the Rotary Club. Volunteer at the free document-shredding event. Build a float for the Fourth of July parade. Stuff like that. Today there was a flyer posted for a community potluck at Skagiton Methodist happening this Sunday that would support the food bank. Noelle had seemed to hit it off with Pastor Olivia the other night. Maybe this would be a nonthreatening event that he could invite her to without making her feel uncomfortable. Daniel could come too.

"I was wondering," Peter said as he spun around. "You know—"

"Would you like to come to a potluck with me this Sunday?" Noelle blurted out. "I mean with Daniel and me? It's a fundraiser for the food bank and—"

"I'd love to." Peter grinned. "That would be fabulous." It was like they could read each other's minds.

"Really?"

Peter nodded. "But I'll need help figuring out what to bring." He held up his hands. "Can't cook, remember?" No way would he ask Vanessa for assistance—not until she got over herself and was willing to drop her animosity toward Noelle.

"I'll bake an extra pie for you." Noelle smiled shyly.

"You would?"

"Homemade crust and everything."

"What flavor?"

"Rhubarb. There's a whole bunch of it in my garden."

"It sounds like I lucked out, then. I get to eat homemade, homegrown pie; support a good cause; and hang out with you and Daniel. That sounds like the perfect Sunday."

Noelle's cheeks turned pink. "Um . . . well . . . since it's for the food bank, they'll probably ask us for a donation."

"I would hope so. Since you're bringing the pies, I'll bring my checkbook." Peter leaned against the counter. "It's a date," he added, casually, watching to see how she'd react.

When she lifted her eyes to meet his, he felt a zap of electricity. When she smiled, his heart melted. "Yeah," she said. "A date." She darted away to the bullpen before he could say anything else.

SKAGITON MOMS FACEBOOK GROUP

Wendy Basi
Saturday, March 12

There's an owl acting funny in front of the Lumberjane Shack. It's been there about three hours now, sitting in a puddle. I've kept my distance because I don't want to be attacked, but this seems weird. What should I do besides keeping an eye on him in between making lattes?

Tracey Fukui
A real live owl?

Wendy Basi
Yes, *Tracey Fukui.*

Tracey Fukui
I never saw that in California, *Wendy Basi.*

Courtney Nettles
Sometimes owls hang out near water after they've eaten a poisoned rat. This is why when people have a rat problem they should use traps instead of bait. Or get a cat! Visit Skagiton Cat Rescue for a list of kittens we currently have available for adoption.

Corine Reeder
I love your heart for rescuing felines, *Courtney Nettles*, but cats should be kept inside, otherwise they prey on birds. A volunteer from the Audubon Society came to speak to my Girl Scout troop about that.

Courtney Nettles
We keep our cats inside at the rescue, but they get fresh air in our fully enclosed catio, *Corine Reeder*.

Corine Reeder
LOVE! *Courtney Nettles*.

Melissa James
I'll pm you the number of the parks and recreation department. Maybe they can come help?

Maggie Swan
Call my son Mike. He'll know what to do. If all else fails he has a pellet gun.

Vanessa Collins
Gross, *Maggie Swan*.

Carmen Swan
My mom was kidding. Can't you take a joke, *Vanessa Collins*?

Corine Reeder
Just so you know, *Maggie Swan*, under federal law it's illegal to harm birds of prey.

Carmen Swan
SHE WAS KIDDING, *Corine Reeder*!

Maggie Swan
No wonder this group has such a bad reputation. You can't say anything without being attacked.

Vanessa Collins
No one is attacking you, *Maggie Swan*.

Carol Durango
I stepped outside the diner just now to take a look and the barred owl is still there.

Katie Alexander
There's a wildlife rescue in Lynnwood that might be able to help. Have you tried calling PAWS?

Angela Grosset
Wendy Basi is working at the Lumberjane Shack right now. She doesn't have time to call anyone.

Alastrina Kelly
I drove a hawk down to PAWS once and they ended up needing to put it down. Broke my heart. But it was a little hawk. I wouldn't recommend trying to pick up an owl unless PAWS tells you what to do.

Melissa James
Update! I called my husband and he's sending someone from parks and rec over there right now.

Vanessa Collins
Thank you Mayor James!

Chapter Fourteen

Noelle kept thinking about the owl as she baked pies Sunday morning. She rolled out the piecrust and checked her phone. She slid the pies into the oven and checked again to see if there were any new comments. Noelle had a lot that she could have added to the conversation on Skagiton Moms, but she kept out of it, not wanting to involve herself in mom drama. The old wooden barn on the family farm was over a hundred years old and had plenty of nesting sites. Noelle had a soft spot for owls, and whenever she had found one injured on the ground, she'd brought it to her mother. Anika had nursed them back to health, if possible. But sadly, rodenticide wasn't something they could usually recover from. After Noelle removed the pies from the oven and set them on the cooling rack, she considered chiming in on the thread. But even though Noelle had valuable knowledge to contribute, she held back from commenting. Instead she chided herself for checking Facebook so often. What was she doing obsessing over a Skagiton Moms post anyway? Peter would be here soon, and she still wasn't ready.

"You made three pies for this thing?" Joyce came into the kitchen wearing jeans, a bright-purple flannel, and a matching puffer vest. "Where'd you get all the pie plates? I thought we only owned one."

"I picked up some disposable aluminum ones when I was at the store buying lard." Noelle untied her apron and folded it before putting it away in the drawer. "This way I can abandon them at the potluck if necessary."

"Clever." Joyce leaned over the counter where they were cooling and closed her eyes, and she breathed in the sweet aroma. "Two rhubarbs and a blueberry. You outdid yourself."

"We had all those frozen berries to use up." Noelle took out her two largest baking sheets to transport the pies on. Joyce's approval helped temper her shaky nerves. Weaving the lattice atop the blueberry hadn't been nearly as hard as the idea of going on an almost-date with Peter. Or was it a real date? On Friday he did say "It's a date," after all, but she assumed that was just a figure of speech. Still, she'd repeated it back to him, and he hadn't corrected her.

"When does Peter arrive?" Joyce asked.

"At eleven forty-five." Noelle glanced at the oven clock. "Oh no! That's almost now, and I haven't brushed my hair yet."

"Um . . . about your hair. It's fine in a ponytail, but I noticed this morning at breakfast that it was lopsided. Did you trim it recently?"

Noelle nodded. "Last night after my shower." She raced to the bathroom and took down her hair. "Oh my goodness—you're right! The left side is longer by at least an inch."

Joyce leaned against the doorjamb. "I'd be happy to schedule you an appointment with my hairdresser. My treat. It's the least I can do after you bought me my new exercise outfit. I'm going to wear it tomorrow to yoga."

"Pay someone to cut my hair?" Noelle picked up a lock and inspected the uneven ends. "I don't know. My mom always cut my hair, and I really think you'd be able—"

"No," said Joyce. "We've been over this before. Cutting hair isn't in my skill set."

"It's not in my skill set either, but I usually manage." As soon as she'd moved to Skagiton, she'd purchased a handheld mirror so she could see the back of her head when she held the scissors. That trick had been foolproof until now. Well, not exactly foolproof, but Noelle's blunt cut wasn't fancy. It was hard to screw up.

"Why don't you braid your hair for now and then schedule a haircut appointment for this week?" Joyce suggested.

"Lexie Britt did offer to give me a twenty percent discount at Beach Blonde when I helped her buy her condo a few years ago."

"Was there an expiration date on that offer? That was a long time ago."

Noelle sighed. "You're right. And Lexie deserves to earn full price anyway. I just don't know if I should—"

"This isn't a *should* or *should not* scenario. You deserve a hairstyle with some shape to it, and I'm offering to pay. I don't know how much Lexie charges, but my hairdresser isn't cheap either. Now finish getting ready, and I'll rustle up Daniel. Peter will be here any minute."

"Okay. Thanks." Noelle grabbed a hairbrush from the counter and began French braiding. "But hey," she said, suddenly noticing Joyce's makeup and earrings. "You look like you're dressed to go someplace. Are you coming with us?" *Hopefully not,* she thought but kept the words to herself.

"On your date?" Joyce laughed. "No thank you. Actually Stone and I are driving down to Lynnwood to check on an injured owl that his daughter helped rescue."

"The owl in front of the Lumberjane Shack?"

Joyce nodded. "That's the one. Alastrina—that's his daughter—heard about it on Skagiton Moms and went down there yesterday afternoon with a cardboard box and an old blanket to collect the poor creature; bless her heart. But then it flapped its wings and scared her when she tried to move him into the box. She called her dad, and Stone rushed to the rescue as soon as he was done with his meditations." Joyce's cheeks turned pink. "Stone is very serious about his meditations. He meditates every single day and said I might be able to join him one afternoon, when I'm not watching Daniel. Anyhow, he has such a naturally calming presence that he was able to move the owl to the box no problem, and then they took it to PAWS."

"That's a good sign that it made it through the night," said Noelle, hoping maybe she'd been wrong and that the owl hadn't been a victim of rodenticide. "I'm sorry watching Daniel is impacting your social life."

"Oh, I wasn't complaining." Joyce looked down at the wood floor. "I love my grandson."

"I know." Noelle finished her braid and secured the end with elastic. "I want to hear more about Stone too—just not right now when I'm in a rush." Out in the distance, there was the sound of a car pulling into the driveway. "Oh no! That's Peter. He's here."

"I like people who are punctual." Joyce tried to scoot her out of the bathroom, but Noelle didn't budge. "You finish getting ready and I'll stall Peter."

"Finish getting ready? I *am* ready."

"Don't you want to change into a shirt that doesn't have blueberries on it?"

"What?" Noelle looked down at her shirt. "How did that happen? I was wearing an apron."

"I don't know. But the way that smear is placed, it looks like you've got a nipple ring." Joyce chuckled.

"Maybe I do and you just don't know it," Noelle said, feeling herself blush even as she said it.

"Sweetie, I love you, but I wager you can't even say *nipple ring*."

"I can too," Noelle said with more confidence than she felt.

Joyce pointed at her. "Prove it."

Noelle opened her mouth to speak, and nothing came out. Luckily, she was saved by the doorbell.

"That's what I thought." Joyce sighed. "We really need to get you to loosen up."

"I'm plenty loose. I'm the loosest person you know." It felt good sticking up for herself. "Nipple ring." She pointed at her blotched shirt. "Nipple ring. Nipple ring. Nipple ring."

"Um . . . Mom," Daniel stood in the hallway, staring into the bathroom. "Peter's here."

Noelle felt all the blood drain from her head as she looked up at Peter and his bemused expression. Embarrassment dizzied her, and she gripped the bathroom counter.

"Hi, Peter," Joyce said, speaking for both of them. "Noelle was just about to change her shirt after an unfortunate blueberry accident."

"How *berry* unfortunate," Peter said, with a quick smile.

Noelle remained speechless. She wished a giant sinkhole would open up in the floor and swallow her into the basement.

"Ah . . . that was punny." Joyce took Peter by the elbow and led him toward the kitchen. "Let me show you these beautiful pies Noelle baked."

As soon as they were gone, Noelle splashed water on her face to cool her now-burning cheeks. Still feeling mortified, she mopped her face with a towel. What a horrible way to start an almost-date. Maybe if she barreled through and pretended like nothing had happened, she wouldn't die of embarrassment. There was nothing wrong with shouting . . . *those two words* . . . three times in a row. Noelle couldn't even *think* of them without her blush returning. No, she would move forward like nothing had happened. That meant changing into a shirt that didn't look like it had a purple *something something* peeking through.

Noelle raced to her bedroom and threw on the first shirt she saw in her closet. It was a shapeless top she'd sewed herself ten years ago, but with her new jeans and boots, it didn't look as bad as when she wore it with a peasant skirt. She added one of the only necklaces she owned: a simple gold chain with a daisy pendant that Jeff had given her for their five-year anniversary. *"You're as sweet as this flower,"* he'd said. *"I love you."* Noelle pressed her fingertips to the flower for a moment, settling her racing heartbeat, and left her bedroom, headed for the kitchen. Peter was already there, admiring her pies.

"Wow," he said. "You really know how to bake."

"Thanks." She selected three of her best dish towels from a drawer and gently placed them over the pies, which were already on the baking sheet. "I've thought about this a lot, and I think I should drive. Daniel's car seat is already in my van, and it'll be easier to transport these in my Honda than your Mercedes."

"My leather interior thanks you." Peter picked up a baking sheet. "I'll hold this tray so the pies won't slide around."

Noelle nodded. "Good idea." She picked up her purse and keys.

"And I can help you load the van," said Joyce, gathering the third pie. "Daniel, go get your shoes. You can put them on in the car."

"Is there going to be food that's good at this thing?" Daniel asked as he stuffed his feet into his lace-ups.

"Yes, and it'll be delicious," said Joyce. "You'll see."

"I hope you're right." Noelle touched the daisy pendant, adjusted the clasp so it was at the back of her neck, and made a wish. *Please don't let me embarrass myself again.* On the way to the garage, she looked at Jeff's picture hanging in the hall and felt like he was smiling just for her. Jeff was gone; Peter was here, and she was really doing this. "Are you ready?" she asked, feeling her confidence return.

"Sure am." Peter smiled at her. "I can't wait."

"So how'd your math quiz go?" Peter asked Daniel as they drove through town. It seemed like a safe topic of conversation. Noelle was obviously embarrassed over nipplegate. The color still hadn't left her cheeks. She kept her eyes on the road and barely looked at him. As pretty as she looked with flushed cheeks, he knew she was uncomfortable, and he wanted to ease the tension. "You seemed like you had those math facts down cold at practice Thursday night." He turned so he could see the back seat.

Daniel shrugged. "I thought so, too, but that test was hard. The timer went off before I finished."

"My sister says that timed tests are wrong and that—" Peter stopped himself just in time. Mentioning Vanessa seemed like a bad idea considering how rude she'd been to Noelle. "Never mind."

"Greg's mom?" Daniel asked. "What does she say about them?"

"Yeah?" Noelle glanced at him before looking back across the steering wheel. "I'm curious too."

"Oh, well in that case, Vanessa read somewhere that timed tests are bad for kids and that they're an old-fashioned teaching technique that does more harm than good. Daniel has Mrs. Hendricks, right?" He checked with Daniel for confirmation.

"Yup." He nodded. "She's older than Pokémon."

Peter chuckled. "My older nephew, Milo, had her too. Vanessa got into it with Mrs. Hendricks over timed tests—and some other things." Peter readjusted his grip on the baking sheet. "You know Vanessa; she has strong opinions."

"I gathered," Noelle said with a wry smile.

Peter was relieved to see her loosen up, even if it was at his sister's expense. "There was the timed-test thing and also a big brouhaha over Milo reading *Captain Underpants*."

"Mrs. Hendricks hates that book," said Daniel. "She said that if she caught us reading it, she'd put it in the trash where it belongs."

"I've never heard of *Captain Underpants*," said Noelle. "What's wrong with it?"

"Nothing." Peter stretched out his legs. "That was Vanessa's point. It's full of crass little-kid humor, but it also motivates kids to read. Milo didn't start reading on his own for fun until I gave him that book for Christmas. An old girlfriend recommended it."

"Who was she?" Daniel asked.

Shoot, why'd I have to go and mention Rochelle? Peter wondered if he was more nervous than he had thought. "She was a woman I met online who worked for Google. We dated a couple of years before she moved back to California for work," he explained. "But back to *Captain Underpants*—Mrs. Hendricks really did put Milo's copy in the trash after he brought it to school. He wasn't even reading it in class either. He brought it for recess. Vanessa was furious. That's why when it was Greg's turn for first grade, she put in a special request for him to get the other teacher."

"I thought parents weren't allowed to request teachers." Noelle cruised to a stop at a red light.

"Sure, they say that, but anyone who works at the school or volunteers a lot gets special treatment," said Peter. "It's been that way ever since I went to Skagiton Elementary twenty-five years ago. All my friends whose moms volunteered knew who their teachers would be the next year, but Vanessa and I never found out until we got our classroom-placement letters three days before school started."

"Did your mom work too?" Daniel asked. "Is that why she couldn't help?"

"For a while she did," said Peter. "But by the time I turned eight, she was gone."

"She just left?" Daniel exclaimed.

"Yeah, but don't worry, buddy—your mom's not going anywhere."

"That's right." Noelle reached back and patted her son's knee. "You're stuck with me."

"And your Grandma Joyce, too, I would assume," said Peter. He was fine with his mom leaving him. Totally fine. He never thought about Elaine at all. But he did feel bad for Milo, Greg, and Waylon not having a grandma. Their paternal grandmother was great, but Ian's mom lived in Portland and saw them only a couple of times a year.

"Wait," said Noelle. "Back to the teacher thing—you're telling me Vanessa handpicks her sons' teachers, and the school lets her?"

Peter nodded. "Some just have teaching styles that work better for one kid than another. Milo does better with teachers who are relaxed about making kids raise their hand, for example."

Noelle pulled into the church parking lot. "I wouldn't know which teacher to request."

Peter shrugged. "I'm sure Vanessa could tell you."

"I like Mrs. Hendricks," said Daniel. "Even though she smells like koalas. She lets us play math games on Friday and eat popcorn once we're done with our timed tests."

"That sounds like a good reason to learn your math facts," said Peter. "But how does a person smell like koalas?"

Noelle parked the car. "It's her arthritis cream. It's not necessarily a bad odor, but there's definitely a menthol-eucalyptus scent in the classroom."

"Just like in my scratch-and-sniff book about Australia." Daniel pushed the button in his five-point harness and wiggled out of his car seat.

Peter wasn't sure how the short drive had turned into a conversation monopolized by his sister's opinions on Skagiton Elementary, but he vowed not to mention Vanessa again for the rest of the day. Avoiding the topic of what Mrs. Hendricks smelled like also seemed wise. He opened the door with one hand and carefully exited the van without the pies slipping. "I'm going to feel like a poseur walking in with these masterpieces," he said.

"Like a what?" Noelle opened the back of the van and removed the second baking sheet.

"A poseur," Peter repeated. "It'll look like I'm the one who baked them, even though the only time I turn on an oven is to bake preformed cookies at an open house."

"We really need to work on your cooking skills," said Noelle. "I could teach you if you want," she added softly.

"Private cooking lessons from you? Sign me up."

"Can I come too?" Daniel asked. "I've always wanted to see your house."

"Of course," said Peter as they followed the signs to the potluck. "But why? What's so interesting about my house?"

"Greg says you have a foosball table, and a *Pac-Man* game, and a ball pit, and everything."

"Wait." Noelle gave him a questioning look. "You have a ball pit? Like at McDonald's?"

"Uh-huh." Daniel nodded. "That's what Greg says."

"Not like at McDonald's," said Peter, slightly irritated that his nephew was exaggerating his rec room. "I have a ball pit for toddlers I bought for the boys to use when they were little. Now Waylon is the only one who can still squeeze into it."

"I bet I could fit too," said Daniel. "I'm the shortest boy in my class."

"Well, you can find out when you both come to my house this week for the cooking lesson." Peter tried to picture his work and coaching schedule. "How about this Wednesday?"

"That'll work." Noelle smiled. "I'll have to think about what to teach you."

"I bet it'll be delicious, whatever it is. I've seen those lunches you bring to the office."

"Leftovers," she said modestly. "They're only leftovers."

"Your leftovers look ten times better than what's in my fridge right now."

"And what's that?" she asked.

The correct answer was moldy cheese, but that was too gross to admit to. "Ketchup and mustard," he said instead, since that was technically also true.

"You can do a lot with ketchup and mustard," Noelle said. "Those are two of my favorite ingredients." She paused in front of the heavy door leading into the church's daylight basement. "Hey, Daniel, could you open the door for us? Our hands are full."

"Sure." Daniel opened the door, and they were instantly greeted by the hum of conversation and a whoosh of warm air.

"After you," said Peter, waiting for Noelle to enter first. But once inside, he saw her hesitate. She hung back near the door, as if she was uncertain what to do.

Peter scanned the room, which he was already familiar with after having volunteered here for several Rotary events. Along the back of the room was a long line of tables laden with food. Signs hung on the wall behind them, saying **Salads**, **Entrees**, **Side Dishes**, and **Baked Goods**. "Let's put these on the end with the other desserts," he said, leading the way.

They'd barely approached the table before an older lady wearing an apron rushed over to help. It was Arlene Davis, the wife of his former Boy Scouts leader. "Those look like pies," she said. "I can tell from the silhouette."

"Rhubarb and blueberry," said Noelle. "All three are dairy-free. I brought labels."

"Wonderful. Hi, Peter. Fancy seeing you here." Arlene helped herself to one of the pies Peter was holding and made room for it on the table. She put the second next to it. "We'll put the third pie in the back for the volunteers," she said, taking the tray from Noelle. "My husband's back there washing dishes, and he has a real sweet tooth, but I promise I won't let him eat the whole thing."

"Good luck with that," said Peter. "I've never known anyone who could eat as many roasted marshmallows as Dale. He's the one who taught me how to cook them to a golden-brown color."

Daniel poked him in the arm. "I thought you said you couldn't cook?"

"Not unless there's a campfire involved." Peter lifted up the empty baking sheet. "And then I'm a pro. Do we need this, or should I put it in the car?"

"Let's put it in the back with the other carrying trays," said Arlene. "You might need it if there are leftovers, although those pies are so gorgeous, I doubt there will be one bite left. Follow me."

"Okay." At first, Peter wasn't sure about leaving Noelle on her own in a new situation, but she seemed fully capable of taking care of herself. At the moment she was setting homemade labels next to the pies. He read one as he walked past: **Dairy-Free Rhubarb Pie. Ingredients: Organic rhubarb, white sugar, flour, margarine, lard, and salt.** Boy, she wasn't taking any chances after the peanut butter cookie incident. Everyone would know exactly what they were eating.

Peter hoped he could drop off the pans and go, but once he stepped into the kitchen, it would have been rude to not say hello to his former scoutmaster.

"Peter Marshal!" Dale hollered over the rumble of the commercial dishwasher. "Is that you? I haven't seen you in months."

"Hi, Dale." Peter put the baking sheets and dishcloths on a table next to other carriers. "It's good to see you."

"Still coaching Little League?" Dale asked.

Peter nodded. "It keeps me busy."

"Okay, but I still think you'd make a great assistant scoutmaster." Dale dried his hands on a towel. "You let me know if you change your mind."

"Will do." Peter turned to go and almost ran straight into Rick, the owner of Windswept Realty. Rick sported a deep-brown tan after his vacation in Jamaica.

"Peter!" Rick exclaimed, slapping him on the back. "I'm so glad you came. Come sit with me at my table."

"Um . . ." Peter scrambled to figure out a way out of this. He didn't want to have to eat lunch with their boss. "I'm here with Noelle and her son," he said, hoping that would dissuade Rick.

"Even better." Rick grinned. "Now I'll have my two bestselling real estate agents there with me." He dragged Peter out of the kitchen and into the main room.

Peter caught Noelle's eye as Rick pulled him along by his sleeve. She rushed over to catch up with them. "Hi, Rick," she said. "Where are you taking Peter?"

"Not just Peter; you're coming too. This is perfect." Rick let go of Peter's shirt and threw his arm around both their shoulders. "I'm bringing you to the table of power; all of Skagiton's elite in one place. This is a networking gold mine. Make the most of it." Rick slapped them on their backs.

"But Daniel," Peter blurted out.

"Who?" Rick raised his eyebrows.

"Daniel, Noelle's son," Peter explained, irked that after all these years of Noelle working for Windswept, Rick didn't know Daniel's name.

"Oh, of course," Rick muttered. "He's a toddler, right? I think they are offering childcare in the nursery."

"He's six," Noelle said curtly. She pointed across the room to a tableful of kids. "But he's already found friends he knows."

"What a trooper." Rick whacked them on their backs one more time. "Now, you two grab plates of food and meet me over there at the front of the room."

"I'm not sure—" Peter began to say.

"Okay," Noelle said, interrupting him. "Thanks."

"Are you sure about this?" Peter asked once Rick was out of earshot. "If you hadn't agreed, I would have pushed back on Rick's plans." A nagging thought occurred to him. Maybe Noelle had agreed to eat with Rick because she didn't want to spend alone time with him.

"This is a chance I can't pass up," said Noelle. "Rick never gives me special opportunities like this. You heard him a minute ago. He barely knows that I have a son. This could be the moment where I finally make a good impression on him."

"He's stupid not to notice you. You're an amazing asset to Windswept."

"Oh, Rick notices me all right." Noelle frowned. "He catches me every time I crank the thermostat up past sixty-six."

"Well, I certainly don't want to deny you your well-earned seat at the table. Let's do this."

"Great!" Noelle smiled. "Thanks for understanding." She darted away to the buffet and picked up a plate.

Peter took his wallet out of his pocket, removed the check he'd made out at home, and dropped it in the donation basket. Then he loaded up a plate with food.

The potluck had something for every eater. Fried chicken, barbecued chicken, macaroni and cheese, and meatballs. Rice noodles with crisp vegetables, platters of sushi, and egg rolls. Pasta salad, green salad, and fruit salad. Large platters of cookies and every flavor of cake. Doughnuts, fresh rolls, and cinnamon bread. Peter's plate was so heavy he had to hold it with two hands.

"Are you sure you can eat all that?" Noelle asked, with a smirk, when he reached the end of the buffet line.

"This is my lunch *and* dinner," said Peter. "I can't cook, remember?"

"After Wednesday night, you won't be able to use that as an excuse anymore," said Noelle. "I'll teach you how to make three meals out of a rotisserie chicken from the food co-op. I have it all planned out."

"I like hearing that you have plans for me," Peter said, feeling a rush of excitement. "I might have some plans for you too."

"I hope so," she said, smiling shyly. "Thanks for coming with me today."

"I wouldn't have missed this for the world." He stared into her brown eyes and saw something he'd never seen before: an invitation. If it weren't for the roomful of a hundred people and the giant plate of food he was holding, he would have kissed her right there. Instead, he would have to wait for that first kiss a little while longer.

SKAGITON MOMS FACEBOOK GROUP

Alastrina Kelly
Sunday, March 13

Great news mamas! The owl is safe and slowly improving. My father drove down to PAWS today to check on him, and sent me a cute picture. The wildlife vet said the owl has inflamed retinas and that medication will help. There's no need for a GoFundMe, but if you'd like to make a donation please visit their website.

Wendy Basi
What a relief!

Anissa Solas
Proud of you!

Maggie Swan
That's so good to hear!

Courtney Nettles
Yay!

Chapter Fifteen

This day was supposed to be about her and Peter, but when Noelle saw two empty seats at Rick's table, she knew she wanted one of those spots. Instead of being the ignored woman from a dairy town nobody cared about, Noelle would be eating lunch with a city councilman, a school board member, the mayor and his wife, and two people Noelle didn't know. Rick was right; this really was the power table. Expressing an opinion about local politics might be bad for business, but schmoozing with the bigwigs was helpful.

"Hi, Peter and Noelle." Melissa James lifted her glass of lemonade. "Have you met my husband, Ryan?"

Noelle, who had never seen the mayor in person before, except in the Fourth of July parade, shook her head. "No," she said as she set down her plate next to Peter's. "I haven't. It's nice to meet you."

"Nice to meet you too," said Ryan. "As for Peter, he and I go way back. We used to be neighbors."

"That's right." Peter picked up a piece of fried chicken and looked at it grimly. Noelle wondered what had caused his sudden frown.

"How did I not know this?" Melissa wiped her mouth with a napkin. "You grew up next to Vanessa and her brother, and you never told me?"

Ryan popped a bite of salami in his mouth and spoke before he'd finished chewing. "Because that's not how it went. Peter and I were next-door neighbors in college. Or dormmates, or whatever. He was famous on our floor for having the worst bath towel. I mean, that thing was practically a rag. Remember, Peter?"

"Vaguely," Peter answered in an annoyed tone.

"You should have seen how the girls ogled Peter as he walked down the hall after his shower." Ryan chuckled. "I bet every one of them was hoping that the scraggly towel would fall. And then one fatal day, it actually did."

"Thanks to you," said Peter. "That towel didn't slip on its own."

Ryan tossed his head back and laughed. "The pranks we used to play! You couldn't get away with that type of crap now."

"No, and for good reason." Melissa elbowed her husband. "No wonder you didn't tell me that story before now. Did you ever apologize to Peter for being an asshat?"

"No, I didn't." Ryan's smirk vanished. "Sorry, Peter. I'd say 'Boys will be boys,' but . . ." He glanced at Melissa. "We don't say *that* anymore either."

"Apology accepted," said Peter.

"At least you gave those coeds quite the show," said Rick, with a laugh.

Dorothy Caulfield, the city councilman's wife, put down the slice of bread she was meticulously nibbling. "That's why boys and girls shouldn't mix together in the same dorm. In my dorm, girls didn't even have bedrooms. We all slept on a sleeping porch."

Noelle wasn't surprised that Dorothy had strong opinions about education. Some of the things Dorothy had posted on Skagiton Moms about public schools reminded Noelle of hateful thoughts her father had shared too. Phil had often cited coed dormitories as a reason he'd never allow his daughters to go to college.

"How did that work?" asked Fern Sharp, the school board member, raising her brows. "Did everyone wake up at the same time?"

"And where did you keep your clothes?" asked Peter.

"There was a sign-in sheet," Dorothy explained. "We'd write down when we needed to wake up, and the girl on duty would tap on our shoulder at the appropriate time." She tilted her head at Peter. "As for our clothes, we shared a room with three other girls for our desks and wardrobes."

"You mean women, right?" Melissa raised her perfectly arched eyebrows. "Women go to college, not girls. And I fail to see how single-sex dorms prevent women from seeing naked men in other places. I mean, I don't like to brag, but I saw a lot of naked men in college."

"La la la." Ryan plugged his ears. "Give me a warning next time so I can sing through it."

Seeing as how she hadn't gone to college, Noelle felt decidedly left out of the conversation. She turned to the woman sitting next to her instead. "Hi, I'm Noelle Walters. I don't think I caught your name."

"Nice to meet you," said the woman. Her gray hair fell softly against her shoulders, and she wore a crisp blue shirt that matched her eyes. "I'm Deirdre DeBoer. And this is my husband, Marty."

"From the DeBoer tulip fields I pass driving to Hollenbeck?" Noelle asked, recognizing the name, both from the fields and the grocery store.

"That's right." Deirdre nodded. "We take part in the festival each spring, but our main business is supplying bulbs for mail-order catalogs."

"Deirdre and her husband, Marty, are also co-owners of DeBoer's Food Co-op," said Rick.

"I would have phrased that the other way around," said Marty. "We're farmers first, grocers second. Deirdre's brother runs the food co-op. We're investors—that's all."

"I never shop at the co-op," said Dorothy. "It's ridiculously expensive."

"Good food raised humanely is expensive." Fern folded her hands. "The co-op is the only place I shop. They have the best selection of organic foods I can find."

"And they'll charge you an arm and a leg for it too," said Dorothy.

"I've always found the co-op prices to be quite competitive," said Melissa. "Unless I'm going to drive down south to Everett. It's hard to beat WinCo prices."

Marty snorted. "Good luck keeping *their* produce fresh. It'll wilt before you drive home."

"So true." Melissa nodded.

"I buy all my vegetables at WinCo and never have any problems," said Dorothy.

"Well, good for you." Marty shoveled a bite of pasta salad into his mouth.

"I grew up on a farm," said Noelle, trying to make peace but also trying to connect with the DeBoers. "My brother still owns it. Jansen Farms up in Hollenbeck. It's a dairy farm."

"I've heard of them." Deirdre speared a piece of broccoli with her fork. "Aren't they having a fundraiser this spring to save their historic barn from demolition?"

"That's right." Noelle nodded. "It needs a complete overhaul, but since it's not a working structure anymore, the repair cost isn't a good return on investment."

"Noelle here is a former Washington State Dairy Ambassador," said Peter as he rested his hand on the back of her chair. Noelle leaned lightly against his arm and was happy when he didn't move it.

"I used to work at the creamery where they sell ice cream and cheesecake," said Noelle.

"I've been there." Deirdre smiled. "The cheesecake with blueberry topping is my favorite."

"Are they organic berries?" Fern asked.

"No," said Noelle. "But they're locally grown."

"If you like blueberries, you should grab a slice of Noelle's homemade blueberry pie before it's gone," said Peter. "It's beautiful."

"I'll be sure to do that," said Marty.

"Noelle is my number two bestselling real estate agent at Windswept," said Rick. "After Peter, of course." He looked at Councilman Caulfield sitting next to him. "If you and Dorothy ever decide to downsize, you let me know. Peter could sell that place of yours in a couple of days."

"Now, now," said Dorothy. "Let's keep the shoptalk out of it. Today's supposed to be about having fun and raising money for the food bank. They should be putting up the list of donations soon."

"The what?" Peter asked.

"The grand tally," said Melissa. "To see how much the potluck raised."

"Oh." Peter's shoulders relaxed. "I thought you meant they were going to put up how much each individual person had donated."

"Only the big donors," said Mayor James as he ripped apart a yeast roll. "You have to donate a minimum of two hundred and fifty dollars to make the honor roll."

Two hundred and fifty dollars? That was a lot of money, but Noelle could have managed it if she'd pinched her grocery budget for the next two months. That was what this event was about, after all—supporting the food bank. Noelle wished that she had brought her checkbook in addition to the pies. She'd never gone to bed hungry herself, unless she had been in trouble and her parents had been punishing her, but she did know what it was like to survive hard times. That year in Kerry's trailer had been grim, especially since the heater had never worked properly. Sometimes Noelle wondered if she'd be cold the rest of her life because of the conditions she'd endured when she was nineteen and twenty. But she didn't have time to think about that now because Deirdre was speaking to her.

"What was that?" Noelle asked. "I'm sorry—could you repeat yourself? I couldn't hear."

"I was asking if you missed farm life," said Deirdre.

"I miss the animals every day." Noelle scooped up a spoonful of Jell-O. "And the open spaces and glorious views. I'll never get used to my neighbors living so close to me. But I don't miss the smell. I did grow up on a dairy farm, after all."

Deirdre chuckled. "That's not the same as a tulip farm, for sure."

Noelle shook her head. "Nope. I'll always be a farm girl at heart, but I can't go back. My son is here, and so is my mother-in-law."

"What did you say your last name was again?" Deirdre put down her fork.

"Walters. It used to be Jansen, but now it's Walters."

Deirdre gasped. "As in Jeff Walters, the teacher who died in the biking accident?"

Noelle nodded, and Deirdre's eyes grew big with understanding. "I'm so sorry for your loss."

"Thank you."

"Are you on Skagiton Moms?" Deirdre asked.

"I am." Noelle picked up her water glass. "But I never post."

"Me either," said Deirdre.

"Which is hilarious, considering she's the moderator," said Melissa.

"Really?" Dorothy asked. She pointed her fork at Deirdre. "You're the moderator of Skagiton Moms?"

"Guilty as charged," Deirdre said without a smile.

"You mean you didn't know?" Melissa's mouth gaped open for a second. "Not only is Deirdre the moderator; she's also the founder of Skagiton Moms."

"Oh, that's no big deal." Deirdre poked at a piece of roast beef with her fork. "I invited a few friends to join about ten years ago, and it grew on its own."

"I hear about that group all the time," said Ryan. "It's the best way to find out what's happening in this town. I tried to join, but my application was denied." He looked pointedly at Deirdre. "That must have been a mistake, right?"

"He's kidding." Melissa gently slapped her husband on the arm. "I promise."

"We don't let men join," said Deirdre.

"*We* meaning you and who else?" asked Fern. "I've always wondered who was running that group."

"Yeah," said Dorothy. "Surely you don't run that pit of vipers by yourself."

A pit of vipers is right, Noelle thought. *And Dorothy has some of the sharpest fangs.*

Deirdre twisted her napkin around her finger. "It's complicated."

"It sure is," said Dorothy. "That place is a mess."

Privately, Noelle agreed. But when she saw Deirdre's mouth press together into a thin line, she wondered if maybe Deirdre's feelings might have been hurt.

"Skagiton Moms might have its fill of drama—like all Facebook groups do," Noelle said, coming to Deirdre's defense, "but it's also a wealth of information. I've learned so much from Skagiton Moms over the years. That's why I stay in it."

"That's right," said Melissa. "Whenever I have a problem, I know I can post on Skagiton Moms and there will be over a thousand smart women to help me."

Dorothy sniffed. "A thousand know-it-alls without a cupful of common sense between the lot of them."

"Tell them about the barn owl," said Ryan. "The one I helped rescue."

"That's a great example of Skagiton Moms doing good." Melissa sat up straight. "It was all over Skagiton Moms yesterday. There was an injured barn owl on Main Street, about ten yards from Carol's Diner. Ryan called the parks department, who then called PAWS, who then contacted a local mom in Skagiton, who helped the owl."

"It was Alastrina Kelly and her father who rescued the owl," said Noelle, not wanting the mayor to take full credit.

"Yes!" Melissa said brightly. "That's right."

"I would have had no idea what to do for an injured owl," said Peter. "I have zero experience with wildlife."

"Oh, we get owls on our farm all the time," said Marty. "They're great for keeping down rodents."

"It's still unclear if the owl was injured or poisoned," said Noelle. "My mother-in-law is driving down to Everett this afternoon to check."

"I didn't know that Joyce was interested in wild birds," said Peter.

"She's not," Noelle admitted, unsure how to explain Joyce's relationship with Stone. She wasn't sure if Joyce knew how to define it yet either. "Her, um . . . friend was driving down there to visit the bird, and she decided to go too."

"I'll be surprised if the bird makes it," said Deirdre.

"Rodenticide," Noelle and Deirdre both said at the same time.

"Jinx." Peter grinned.

Deirdre laughed and then grimaced.

"How old are your kids?" Noelle asked her.

"Two college students who think they know everything," said Deirdre.

"And who would make great aristocrats," grumbled her husband, Marty. "What a twist of fate that they grew up farmers instead."

Noelle chuckled. "When my brother, Sam, was younger, he could barely wake up in the middle of the night to help with calving season."

"What about you?" Peter asked her. "Were you bright eyed in the dark?"

"Not really." Noelle grinned. "But at least my parents didn't have to drag me—literally drag me—out of bed. Now Sam runs the whole farm and does a great job, but he hires calf-care specialists to help with the newborns."

"That sounds like a wise move," said Deirdre. "Farming is a round-the-clock job."

"Which is one of the many reasons that Noelle has such a strong work ethic," said Peter, giving her a quick side hug with the hand that rested on the back of her chair. It was the closest they'd ever come to hugging, and the small gesture made Noelle's heart flutter.

"Farm women always have strong work ethics." Marty set down his glass of milk. "My wife works two full-time jobs. One as a farmer and another as a billing specialist for a dentist in La Conner."

"Wow," said Ryan. "That's one hell of a workweek."

"Does your job come with health insurance?" Noelle asked, knowing that many spouses worked off their farm for that reason.

Deirdre nodded. "That's why I took the job. I carry our whole family on my policy."

"My friend's dad ran for the school board in Hollenbeck so that his family could go onto the school district's plan," said Noelle.

"Not because he cared about school?" Fern rolled her eyes. "What a jerk."

"He cared about schools too," said Noelle, wishing she hadn't mentioned it.

"Health insurance is a huge issue for farmers," said Marty. "Rates go up every year, and for a lot of us, the premium is one of our biggest expenditures."

"Then maybe they should spend less money on pesticides." Fern twisted her napkin. "Everyone's health insurance costs would go down if farmers used less chemicals. That's why I only eat organic."

"Organic farmers use pesticides too," said Noelle.

"That's not true," said Fern.

"It *is* true," said Noelle. "Pesticides, insecticides, and fungicides."

"You don't know what you're talking about." Fern clicked her manicured fingernails against the table. "I just watched a documentary about it last weekend."

"She absolutely does know what she's talking about," said Marty. "Organic farmers use pesticides from a list approved by the EPA's National Organic Program."

"Huh?" Fern's forehead wrinkled in confusion. "But I pay extra to buy organic so that my family doesn't eat any pesticides. That's what organic means. The soil on organic farms is better too."

"That's not what it means," said Marty. "Organic farmers use pesticides that are naturally derived instead of synthetically. Don't let the marketing fool you."

"Well," Fern said with a sniff. "That marketing is there for a reason."

"Because farming is a business that needs to meet consumer demand," said Marty. "If people want to pay extra for organically grown tulip bulbs, sure, I'll grow them. But I take care of the soil in my conventional fields too. I'm sure Noelle here would say the same thing about the care and well-being of dairy cows." Marty looked at her expectantly, and so did Deirdre. Suddenly, every pair of eyes at the table was glued on her.

The last thing Noelle wanted to do was get in the middle of an organic-versus-conventional-foods argument. Many farmers she knew, not just her parents, thought organic farming was a marketing hoax, but women like Fern didn't want to hear that. Fern was probably moments away from googling "Do organic farmers use pesticides?" on her phone.

"Oh, I don't know if I should get involved," Noelle said, trying to stay out of it.

Rick speared her with an annoyed look. "The man asked you a question. Why not answer it?"

"Go for it," Peter whispered, scraping his chair closer to hers. "You got this."

Noelle rolled her shoulders back and lifted her chin. "Okay, then," she said, looking at Rick. "Fine." She spoke in a clear voice, ad-libbing from her Dairy Ambassador speech that she still knew cold. "Dairy is a billion-dollar industry in Washington State, and I'm proud of

Hollenbeck County's part in this. My great-great-grandparents were Dutch farmers who cared for their livestock with skill and heart. Most farmers in Hollenbeck County sell their products to two different co-ops—one for conventional, and one for organic. I'd be happy to drink either variety, and I know the cows are well cared for. America has one of the safest food supplies in the world." She nodded reassuringly at Fern. "When I want to know about how my food is grown, I trust farmers for that information, not Netflix producers or celebrities."

"Well said." Deirdre patted her knee.

Peter patted her on the shoulder and left his hand on the back of her chair.

"If you've forgotten that farmers are the backbone of this country, Fern, then I suggest you take a drive up I-5 and observe how hard people are working to put food on our tables," Marty said, his face turning red as he stared at Fern.

"I know that farmers work hard," said Fern. "That's why I shop at the co-op. So that I can support farmers." She looked at Melissa. "I said that, didn't I? Jeez Louise, I don't know what people are getting so upset about."

"It's because you can't say anything these days without someone being 'triggered.'" Dorothy lifted her hands up to make air quotes.

"You're one to talk," said Melissa. "Half the drama on Skagiton Moms happens because—"

"Okay there, love," said Ryan. "We're all on the same side here, trying to raise money so everyone can eat."

"If all farmers switched to organic methods, we wouldn't be able to feed everyone," said Marty.

"At what cost?" Fern asked. "You're killing the planet!"

"Mayor James is right," said Noelle, who took it personally whenever ag came under attack. But she'd also been trained to help educate people about the industry. She was an ambassador, after all. "We are on the same side." She pointed at Fern and Marty. "Especially you two.

Fern, thank you so much for supporting local farmers by shopping at the co-op. Every dollar counts, and I know it gives my family great satisfaction knowing that they are feeding their neighbors. Sometimes I buy organic food, too, if it's locally grown and not flown in from Australia. Marty, Fern is not your enemy. She is a leader who holds great influence over what people think, especially the ones pushing the grocery cart." Noelle put her hand down. "Why don't you two learn from each other? Marty, maybe you could invite Fern to tour your farm so she can see firsthand how well you care for your land?"

"Well," Marty mumbled. "I guess that could work."

"I have an idea too," said Peter, surprising Noelle by speaking. "Fern, why don't you come up to Hollenbeck this Mother's Day and eat brunch at Jansen Farms? I have an extra ticket to the barn fundraiser."

"You bought tickets?" Noelle asked, looking into his green eyes. The fluttery feeling she'd felt earlier turned into full-grown butterflies. Peter wouldn't have purchased tickets for an event so far away unless he really did care for her. She felt nervous and excited at the same time.

Peter smiled sheepishly. "A whole table."

"I'd love to visit your farm," said Fern. "But I already have plans that weekend. I'll be sure to make a donation to save the barn, though." She leaned forward and spoke to Marty. "I'd like to tour DeBoer Farm as well, if you'd be willing to have me."

"That would be excellent," said Deirdre. "I'll email you to set it up."

"I always learn something new when Noelle is around," Rick said as he looked worriedly at the Caulfields. "She's very, uh . . . rural."

"And that's why if we ever sell our house in town, Noelle will be the person we call to list it," said Marty. "Isn't that right, Deirdre?"

"Absolutely." She nodded.

"No offense to you there, Peter," Marty added.

"I can't think of a better agent at Windswept." Peter looked at her with pride. "Noelle's unstoppable."

"And isn't that what today is about?" asked Melissa. "Our community's unstoppable commitment to reducing food insecurity in Skagiton?" She waved her hand in the air like she was trying to catch someone's attention. "Pastor Olivia! Father Gabriel! Rabbi Benjamin! Ryan's ready to announce the list of big donors when you are."

"I am?" Ryan put down a chocolate chip cookie.

"Of course you are, honey." Melissa licked her napkin and used it to wipe crumbs off the mayor's face.

"Are you ready to go?" Peter whispered. "I'm ready when you are."

Noelle looked down at her plate of unfinished food. She'd been so busy talking she'd consumed only half of it. "Sorry." She picked up her fork. "I can eat faster."

"I'm not trying to rush you." Peter squeezed his eyes shut like he was in pain.

"Are you okay?" Noelle asked. "Are you getting a headache? Joyce gets those, especially around fluorescent lights."

Peter massaged his forehead. "No, I'm fine." He bit his lip and looked away, not meeting her gaze.

That was weird. Noelle worried that perhaps she'd inadvertently done something to offend him. Or maybe Marty's declaration about choosing her for future real estate needs had ticked Peter off. Sitting at this table might have been good for her career, but if it had torpedoed her chances with Peter, she'd never forgive Rick for herding them over here.

"Thank you, friends, for coming today." Pastor Olivia spoke at the front of the room. She wore a long emerald maxi dress and a thick belt. "I promised the kitchen crew that I'd keep my comments brief so that we could all finish enjoying the delicious food everyone brought. Did you see the dessert table?" She clicked her tongue. "It's a good thing this dress has an elastic waist. Let's start off with some facts and figures, and then I'll pass the mic over to Mayor James so we can find out how much money we've raised today. Thirty-seven percent. That's how many Skagitonians live beneath the poverty line. And let me tell you—if you've never had the privilege of volunteering with us—that these friends are not whom you'd expect. We see moms who work two jobs and still can't afford diapers, retirees living on fixed incomes that can't keep up with rising rents, students working long hours and attending community college, as well as folks who are weighed down by medical bills. Your donations tonight will help us serve over four hundred households a week. Now let's find out how much we've raised!" Pastor Olivia handed the mic over to Mayor James and joined in the round of applause.

"How's Daniel doing, do you think?" Peter whispered. "This is probably really boring for him. Now that you've finished eating, maybe we should take off."

"Well, okay." Noelle gulped down the rest of her lemonade. It was a good thing she'd baked those pies in disposable aluminum. "I just need to get my baking sheets and dish towels, and we can go."

"I'll go get them." Peter stood and walked quickly away, without pushing in his chair.

Noelle scanned the room for Daniel and saw him attempting to throw grapes into the mouth of the boy sitting next to him. *Yikes.* They looked like they were having fun, but she'd taught her son better table manners than that.

Ryan was reading off the lists of large donors one by one, and there was a smattering of applause after each name. Noelle waited for a break in the clapping and then said her goodbyes to the table.

"It was nice to meet you." She collected her plate and silverware and Peter's, too, to bring to the trash can and compost bin.

"Leaving so soon?" Rick asked. "You just got here."

"I have clients to message." Noelle pushed in the chairs. "It's Sunday, after all."

"Attagirl," Rick said, reminding Noelle of her father. He nodded his approval. "Good luck."

"Shh!" Dorothy whispered, right as the mayor spoke.

"Ernest and Dorothy Caulfield." Mayor James nodded at them. "Thank you for your generous donation of five hundred dollars."

Dorothy flashed a superior smile and linked her arm through her husband's.

That was definitely Noelle's cue to leave. She dumped the picnic items into the wastebasket and went to Daniel's table. Crouching down so she wouldn't block the view of the people behind her, Noelle whispered that it was time to go.

"Do we have to?" Daniel asked. "I'm having fun."

"It's a school night." Noelle helped him collect his trash. "Sorry."

"And finally," said Ryan. "I'd like to say a special thank-you to our most generous donor, who has been my personal friend for years, ever since college."

Noelle stopped what she was doing and looked up at the podium.

"Peter Marshal, where are you, buddy?" Ryan looked out across the audience.

"Here he is," boomed a voice from the corner. An older man wearing an apron grabbed Peter by the shoulders.

Holding both sheet pans under one arm, Peter's eyes opened wide like he was a deer being mowed down by a motorist. Noelle was surprised by his discomfort. How much had he donated, and why did he feel bad about it?

"Ten thousand dollars!" Ryan said in an excited voice. "That's more than all of the other donations combined."

"Praise the Lord!" Pastor Olivia tossed her head back and gazed at the ceiling as the whole room burst into thunderous applause. Father Gabriel and Rabbi Benjamin high-fived each other.

"And he's a Windswept Realty agent!" Rick hollered.

"Are they all clapping for Peter?" Daniel asked.

Noelle nodded. "Yep. They are." Peter's generous donation stunned her, and she wondered how he might surprise her in other ways too.

SKAGITON MOMS FACEBOOK GROUP

Olivia Doyle
Monday, March 14

Thank you to everyone who came to the community potluck supporting the Skagiton Food Bank yesterday. Together we raised enough money to purchase a new walk-in freezer. This blessing will be shared by many. The interfaith leaders, who put this event together, are grateful for your support.

Melissa James
Did you hear how much your brother donated, *Vanessa Collins*?

Vanessa Collins
No. I didn't, *Melissa James*.

Melissa James
$10,000, *Vanessa Collins*!

Lexie Britt
Is he still single, *Vanessa Collins*?

Renee Schroth
He's seeing someone, *Lexie Britt*.

Vanessa Collins
He absolutely is still single. Swing by the play fields tomorrow night and you'll catch him at Little League practice, *Lexie Britt*.

Chapter Sixteen

Figuring out what to do with big chunks of cash was a problem Peter didn't talk about with anyone. How could he? Nobody he knew could offer any sympathy for having too much money. Even Rick, who had been in the real estate business a long time, had alimony payments to make and three grown daughters whose college and wedding expenses had almost broken him. But yet here Peter was, at the Skagiton Credit Union ATM, staring at his bank account balance and not knowing what to do with it all. Sure, he could finally purchase living room furniture, but that seemed so permanent. What if he picked something ugly by accident and was stuck with it the rest of his life?

Donating a chunk to the food bank had helped, but his checking account was still too high. Tapping his finger on the screen, Peter withdrew three hundred dollars from the ATM and slipped the cash and card back into his wallet as quickly as possible. Despite the awning over the ATM, rain drenched him. Peter clenched the hood of his raincoat and charged into the storm.

As he walked down the boardwalk toward Carol's Diner for breakfast, he thought about his own college days working two jobs to survive. His Future Business Leaders of America scholarship had paid for part of his tuition, but it had been up to Peter to pay for everything else. During the school year, he'd worked thirty hours in an arcade, wiping down machines and selling popcorn and candy. He'd loved that job. It had been more like fun than work, especially compared to his summer employment. Over the summers he and Vanessa had gone up to Alaska and processed fish. His dad had gotten them the job working in the cannery, and it had paid extremely well, but Peter never wanted to decapitate another salmon for as long as he lived. When he'd returned home to Washington, his clothes had smelled so bad he'd had to burn them. Vanessa had cut her hair short because no matter which shampoo she used, she couldn't wash away the stink of fish.

Peter opened the door to Carol's Diner and stepped out of the rain.

"Hello, Mr. Money!" Carol called out before Peter had even taken off his raincoat.

"What?" Peter looked over his shoulder. "Are you talking to me?"

She spritzed disinfectant spray on the counter and wiped next to the cash register. "Of course I'm talking to you, you adorable idiot. It's all over Skagiton Moms."

"What is?" Peter felt his ears turn red. Gifting money to the food bank yesterday had felt good until Ryan had called attention to his donation. Now it was on Skagiton Moms? How embarrassing!

"Your donation to the food bank." Carol put down the rag and picked up a pitcher of orange juice. "Pancakes are on me today because I admire your community spirit."

Peter eased himself onto a barstool. "Thanks, but I didn't write that check because I wanted the spotlight. I had no idea they'd make a big deal like that. If I could have donated anonymously, I would have."

Carol poured him a glass of orange juice. "The important thing is now the Skagiton Food Bank can replace the walk-in freezer that's been on the fritz."

"Yeah, you're right. It still feels weird that everyone knows about it."

"You'll get used to it." She rapped her knuckles on the counter. "I'll be right back with your stack and syrup."

"Thanks." Peter picked up a copy of the *Skagiton Weekly Gazette* and read the front page while he waited. The news was already four days old, but the cranky letters to the editor about the new library tax were worth rereading.

"Mind if I sit here?" asked a deep voice.

Peter looked up and saw a man with tan skin and shoulder-length white hair standing behind the empty seat. "Sure," he said, even though he wondered why the guy didn't pick one of the other available seats. It wasn't quite as bad as a total stranger peeing next to him in a urinal, but it was close.

"This spot has the best view of Carol," the man said, right as she came out with Peter's syrup. "Well, hello there, Butter Biscuit. Fancy meeting you here." He winked at her.

Carol stumbled and almost dropped the syrup. "Maybe you should call me Butterfingers," she said, steadying herself against the bar. She set the syrup in front of Peter without taking her eyes off of the man with white hair.

The man took off his wet jacket. Underneath he wore a faded Henley shirt and a leather necklace. "Any type of butter is fine with me so long as you're the one serving it." He leaned forward. "I've been dreaming about your coffee all morning."

Carol fanned herself with her hand. "There's a fresh pot brewing. I'll be back in a jiff."

The man reached out and caught her apron, pulling her forward, the counter wedged between them. "Don't be too long. You know what I'm like without my morning coffee."

"Oh, Stone," Carol said, with a breathy laugh. "You've got me trapped against the bar."

"Wouldn't be the first time," he said with a wink.

Peter dropped his gaze and stared intently at the newspaper. What Carol did after hours in the diner was none of his business, but he hoped that disinfectant spray she used to clean the counters had bleach in it.

"What a woman," the man said, once Carol walked away. "And boy can she cook."

"That's the truth." Peter spread out the paper, trying to claim some territory away from Stone's and Carol's lines of sight. "Are you new in town? I don't think we've met."

"Stone Abrams." The man held out his hand and gave a bone-crushing handshake. "I moved here three months ago from Yakima."

"Welcome to Skagiton. What brought you to town?"

"My baby girl lives here. That was the driving force. But the spirit within my yoga community had also become unhealthy."

"The what?"

Stone's shoulders rolled forward, and he sighed. "They were co-opted by conspiracy theorists. Unfortunately, that's become quite common in the health-and-wellness community."

"I had no idea." Peter pushed the newspaper aside so he could give Stone his full attention. This conversation seemed much more interesting than the cantankerous letters to the editor he'd been planning to reread.

"It's a big issue." Stone pulled a lock of his thick white hair behind his ear. "It started with 'Eat healthy food, and you'll be healthy.' Then it moved to 'If you're practicing yoga and eating clean, you shouldn't seek Western medicine to help you.'" Stone planted his palm on the table. "My wife was a vegan yoga teacher, but she still died of cancer last year."

"I am so sorry," said Peter.

"Thank you. It spread before the doctors could help. She might have had a chance if she'd gone in sooner instead of sticking to that damn juice cleanse her friends were raving about."

"Here's your coffee," said Carol, hurrying over with an extralarge mug. She was also, Peter noted, now wearing bright-red lipstick.

"Thank you, Butter Biscuit."

"Careful," she warned. "That's hot."

"It sure is." Stone took a sip and stared into her eyes.

"Order up!" shouted someone from the kitchen. "Blowout patches ready."

Carol shot Peter an annoyed look. "You and your damn pancakes. What are you, eight years old?" She rushed off to get them.

"Um . . . sorry about that," said Peter, unsure of why he felt the need to apologize. "You were telling me about your wife?"

Stone put down his mug and nodded. "I was so focused on yoga and my candle-making business that I didn't see what was happening until it was too late. The change happened rapidly in our community, and my wife got caught up in it. I blame social media. Before I realized it, most members, including my wife, had turned antimedicine. They didn't trust doctors or science. Instead of encouraging my wife to go to an oncologist, her friends told her to fast on alkaline water with a slice of lemon."

"That's awful."

Stone wrinkled his lined forehead and stared into the depths of his coffee mug. "After my wife passed, a lady friend of mine developed a thyroid the size of a golf ball sticking out of her neck, but she refused to seek treatment. She was convinced vitamins would help her. My best friend refused to get his shingles shot. One of my fellow yoga instructors was convinced that our local state representative was a Satan worshipper." He shook his head in disgust. "My yoga paradise had become hell."

"That's tragic," Peter said, feeling compassion for the man.

"Why the long face?" Carol asked as she brought Peter his pancakes. "I had the cook add chocolate chips for a special treat." After setting down his plate, she turned to Stone and smoothed her hair. "Can I get you anything besides coffee?"

"My body is craving avocado toast," he said, looking at her intently. "Among other things."

Carol blushed. "We don't have that on the menu, but I'll see what I can do."

Peter scratched his head after she left. "Back to the fast thing—isn't lemon juice acidic?"

Stone shrugged. "Fellow yogis claimed your body would react to the lemon in the digestive process or something like that. Fine. Whatever. But five days into her fast, I came home from my candle shop and caught my wife eating a hamburger."

"No."

"Yes." Stone nodded. "From McDonald's. She'd been vegan for ten years, and that fast broke her. Plus she was in pain. I confronted her and finally convinced her to go to the doctor."

"But it was too late?"

Stone nodded.

Peter lapsed into silence, not knowing what to say. He drizzled syrup over his pancakes.

"Nine months after my wife died, an investor offered to buy the building where my candle shop was. I chose to see it as a sign. It was just enough money to help me move closer to my daughter."

"That sounds like a wise choice."

Stone shook back his hair. "Life is short, and family is everything." He wrapped his hand around the coffee mug. "Do you have relatives in Skagiton?"

Peter stabbed a bite of pancake with his fork. "Yes. I do." Not that he'd spoken to his sister in four days. This was the longest he'd gone without talking to Vanessa since her honeymoon.

"You're a lucky man."

"Peter?" Carol asked as she came back holding a plate. "He's more of an idiot if you ask me. A lovable idiot, but still . . ." She set down the toast. "Here you go. Fresh bread with an avocado and a sprinkle of sesame seeds."

"You spoil me," said Stone. "Thank you, my darling."

"Why did you say I'm an idiot?" Peter asked. *Where had* this *come from?* "Is this about my standing order for pancakes?"

"No, *idiot.*" Carol rolled her eyes. "It's because you have half the women in this town falling all over you, but you won't pick one."

"Half the women in town, eh?" Stone gave him a sly look. "Impressive."

"I don't know where you're getting that information, Carol, but it's not true. And as it so happens, I have plans with a very special woman in particular on Wednesday night."

"You do?" Carol tightened her apron. "Who?"

"How is that any of your business?" Peter asked, regretting having brought it up.

"You mean you won't tell me?" Carol crossed her arms. "What are you going to make me do, wait and find out on Skagiton Moms?"

"Why would Skagiton Moms know about my love life?"

Carol shook her head again. "Idiot," she mumbled.

Stone reached forward and drew his finger down her arm. "I love it when you talk tough."

"You do, huh?" She jiggled her chest as she leaned forward. "Maybe I should boss you around tonight."

"I'd like that," he said. "I have a yoga class to teach, but afterwards?"

"And that's my cue to leave," said Peter. He shoveled the last bite of pancakes into his mouth and took off. Maybe he should ask Noelle to start his cooking lesson with breakfast items first. Eating pancakes at Carol's was becoming too weird.

"Okay," said Noelle as she opened the back of her van. "We're starting with breakfast recipes like you asked. I wasn't sure what ingredients you'd have on hand, so I brought the basics." She picked up one of the reusable grocery bags and waited as Peter picked up the other two. It was Wednesday night, and she was visiting Peter's house for the first time ever to give him a cooking lesson. She was familiar with the expensive housing development he lived in but had never signed a client who lived here. The homes had been built fifteen years ago, and most residents were original owners. Peter must have made a killing on this place, buying when he did eight years ago. Clumps of daffodils bloomed by the front door along with some tiny purple flowers.

"Thanks for the groceries. I hope you kept receipts so I can pay you back." Peter held two bags in one hand and took the third from her arm. "I'll carry this."

"Careful," Noelle cautioned. "That one has eggs in it. And no need to repay me. Daniel's been talking about your arcade for days now."

"Yeah," said Daniel. "When can I see it?"

"Right away, but don't get your hopes up." Peter led them up the front steps to his house. "Greg might have oversold my bonus room to you."

"What does that mean?" Daniel carried Noelle's hand mixer and a muffin pan.

"A bonus room?" Peter asked. "Or overselling something?"

"Both," said Daniel. He had such a loose grip on the hand mixer that Noelle was afraid he'd drop it.

"Careful with the beaters," she cautioned.

Peter opened the front door and waited for them to enter. "A bonus room is a large space that can be used for anything. Mine isn't a real arcade, though. Greg probably made it sound cooler than it actually is. That's what overselling means."

"Speaking of cool, I love these wood floors." Noelle slipped off her shoes and motioned for Daniel to do the same. The entryway basked in the golden light of a carriage house lantern, but the rest of the downstairs was dark.

"Oh, you don't have to take your shoes off." Peter shut the door. "This isn't an open house."

Daniel, who had already untied his laces, looked up at Noelle for confirmation. "Your choice," she said with a shrug, but she kept her shoes off. Her work shoes had a low but angry heel on them, and it felt good to take them off. "I hope you guys are hungry, because we're making three different things tonight."

"I'm always hungry." Peter flicked a light switch with his elbow and lit up the house.

"Whoa!" Daniel exclaimed. "Were you robbed?"

"No, I wasn't robbed. I just haven't bought much furniture yet." Peter walked into the kitchen and set the bags on the island.

Noelle stood rooted to her spot, still staring in amazement at the empty living room. It was large and spacious with windows that faced the Skagit River. A flat-screen TV hung over the fireplace, facing a lone recliner, but that was the only furnishing. "How long have you lived here?" she asked. "I thought you said eight years?"

"Yeah. Um . . . I did . . . but I haven't dealt with the living room yet. I figure if I ever move, stagers would come in here anyway, so it's actually easier *not* having furniture."

"Are you moving?" Daniel asked, climbing onto a barstool at the island.

"No—at least I don't think so." Peter took a can of baking powder out of a grocery bag and set it next to a bottle of vanilla. "But I like to keep my options open. I see houses all the time. Maybe someday I'll find one I like better."

"But you haven't in eight years?" Noelle came over to help with the groceries. Hopefully Peter's inability to commit to furniture didn't extend to other areas of his life, like dating.

"Nope." Peter shook his head. "This one has a great view. You can't see it now because it's dark, but it's there."

"What about window coverings?" Noelle took out a bag of flour. For all she knew, the people across the street might be in Skagiton Moms and spying on Peter's every move. "Doesn't it bother you that your neighbors can see inside?"

Peter scratched the back of his head. “I don’t think about it. There are blackout shades in my bedroom, and that’s all I really need.”

“Can I see the arcade now?” Daniel climbed off the barstool.

“Sure. The bonus room’s upstairs.”

“I’d like to see too.” Noelle pulled her hair back and secured it with a band so she’d be ready to cook.

“Like I said, don’t get your hopes up.” Peter waved for them to follow and walked up the stairs. “Mainly I bought some stuff so that Milo, Greg, and Waylon would have something to do when they came over to visit. We have boys’ night a couple times a month so that Vanessa and my brother-in-law, Ian, can go out.”

The carpet on the stairs was spotlessly clean. There weren’t any pictures on the walls or knickknacks to dust either. But when they reached the upstairs and entered the bonus room, the minimalist aesthetic disappeared. There were half a dozen full-size arcade games, a deflated bouncy house, a swing, a tiny ball pit, and a Nerf gun shooting range. Along the back wall was a shelving unit stuffed with board games and toys.

Daniel’s jaw dropped. “It’s like Chuck E. Cheese exploded in here.” He looked at Peter with awe. “Do I need tokens?”

“No.” Peter chuckled. “The games work without them. Alexa, turn on the fun house.”

A few seconds later, a blower whooshed to life as air began inflating the bouncy house. The arcade games twinkled one by one, and neon lights lit up dark corners. “Alexa,” Peter said again. “Play ‘Fun Uncle’ playlist.” The theme song from *Rocky* came on right as Daniel was playing his first round of *Pac-Man*. Noelle recognized the music because she’d watched the movie with Jeff.

“This is so cool!” Daniel shouted over the noise.

Noelle still hadn’t said anything yet. She was taking it all in. Here she’d spent the past eight years working with Peter almost every day, thinking she knew everything about him, and he had this whole other side to him that was . . . what? She didn't know how to articulate it. Childlike, maybe?

"So . . . um . . . what do you think?" Peter mussed up his hair and dug his toes into the carpet. "It's a lot, I know, but probably not as amazing as Greg advertised."

"Ahh . . ." Noelle's gaze darted around the room as she scrambled for words to respond.

"Wait. We should be armed." Peter jogged to the corner and took three Nerf guns off the wall. "This one's Waylon's," he said as he gave it to her.

"How do you know it's his?" she asked. The Nerf guns looked the same to her.

"It has his name on it." Peter pointed to the label. "Don't tell him I let you use it, or he'd be mad. We'll make sure the cartridges are refilled when we're done so he won't know."

Daniel turned from his *Pac-Man* game, the **Game Over** sign flashing. "Can I use Greg's gun?"

"That's just what I was thinking." Peter handed him the second weapon. He cocked the third Nerf gun and rested it on his shoulder. "There are extra darts over there," he said, pointing at the shelf. "But these are the rules. The floor is lava. Anyone who steps on the carpet is dead."

"Wait a sec." Daniel ran to the arsenal and helped himself to extra darts, stuffing them in his pockets. "Okay," he said. "I'm ready."

"Three. Two. One. Go!" Peter shouted, hopping onto a stool that bumped into the ball pit. Plastic balls flew everywhere.

Daniel dove into the bouncy house. "The floor's lava, Mom!" he cried. "You gotta move, or you'll be burnt alive!"

"But where?" Noelle spun around, frantically looking for a safe place to land.

"The swing!" Peter hollered. "Try the swing."

Noelle wasn't sure if it could hold her, so she carefully stepped on the Sit 'n Spin instead. Hopefully her weight wouldn't crack the plastic.

"Great choice!" Peter called before pelting her with Nerf darts. "Now you're an easy target."

"I'll protect you, Mom!" Daniel crawled out of the bouncy house, onto the shelving with the board games. He blasted Peter with bullets.

"Don't climb on those shelves!" Noelle cried. "You might fall."

"They'll hold." Peter lunged forward and landed on the swing. Noelle eyed it nervously, but it didn't fall down.

"Oh no!" Daniel yelled. "I'm out of Nerf bullets!"

"But I'm not!" Peter reloaded his gun with another cartridge and aimed at Daniel.

"Mom!" Daniel laughed. "Save me." He toppled into the ball pit.

"Hold on, sweetie; I'm coming." Noelle searched to the left and right as she tried to figure out what to do, but there was lava everywhere. She took off her sweater and threw it on the floor, right in front of the Nerf supplies. After leaping onto her sweater, she grabbed another cartridge just in time to reload and aim at Peter.

"You got 'em, Mom. You got 'em!"

"Oh no!" Peter clutched his chest. "I've been hit!" He slumped forward off the swing and landed on the carpet. "I'm burning alive!" His arms and legs flailed like a dying daddy longlegs. "I'm in agony!"

"That was awesome!" Daniel cheered. "Now let's jump in the bouncy house."

Noelle lowered her Nerf gun. "I don't think that's meant for adults. Besides, we should pick up all these Nerf bullets."

"I can do that later," said Peter, still stretched out on the ground. "But how about that cooking lesson?"

Noelle held out her hand and helped pull him up. "That's the least I can do after causing you to disintegrate."

"Great. But bad news about the bouncy house, Daniel. The instructions say it needs an adult to supervise. You can stay in there while I deflate it. That's kind of fun too." Peter scooted behind the structure and unplugged it.

"Wheee!" Daniel lay flat as a pancake as the bouncy house collapsed.

"I'll set it up for you again after dinner," said Peter. "In the meantime, you can play the arcade games."

"That'll keep him busy." Noelle picked up her sweater and put it on.

"Are we making pancakes?" Peter asked. "Those are my favorite."

"You've mentioned that before. That's why we're making pancakes tonight but also muffins and scrambled eggs for variety. You'll be a breakfast master."

"Excellent." Peter smiled, his face illuminated by a neon-green glow reflecting from the lights behind him. "It's a good thing I bought those barstools. Otherwise there'd be no place for us to sit."

Noelle laughed. "That was some clearheaded thinking." She began walking down the stairs. Peter's smile made her feel happy. No, more than happy. Lighter, perhaps, like the weight of the world had been lifted off her shoulders and she was once again capable of fun.

Peter brushed past her as he jogged down the stairs, and the static electricity from their encounter sparked in the dark. "Oops," he said, pausing next to her. "I must have brought some of that hot lava with me."

"What a spark!" She leaned forward ever so slightly to where he stood against the stairwell. Her leg was against his leg, and if she lifted her chin, their lips would be inches apart. It would be so easy to do. She wouldn't even have to crane her neck. But then an arcade game jingled, breaking the moment. Noelle looked up the stairs to where she could see Daniel playing. Now wasn't the time for the kisses her heart yearned for. She kept her eyes focused on Daniel, thinking about that realization. *Does my heart yearn for kisses? Yes,* she realized. *It does.* She turned her focus back to Peter, who was studying her tenderly. *But not just anyone's kisses.* Her heart yearned for Peter.

SKAGITON MOMS FACEBOOK GROUP

Alastrina Kelly
Thursday, March 17

Morning mommies. I hope you've had your coffee already because I need some help. My dad has a girlfriend and I don't know what to do about it. It's been just over a year since my sweet mama passed from cervical cancer. Three months ago he moved here from Yakima. I encouraged him to join the YMCA to make friends but I didn't mean for him to start dating. I don't think he's ready. Help! What should I do?

Melissa James
This is really hard. I'm sorry for your loss. Are you sure this isn't a situation where he might be ready and you're not? How can we help support you?

Vanessa Collins
Seconding what *Melissa James* said. When people leave you it messes you up. But it messes people up in different ways. Everyone has their own ways of coping. He was the one with the box of condoms under the sink, right?

Alastrina Kelly
Yes, *Vanessa Collins*. Don't remind me. Gah!

Maggie Swan
Is the box open or closed? Are any of the condoms missing?

Carol Durango
Don't answer that, *Alastrina Kelly*. It's nobody's business.

Corine Reeder
Let's bring the conversation back to *Alastrina Kelly* and her grief. *Carol Durango* is right. What her father does is none of our business. How can we support Alastrina?

Anissa Solas
I will get a Mass card for your mami and we can go together.

Alastrina Kelly
Thank you, *Anissa Solas*.

Jessica Luoma
Do you have a backyard? Maybe you could plant a garden in honor of your mother.

Alastrina Kelly
I do have a yard, *Jessica Luoma.* But it's just the grass that the builders put down. When I bought the house my mom said that the side yard would be good for roses. Maybe I should do that. Thank you!

Fern Sharp
February and early March is the right time to plant bare root roses. What was your mother's favorite color? I can offer some suggestions.

Alastrina Kelly
Yellow. She loved sunshine, *Fern Sharp.* That's why she said she wanted to stay in Yakima even after I moved here.

Fern Sharp
I have a Henry Fonda rose in my garden that's a beautiful yellow color. It's organic. I've never used any pesticides on it and it seems to hold up well. Peace roses also have yellow in them. I'll PM you pictures.

Alastrina Kelly
Thank you, *Fern Sharp*!

Olivia Doyle
Grief is a difficult thing. If you feel comfortable with it, I will pray for you and your father as you navigate this transition.

Alastrina Kelly
Yes, please, and thank you, *Olivia Doyle.*

Jourdaine Bloomfield
I don't make it to Mass very often but I'll say the rosary and Eternal Prayer for her.

Alastrina Kelly
Thank you, *Jourdaine Bloomfield*!

Vanessa Collins
I always forget that you're Catholic, *Jourdaine Bloomfield.*

Jourdaine Bloomfield
If you scratch me real hard, my true colors come out, *Vanessa Collins.*

Vanessa Collins
I see your true colors and they're beautiful, *Jourdaine Bloomfield.*

Alastrina Kelly
That was my mother's favorite song, *Vanessa Collins*! We played Cyndi Lauper at her memorial service.

Jourdaine Bloomfield
I have chills, *Alastrina Kelly*!

Vanessa Collins
Same. Go have some fun today in your mother's honor, *Alastrina Kelly*.

Alastrina Kelly
I'll do that, *Vanessa Collins*. I'll talk with my dad too. Life is too short to be angry with those we love.

Vanessa Collins
I needed to hear that today. Thank you, *Alastrina Kelly*. I am sorry for your loss.

Chapter Seventeen

The muffin he ate for breakfast was golden brown on the outside and had just enough streusel topping to satisfy his sweet tooth, yet it also had wheat germ in it for extra nutrition. Peter peeled back the wrapper and took a bite, remembering last night. Noelle had taught him a hundred small things he hadn't known. The hand mixer had two different beaters, one designed for each slot. Before you flipped pancakes, you watched for bubbles to form in the batter. When you made muffins, you never filled the tins all the way, or they'd overflow. Scrambled eggs cooked better on a nonstick pan, which Peter didn't own, so they had to use butter instead. She had been a patient teacher, and Peter had paid attention to every word. He'd hoped that their time together might progress toward something other than a cooking lesson, but with Daniel upstairs and the downstairs' lack of window coverings, they didn't have any privacy. Still, as Peter wiped crumbs off his fingertips, he considered the night a success. He'd spent quality time with Noelle and Daniel and had finally used the measuring cup set Vanessa had given him as a housewarming present eight years ago.

The phone rang, interrupting his thoughts. Peter answered it without looking at who was calling. "Peter Marshal," he said.

"It's your sister," said Vanessa. "I am officially extending the olive branch and inviting you to dinner before T. Rex practice tonight."

Hearing Vanessa's voice filled him with relief, even though he was still angry with how she'd treated Noelle. Even so, the best path moving forward was one where Vanessa and Noelle became friends. Okay, maybe friendship was too much to ask, but if Vanessa could tolerate his new relationship without making passive-aggressive side comments, that would work too.

"Thanks for the invitation." Peter adjusted his grip on the phone. "I would love to come to dinner. What can I bring?"

"What can you bring? Peter, you have never—not once—offered to bring something."

"How about corn muffins?" Peter remembered seeing the recipe for those on the back of the muffin wrapper box. Noelle had taken her muffin pan home, but maybe he wouldn't need that.

"We're having spaghetti, so muffins aren't needed. Just come an hour before it's time to leave for practice, and bring yourself."

"Okay." Peter felt slightly deflated that Vanessa didn't want him to bring anything—not that he would have known what to bring to go with spaghetti. Breadsticks, maybe? That sounded complicated.

"Is it true that you're dating Noelle?"

"Yes. Although we haven't managed to go out on a real date yet." Between the T. Rexes and work, there hadn't been an opportunity.

"Why?"

"Because our schedules are so busy and—"

"No, I mean why Noelle? This town is full of so many other women who'd be better choices for you."

"Is this what dinner is going to be? You badgering me about Noelle? Because if so, I'm not coming."

"No, I won't badger you." Vanessa's voice softened. "I just want to know. I'm trying to understand it."

"I didn't use to like her that way. I always thought of her as just another coworker up until Jeff died. Then I started noticing things that I admired about her, and once I began noticing them, I couldn't stop."

"Like what?"

"Like how every time she's on the phone with Daniel or one of her family members, she always says 'I love you' before hanging up. Even with Joyce."

"Lots of people do that."

"We don't."

"We could." Vanessa paused. "I love you, Peter."

"I know. I love you too."

"So what else about Noelle made you like her?"

"When Debbie, our receptionist, sprained her wrist, Noelle brought her an ice pack every forty-five minutes. She set a timer on her phone."

"So?"

"That was kind of her."

"Lots of people are kind."

"Yeah, but Noelle takes it to an extra level, like she knows how people are hurting. Each year when Windswept hosts a 'New and Used Coats for Foster Kids' drive, she takes all the used coats home and washes them. Sometimes she patches them too."

"It's easier to do things like that when you only have one kid."

"This isn't a competition," Peter said, annoyed that Vanessa kept making this about her. "And that's another thing I admire about Noelle: her humility."

"You're humble too," Vanessa pointed out. "Sometimes I feel like I have to do all your bragging for you."

"And I'm grateful. I brag about you too. At least I used to before you lashed out at Noelle."

"About that . . ." Vanessa started to say something, but Peter couldn't hear what it was.

"Are you there?" he asked, wondering if the line had gone dead.

"I'm still here," Vanessa said morosely. "Last week when we argued, I was having a really bad morning. I'm sorry I took it out on you."

"You didn't just take it out on me; you took it out on Noelle too. I'm only glad she wasn't there to witness it."

"Yeah. Again, I'm sorry about that."

"What was so bad about your morning?"

"They changed my hours at the elementary school. Instead of serving lunch every day and working in the third-grade classroom on Mondays and Tuesdays, now my only regular hours will be lunch duty. Instead of working with the same two students on Mondays and Tuesdays, I'll be a floating paraeducator substitute five days a week. I'll never know what my schedule is until six a.m. the morning of."

"That's rough."

"Yeah, tell me about it. And it's not fair either because I know the teachers at Skagiton Elementary. I went to school with half of them. The only difference between them and me is they have a college diploma, and I don't."

"Maybe you could go back to school and get your teaching certificate?" Peter carefully opened his water bottle with one hand and took a sip.

"Ian and I have talked about it, but I'm not sure I could keep up with the boys and go to school at the same time. His hours have become really intense because of all the budget cuts at the USPS."

"What if you took classes during the day when the boys were at school?"

"But then how would we make ends meet?"

"I could—" Peter started to say.

"I wasn't asking for money. If I did go back to school, I'd take out student loans. Ian and I have talked about it."

"That sounds like a good conversation, and I'm glad you're considering your options. But I fail to see how any of this warrants you hating Noelle."

"I don't hate her." Vanessa paused for a beat. "I'm jealous. There, I said it. Noelle seems to have things so easy. She's younger than me, and she has more money and a cooler job. Her mother-in-law is so helpful. Daniel has a great relationship with his grandma, and my boys don't. It doesn't seem fair."

"You're way more popular, if it makes you feel any better."

"Har har, very funny. This isn't high school."

"No, it's life. You're only seeing the things you want to see about Noelle. You're not focusing on all the hardships she faces that are hidden."

"Like what?"

"That's not my story to tell." Peter didn't think Noelle would want Vanessa knowing how messy her house was or how she was too afraid of Rick to turn up the thermostat. He didn't want to expose Noelle's fear of public speaking or how sometimes he walked past her desk and caught her staring at Jeff's picture. "Noelle's had a hard life," he said instead. "Imagine what yours would be like if Ian was gone and your in-laws came up here from Portland and moved in with you."

"I'd go berserk. I told you they sleep in the nude, right?"

"Yes, and I've been trying to forget that fact for years."

"So you'll come to dinner tonight, and you'll forgive me for being a jerk?"

"Yeah, I'll come to dinner. As for forgiving you, that depends. Will you be nice to Noelle from now on?"

"I can't promise you nice, but I can promise you neutral. If I was nice, Noelle would see right through that and wonder what was up."

"Which shows you've realized how smart she is."

"Smart enough to get out of volunteering to chaperone the field trip to the tulip festival next month. I'll give her that. She won't have to spend all day telling kids not to run between the rows."

"But running between the rows is fun."

"You're like my fourth kid. You know that, right?"

"At least I do my own laundry."

"And you clean up after yourself. Has Noelle seen your unfurnished house yet?"

"It's furnished!"

"The bonus room and exercise room don't count."

"And my bedroom. My bedroom has furniture in it."

"And has Noelle seen your bedroom yet?"

"No, though that's none of your business," Peter grumbled. "We haven't even gone on a real date; I already told you."

"Why the hell not?"

"Because of our schedules and Daniel, I guess—not that I'm blaming Daniel; he's great."

"Well, why don't you take her out to dinner tomorrow? You can drop Daniel off at my house. It's pizza night, and we're watching Disney Plus."

"I thought you didn't get Disney Plus."

"Greg finally passed his math-facts test, so we signed up for one month. They've been binging *The Mandalorian* all week as soon as they finish their homework."

"Good for Greg. Are you sure you wouldn't mind babysitting Daniel?"

"Of course not. One more kid isn't really that hard unless you don't have enough seat belts."

"Thanks. I'll owe you."

"I'll add it to your bill. But be sure Noelle knows I won't be offended if she doesn't want Daniel to come over. Maybe she'd rather Joyce babysit."

"It won't bother you if she turns you down?" Peter asked with a note of skepticism.

"No, but it'll shock me if she says yes."

Peter sighed. He didn't want to admit it, but Vanessa was probably right. An olive branch was an olive branch, though. "Thanks," he said. "I'll see you tonight for dinner."

"Your plate of spaghetti will be waiting."

"Love you," Peter said before hanging up.

"Love you too."

After the call ended, Peter set down his phone. Heartbeat climbing, he thought about Friday night and what it would be like to finally have a romantic evening with Noelle.

From the angle where Noelle sat on her yoga mat, it appeared as though Joyce had learned her lesson about panty lines and leggings. Her mother-in-law stood in a powerful warrior two pose, made even stronger by the performance fabric in her new athletic wear. Noelle wasn't trying to admire Joyce's backside, but it was pretty hard not to notice, considering Stone stood right in front of her, giving Joyce "adjustments."

There was something about the yoga teacher that creeped her out, but Noelle tried to push those feelings aside now that Joyce and Stone were officially dating. When Noelle and Daniel had arrived home from Peter's house last night, Joyce hadn't been there, even though it had been past eight o'clock. Noelle had put Daniel to bed and put on her pajamas. When she had come into the kitchen to pack lunches around ten, Joyce still hadn't been home. Growing worried, Noelle had been just about to text her when Joyce had walked in through the front door smelling like patchouli and humming a song about red wine. She'd told Noelle all about their trip to the wildlife center and their dinner afterward—Applebee's at the outlet mall. Joyce had been so happy it was like she was a bunch of helium balloons at a birthday party. She'd practically floated.

"I can't unsee this," Zara whispered from her yoga mat next to Noelle. "There's no reason for Stone to put his hand on her hips like that."

"There's not?" Noelle asked. "This is only my second class, so I didn't know."

"Some adjustments are fine, but that's really taking it to extremes." Zara raised her eyebrows.

"It doesn't seem like Joyce minds one bit." Helen smiled at her daughter. "She's really getting her money's worth from her YMCA membership."

"But she's on the SilverSneakers plan," said Noelle. "She comes here for free."

"My statement stands." Helen stretched out her legs. "I'm on the SilverSneakers plan, too, and I'm not getting perks like that."

"You're married." Zara pointed at her mother. "Behave."

"Oh, I do." Helen wiggled her foot. "Unless your father's involved, in which case I'm very naughty."

"Mom!" Zara covered her ears. "Don't be gross."

"My parents are never naughty," Noelle said before instantly regretting she'd volunteered that information. It was so unlike her to share personal stuff that she didn't know why she had spoken. Maybe because Zara and Helen weren't on Skagiton Moms, so they seemed like safe people to talk to.

"How can you know that?" Helen asked.

"Because they sleep in different rooms." Noelle fiddled with the cuff of her sweatshirt. "They have since my mom hit menopause."

"Well, that doesn't mean anything," said Helen.

"Yeah," Zara added. "Just because they are in different rooms doesn't mean . . ." She swirled her finger around.

"It does, though, I think." Noelle bit her bottom lip. What the heck was she doing? No way would her mom want her to talk about this. But then again, her mom wouldn't have wanted her to make breakfast for a man she wasn't married to either, and Noelle had done a pretty good job of whipping up eggs for Peter last night. Nothing had gone beyond baking, and Noelle felt frustrated by that. There were so many moments when if she had just stepped forward . . . leaned in . . . looked up . . . something different might have happened. Heck, Noelle could have hopped up and sat on the counter, grabbed Peter by the shoulders, and planted one on him, but she hadn't. No, all she'd done was teach him how to flip pancakes. Even she could see that was pathetic. If she wasn't careful, she'd end up like her mom. Thinking so harshly about Anika made her ashamed.

"There are lots of ways to alleviate the symptoms of menopause these days," said Helen. "Separate bedrooms doesn't have to be one of them—unless that's what the woman wants."

Zara pulled her arm across her torso, stretching her shoulder. "My mom's an ob-gyn, in case you didn't know."

"I didn't." Noelle bit her bottom lip for a moment. "I have an ob-gyn. She helped me deliver Daniel in the hospital. I was in labor for over twenty hours." It was a simple thing to admit, even though it had been the tip of an iceberg. Anika had flipped out when she'd learned that Noelle had chosen that option instead of a midwife-assisted home birth.

"First-time deliveries can often be long. What practice do you go to?" Helen asked.

"Skagiton Family Medicine. That's what was covered by Jeff's insurance—and still is now that I'm the policy subscriber."

Helen nodded her approval. "Skagiton Family is a good choice. Two of my friends from med school work there. My practice is in La Conner."

"Growing up, my mom was always rushing off in the middle of the night to deliver babies." Zara unscrewed the cap to her water bottle. "It was so annoying because I'd wake up every time the garage door opened."

"What a sacrifice." Helen rolled her eyes.

"But now I realize how cool that was, and I'm super proud of her."

"I bet," said Noelle. Maybe this was her opportunity to find out information about a problem Anika lived with that had been worrying Noelle for years. Google had given her answers, but she'd never confirmed them. Every time she'd visited her own ob-gyn, she'd had other things to talk about, and bringing her mom's troubles up didn't seem appropriate. "Um . . . Helen, have you ever had a patient whose uterus was falling out?" There, she'd said it. She'd told her mother's darkest secret to two almost strangers.

"You mean literally or figuratively?" Helen asked, looking at her with concern.

"Literally." Guilt overwhelmed her. If only the earth could swallow her up. "I shouldn't have said anything."

"Is this about you?" Zara sat up straight.

"No." Noelle quickly shook her head. "My mom." She twisted the edge of her shirt into a knot.

"Does she have uterine prolapse?" Helen leaned forward.

"I think so. I've googled it, but I'm not sure." Noelle held tightly to the knot in her shirt. "She had another baby after my brother that didn't live. That's when it happened. The midwife said that it wasn't her fault."

"Your mom's fault or the midwife's fault?" Helen asked. "Was the midwife licensed?"

"I don't know. My sister lives up there, and she didn't use the midwife when she gave birth to her six kids. She intended to, but her husband said no. Hank is a science teacher at our old high school and also the principal. He made sure Kerry delivered her babies at the hospital in Bellingham."

"I'm not against home births so long as the midwife is licensed and working in conjunction with a doctor," said Helen, "but what you're telling me about your mother concerns me. An infant death combined with uterine prolapse would absolutely require medical attention. Did the midwife refer your mom to a doctor?"

"I don't know," said Noelle, because it was easier to say *that* than that her mom wouldn't go to a doctor even if she was bleeding from a head wound.

"Uterine prolapse is treatable," said Helen.

"My mom does brew a special tea with herbs from the garden that she says helps." Noelle loosened her grip on her T-shirt and let the knot flow free. She was glad she had asked. Now that she had confirmation from a doctor about what she'd already learned from the internet, maybe she could convince her mom to see a specialist.

Helen took a sharp breath. "She should see a doctor. In severe cases, uterine prolapse can obstruct the bowels or even hinder walking. She might need to see a urogynecologist."

"Wow." Zara rubbed her arms to warm herself. "That's really sad. I'm sorry your mom's been dealing with that, Noelle."

"Me too. I'll talk to my sister. Maybe together, Kerry and I can convince our mom to see a doctor if I offer to pay for it."

"Your mom doesn't have insurance?" Zara asked.

Noelle shook her head.

"She could go to Planned Parenthood," said Zara.

"Yes." Helen nodded. "They could refer her to a physical therapist or perhaps a surgeon depending on the severity of her condition."

"My mom would never go to Planned Parenthood in a million years." *Unless she was picketing it,* Noelle thought to herself. "She doesn't think it should be federally funded."

"But it's not federally funded." Zara stretched out her legs. "Funding comes from Medicaid reimbursement, donations, and patient fees."

"Okay, but still," said Noelle. "I don't want to talk about politics, but my mom would absolutely not go there."

"Look, I get it," said Helen. "I'm Catholic. Have been my whole life."

"Mom, please. Spare us."

"I now have one daughter who's agnostic and another who's an atheist."

"I'm the atheist." Zara waved.

Ignoring her daughter, Helen continued. "I don't perform abortions, but I agree with Zara and Jourdaine that all women, regardless of income, have the right to health care. God wouldn't want your mom to suffer."

"And I believe that abortions are part of health care, and you can't say you're pro-life if you'd force a woman who was raped to bear a child," said Zara.

"That's not what we're talking about!" Helen threw up her hands.

"My mom's not going to get pregnant anytime soon," Noelle said, trying to lighten the mood. The joke fell flat, and nobody smiled. "But . . . um . . . since I've already explained that I'm unlikely to convince her to go to Planned Parenthood, what are her other options?"

"There's a community health clinic in Bellingham that could help," said Helen. "The wait time for an appointment might be longer, but they'll see her. Remind me after class, and I'll text you the information."

"Thank you," Noelle said with sincerity. "I would really appreciate that." Her armpits were already sweaty even though she hadn't done one yoga pose yet.

"What time is it?" Zara asked, turning around to look at the clock. "This class was supposed to start five minutes ago."

"So far it looks like Joyce is the only one getting a workout." Helen tilted her head to the front of the room, where Stone had his hands on Joyce's hips as she balanced in tree pose.

"Maybe he doesn't realize what time it is," said Noelle.

"Or maybe he's trying to figure out if Joyce is going commando," said Helen. "Seriously, how does she not have a panty line in those things? Her leggings are skintight."

"She's probably wearing no-show underwear, Mom. Like the ones I got you for Christmas that you threw away."

Helen wrinkled her nose. "Because they bunched up into wedgie territory."

"Were you wearing them with leggings or jeans?" Noelle asked, feeling proud of herself for her newly acquired knowledge of the intricacies of athletic wear.

"With scrubs," said Helen.

"Why would you do that?" Zara asked. "Your scrubs don't get panty lines to begin with."

"Because they were my new underwear and I wanted to try them. Okay? What's wrong with that?"

"Nothing," said Noelle. "But they won't stay in place unless you have high-tech leggings fabric holding the underwear in position."

"Noelle's right." Zara nodded in agreement. "Personally, I prefer thongs."

Helen shook her head. "You know that's a bad idea. Most of them are made from synthetic fabric that traps bacteria."

"Mom! Please! Don't be gross."

"Thongs are gross." Helen pointed at her daughter. "I've raised you better than that."

"Have you, though? Really?" Zara smirked and slapped her bottom. "Look, Ma, no panty line."

"Are we going to start class, or what?" someone shouted from the back of the room.

"Yeah," said another voice. "We're eight minutes late."

"Oooh . . . ," said Zara. "Yoga's getting spicy."

Stone brought his hands to prayer position and bowed to the class. "My apologies, yogis. As a person untrapped from time, I sometimes forget that the rest of humanity remains enslaved to the clock." He nodded toward Joyce, dismissing her to her mat. Bending down, he lit a pillar candle and then strode to the back of the classroom, where he dimmed the lights. "The next hour is for you," Stone said, his deep voice resonating across the room. "This is your opportunity to let go of wanting and simply be."

"Thanks for saving a spot for me," Joyce whispered as she stepped onto her mat. Her cheeks glowed rosily, even in the semidarkness.

"It looked like you and Stone were turning this into hot yoga instead of hatha," Helen whispered, with a twinkle in her eye.

"Shh!" Zara hushed them. "I'm trying to find my zen."

Noelle was trying to concentrate, too, especially when they rose to their feet for mountain pose. Yoga was still new to her, and she had to pay attention to Stone's instructions to not screw up her breathwork.

"As you stand on your mat, think of yourself being rooted to the earth," Stone said as he snaked through the studio. "Your head is in the clouds, ready for ethereal thought, but your feet are grounded, giving you the stability you need to feel safe." He was right next to them now. "Earthiness is your friend," he said as he swept past Joyce.

Noelle opened her eyes and looked at her mother-in-law. Joyce was smiling like a young girl without a care in the world.

Noelle closed her eyes again, challenging her balance. But even in darkness she knew that Joyce was to her right and Zara and Helen were to her left. She was here, trying something new, and she'd just survived a difficult conversation. If she was brave enough to endure that, maybe when class was over, she could have one more. She could call her mother and encourage Anika, yet again, to visit a doctor. Helen was right. Women deserved doctors—*real* doctors, not strangers pedaling essential oils and homegrown teas.

"With your hands on your heart, bend down to standing forward fold," said Stone. "Then slowly release your hands, letting all the burdens you carry flow down your arms and into the ground."

Noelle leaned forward and felt tension ripple across her muscles until it quietly fell away. She wondered what Anika was doing right now. Enduring her discomfort, probably, or agreeing with Phil about one of his crazy antigovernment rants. Noelle couldn't control any of that, she realized as she touched her toes. But she could take care of herself. She walked her hands out to downward-facing dog, her muscles protesting as they warmed up. It was hard, especially since this was only her second yoga class and Noelle wasn't used to regular exercise. But it also felt good to know she was strengthening her body. She could do difficult things like plank pose and baby cobra. She could talk about difficult things, too, like she'd just done with Zara and Helen.

Zara was right. It was sad that Anika lived in pain. But Noelle wasn't Anika. Her body was her own, and her life was her own. Noelle filled her lungs with air and blew it out with her lips pursed together. Her mind was her own too. Jeff had given her wings, and now it was time to use them.

SKAGITON MOMS FACEBOOK GROUP

Lexie Britt
Thursday, March 17

I keep getting bombarded by Facebook ads from that new restaurant in La Conner called the Western Cedar. Has anyone been? Is it good? Is it as romantic as the pictures or are those stock photos? Also, how expensive is it? I think my date will pay but I want to bring enough cash with me in case we split the bill.

Melissa James
It's outstanding! The owners are from Harper Landing. This is the second location. Think Pacific Northwest cuisine with an emphasis on farm (and sea) to table.

Fern Sharp
I looked at the menu online and was happy to see that they use organic produce whenever possible.

Rachel Glass
Following. Our kitchen is in boxes right now because we're moving to Harper Landing. It would be good for my husband and I to eat something besides frozen dinners.

Anissa Solas
I took my mami there for her birthday last week and it was wonderful. As for price, expect to pay $35 a person, not counting drinks. But if you do order a drink, I highly recommend the Tulip Tonic or the Snow Geese Gimlet. My mami kept calling it the "Snow Geese Giblet" but that's not something anyone would want to drink, hee hee.

Melissa James
I should think not!!!! But I love that your mami drinks cocktails, *Anissa Solas*. How old is she?

Anissa Solas
She's 29, *Melissa James*. At least that's what she tells people. But I'm 48, so . . .

Melissa James
I'm 29 too, for over a decade now, and should have known better than to ask a woman her age, *Anissa Solas*.

Anissa Solas
Forever young! You and my mami would get along great, *Melissa James*.

Chapter Eighteen

It was Thursday night, and Noelle had just parked her van in the parking lot by the baseball fields. T. Rex practice started in ten minutes. When she saw that Peter was waiting for them, she flushed with pleasure.

"Could you bring this bag of balls to the field?" Peter asked Daniel. "I need to talk to your mom for a second."

"Sure, Coach." Daniel picked up the bag and lugged it away. Mercifully, it wasn't raining, but the crisp forty-degree temperature made Noelle worry her son wouldn't be warm enough, even though she'd insisted he wear a knit hat in addition to his team hoodie. Daniel had protested that the colors didn't match, but she'd talked him into it.

As for herself, she had on jeans, boots, and her new puffer coat, which she'd purchased online after trying on a similar model at the outlet mall. This one was in a soft-brown color that matched her eyes, and it had a hidden pocket for her cell phone. She closed her van door, stuffed her hands into cozy pockets, and looked at Peter. "What's up?" she asked with a smile.

Peter stepped closer. "Would you like to go out to dinner with me tomorrow? Vanessa offered to have Daniel over for pizza night with Greg. I thought you and I could go drive down to La Conner and try that new restaurant everyone's been talking about."

"What? I mean, yes, I'd love to." Noelle removed her hands from her pockets but didn't have the courage to do anything beyond that.

"Are you sure Vanessa wouldn't mind watching Daniel? I could ask Joyce—"

"It's entirely your call. Whatever you feel comfortable with. Daniel would probably have a great time hanging out with Greg, Waylon, and Milo. He might learn a few words you didn't want him to know, but—"

"That would prepare him for his next visit with my dad." Noelle touched Peter's arm, placing her hand lightly on his tricep. The courage that had been missing moments ago flowed through her with vigor. "Thanks for inviting me. It sounds like fun."

"I was hoping you'd say that." Peter stepped even closer. His green eyes locked with hers, and he swept a lock of hair off her cheek and hooked it behind her ear, under her hat. "But I wasn't sure how you'd feel about going on an official date." He paused. "Or if you'd be ready."

Her heart hammered in her chest. Flutters of excitement rippled from her head to her toes. "I'm ready." Noelle parted her lips. It was now or never. She slid her palm up Peter's arm and hooked her hand behind his neck. Then, before she could think about it too hard and lose her nerve, she pulled him closer and pressed her lips against his. Their mouths crushed together with more intensity than she'd anticipated. She was out of practice, after all, and hadn't kissed anyone besides Jeff until now. Peter was taller than Jeff, and as his arms wrapped around her, their bodies lined up differently. Noelle barely had time to notice that before her lips, of their own accord, parted and deepened the kiss. Her tongue touched Peter's with a delicious thrill that made her cling to him harder. Her hands roamed across his shoulder blades, and her head tilted to the side as Peter's lips left her mouth and wandered down her neck and back up again.

"Noelle," he murmured. "I've been dreaming about this moment for so long."

"You have?" she asked, slightly out of breath.

Peter nodded and then rested his forehead against hers, against the brim of her stocking cap. They stood there, clasped together, toasty warm despite the cold atmosphere around them. Noelle wondered why Peter had stopped kissing her—and if she had perhaps done something wrong. She was wildly out of practice, after all, and not that experienced to begin with.

"I need to go set up before the other T. Rexes arrive," Peter said in a husky voice. "They could walk past us at any moment."

"Oh." That made sense. For a moment, Noelle had forgotten where they were and that her own son was out there on the field somewhere dragging the bag of balls. "Good point."

"Can we pick up where we left off tomorrow?" Peter's lips brushed gently against her cheek.

Noelle nodded. "I'll be looking forward to that."

"Not as much as I will." Peter groaned as he stepped away. "Okay, well, I better go." His tone was filled with reluctance.

Noelle shivered as the cool air hit her from where Peter's warmth used to be. "How did it get so cold? I was burning up a second ago."

Peter chuckled. "It's a mystery." He kissed her palm and waved at her before jogging off toward the field.

Noelle paused for a moment, there by her van, and let her heartbeat steady. What had just happened? Had that really been her? Kissing Peter like she was a young woman without a care in the world instead of a thirty-year-old widow with a son depending on her to make smart decisions?

"There's nothing wrong with kissing." That's what Jeff had told her that first day they'd gone for a drive after her shift at the creamery. They'd arrived at Peace Arch Park, at the border between the United States and Canada. Noelle remembered the feeling of Jeff's hand in hers and the way his arm had kept brushing against her.

Their first kiss underneath a rhododendron had changed her whole world. It had been sweet and innocent, yet Noelle had felt immediate guilt. "My parents don't know you," she said. "My dad needs to approve who I date."

"What?" Jeff asked. "That makes no sense."

"He'd be furious with me," Noelle admitted.

"There's nothing wrong with kissing. All we did was kiss."

"But you don't understand," Noelle explained. She'd known this was a bad idea when she'd agreed to the outing, but she'd been so enamored with Jeff that she'd left with him anyway.

"You're nineteen years old." Jeff shook his head in confusion, standing underneath the rhododendron. "Your father doesn't have a say in who you get to date."

"But he does."

"Are you superreligious?" Jeff asked. "Fundamentalists or something?"

Noelle shook her head. "No. We used to go to church until my dad got into an argument with the pastor over tithing, and we never went back."

"So what is it, then?"

"What's what?"

"Why would you let your dad control you like that?"

"Because he's my father." Noelle couldn't understand Jeff's reaction until she remembered his circumstances. "You were raised by a single mom, so you don't understand."

"What's *that* got to do with it?" Jeff asked, with an edge to his voice.

"Fathers lead families, not mothers." Noelle said it as kindly as possible to not make Jeff feel bad. The kisses with Jeff had been sweet, but the guilt was overwhelming her.

"That's not true. Mothers lead families all the time and do a great job of it."

"My dad would be able to explain this better than me. You need to meet my parents first so that I can get my father's approval before our relationship continues."

"What the hell?" Jeff palmed his forehead, lifting up his unruly hair by the roots.

Noelle gulped air before she spoke in a rush. "I really like—I mean, I really like you, which is why I came today, but if we're going to go out again, then you need to come to the farm first so this can be official. Otherwise my dad will think we're sneaking behind his back."

They stood there for a moment, neither one of them saying anything further. Noelle worried that she had destroyed things before they had even begun. Her first kiss seemed ruined. One minute Jeff's sweet lips were on hers, and the next minute he was looking at her like she was a mad cow. But then he took both her hands in his own and kissed her fingertips. "I really like you too. I must, or else I wouldn't be agreeing to something so stupid. When can I meet your parents?"

That fateful visit had happened a week later and had gone horribly wrong. But Noelle couldn't think about that now. She tried not to think about it ever.

"Are you okay?" asked a voice.

Noelle spun around and saw Vanessa standing in the parking lot, holding a blanket in one hand and a thermos in the other. Greg was next to her with his baseball glove.

"Yeah," Noelle said with a hitch to her voice.

Vanessa studied her for a second before looking down at Greg. "Go on and run to practice. I'll be right there." After he'd taken off, Vanessa shifted the blanket to her other arm so that she could open the thermos. "I made coffee. Do you want some? It's half-and-half."

"Milk?"

"No, I mean half-caffeinated, half-decaf." Vanessa poured the steaming brown liquid into a cup. "I have extra if you'd like to share. It's cold out."

"Thanks but—" Noelle was about to say no when the rich scent reached her nostrils. "Actually, yes. I'd love some." She clicked open her van. "Let me get my travel mug." Poking her head into the safety of her vehicle, Noelle took a deep breath. This was hard. Making peace with Vanessa was difficult, but Peter was worth it. Relationships were ten times harder when families didn't get along. She closed her door and held out her mug. "Thanks. Coffee was a good idea."

Vanessa filled her cup. "I hope you like Folgers."

"That's what my parents drink."

Vanessa pressed her lips together but didn't say anything until she'd closed the lid on the thermos. "My boys are having a pizza-and-movie night tomorrow, and Greg asked if Daniel could come over." She stood up straight and looked Noelle in the eye. "I'd like that too. He seems like a great kid. You've done a real good job with him."

"Thank you."

"Um . . . has my brother talked to you?"

Noelle felt her cheeks go hot. "Peter told me you'd offered to watch Daniel so that we could go out to dinner."

"Yeah. If you want. But the offer still stands for Daniel to come over no matter what."

"You need my family's blessing . . ." She'd said those exact words to Jeff all those years ago, and he'd cared enough about her to try. It had turned into a disaster, but Jeff had made the effort.

Noelle wrapped her fingers around her travel mug. "Daniel would love to come over for a movie night with Greg. Thank you."

"Great." Vanessa looked down the path toward the field. "And, uh, what'd you tell Peter?"

"I told him yes."

"Great. He'll be so pleased."

Vanessa was making an effort. Noelle could clearly see that. She needed to do something to show that she was making an effort too. But what? She scrambled to think of what she could say to patch things up with Vanessa. "Would you like to sit together on the bleachers?" This seemed like a long shot, but maybe it was worth the try. "I could show you how to manage Facebook ads so you could monitor Peter's phone instead of me."

"Do you think I could figure it out even though I'm not a real estate agent?"

Noelle couldn't tell if Vanessa's question was serious or if she was baiting her for a snarky retort. "You're great on Facebook," she said with care.

"But I've never done ads before," Vanessa said as they walked toward the fields.

Noelle relaxed a bit. Maybe Vanessa was being serious after all. "Ads aren't that hard to learn," she said. "Monitoring them, that is. Setting them up is complicated. I had to take an online workshop to learn how to do them well."

"Like at the community college?"

Noelle shook her head. "No, this one was through the Windswept franchise."

"Oh."

"But the community college is where I got my start." They were at the bleachers now, and she could see Daniel standing with Greg under the lights with some of the other boys. Peter spoke to one of the dads, a huge smile on his face.

"I've thought about taking classes—for something. I'm not sure what." Vanessa climbed the bleacher steps and scooted into the middle of the row. She spread out the blanket she was holding. "Sit on this so your butt doesn't get cold. There's plenty of room."

"Thanks." Noelle sat next to Vanessa and sipped her coffee. She couldn't believe this was happening. Peter asking her out was one thing; she had kind of been expecting that. But hanging out with Vanessa like they were friends? No way. Noelle had not seen that one coming.

"When you took the online classes . . ." Vanessa curled the edges of the blanket around her legs. "How did that work exactly, considering you also had Daniel and your job?"

"It wasn't easy, but I made it work, and as soon as I mastered ads, my sales shot up. I even taught Peter a few tricks."

Vanessa snorted. "Sorry," she said, blowing her nose in a tissue. "The cold gets to me."

"Me too." Noelle pulled her hood up over her hat and wrapped the edges of the blanket around her like Vanessa had. Then she pulled out her phone. "Still want to learn how to monitor ads?"

Vanessa nodded. "Yup. Let's do this."

Noelle opened up her account to her latest ad and launched into the minilesson.

"If it wasn't dark out, we could see the daffodils," said Noelle as they drove to La Conner. As soon as she said it, Peter wished he had brought her flowers. He'd thought about it on the way to pick her up but then decided against it because it might look like he was trying too hard.

"They're coming up in my yard too." He sped up the windshield wipers so they could compete with the pounding rain. "I have some new ones growing this year with gold centers."

"I saw them when we came for the cooking lesson. They looked pretty with those purple flowers growing next to them. What were they?"

"Crocuses. They come up first. I wanted to naturalize them in the lawn, too, but that would be a violation of the homeowners' association because of the rules about mowing."

"I don't understand."

"Exactly! I get why homeowners' associations are desirable to certain buyers, but the naturalized lawn would have been a showstopper."

"No, I mean what does naturalizing mean?"

"Oh, sorry. You're such a gardener I thought you knew."

"Vegetables and herbs. Not flowers."

"Similar principles—to garlic, maybe. I'm not exactly sure." Peter scratched his ear. "Naturalizing is when you let bulbs do their thing year after year and don't mess with them too much. So with crocuses, for example, you can plant them with the grass, and they'll come up in the middle of the lawn every spring. But you can't mow while they're blooming, and if you really want the bulbs to recharge for the following year, you should let them keep growing for a while longer until you cut them down."

"Wouldn't that turn the lawn into a pasture?"

Peter nodded. "That's why the homeowners' association wouldn't allow it. I was planting them when I first moved in, and the president of the association walked by and flipped out."

"That's too bad."

"But they're fine with bulbs in flower beds. Wait until you see my tulips this year. I went a bit overboard."

"More overboard than your summer dahlias? I don't think that's possible. You brought at least twenty bouquets into the office last year."

"Don't laugh," Peter said with a grin. "Those flowers are a tax write-off."

"How?"

"I use them for staging open houses."

"I'm not sure that qualifies as a work expense."

"Of course that counts. The pictures are on every flier, website, and social media ad I create. If I paid a stager to buy fake flowers, that would count, right?"

"I suppose."

"See? That's why I should definitely expand to gladiolas this year. You've talked me into it."

"What?" Noelle laughed. "I did no such thing."

"You did." He patted her knee. "And I thank you for it."

"I don't think I realized you knew so much about bulbs. Why didn't you say anything the other day at the potluck when the DeBoers were there?"

"And get in the middle of the organic-versus-nonorganic showdown?" Peter shuddered. "No thank you. I just put down a thick layer of mulch in late February, and that does the trick as far as weed control goes."

"Mulch or manure?"

"Ha! I forgot who I was talking to there for a second. Compost, actually. Manure is too stinky, and mulch doesn't have enough nutrients to feed the bulbs the way I like."

"Manure is *not* too stinky. Take that back."

Peter took his eyes off the road for a second to see if she was serious or not. When he heard her giggle, he knew she was kidding. "What do you use for your raised beds?" he asked.

"Compost," she admitted. "I like that better for growing vegetables. My sister, Kerry, has a friend who processes it, and usually my dad picks me up a load and drives it down in February."

"That sounds helpful. Free compost is like black gold."

"It'd be more helpful if my dad wouldn't get into a fight with Joyce every time he saw her. They hate each other's guts, and it's really hard to be stuck in the middle of that, especially now that . . ."

"Now that what?"

Noelle shifted in her seat. "Now that Jeff's not there to intervene. He and my dad didn't get along either, but my dad at least would listen to Jeff, up to a point."

"How's that?" Peter asked, genuinely curious. She so rarely spoke about Jeff or her family that every nugget she offered was a piece of information to be closely examined.

Noelle pulled a lock of hair behind her shoulder. "Jeff would say things to my dad like 'What Noelle earned on that house sale is none of your business. Don't tell her what to do with her money,' and then my dad would stop. He'd just stop." She clasped her hands in her lap and stared at her thumbs. "He wouldn't tell me what to do with it or how to hide it from the government's tax collectors. He wouldn't call me each day to talk about the price of gold. He'd stop inviting me to gun shows."

"Gun shows?" Peter looked at her sideways.

"Guns can be a great investment." She scrunched up her nose. "But I'm not interested in guns, and Jeff was a hiker, not a hunter." She turned her head and looked at him. "Do you hunt?"

"No. I can fish, though—not that I ever do."

"Why not?"

"My dad works in fishing. Vanessa and I grew up on frozen salmon and halibut. Then over the summers, I'd move up to Alaska and earn money at a cannery. I never want to eat fish again. Even the smell bothers me."

"Wow, that's too bad. I don't like fish either, but so many people around here love Dungeness crab, oysters, razor clams, and salmon, of course."

"You grew up on a dairy farm, and you still love milk, but it wasn't like that for me." They were approaching La Conner now, the small town known for its artist vibes. "Maybe if I'd had more variety in my diet, I'd like fish more, but not when we ate it five nights a week."

"That's a lot. I mean, for us Americans, it's a lot. That's probably normal in other parts of the world."

"Could be." Peter pulled into a parking spot half a block away from the restaurant.

"How did your mom—or your dad—cook it?" Noelle asked. "I usually make fish in the oven."

Peter turned off the car. "Well, that's another thing. When my mom still lived with us, she knew I didn't like fish, so she'd make something else for me to eat instead, like waffles or a jelly sandwich."

"That's sweet."

"Yeah." Peter nodded. "It was. But then once she left, my dad would usually barbecue it or nuke it in the microwave."

"The microwave?"

"It was gross. The whole house would smell."

"Yuck."

"Yeah. Vanessa hated that too. She taught herself how to make fish sticks with bread crumbs, which were just barely better, and chowder with canned corn and powdered milk. I actually liked that a little bit. By the time she was thirteen and I was ten, she did all the cooking, and I did the dishes."

"And you never learned to cook?"

Peter shook his head. "That's what restaurants are for." He reached into the back seat and plucked out her raincoat. "Would you like me to get the umbrella from the trunk?"

Noelle unbuckled her seat belt and pulled on her jacket. "Do I look like a woman who needs an umbrella?"

He laughed. "No."

"It's not three a.m., I don't have a calf to feed, and this new coat I'm wearing doesn't have one rip. I'll be fine." She eyed him critically. "But what about you? You're only wearing a softshell."

"I'm the son of a fisherman." He opened the car door and faced the squall. "I'll be okay!" he shouted over the rain.

They held hands as they splashed through puddles on the way to the restaurant. The hostess opened the door for them and invited them into the cozy space. Soft music played in the background, and the air was rich with the scent of fresh bread.

"Table for two, please," said Peter. "The reservation is under the last name Marshal."

"It'll just be two minutes," said the hostess. "Let me check to make sure your table's ready." She tottered off in her high heels.

Peter and Noelle removed their coats while they waited and read the framed newspaper article about the restaurant's recent opening.

"It looks like this is a new chain," said Peter as he held tightly to Noelle's hand, lacing their fingers together.

"Do two restaurants count as a chain?" Noelle asked. "There's only one other location, and it's in Harper Landing."

"Good point. Maybe this isn't in chain territory yet. But at least we don't have to drive down to Harper Landing in this storm."

"Yeah." Noelle stepped closer as the door opened, and a family of six entered the lobby. "It's getting crowded in here. I wonder where the hostess went?"

"I don't know. But we have a reservation." Peter turned his body slightly to protect Noelle from the influx of people. Before he could stop to think about it, his lips brushed against her forehead in a gentle kiss. She surprised him by hugging him back.

"I don't mind waiting," said Noelle as she rested her head on his shoulder.

Peter breathed in the sweet floral aroma of her hair. "Me neither." He was almost sad when the hostess returned a minute later and led them to their table.

Noelle opened her menu first. "Well, I guess you won't be ordering the cedar-plank salmon."

Peter chuckled. "Nope." He opened his menu and scanned the offerings. "But the pasta with cream sauce looks good."

"You like mushrooms?" Noelle glanced at him over the top of her menu.

"Is that what they mean by chanterelles?"

"Yes. They're a golden color. Jeff used to point them out when he took me on hikes sometimes."

"I'm okay with mushrooms so long as there's enough butter or olive oil with them. Vanessa makes an appetizer in her Crock-Pot with mushrooms and red wine that's good too."

"That sounds delicious." Noelle looked back at her menu. "I'll get the pork."

"Do you want a drink?"

"Water's fine. I don't like the taste of beer, and wine makes me sleepy."

"How about a cocktail?"

Noelle picked up the menu. "Fourteen dollars for a Tulip Tonic?" She set it down. "That's almost minimum wage."

Peter, who liked only fruity drinks but was too ashamed to admit that in public, agreed. "They're pricey—that's for sure. I'll stick with water, too, since I'm driving home. Maybe we could order coffee with dessert."

"Coffee's kind of our thing."

Was it Peter's imagination, or did Noelle's foot just brush against his underneath the table? He scooted his foot forward slightly to find out, and his shin lined up with hers, but she didn't move it. A warm coziness spread over him, and he buzzed with joy.

Their easy conversation continued for the ten minutes it took for the server to come take their order. Peter kept thinking he should pinch himself to make sure he wasn't dreaming. After such a long wait for Noelle to finally be ready to date, there she was, right in front of him, the soft glow from the candle basking her in a warm light, playing off the chestnut highlights in her hair. Hair that looked different, now that he studied it. Shorter, maybe?

"Did you get your hair cut?" he asked.

"Yes." Noelle blushed. "And it was so expensive," she mumbled.

"It looks really nice."

"Thanks. I'd never gone to a professional hairdresser before. Lexie had these weird scissors." She made snipping motions with her fingers. "After she cut my hair with normal ones, she layered with these other ones that seemed to cut at random. It made me so nervous." She raked her fingers through her hair, and it settled in a face-framing shape against her collarbone.

"It looks beautiful." Peter leaned forward. "You're beautiful."

"Thank you." She smiled shyly. "Lexie tried to talk me into babylights, but I said no. Too expensive. Plus, I like my hair color the way it is, even if it's brown."

"It's a wonderful shade of brown."

After they ordered, they talked about various things: how long the hot real estate market would last, whether the Little League ref at last week's game had recovered from laryngitis, and if Daniel should be allowed to move his bedtime up to 8:45 like he wanted.

"I didn't have a bedtime once my mom left." Peter shrugged. "I just learned to go to sleep when I felt tired instead of what the clock said."

"How did that work waking up in the morning?"

"I'm an early riser, so it wasn't a problem, but sometimes Vanessa had trouble. I'd have to drag her out of bed so we'd make it to the bus on time."

"She was lucky to have you, then."

"Not really. It was usually the other way around. If it weren't for Vanessa, I would probably have starved." He chuckled, even though it wasn't something to joke about. Vanessa had learned early on that they could visit the food bank once a week and get food they actually liked to eat. If it had been up to their father, Jerry would have fed them frozen fish and baked potatoes every night and called it good.

"Well, look who's here," said a familiar voice. "I had to come by and say hello." It was Peter's client Rachel Glass.

"Rachel, hi. Is Al here?"

"He sure is." She waved at a table across the room. "He would have come to say hello, too, but was convinced we'd lose our table. This place is packed."

"It definitely is. Rachel, I'd like you to meet my—er, friend, Noelle Walters." Peter felt bad for stumbling over the introduction, but he wasn't sure what else to say. He took a drink of water.

"It's a pleasure to meet you," said Rachel.

"You too," said Noelle. "Your house was lovely. I showed it to one of my clients, but it was a bit out of their price range."

Rachel sighed. "It's not lovely now. The whole place is torn up with moving boxes. I'll be glad when we're done and in our new place." The server arrived with a tray of food, and Rachel stepped to the side. "Well, that's my cue to leave. You two have fun." She slapped Peter on the back. "This one's a gem. Half the women on Skagiton Moms are after him."

"They're what?" Peter put down his water glass.

"Noelle, are you on Skagiton Moms?" Rachel asked.

"I am." Noelle leaned back as the waiter set down her plate of pork roast.

"You know what I'm talking about, then," said Rachel. "I really should go now that your food's here. Good night, Peter. Have fun tonight."

"What was that about?" Peter asked as soon as Rachel and the waiter had left. He twirled his fork in the pasta.

"Um . . ." Noelle switched her fork into her left hand and picked up her knife. "Vanessa brags about you on Skagiton Moms a lot. You know that, right?"

Peter nodded. "That's one of the reasons I get so many clients."

"Yes, and she also—"

"Wait. Shoot." Peter cringed. Was everyone he knew driving down to La Conner tonight? "Mike Swan is here," he whispered.

"What?" Noelle turned her head just as the hostess led Mike and Lexie Britt to a table.

"Noelle!" Lexie scampered over to say hello. Her skintight dress sparkled in the light. "You look fabulous." She fluffed up Noelle's hair. "When you were in the chair this morning, you didn't tell me your hot date was with Peter." She held up her hand. "High five, girlfriend."

"Ah, thanks." Noelle tapped her hand to Lexie's.

"Come on back to the table, babe," Mike hollered across the restaurant. "Let's order the lobster."

Lexie giggled. "I've got a hot date too." She peeked over her shoulder and blew Mike a sultry kiss. "Mama's gonna have fun tonight."

"Take it slow with Mike; he has a bad track record with women," Peter said, eyeing the ice cubes in his water glass. Delivering an Alaskan hello wasn't his style, but he understood the temptation.

"Oh, Peter, you're so funny." Lexie's smile transformed into a cringe. "And so serious in that polo shirt. Look at you guys—drinking water with dinner. Both of you could be the designated driver. Ha! To each their own. See ya." Lexie strutted away.

"That was good that you warned Lexie about Mike." Noelle frowned. "I should have said something, too, but didn't know how."

"People can change and be better than what they were in high school, but . . ."

"I don't think Mike has." Noelle sliced into her meat. "I wonder if I should tell Zara since she has that bad history with him."

"You know Zara?"

"Yeah. She and her mom, Helen, are in my yoga class. Zara's really nice."

"She is, even if she thinks I'm boring."

Noelle laughed. "You are the least boring person I know."

"Are you sure about that?"

"Peter Marshal, are you fishing for compliments again?"

Peter grinned. "I told you I was the son of a fisherman."

"You did give me fair warning." Noelle took a sip of water, and her expression became serious. "About Lexie and, um . . . what Rachel said earlier about Skagiton Moms."

"Yeah? What about it?"

Noelle froze, her eyes wide open. "Vanessa loves you a lot," she finally said. "She wants you to be happy and successful. That's clear to anyone who's a part of Skagiton Moms, even the people like me who never post."

"Are you saying she talks about me? She's paraded me about as the younger brother she can boss around her whole life."

"Yeah. That. But in a loving way. And she'll do what she can to make you happy."

"Exactly." Peter wiped butter off his lips. "It's embarrassing, but I'm used to it."

"Good." Noelle's shoulders relaxed. "Then I don't need to say anything." Her hand slipped underneath the table and rested on his knee. "Except that I'm glad it's you and me out tonight. So glad."

He covered her hand with his and squeezed. "Me too."

Noelle held his gaze for a moment, and then she looked at her purse. "I don't mean to be rude, but would it be okay if I sent Lexie a quick text? Helen told us that Mike's mom told her that he's broke. I don't want Lexie to order the lobster if she can't afford to pay for it."

"Noelle, you don't have to ask me for permission for anything."

"Oh. Right." Blushing again, Noelle typed quickly into her phone.

"And I'd love to hear more about what Mike's mom told Helen about his bad finances." Peter loaded up his fork with pasta. "Not that I'm vindictive, but . . ."

"I know exactly what you mean." Noelle slipped her phone back into her purse right as there was a shriek on the other side of the dining room.

"Waiter!" Lexie called, holding up her hand. "I'd like to change my order to a side salad."

SKAGITON MOMS FACEBOOK GROUP

Vanessa Collins
Wednesday, March 23

Need answers ASAP! My husband was bitten by a dog. The damn thing sunk its teeth into his ankle and broke the skin. Now it's oozy. I think he should go to the doctor but he thinks all he needs is rubbing alcohol and a bandage. This could be serious, right?

Courtney Nettles
Was the dog's owner there? Did your husband ask for information about the dog's shot records?

Vanessa Collins
No, he didn't, *Courtney Nettles.*

Courtney Nettles
Okay, well, I know more about cats than dogs obviously, but bacterial infections

from animal bites are a big deal. That's what I would worry about, *Vanessa Collins*.

Corine Reeder
Plus rabies, *Courtney Nettles*. Yikes! How did Ian get bit, *Vanessa Collins*? I thought he was working the counter these days instead of a route?

Vanessa Collins
It happened as he was taking the trash cans out this morning, *Corine Reeder*. You know the woman who lives two streets away with the terrier?

Corine Reeder
The one who power walks and smokes at the same time, *Vanessa Collins*?

Vanessa Collins
That's the one, *Corine Reeder*.

Carmen Swan
Stop talking about my aunt, *Vanessa Collins*! She's not even on Facebook! Little Rascal does not have rabies!!!!

Vanessa Collins
That's your aunt, *Carmen Swan*? Could you have her send me a picture of Little Rascal's vaccination record?

Vanessa Collins
Please, *Carmen Swan*?

Vanessa Collins
Pretty please, *Carmen Swan*?

Katie Alexander
He needs rabies shots and possibly some antibiotics. Take him to the walk-in clinic or urgent care.

Sabrina Kruger
I second this, *Katie Alexander*. The doctor will also be able to flush the wound better than you can at home. Sometimes dog bites are really deep.

Angela Grosset
I got a dog bite once and thought I was fine. The next day I couldn't move my arm. The doctor said it was infected and gave me three bottles of antibiotics. I still have the scar.

Vanessa Collins
Update. My husband is running a fever. We're headed to urgent care. *Jourdaine Bloomfield*, can you ask Carmen Swan to send you a picture of her aunt's dog's vaccination records? I can't tag her because she's blocked me.

Chapter Nineteen

Sure, she'd seen Peter almost every day since their date on Friday, but tonight was different. It was Wednesday, and she and Daniel were once again going to his house for a cooking lesson. Spending time with him at his house was different from seeing him coach a T. Rex game on Saturday or trying to sneak kisses at the office before Debbie walked in on them to brew coffee. Noelle walked up the steps to Peter's porch, admiring the daffodils and crocuses growing along the pathway. She held tightly to the grocery bags as her excitement grew.

"Whatever you do, Mom, don't interrupt me when I'm playing *Frogger*." Daniel lugged a jug of unfiltered apple juice from DeBoer's Co-op. "Last time you called me down to dinner right when I was winning. I'll come down when I can, okay?"

"You'll come down when I call you." Noelle shot him a look. "Or you won't play at all."

"But, Mom, that's—"

The door swung open, interrupting Daniel's complaint. Peter stood in the entryway with total chaos behind him.

"Got 'em!" Greg shouted, pelting Peter with Nerf darts.

A blip of orange Styrofoam bounced off of Peter's head. "Hold your fire for one minute, will ya?" he called over his shoulder. Greg and two other boys, one older and one younger, ceased shooting. All three were spitting images of Vanessa.

"Greg, Milo, Waylon!" Daniel handed Peter the apple juice and ran into the house. "I didn't know you'd be here."

"I didn't know either," Peter explained. "But my brother-in-law was bitten by a dog and—"

"It's horrible." Noelle stepped inside and kicked off her shoes. "I heard all about it on Skagiton Moms. It sounds like it's infected, what with the fever."

"They're at urgent care right now." Peter took the groceries from her. "I said I'd watch the boys to make it easier for them."

"That's what I would have done too." Noelle lifted up on her toes and kissed Peter on the cheek since Daniel was in the room. "It's good to see you."

"Eew!" Daniel screeched. "Kissing!"

"You should see my parents," said Greg. "They're totally disgusting."

"You already know Greg," said Peter, "but these other two animals are Milo and Waylon."

"Hi. I'm Noelle." She looked around the room. "And I'm seriously outnumbered."

"Come on." Milo grabbed Daniel's hand. "Let's get you armed." All four kids ran upstairs, and it sounded like a stampede of elephants. Noelle was glad that Daniel was included in the herd.

She followed Peter through the empty great room and into the kitchen. There still weren't any furnishings besides the recliner and TV, but unlike last week when she'd visited, now there were window treatments. "You got blinds." She looked around in amazement. "Custom ones, by the look of it."

"Yeah." Peter set the bags on the counter. "They did a rush order for me for free since I've referred so many customers to them. I was tired of living in a fishbowl. The lack of privacy never used to bother me, but . . ." He swooped her up in his arms. "Last week I really wanted to do this without the neighbors watching." He leaned her back for a kiss.

Noelle laced her hands around his neck as their lips locked together. She felt like she was in one of those old black-and-white movies that Joyce liked to watch, the ones where the orchestra swelled at just the right moment. When their lips parted, she sighed. "Peter, I'm so happy."

"You are?"

"Yes." Her heart bubbled with joy. "I've been sad. Stuck, really. Not knowing how to move on or if happiness was even possible after Jeff."

Peter stroked her hair. "You've been so brave."

"I don't know about that." Noelle wasn't sure she deserved the compliment. She rested her head on his shoulder for a moment. "I did what I had to do for my son." She looked back up at him. "But being here with you is for myself. Well, for Daniel, too, because you're so great with kids, but mainly I'm here for me." She leaned into him, enjoying the weight of his body against hers. "I have so much fun with you, Peter." She kissed him. "So much fun." She kissed him again, and this time, heart beating hard, her tongue explored the mystery of his mouth.

"Life's too short to be miserable," he said a couple of minutes later, his arms keeping a firm grip on her back. "You deserve all the fun in the world."

"Starting now." Noelle chuckled and then paused as she heard shouts upstairs. Were they playful shouts, or was someone injured?

"It sounds like mayhem up there," said Peter. "I'll go check to make sure nobody's ended up with a Nerf dart up their nose."

"That's probably a wise idea." Noelle slid her hands down his chest and gently pushed him away. "You go do that while I get out the ingredients to make dinner."

"Okay. Be right back."

Noelle grabbed his polo shirt and pulled him forward. "Not so fast," she said breathlessly. "One more kiss."

After Peter left, Noelle snapped pictures of the ingredient labels on the chicken, mayonnaise, and frozen vegetables so she could double-check that they were safe for Vanessa's son with the peanut allergy.

"No broken bones up there," said Peter when he returned. "No broken anything except a tissue box that never saw it coming. They promised to clean that up after the battle."

Noelle laughed, picturing the tissue explosion. "I hope Daniel's not revving them up. He can get loud when there's excitement to be had."

"Don't worry about it. Loud, we can handle. All four of them are having a blast."

"What's Vanessa's phone number? I want to make sure the food we prepare is safe for her son with the peanut allergy."

"Milo? That's a good idea." Peter told her the number, and Noelle sent the pictures.

Are these foods along with celery, grapes, salt, pepper, and dairy-free mayonnaise safe for Milo to eat? she texted.

Yes, Vanessa responded seconds later. Thx for checking.

Relieved that she wouldn't be accused of releasing "death bombs on unsuspecting innocents" again, Noelle waited for Peter to finish washing his hands, and then she took a turn at the sink. After she dried off with a towel, she tied on the apron Joyce had given her for her first Mother's Day without Jeff, the one that was covered with cows and said **I UDDERLY LOVE YOU**. Her hair was pulled back in a band, and she was ready to cook.

"What are we making?" Peter asked.

"I call it 'three ways with rotisserie chicken.' After tonight you'll know how to make breakfast, lunch, and dinner."

"Another breakfast recipe? Cool."

"No, breakfast was last week. I meant after tonight, combined with last week's lesson, you'll be a full-fledged cook."

"Gotcha. And this is the rotisserie chicken?" Peter took off the lid and inspected the fully cooked chicken. "It smells so good. I've always wondered how they tasted but didn't think I could eat a whole one by myself." He wiggled a drumstick. "How do you slice it?"

"I'll show you. Which is why . . . ta-da!" She uncovered the present she'd purchased for him at the outlet mall. "I bought you a knife."

"Whoa!"

"Last week I noticed you didn't have anything sharper than a butter knife. You can't be a proper chef without a real knife."

"Thank you, but that looks expensive. Can I pay you back?"

"Nope." Noelle shook her head. "You bought me that fancy dinner in La Conner last Friday, and you're coaching Daniel. My treat."

"But all these groceries too."

"I can afford it. I might be the *second* bestselling real estate agent in Skagiton, but I still make a comfortable living." It felt good admitting that. She'd been scared the first two years after Jeff had passed—frightened that she wouldn't be able to support Daniel on her own and that she'd have to rely upon her parents for help. Move back home, even. But Jeff's pension combined with her real estate commissions provided for them well. "I took a hard look at my finances a few days ago when my tax refund cleared and realized I should loosen the reins. I've been living like I'm broke, but I'm not." Noelle fiddled with her apron strings. "I'm taking what Social Security sends Daniel and investing it in the 529 account that Jeff started for him when he was little." She smiled, that thought adding to her happiness. She wasn't the same person who used to hand her paycheck from the ice cream shop over to her father—or to Kerry and Hank—anymore. She wasn't the young wife who relied on Jeff to make all the financial decisions. She was herself, Noelle Walters, and she was capable.

"Nice." Peter nodded his approval. "Act broke; stay rich."

Noelle laughed. "Is that why you don't have any furniture?"

"Furniture is so permanent, and I have no idea what to buy. I'd rather have nothing and wait for my dream couch to come to me in a vision."

"Your dream couch?"

"I'm assuming comfort will be involved. Aside from that, I don't know. Leather sticks. Fabric stains. Sometimes couches develop a weird odor. My dad's old recliner suits me fine at the moment. It barely smells like fish anymore."

"That doesn't encourage me to sit on it."

He tugged on the waistband of her apron. "What if you were sitting with me?"

"It would take more convincing than that." She giggled as he nibbled her neck. "We're never going to get dinner going if we continue like this." She closed her eyes and enjoyed the moment before scooting away to work. "Okay," she said, slapping the cutting board on the counter. "This is how you carve and debone a chicken. First thing you're going to do is take it out of the tray."

"That got scary fast. One moment we're kissing; the next you're dismembering a bird?"

"*I'm* not dismembering it; *you* are."

"At least give me tongs or something."

Noelle shook her head. "Your hands will do, or sometimes I stick a fork into the cavity and lift it up."

"Okaaaay, but this seems weird." Peter wrinkled his nose as he picked up the bird.

"Good job. Now set it on the cutting board."

Noelle spent the next ten minutes showing Peter how to carve the chicken. She demonstrated on one side and let him do the other. When they got to the back, she taught him how to pull off the little bits of meat with his fingers. When they were all done, they dropped the carcass into the one pot Peter owned and covered it with water.

"I still don't understand how these bones will turn into soup," said Peter.

"You'll see." She passed him a bag of frozen vegetables. "Rip this open, and pour it in. I bought a mixture with onions for extra flavor." After Peter added the veggies, Noelle had him sprinkle in salt and pepper. “Look at me,” he said as he shook the shakers. “I’m cooking soup from scratch!”

“Yeah.” Noelle gave him a thumbs-up. “Way to go.” She didn’t have the heart to tell him that real cooks would have sliced their own vegetables. “That’s enough salt there; you can put the shaker down.”

“Oh. Sorry. I got a bit carried away.”

“That’s fine. Salt will bring out the flavor. Okay, next up is chicken salad, but here’s the twist. We’re going to serve it two ways. Tonight with lettuce as a chicken salad, and tomorrow you can eat it spread on this loaf of bread I bought to make sandwiches.”

“Lunch and dinner. That sounds great.”

“It *is* great, except maybe I should have brought more food since we have three more mouths to feed. But don’t worry.” Noelle took out a can of green beans. “That’s what these are for, plus apple juice to wash it all down.” It was a simple meal but one that she guessed Peter would enjoy since he liked neutral flavors and things that were sweet. “All you gotta do is slice some cucumbers, grapes, and green onions. Then we’ll mix it up with the mayonnaise.”

“I can handle that.” Peter took the grapes out of the bag. “I should wash these first, right?”

“You got it.”

“How’d you learn to cook? Did your parents teach you?”

“My mom did. She always had a big garden, and our freezer usually had a side of beef in it. Plus we raised chickens—just for eating, not for selling. But the best part of growing up was drinking milk before it even went on the truck.”

“You’d drink it raw?”

“That’s right. Jeff freaked out when he found out and said we could have gotten listeria.”

“Um . . . he had a point.”

Noelle picked apart the head of lettuce. “I know. I can see that now. At the time I thought it was normal. My dad said pasteurization was just another way for the government to harass farmers. It's one of the reasons he got in trouble with the co-op. They caught him selling raw milk from our farm stand and refused to buy from Jansen Farms after that for almost a year until my dad got back into their good graces."

"How did he manage that?" Peter had finished at the sink.

Noelle shuddered, not wanting to think about that awful year any longer than she had to. With almost no money coming in, they'd had to live off the land. "Now that the grapes are washed," she said, trying to change the subject, "you can slice them in half. I'll wash the cutting board for you since it has chicken juice on it."

"You were telling me about your dad and the dairy co-op," Peter prompted.

"Oh. Well . . . I don't exactly know how it happened. All I know is that the dairy co-op has an outstanding reputation and takes the USDA regulations seriously. In addition to obeying the rules, my dad owed them a hefty fine he refused to pay. But right around the time Kerry got married, he must have paid it, because they took him back, and Jansen Farms started supplying the co-op again."

"What do Kerry's in-laws do?"

"Her father-in-law is retired now, but he used to be the principal at Trivium. Her mother-in-law is a stay-at-home mom."

"Do you think they might have pulled some strings?"

"That's not how it works. The USDA does not mess around."

"I get that, but maybe Kerry's in-laws paid your dad's fine?"

Noelle bit her bottom lip and mulled that thought over. "Could be. It would have been embarrassing to them otherwise. My dad was—or is—vocal about his distrust of the government. The local sheriff's a buddy of his from way back, or else he might have been charged with something by now."

"Charged with what?"

"Lots of things. Driving without a license. Letting the tags on his truck expire. Things like that. My dad feels like he doesn't owe the government a dime."

Talking about her parents was exhausting, so Noelle changed the subject to Rick's email about Windswept's shredding event happening in a few weeks. Soon they were mixing up the last few ingredients of the chicken salad and calling the boys down for dinner.

Daniel, Greg, Milo, and Waylon took their seats at the four barstools.

"Where are you gonna sit, Uncle Peter?" Waylon asked.

"Yeah," said Milo. "This is why you need a kitchen table. Mom says that the next time Costco has furniture in stock, you should just buy some."

"What do you think, Daniel's mom?" Waylon asked.

Jeff's wife. Joyce's daughter-in-law. Daniel's mom. Could she ever be known as Noelle? She was about to say something when Peter spoke first.

"Her name is Noelle Walters," said Peter. "Noelle, like Christmas."

"Thanks." Feeling grateful, Noelle poured multiple cups of apple juice. "I think Vanessa's right. A kitchen table would be a good idea."

"Yeah," said Greg. "Especially since Daniel took your barstool."

"Where else am I supposed to sit?" Daniel asked.

"Furniture is on my list of things to do, I promise." Peter picked up a cup of apple juice. He looked at Noelle. "Would you help me shop?"

Noelle shook her head. "Sorry, but no. It's not my living room. I have full faith in your ability to pick out a couch on your own."

"Or my mom could do it for you," Waylon offered.

Peter rubbed the back of his head. "No. Noelle's right; I can do this on my own. I just hadn't gotten around to it yet."

"If you buy a new couch, I promise we won't trash it." Milo eyed his younger brothers. "At least *I* won't."

"Hey!" said Greg. "Who spilled Snapple down the heater vent last week?"

"That doesn't count," said Milo. "Waylon pushed me."

"Did not," Waylon grumbled.

"Did too," Milo insisted.

"I once sprinkled a whole box of Cheerios down the heater." Daniel laughed. "It was sick."

"That's not something to brag about," Noelle chided. It had happened on Joyce's watch, a couple of months after Jeff had passed. Noelle had come home from a meeting with clients, and the whole house had smelled like oats.

"Maybe you and I should go eat in the living room?" Peter suggested. "We can leave the kitchen to the boys."

"But there's only one chair in there," said Daniel.

"That's fine." Noelle picked up her plate and winked at Peter. "We'll manage." Until Peter bought a new couch, she was going to enjoy squeezing onto that recliner with him. If they pushed it away from the kitchen's view, nobody would be able to see them snuggle.

SKAGITON MOMS FACEBOOK GROUP

Carol Durango
Thursday, March 24

Announcing a brand new pie at Carol's Diner: Blueberry Ripple. I know what you're thinking, it's not blueberry season. But DeBoer's gave me a great deal on frozen blueberries and my pastry chef has whipped up a new treat. Come in to try it and—this week only—get a free cup of coffee with your slice.

Melissa James
Sounds delicious!

Lexie Britt
Stop by to see Carol's new hairdo while you're at it. She's gorgeous!

Carol Durango
Thanks to your handiwork, darling, *Lexie Britt.*

Rachel Glass
Al and I leave for Harper Landing in a few days, but we'll be sure to stop by for one of our last meals in Skagiton.

Fern Sharp
Are the blueberries organic?

Carol Durango
They are not organic but they are locally grown from a no-spray farm, *Fern Sharp*.

Corine Reeder
Yum! I will stop by. Btw, my Girl Scouts learned so much from you. Thank you for speaking to my troop about what it's like running your own business.

Carol Durango
You're welcome, *Corine Reeder*.

Chapter Twenty

"Thanks for meeting me." Joyce took a seat in Peter's booth at Carol's Diner. It was Thursday at 11:00 a.m., and the lunch crowd hadn't picked up yet. "I appreciate your discretion."

"I didn't agree to anything." Peter folded his hands. When Joyce had contacted him this morning asking him to meet her after her water aerobics class, he hadn't known what to say. But now here he was because curiosity had gotten the better of him. "I don't feel right keeping secrets from Noelle."

"Neither do I. I'm going to tell her that I ran into you today, and then it won't be a secret." Joyce unrolled her silverware packet and put the napkin in her lap. "You can tell her too."

"Okay," Peter said dubiously. "But that still doesn't explain your mystery text." Meeting with Noelle's mother-in-law was weird. He wondered if maybe it was hard for Joyce to see Noelle move on from Jeff—and she was here to shoo him away.

"I'll explain everything once we order." Joyce opened her menu but didn't look at it.

"Well, this is a duo I don't see too often." Carol came over with a pencil and a notepad. "Can I get you something to drink?"

Joyce looked up. "Coffee and cream would be great. Thanks, Carol."

"See?" Carol pointed her pencil at Peter. "Joyce likes my coffee."

"Your coffee's fine, but I already tanked up at the office." Peter smoothed the collar of his polo shirt. "I'll take a Diet Coke."

"One coffee and a Diet Coke it is." Carol spun on her toe to head back to the kitchen when Peter stopped her.

"Wait a sec," he said. "There's something different about you."

"It's her hair." Joyce smiled and nodded her approval. "I love the red."

"Thanks." Carol patted her newly auburn tresses. "Lexie Britt over at Beach Blonde did it for me. She added golden babylights if you look closely."

Peter peered closely to try to spot the gold. "Sassy," he said. "I like it."

"Aw, aren't you a sweetie pie." She pinched his cheeks. "New hair. New man. New pie on the menu. I haven't felt this great in years."

"New pie, do you say?" Joyce asked. "I'll have a slice of that, whatever it is."

"It's blueberry ripple, and you'll love it," said Peter. "I've already tried it."

"Several times, in fact." Carol laughed. "I don't see him as much as I used to now that his girlfriend's teaching him to cook, but he still stops by a few days a week. Don't you, Peter?"

"Your pancakes will always hold a special place in my heart."

"Ha! I'll be right back with the drinks and the pie."

"Make that two slices of pie," said Peter. "Then, when you come back, we'll order lunch."

As soon as Carol was gone, he looked at Joyce. "So what did you want to tell me?"

"Not yet." Joyce tapped her finger on the menu. "I'm still deciding what to order. Is the club sandwich any good?"

"It's delicious."

"I'll get that, then." Joyce pushed her menu to the side and clicked her fingernails on the table like she was antsy. "I don't know how to say this—how to say any of this—but I think Jeff would want me to."

"Okay." Peter gulped. Here it came.

"Jeff would like you. A whole bunch." Tears filled Joyce's eyes, but she didn't wipe them away. "I like you too. You're one of the best things that's happened in Noelle's life in a long time, and that's good for my grandson too."

"I appreciate you saying that." Peter offered her his napkin.

"Thank you." Joyce blotted her eyes. "Here's the thing. The way I see it, you're really good for both of them, and I want you to succeed. So I think you should know some things about Noelle's upbringing that it took Jeff years to find out. He would want you to know so you could help protect Noelle."

Peter racked his brain for things Noelle had already told him that might be what Joyce meant. "You mean about Trivium High School using corporal punishment?"

"That and a whole bunch of other stuff."

"I'm not sure I feel comfortable hearing Noelle's secrets unless she tells them to me herself."

"That's fair. I respect that." Joyce blew her nose. "But I can tell you *my* story, right? I can tell you my experience these past ten years, and I can tell Jeff's story too." Her voice broke. "I can speak for my son."

"Okay." Peter's heart dropped into his stomach. "Please do."

"Here's your drinks," said Carol, zipping in with the soda and coffee. "I'll be right back with the pie."

"Thanks." Joyce forced a smile, tears glistening on her cheeks.

Carol stared at her for a second, not moving, before rushing away.

"Jeff met Noelle at a friend's wedding a little over ten years ago," said Joyce. "He told me all about it after it happened. 'Mom,' he said. 'I met the sweetest girl. You'd love her. She's so kind and easy to talk to.'"

"That sounds like Noelle, all right."

Joyce nodded. "Jeff asked for her number, but she didn't have one. That should have been his first clue that something weird was going on, but at the time Jeff wrote it off and thought she was broke or something."

"Not having a phone number is unusual . . ."

"Yeah. So since he couldn't call her, Jeff drove up to Hollenbeck the next weekend after he went hiking at Mount Baker. He knew she worked at the ice cream stand."

"I've already gathered this. Noelle told me about working at the creamery before." Or Vanessa had. Peter couldn't remember how he'd first learned that detail.

"Jeff came home after that second meeting and told me, 'Mom, I like this woman a lot, but she says I have to get her dad's approval before I can see her again.'"

"What?"

"I know, right? Like it was the olden days and he was courting her. But Jeff agreed because he thought Noelle was worth it."

"*Knew* she was worth it," Peter corrected.

"Yes. I misspoke." Joyce rubbed a hand over her face and then stirred cream in her coffee. "Look, Peter. This isn't easy, and I do love the both of them. Jeff drove up there the next weekend to have dinner on the farm with Noelle, Phil, and Anika—those are her parents—and Sam, who was a senior in high school and still living at home at the time. Noelle was living at home too. That's important to note. She was nineteen years old and still under her parents' control. They didn't pay her anything for her labor on Jansen Farms, but they did expect her to pay rent. She passed over all of her money from the ice cream stand to Phil each payday, and he gave her a small allowance."

"Shit. Sorry—I didn't mean to swear."

"No, I get it. And I realize you said you didn't want me to tell you Noelle's secrets, but these aren't just her secrets anymore; Jeff knew them too."

Peter nodded. Carol caught his eye from the bar and held up the pies, like she was asking if it was okay to deliver them, and he nodded again. She came over and slid them onto the table. "Are you ready to order?" she asked in a quiet voice.

"Yes, thank you," said Joyce. "I'll have the club sandwich on white bread with an extra pickle."

"I'll have the same." Peter picked up his fork.

"I'll get that going for you." Carol collected the menus and walked away.

"That first meeting with the Jansens did not go well." Joyce grimaced. "Jeff discovered that Phil is a total nutjob. A doomsday prepper. An antigovernment conspiracy theorist. A misogynistic, antiwoman, controlling pig."

"But how do you really feel about him?" He tried to take the intensity down a notch.

Joyce scoffed. "Like he should be on the Homeland Security's watch list. Hell, for all I know, he already is. Half the house wasn't even finished, even though they'd lived there since before Noelle was born. The sides had tar paper instead of siding."

"What about the farm buildings?" Peter thought about the fundraiser coming up.

"The barns were in fine condition, except for the old one. Phil's parents were good people. It was their son who went wrong. I'm not sure how that happened, but maybe it's because Phil listens to so many extremist shows on AM radio. When Phil found out that Jeff was a public school teacher and therefore a government employee, he went ballistic. He accused Jeff of spying on him for the governor and trying to steal his daughter."

"Damn. What about Noelle's mom? Did she intervene?"

"Anika?" Joyce shook her head. "That woman is a mouse. She doesn't so much as raise her voice to her husband. I never understood how she could stand him until Jeff learned that in one of the outbuildings, she grows her own stash of pot. Mint and echinacea are not the only things in her medicinal tea." Joyce rubbed her temples. "I've tried it for my migraines, and it's pretty strong."

"Wow. I did not see that coming."

Joyce grinned, but then her smile dissolved. "Jeff knew that Noelle came from difficult circumstances. After that dinner, how could he not know? I told him to stay away and find another girl that he liked who wouldn't have so much baggage."

"That was harsh."

"It was," Joyce admitted. "But if you were in my position, you might have done the same. Nobody wants their son to have a future father-in-law who threatens him."

"I can see that."

"But Jeff was adamant about seeing Noelle. I'm not saying it was love at first sight because their relationship definitely deepened over the following year, but he cared for her right from the beginning. Privately, I worried that Jeff viewed Noelle as a project to fix, like one of his broken bicycles. It took me a while to see that he was truly in love with her. What Jeff didn't know were the sacrifices Noelle made to keep seeing him. Phil kicked her out of the house."

"He what?"

"She had no place to go. No car. No driver's license."

"No driver's license? She mentioned Phil driving without one, but I didn't know Noelle did too."

"She didn't know any better. And even if she did, it gets worse. Noelle didn't have a birth certificate or a social security card either."

"How was she employed? How was the ice cream stand paying her?"

"In cash, which Noelle would then hand over to Phil. When Phil kicked her out, Kerry and her husband invited Noelle to move into a camping trailer on their property. Kerry and Hank are extremely religious and hoped that by forcing Noelle to attend their church each Sunday, Noelle would forget Jeff and marry someone from their congregation. Which was the same congregation that sponsored Trivium High School, by the way."

"Where they allow corporal punishment." Peter raked his fingers through his hair and leaned his elbow on the table.

Joyce held up her palm. "On the one hand, you have Noelle's father, who is a narcissistic, controlling asshole, and on the other, you have Kerry and Hank, who wanted to control Noelle through their specific religious beliefs. Kerry loves Noelle but not enough to invite her into the house where she might 'corrupt' her children."

Anger coursed through him. "She couldn't enter their house?"

"No, not unless she was going to church that day, in which case they'd let her come in to take a shower. The trailer Noelle lived in didn't have heat or running water, which is one of the reasons I think that she's always cold."

"I've noticed that too." His heart shattered, like it had been smashed by a boulder.

"When Jeff realized how she was living, he proposed, then and there, even though he was twenty-eight, she was only twenty, and he hadn't been planning on getting married until later." Joyce lifted her chin. "Jeff was a good man. My son was a hero. He loved Noelle and knew that her only way out of that awful situation was to marry and move away."

"Jeff's my hero too, then." Peter blinked. He wasn't crying. His eyes were just moist from the weather.

Joyce stabbed her pie with her fork. "But marrying Noelle wasn't that easy."

"Why?"

"She didn't have a birth certificate. Remember?"

"Hold on; how could she not have a birth certificate?" Peter was shocked by that. "I should have asked about that earlier."

"It was a home birth. Anika delivered all her babies at home—the ones who lived and the ones who didn't," she added ominously. "Jeff had to hire a lawyer through the teachers' union to sort it all out. As soon as they got married, he put her on his health insurance, got her vaccinated, and—"

"Holy—"

"Yeah. She wasn't even vaccinated for tetanus. Her mouth was a mess too. Her poor teeth . . ." Joyce put her face in her hands. "I love Noelle like she's my daughter. My own daughter that I never had." Her shoulders shook, and when she lifted her face, she was openly crying.

Peter pulled napkins out of the dispenser and handed them to her. Joyce blew her nose, and as she settled herself, Carol came over with a box of tissues and then rushed off.

"This is what I want you to know," Joyce said, her voice as hard as steel. "If Noelle wants to keep up communication with her family for some reason, fine; she's an adult. I don't like it, but she doesn't deserve anyone, including me, trying to control her." Joyce raised her fist. "But under no circumstances do I want those people to hurt Daniel. Jeff wouldn't let them near him. They saw Daniel three times total the whole time Jeff was alive." She opened her fist and counted on her fingers. "First a few weeks after Daniel was born, then at one of Kerry's baby showers, and then at Sam's wedding. That's it. That's all Jeff felt comfortable with. Now Phil calls Noelle on a regular basis, pestering her to move home."

"Sam. What about Sam? Where does he fall into this?" Peter wondered if sponsoring a table at the barn fundraiser had been a bad idea. The last thing he wanted to do was support people who were cruel to Noelle.

"Sam's different." The creases in Joyce's forehead softened. "He came back from college with an education and a woman with a good head on her shoulders. Shayla is the only member of the Jansen family besides Noelle that I like. Under her and Sam's stewardship, they've turned Jansen Farms around. Cleared up regulation issues and some environmental mishaps. Noelle said that they even filled in the bunker.

I like Sam a lot, but at his wedding, Phil and Jeff got into it over school levies. Phil said Jeff and public school teachers like him were parasites and that he wasn't a real man anyway because Noelle made more money than him."

"Oh, jeez."

"Jeff wanted Noelle to turn her back on her parents and Kerry, but she never did. I don't know why exactly. It's like they have tentacles in her and keep pulling her back into the swamp."

Carol brought their sandwiches, and nobody spoke until Peter said: "Thanks, Carol. These look good." He looked over at Joyce, who twisted the tissue she held in her hand.

"Yes," said Joyce. "Thanks."

"No problem," said Carol. "I'll be right over there if you need anything else."

Joyce put away the tissue and pulled the decorative toothpick out of her sandwich. "My greatest fear is that Noelle will move back to Hollenbeck. She's never felt fully at home here in Skagiton. I know she still has friends in Hollenbeck—normal friends, not just toxic family members. What if Phil convinces her to move up north and I never see my grandson again?"

"That would be cruel—to you, Daniel, and Noelle, it sounds like."

Joyce nodded. "See why I'm rooting for you? It's not only that I like you. It's because Jeff would want your help to protect Noelle and Daniel."

Peter took a deep breath and pondered what he'd just learned. Noelle had told him some of this information and hinted at the rest but always with a rosy glow to everything that she'd shared about her life in Hollenbeck. He could see what Joyce meant about dark forces rooting her to a bad situation. But he also saw something more in Noelle than what Joyce was sharing.

"Noelle's not twenty anymore. She's a grown woman capable of doing amazing things. She pays bills, takes care of her son, manages clients, and so much more. With or without me, I have confidence that she'll make good decisions. Daniel's well-being means everything to her. I know that in my soul, and you should see that too. The number one reason I fell in love with Noelle was because of what a great mother she is." Peter stopped, shocked at his own admission. Had he really said he was in love? Yes, he had because it was the truth. "Noelle's not Phil, or Anika, or Kerry; she's her own person. Take faith in that."

"I will." Joyce nodded. "I mean, I do. But I'm still awfully glad you love her."

"Me too." Peter bit into his sandwich and savored the taste of the salty flavors. He and Joyce ate in companionable silence, neither one of them speaking for the next few minutes. The weight of what had already been shared sat with them, like a heavy presence in the booth. By the time Peter was crunching through his pickle, he felt ready to speak again. "Do you think attending the barn fundraiser is a bad idea? I sponsored a whole table and was going to bring Vanessa and her family."

"I'm not going, but I think that was sweet of you to try to help. It'll make me feel better knowing that you and Vanessa will be there to watch over Daniel when Noelle is serving food. Phil's likely to give Daniel a hard time about not drinking milk."

"I'd like to see Phil try, with my sister there." Peter folded his arms across his chest. "He won't know what's coming for him."

Joyce chuckled. "I hope there's ice water." She was about to take another bite of her sandwich when an enormous smile spread across her face, and she giggled. "Oh my goodness." She hunched her shoulders and then sat up straight. "Look who's here. Have you met my new boyfriend?"

Peter turned to see whom Joyce was looking at and saw a head of thick white hair he recognized. *Crap,* he thought. *This isn't good.*

Stone stood in the doorway of the diner wearing faded jeans and a leather jacket. "Where's my Butter Biscuit?" he called. "Papa's hungry for some love."

"Oh, you fool." Carol strode across the diner and threw her arms around Stone. He grabbed her by the buttocks and pulled her in for a juicy kiss.

Joyce gasped. "Stone?" she squeaked a second later. "What? I thought—"

Stone turned at the sound of Joyce's voice. Still keeping one hand on Carol's derriere, he opened his other arm out wide. "Babe. Good to see you too. Come give me a hug. It can be a papa-bear sandwich."

"Gross." Carol let go of Stone and looked at Joyce. "Are you seeing him too?"

"I *was* seeing him." Joyce's cheeks burned red with indignation. "I was seeing a lot of him."

"You scumbag." Peter crumpled his napkin. "You were dating Carol and Joyce at the same time without telling them?"

Stone ran his free hand up and down the side of his own body. "There's enough of me to go around."

"Peter's right. You're a scumbag." Carol punched him in the stomach and then shook out her hand as she winced in pain. "With rock-hard abs," she gasped.

"Damn yoga." Joyce frowned.

Stone chuckled. "You don't get a bod like this from water aerobics." He looked over at Joyce. "Are we still on for the Y's hot tub later?"

"Absolutely not. And you can find another pickleball partner too. Good luck with that." Joyce picked up her dill pickle and let it flop down.

"Yeah," said Carol. "And good luck finding avocado toast at the co-op that's as soft as you like it."

"I don't need you," said Stone. He glanced over at Joyce. "Either of you. I can get all the ladies I want." He walked out of the diner with a confident swagger.

Peter took out his wallet and fished out a fifty-dollar bill. "This lunch has been illuminating." He placed the money next to his plate. "Unfortunately, I . . . uh . . . have work to do." He was about to stand up and make his escape when Carol sat next to him in the booth, blocking his exit.

"Thanks for defending me." She rested her head on his shoulder. "You're one of the good ones, Peter."

"That he is," said Joyce.

Peter sighed. It didn't look like he would escape this drama anytime soon. He threw his arm around Carol's shoulder in a side hug. "At least you have the hot new hairdo."

"That's right," said Joyce. "It's bitchin'."

"It really is, isn't it?" Carol brightened. "And I love your new workout clothes, Joyce. Are you playing pickleball later?"

"I was, but now I don't have a partner."

"I've always wanted to learn how to play pickleball," said Carol.

"What's stopping you?" Joyce asked.

"I don't know. Is it hard to learn?"

"I could teach you in about ten minutes," said Joyce. "How are your knees?"

"Great." Carol stuck her feet outside of the booth. "These custom orthotics are a lifesaver. But I don't have a YMCA membership."

"That's easy," said Joyce. "You'll get the SilverSneakers discount. It's the workout wardrobe that'll be expensive."

That sounded like a good way out to Peter. He opened up his wallet and swapped his fifty out with a hundred-dollar bill. "Go buy yourself a new outfit on me, Butter Biscuit." He stood up to go.

"Thanks, Peter." Carol scooted to the side so he could pass. "But don't you ever dare call me that again."

"And add another hundred to that," said Joyce. "Sports bras are expensive."

"I did not want to know that," Peter mumbled as he let another hundred dollars flutter to the table.

SKAGITON MOMS FACEBOOK GROUP

Group Member
Friday, March 25

Posting anonymously because I don't want everyone to know my business any more than they already do. Does anyone know of a good dating app? Not Tinder, I'm not a hoochie-coochie type of gal. But I've also reached a certain age where I've decided I like a man's occasional companionship, just not all the bullcrap that comes with it. I don't want to tweeze his ear hair. I don't want to plan Christmas around his colonoscopy. And I don't want a man whose rear end is so flat I could flip it on a griddle. So how do I do it? What app should I try?

Corine Reeder
I've heard Good Catch is popular.

Renee Schroth
Seconding Good Catch. It matched me with some great men. None of them worked out, but I have no regrets.

Carmen Swan
What about Tinder?

Dorothy Caulfield
She already said no Tinder or hoochie-coochie, *Carmen Swan*. Have you tried eharmony?

Group Member
No, should I, *Dorothy Caulfield*?

Dorothy Caulfield
Friends of mine from church met through there, *Group Member*.

Fern Sharp
I don't have any advice other than to say good luck finding a man over 50 who still has a butt.

Vanessa Collins
Fern Sharp, I'm dying. LOL!

Fern Sharp
I see a lot of things during public comments in school board meetings, *Vanessa Collins*.

Chapter Twenty-One

"But I don't understand," said Noelle, sitting at her desk on a cold and rainy Friday morning. Deirdre DeBoer had called her with a strange request. "Why would you want me to become the admin of Skagiton Moms? I don't participate."

"You read it," said Deirdre. "At the food bank potluck I could tell that you follow it closely."

"How?" Noelle looked around the dimly lit bullpen. She was the only one at Windswept so far.

"You knew about the potluck, for one thing. You also knew about the injured owl. Plus, you told me yourself that you're a lurker."

"Okay, that's true, but I still don't see why you'd want me to moderate discussions."

"You wouldn't have to do it by yourself. I'm assembling a small team to take over for me when I leave. My kids are grown and flown. It's time for me to move on. Heck, I might delete my Facebook account altogether. I've been thinking about that. It's not good for my mental health. I feel so much better when I don't look at social media at all."

"Same." Noelle sighed. "But I have to be on Facebook because it's part of my job selling houses."

"And you're good at it too. I've seen your listing ads. Look, this isn't a paid job; it's a volunteer position. But you can do it as much or as little as you want. You don't have to show up at a certain place on a schedule to help out your community. You can do it at home, in your jammies, while you watch TV."

"I *would* like to volunteer . . ." It stung knowing that other moms chaperoned field trips and helped out in the classroom when her work schedule didn't allow time to do that. Well, actually, she could have made time to volunteer an hour a week in Daniel's classroom, but she hadn't. What if she forgot a child's name in math group or grabbed the subtraction games when she was supposed to be helping with addition? The professional-volunteer moms like Vanessa might shame her. Besides, Noelle had only a limited amount of patience for six-year-olds, and she reserved all of it for Daniel. "I still don't understand why you'd want me for this role," said Noelle. "Why not someone who is more active in the group, like Vanessa Collins or Jourdaine Bloomfield?"

"Because the group needs someone neutral, like Switzerland, and Vanessa and Jourdaine aren't neutral. They always take a stand, no matter what the issue is."

"They would say that's a good thing. That they're following their convictions."

"So would the women arguing against them. I've searched your post history, and the only time you were in a heated situation, you handled it gracefully and with a great deal of class. Then, last Sunday at the potluck, you got Fern Sharp and my husband, Marty, to calm down. She's touring our farm next week. Never in a million years did I think that would happen—either that she would come or that Marty would let her. That was your doing. Your good sense, calm thinking, and mediation skills made that happen."

"The only mediation skills I have come from being a middle child."

"Really? It must be more than that."

"No, just that," said Noelle, although she wondered if that was true. She'd spent her childhood doing whatever it took to keep her dad from ranting or Kerry from being caught during her wild high school days of tailgate parties and kegs of beer. When Jeff had come on the scene, she'd been torn in the middle like a rag doll, her family pulling her one direction and Jeff the other. Noelle had had ample practice keeping the peace, but she wasn't usually successful at making people agree with each other. "What would I have to do if I did volunteer?" she asked with hesitation.

"It would be easy. I'd train you." Deirdre spoke quickly. "You could come over to my house for coffee next week, and I'd introduce you to the other volunteers. We'd go over some tips and tricks, and then I'd show you how to use the moderation tools on the dashboard. It's easy. You'll see."

"Really? I've seen some really heated threads there before."

"But life-changing threads too, right? I view it as a mission project for the women of Skagiton. When I think about it that way, I don't feel as frustrated about the work involved."

"You said it wasn't that much work."

"And it doesn't have to be. I've been doing it all on my own for years. You'd be on a team of three. That's a third of the work."

Noelle took a deep breath as she considered. She'd benefited from being a part of Skagiton Moms. It would be dishonest to say that she hadn't. She might not have gotten as many client referrals as Peter had, but she'd learned other things—not just parenting skills but also about being a woman. "Okay. I'll come over for coffee. But this isn't necessarily a yes. I want time to think about it before I make a decision."

"That's fair, and it also shows cool-tempered thinking. Both of those are qualities that would make a good admin."

The front door jingled, and Noelle heard someone, hopefully Peter, enter the lobby. "Text me the details, and I'll be there."

"Will do. Thanks for considering it."

After they said goodbye and hung up, Noelle raced to the lunchroom, eager to see Peter. "Good morning," she sang in a happy voice.

"Good morning to you too, angel." Debbie selected a mug from the cabinet and chuckled. "How about a kiss?" She puckered up her lips.

"I thought you were married."

Debbie laughed. "And I thought you'd never wake up and realize that Peter adored you."

"Really?" Noelle couldn't help shaking her head. "Do you think he adores me? Maybe that's overstating the situation. It could be that he only kinda likes me."

"Oh no, I think *adore* is the proper verb," said Peter, standing at the entrance to the lunchroom.

"Peter," Noelle squeaked. "I didn't hear you come in."

Debbie popped a pod into the Nespresso machine and clamped it shut. "You two better let Rick know what you're up to," she said over the noise of the coffee brewing. "I think there's a form you need to sign or something."

"The consensual relationship agreement from Windswept," said Peter. "I printed it out." He looked at Noelle and brushed his hair back. "I've already signed it, but I didn't want to presume that you'd want—"

"Oh, I'll sign it all right," said Noelle, wondering when Debbie's coffee would finally finish brewing and she would leave. "I'd be happy to."

"Aww." Debbie removed her mug and slowly stirred in the powdered creamer she liked. "Our very first Windswept romance." She leaned against the counter, took a sip, and stared at them.

"Don't you have a front desk to command?" Peter looked sideways at Debbie.

"Is that your not-so-subtle way of asking me to leave so you can French kiss her? Because she hasn't signed the form yet."

"The contract is just a formality." Noelle walked across the small space and put her arms around Peter's neck. "We already have a handshake agreement."

Peter kissed her on the nose. "You are so cute."

"Cute and victorious." Debbie raised her mug. "Cheers to you, Noelle, for beating out all those other women on Skagiton Moms. Vanessa must be happy to know she was finally successful."

"What?" Peter loosened his hold on Noelle.

Glancing over her shoulder, Noelle shot Debbie a murderous look.

"You mean he didn't know?" Debbie raised her eyebrows. "I thought everyone in town knew. I'm not even on Skagiton Moms. My daughter-in-law told me. She thought it was a hoot."

"Thought what was a hoot?" Peter stepped back. "Noelle, what's going on?"

Noelle tugged her collar. "I tried to tell you last Friday at the restaurant. I said: 'Vanessa advertises for you on Skagiton Moms.' Remember?"

"I thought you meant *houses*!"

"That too."

"Oh boy." Debbie added more creamer to her coffee. "Me and my big mouth."

"This isn't your fault," Peter told her. He turned toward Noelle. "*You*, on the other hand. Why didn't you tell me?"

"Because it was none of my business, and I didn't want to give your sister another reason to be mad at me! Then, when it did become my business, I did tell you."

"No, you didn't!"

"I did too. I told you that Vanessa talks about you on Skagiton Moms and that she wants you to be happy."

"The way I heard it," said Debbie, "she was basically pimping for you."

Peter palmed his forehead. "Unbelievable." He stalked out of the lunchroom before Noelle could stop him.

Vanessa had done a lot of dumb things in her life, but this took the cake. Even worse was knowing that Noelle had known about it and hadn't told him. He charged out the front door and into the cold so he could call Vanessa and speak to her privately. After tapping the contact number angrily, he listened to the ringtone as it dialed. Peter couldn't remember if she'd be at work right now or not.

"Hello? Hello?" said Vanessa. "I can't hear you—speak louder. Just kidding; I can't hear you at all because this is my voice mail. Leave a message, and I'll get back to you when I feel like it."

"You've got a lot of nerve!" Peter shouted. "What's this I hear about you pimping me out on Skagiton Moms?"

A dog walker strolling past him mouthed the word "Wow" and kept walking.

"And no, Noelle didn't tell me. She kept your secret, so don't go blaming her. I had to hear it from Debbie, our receptionist. Do you know how embarrassing that was?" A dark thought hit him. That embarrassing moment with Debbie was only a drop in the bucket. Who knew how badly Vanessa had humiliated him in that Facebook group? "You betrayed my trust," Peter growled. "Thanks for nothing." Hanging up, he turned around to go back inside and face Noelle.

She was already waiting for him there on the porch, bundled up in her coat and stocking cap, hugging herself to ward off the cold. "Peter, I'm sorry," she said. "I should have been clearer about what had been happening. But I'm not a gossip, and I think Vanessa truly had your best interest at heart. She didn't say anything bad about you; I promise. Only that you couldn't cook. That's it."

"Can't cook? Is that why you offered to give me cooking lessons? It was some big setup?"

"No, of course not." Noelle dropped her arms. "Let's come back inside and talk about this where we can be warm."

"I'm not sure I'm going back into the office today." He was too angry to focus on work.

"Oh. Okay. Um . . . but I can show you what Vanessa posted. Maybe that'll make you feel better and understand why I didn't say anything to you earlier. It didn't seem bad to me, and Vanessa's plan was working. Suddenly all these wonderful women started noticing how great you are." She looked directly at him. "I've seen how great you are for a long time, and I wanted you to be happy too."

"Wanted me to be happy, eh? With someone else?"

"At first, yes. But then I became jealous." Lines creased across Noelle's forehead. "That's what woke me up. I didn't like watching those other women fall all over you. I knew I needed to act, or I'd miss my chance." She dropped her gaze. "But I understand if you don't want me to sign the form now."

"What form?" Peter's attention was so scattered he was confused.

"The consensual relationship agreement that you printed out."

"Oh. Duh." Peter took a deep breath of cold air. "No, I absolutely want you to sign it."

"You still do?" She looked at him hopefully.

He nodded and took a step forward. "You can even post a picture of it on Skagiton Moms if you want. Make sure people know I'm taken."

"But I never post on Skagiton Moms."

"Would you consider making an exception?" He really wanted that topic shut down—and fast.

"Absolutely." Noelle smiled for the first time since they'd come outside.

Peter closed the distance between them in two big steps and embraced her. She felt different in her puffy coat, and he missed the feeling of her heart beating next to his own. But she was there, safe, and officially ready to be his girlfriend. His heart yearned for her as much as his body wanted to be closer. Cupping her face with his hands, he crushed their lips together. The temperature rose, and he forgot about the cold. "I like you a lot. I mean, I like you a *whole* lot," Peter said when their lips parted. "I adore you." He would have told her he loved her but wasn't sure she was ready to hear that yet. "Yes, I would like to see those posts from Vanessa so I know what she was up to. But I guess I owe her a thank-you as well since it worked out in my favor."

"I'm glad you think so." Noelle nuzzled closer. "Let's go back inside."

"Okay. I need to tell you something too . . . Joyce and I . . . um . . . happened to be at Carol's Diner at the same time, and so we ate lunch together. Did Joyce mention that Stone's been cheating on her with Carol?"

"No." Noelle looked at him. "She didn't. But this explains why when Daniel and I came home from baseball practice last night, I found Joyce halfway into a bottle of merlot. She never drinks wine. It turns her cheeks bright pink, and she has awful sleep the night afterward."

"How'd she seem this morning?"

"She wasn't up by the time I left, so I don't know."

"Hmm . . ." Peter opened the door and waited for Noelle to walk inside first. "Well, keep an eye on her, I guess. She might need extra TLC."

"I'll do that."

Peter thought about the things Joyce had told him before Stone had come into the diner. He was glad to have a clearer picture of the trauma Noelle had experienced, but he would have felt more comfortable if Noelle had told him directly instead of hearing it secondhand via Joyce. Perhaps there was a way to open a conversation that gave Noelle space to do just that.

"Here's the agreement." Peter paused by his desk and picked up a pen. He pulled out his chair for Noelle.

"Thank you." She took the pen and signed her name in elegant cursive.

"I say this with love, but your handwriting does look Victorian," Peter said, taking the pen back from her. "Trivium, I presume?"

Noelle nodded. "Copy work was a big part of my school experience."

"I'm not sure I know what that means."

"Copying things. Like the Gettysburg Address or the Bill of Rights. We had to do it in pen, no Wite-Out. If we made a mistake, we'd start the page over."

"Like you were medieval monks?"

Noelle laughed. "No. Like we were students who studied important historical documents and practiced the art of penmanship."

"How's Kerry and Sam's handwriting? Are they amateur calligraphists too?"

"Sam hated cursive so much that his teachers let him write in block letters. All uppercase. Very masculine. But Kerry's handwriting is a mess. She was a wild one until she started dating her husband senior year. Hank's family is really strict, and that helped her settle down."

Peter sat on the edge of his desk. "Strict in what way?"

"The usual. Obey your parents. Save yourself for marriage. Stay away from corrupting influences. Things like that." Noelle's phone rang. "Uh-oh." She looked at the screen. "I need to take this. It's about the three-bedroom I have listed."

"Sure." Peter reclaimed his desk chair and sat in the warm spot where Noelle had just been. As he turned on his computer, he reflected on what he'd learned. Apparently, Phil's strictness had impacted each sibling in different ways. Kerry had rebelled, Noelle had run away, and Sam had taken over the farm. Noelle had presented a much softer view of Kerry than Joyce had. But there were key words in her description that his brain circled with a red pen: *stay away from corrupting influences.*

That must have been how Kerry and Hank had viewed Noelle—as a corrupting influence because she'd disobeyed her parents and dated someone their insular community disapproved of. The whole thing made Peter feel sick, yet Noelle was so gracious about it, so forgiving. That was the type of person she was: loyal to the core. She never exposed the evil in others. Hell, she'd even covered for Vanessa and those stupid Skagiton Moms posts. Noelle saw the best in people, no matter what.

But Joyce was right. There were a lot of people in Noelle's life who didn't deserve her charity.

SKAGITON MOMS FACEBOOK GROUP

Jourdaine Bloomfield
Saturday, March 26

I am posting on my mom and sister's behalf, since neither of them are on Skagiton Moms. They would like recommendations for yoga classes at the YMCA that are not "taught by creepy douchebags."

Alastrina Kelly
My dad teaches yoga at the YMCA. He's great! Everyone at his studio in Yakima loved him.

Jourdaine Bloomfield
Um . . . thanks, *Alastrina Kelly*. Any other suggestions?

Maggie Swan
Just seconding what *Alastrina Kelly* said. I haven't taken one of Stone's yoga classes

before but after dating him a couple of weeks now I can attest to the fact that he's extremely limber.

Carmen Swan
Mom! Barf, *Maggie Swan*!

Maggie Swan
Hey *Carmen Swan*, I've thought of a new drink Mike could sell at the Lumberjane Shack: The Silver Fox Mocha. It'd be a stiff shot of espresso with white chocolate and extra cream.

Carmen Swan
Maggie Swan, Gross! Mom, stop. Moderators! Please help!

Sabrina Kruger
The YMCA noon classes are great. My wife teaches them. She's not on FB or I'd tag her. Her name is Aurora Lopez and you'll love her.

Jourdaine Bloomfield
Thank you, *Sabrina Kruger*!

Chapter Twenty-Two

Saturday morning was well underway, but Joyce still hadn't emerged from her bedroom, and Noelle was worried. She balanced the tray of coffee and toast she'd made for her and knocked on the door. "Joyce? Are you up? I brought you breakfast."

"I'm here," came a weak voice.

Noelle opened the door and entered the dark room. Joyce lay in bed under a pile of covers. Shipping boxes and wooden floral arrangements were strewed everywhere. "Morning!" Noelle smiled and looked for a place to set the tray. Joyce's nightstand was covered with tissues. "Why don't you scoot up in bed, and I'll hand this to you? I made you toast with raspberry jam. Your favorite."

"You brought me breakfast in bed?" Joyce rubbed her eyes before propping herself up on pillows. "That was really sweet of you, but I'm not sick. I could have come out to the kitchen."

"I know. But I thought you could use a special treat." Noelle placed the tray on her lap and walked around the bed to open the blinds. The March sky was gloomy. Hopefully the rain would hold off until after the T. Rex game.

"I feel so stupid." Joyce picked up her toast. "Stone never said we were exclusive; I just assumed that we were."

"I thought the same thing." Noelle sat on the edge of her bed. "He tricked you."

"It wasn't like he lied to me."

"Omitting pertinent information is almost the same thing."

Joyce hung her head, still not eating the toast. "You must think I'm a real idiot." Tears sprang to her eyes.

"What? No, of course not. He's the one who was being an idiot." Noelle picked up the box of tissues, but it was empty. "I'll be right back with more of these," she said before rushing out of the room.

On her way to the garage to get a fresh box, she ran into Daniel, who was half-dressed in his baseball uniform. "Where's my other sock?" he asked.

"In your dresser."

"I already checked my dresser."

"Look harder."

"I did look."

"If I go in there and find it in three seconds, you're going to be in charge of folding all the bathroom towels for the rest of the week."

"That's no big deal. I like folding towels."

Noelle groaned. "Okay, I'll go find your sock; you go get a tissue box from the garage. Got it?"

"Where do I look in the garage?"

"On the wire rack where we keep all the tissue boxes and paper towels." Sometimes it felt like Noelle was in charge of everything and nobody else living in the house had a clue.

She found Daniel's sock as soon as she opened the top drawer. It was rolled neatly in a ball next to the tiny jockstrap that he must not have been wearing. She passed both items to Daniel when he miraculously returned with a box of tissues. "Here you go. We're leaving in about twenty minutes."

"Thanks." Daniel sat down on the carpet and pulled on his sock.

Noelle returned to Joyce's room and closed the door behind her so they'd have privacy. Joyce plucked a tissue out of the box and blew her nose. "There," said Noelle. "That's better. Now what can I do to help you realize that Stone is a jerk who's not worth your tears?"

"It's not just Stone I'm crying about." Joyce wiped her nose. "It's all of it."

"What do you mean?"

Joyce waved her hand around, indicating the mess. "I can't seem to do anything right. Business is booming because the wedding season is coming up, and I'm behind on shipping orders. Every time my phone dings, it's another angry customer wondering where their package is."

"Oh. I didn't realize that was happening."

"That's why this place looks like a whirlwind. I'm messy, but I'm not *this* messy."

"Yeah. I know."

"I've been spending more and more time at the Y, at first because of Stone but then because of pickleball and water aerobics—those were for me. You know? Something fun. A brief blip of happiness to take the edge off of so much sadness."

"Oh, Joyce." Noelle felt awful. She'd been so focused on her own despair the past two years she hadn't realized how much Joyce was hurting. "You lost your son."

"My only child," Joyce said as a sob overtook her.

"You deserve every bit of happiness out there." Noelle picked up her hand and held it in both of her own. "As for this mess, part of it is my fault. If I didn't rely on you so much to help out with Daniel, you'd be able to keep up with your Etsy shop."

"But I *want* you to rely on me. I'm happy that you've found Peter, but what happens when you go off and don't need me anymore?"

"I will always need you." Noelle scooted closer. "You will always be my mother-in-law and Daniel's grandma, no matter what. As for Peter, I can't predict the future or what will happen, but I can't imagine him not wanting you to be a big part of our lives." Noelle embraced her. "You're stuck with me. So deal with it."

Joyce's body shook as she cried on Noelle's shoulder. "But what happens if you move home to Hollenbeck? I'll never see you or Daniel again."

"That's not going to happen."

"It's not?" Joyce pulled away, her face puffy and red.

"I'm not moving back there. This is home. My business is here. My friends." For a split second, Noelle couldn't believe that word had come out of her mouth: *friends*. But it was true. She had friends now—people she could share her problems with and people who would help her. Even Vanessa, whom Noelle didn't necessarily think of as a friend, would show up if Noelle asked for her help. Speaking of which, Daniel was due at the ball field soon.

Noelle took out her phone. "I'm going to call Peter and see if he can take Daniel to the T. Rex game today. It'll be okay for me to miss one game. You and I can sort out all your orders and take them to the post office before it closes at one."

"But Daniel—"

"Will be fine. Peter will be there along with a whole cheering section of T. Rex parents to clap for him when he comes up to bat." Noelle thought about Vanessa and how she cheered for every player by name. "It's not like we live in a big city," she said. "This is Skagiton. If Daniel ends up hitting a home run, half a dozen people will text pictures to the team chat."

So that's what they did. Peter arrived twenty minutes later to pick up Daniel and his booster seat, and Noelle went to work helping Joyce rein in the chaos that was Wo0d You Be Mine? As she helped process orders and fill boxes with compostable packing peanuts, Noelle thought about how Joyce's life and hers fit together. She had been wanting to broach the subject of Daniel starting after-school care for a while but hadn't known how to do it until now. In the past few weeks, she'd gained practice in having difficult conversations, and if what Deirdre said was true, she had a natural talent for peacemaking to begin with.

"I've been thinking," Noelle said as she deployed a strip of packing tape, "that maybe we should revisit our schedule so that it's healthier for all three of us."

"What do you mean?" Joyce was dressed now and in better spirits.

"The time when I absolutely need your help the most is on the weekends and evenings, when I show houses. You know how it is. My schedule can change at the drop of a hat. But the after-school time slot? That would be an opportunity for Daniel to connect with other kids his age in a program."

"Those can be expensive."

"I can handle it. I've got a good understanding of my budget now, and there's more than enough for me to sign Daniel up for the after-school care at the YMCA."

"That does look like a fun place." Joyce sat down on a chair, holding an orange-yellow centerpiece. "If I had my afternoons back, I'd be able to get to the post office every day before it closed."

"That's right, and your mornings would be free for pickleball and swimming and maybe even dating. I've heard that app called Good Catch is easy to use. Maybe you would meet people there."

"Oh, I don't know if I could handle a dating app."

"No pressure. That was only a suggestion."

Joyce put the centerpiece aside. "Are you sure?"

"Yes." Noelle nodded.

"I thought when you first started talking that maybe you'd ask me to move out since I've been so messy."

"No thank you—not unless you wanted to."

"I've thought about it." Joyce bit her lip. "When Stone and I were together, I thought of what it would mean to have my own apartment again. I think someday I might like that."

"It would be hard to not have another adult around, but if that's what you wanted, I'd want it too."

"Okay, then." Joyce smiled and picked up a box. "That's a conversation for the future. I'm not ready for my own place yet. I sleep easier knowing that you and Daniel are down the hall from me." Tears glistened in her eyes again. "You two are my family."

"And that's never going to change." Noelle held her hand to her heart. "I promise."

It was lucky Noelle had called when she had because Peter had been right about to take off. He'd just barely had time to pick up Daniel and still make it to the fields in time for warm-up.

"Are you my mom's boyfriend now?" Daniel asked from the back seat of the Mercedes.

Peter glanced in the rearview mirror for a second before putting his eyes back on the road. He felt a zing of nervousness, worrying that Daniel might reject him. "Yes. I am your mom's boyfriend, but I'm also still your coach and hopefully your friend."

"Oh."

"What do you think about that?" Peter waited anxiously for Daniel's answer.

"It's okay, I guess. You have cool toys."

"Thanks," said Peter with relief.

"Mom only lets me have toys in one corner of my room. And she said I can't get an Xbox until I'm older."

"I didn't have an Xbox when I was your age either."

"Were they invented back then? Did you even have a TV?"

"Yes, I had a TV, but um . . . no, there weren't any Xboxes. My friends had a Nintendo, though."

"That's cool." Daniel rolled the window down. And then back up. And then back down again.

The change in air pressure made Peter's ears hurt, but he didn't stop him. "Did you have fun the other night with Greg and his brothers? It looked like that Nerf gun war got pretty intense."

"Yeah." Daniel rolled the window back up. "It was fun. We played Mandalorian."

"Let me guess. Milo got to be Boba Fett because he was the oldest."

"Yeah. But who's that?"

"Boba Fett or Milo?"

"Boba Fett. I know who Milo is. But they kept talking about Boba Fett and Jango Fett and the Mandalorian, and I don't know who any of those people are."

"I see. Well, I haven't seen *The Mandalorian*, but Boba Fett is from *The Empire Strikes Back*. You know—he was the armed bounty hunter who flew *Slave One*?" Peter drew his finger in the air. "It kind of looks like a T. Not very aerodynamic, if you ask me. Jango Fett was from *Attack of the Clones* and is the father of Boba Fett, even though, really, they're both clones of each other."

"Huh?"

Peter glanced in the rearview mirror again and saw Daniel scrunch up his face in confusion. "Have you not seen *Star Wars* before?"

Daniel shook his head. "No. But I know about it. Lightsabers, right? We play with pretend ones during recess."

"I see. Well, maybe we could watch it sometime if your mom thought that was okay."

"Like movie night? Greg's family has movie night."

"That's right." *Family movie night with the three of them.* Peter grinned.

"We watched a Marvel movie at Greg's house."

"Fun! Which one?"

"The one with Iron Man in it."

"Oh. Um . . . great." Iron Man was in a lot of movies. Peter would have to ask Vanessa later which one Daniel was talking about.

"It wasn't rated G," said Daniel. "Are you going to tell my mom?"

"Uh . . . I don't keep secrets from your mom."

Daniel was silent for a minute. He was so quiet that Peter could almost hear the wheels in his mind turning. Peter thought hard too. What were Marvel movies rated?

"I watched PG movies when I was in first grade," he said, wondering if Daniel felt guilty for watching something Noelle wouldn't approve of. She hadn't grown up with TV, after all.

"You did?" Daniel asked.

"I sure did. If you tell your mom about the Marvel movie, maybe that's something you could mention."

"That's a good idea. The movie we watched at Greg's house was for big kids."

Peter winced. Had Daniel watched something rated PG-13? *Great, Vanessa, just great.* How was he going to explain this to Noelle? Now he *had* to tell her.

"But Greg's mom fast-forwarded through some of it. 'All the good parts,' Milo said."

"That's something you could tell your mom too. I'll help you with that conversation when you're ready." The last thing Peter wanted to do was detonate Noelle and Vanessa's tenuous truce. "Do you ever watch movies with your mom or your Grandma Joyce?" he asked.

"Yeah, all the time. Grandma Joyce loves musicals. *Oklahoma!* is my favorite. And *My Fair Lady*, and *The Sound of Music*, and *Gypsy*. Those are good too."

"Wow. I didn't know you were so cultured." *In 1960s' Broadway.* Maybe part of his conversation with Noelle could be encouraging her to bring Daniel up to speed on shows that his friends would talk about.

"Can you ride a bike?" Daniel asked.

"I can. What about you?"

"Yeah, since I was three years old." Daniel spoke with a flash of pride. "My dad taught me."

"He was an excellent bicyclist. I remember seeing his picture in the *Skagiton Weekly Gazette* for winning a medal in a triathlon."

"I still have it. It's hanging on my wall next to his other medals."

"That's a special memory to have of your dad."

"Yup."

"Do you ride your bike very often?" Peter asked.

"No. I don't have a bike that fits. Mine's too little."

"Oh. That's a shame. Maybe we could find you a new one."

"Do you think you could? Would you ride bikes with me? My mom doesn't want to."

Danger. Danger. Danger! Peter's brain flashed a warning after it was too late. Probably Noelle didn't want Daniel riding bikes, considering Jeff died in a bicycle accident. What was he going to do now? Peter wanted to establish a positive relationship with Daniel. He couldn't shoot down such a simple idea like riding bikes together. But he also didn't want to interfere with Noelle's parenting.

"Let's talk to your mom first," he said. "If she says it's all right, then maybe the three of us could ride bicycles around the running track one day. That way we wouldn't have to deal with cars."

"That would be fun."

"It sure would be."

Somehow, the twelve-minute drive from the Walters' house to the T. Rex game had become complicated. Peter had loads of experience being a fun uncle, but being the boyfriend to a woman with a six-year-old son was something new. He didn't want to screw up. Daniel was a sweet kid and deserved stability, not someone who would abandon him if things got tough.

Not that Peter intended to abandon anyone.

He shivered, even though the car's heater blasted from the vents. He could never do what his mom had done—not to Daniel, Noelle, or anyone. One day Peter and Elaine had been planting tulip bulbs together, and the next day, she had been gone. She hadn't even put the trowel away. Her pink gardening gloves had sat there for a whole month until they had been buried by snow.

Peter pulled the car into the parking lot with only a few minutes to spare before warm-up began. The assistant coach would be pissed. "We've got to hurry," he said as he opened the door. "Can you help me carry the gear?"

"Sure, Coach." Daniel grabbed his mitt. Too late, Peter realized he was already wearing his cleats. He might need to vacuum out the floor mat before he drove clients around next week. Oh well.

"There you are," said Vanessa as they approached the ball fields. "The other parents were beginning to grumble that you would be late, but I calmed them down." She wore a T. Rex cap and a bright-green scarf.

"We're here now." Peter checked his watch. "With ninety seconds to spare." He readjusted his grip on the bag of equipment he carried. "Noelle is helping Joyce with a business emergency, so I picked up Daniel." Peter looked at Daniel. "I'll be right there, okay? Go start warming up."

"Okay. See ya soon." He ran off, dragging the net of balls behind him.

"Want me to manage your phone for you while you coach?" Vanessa held out her hand. "Noelle taught me how to track comments on Facebook ads and respond to inquiries."

"Er . . . um . . . sure." Peter took out his phone and unlocked the screen. "That would be helpful. Thanks." They were both being extra polite after their tense phone call the night before about the Facebook group. Vanessa had refused to apologize for her actions, saying that since Peter had gotten Noelle out of the deal, she had nothing to be sorry for.

"Great," said Vanessa. "I'm happy to help."

"Um . . . did you know that Noelle only lets Daniel watch G-rated movies?"

"I didn't, but I figured she'd be strict like that."

"Yeah, so why did you let Daniel watch a PG-13 movie when he was at your house?"

"What?" Vanessa looked up from Peter's phone. "I did no such thing."

"Daniel said you watched a Marvel movie with Iron Man in it."

"The Iron Man cartoon." Vanessa chuckled. "It's perfectly safe for kids. I got the DVDs from the library."

"Phew." Peter felt relief wash over him. "That's good to know. But wait a second; why did Daniel think that it was for big kids?"

"Because Common Sense Media said it was for eight-year-olds. But give me a break; they always age up everything."

"Oh." Peter didn't know what Common Sense Media was, but he trusted Vanessa's opinion on it. "What about Milo complaining that you fast-forwarded through the good parts?"

"Wow." Vanessa raised her eyebrows. "It sounds like Daniel gave you a minute-by-minute synopsis of movie night."

"He really had fun. I think he was excited to share that with me."

"It *was* fun." Vanessa rolled her eyes. "Until Waylon spilled soda all over the couch."

"The fast-forwarding?" Peter prompted.

"The trailers. I fast-forwarded through the trailers, and Milo hates that. What's this about, anyway?"

"Hey, Uncle Pete," Greg called from the field. "Are you ready?"

Pressed for time, Peter blurted out what was on his mind. "Do you think I can do this?"

"Coach Little League? Sure, you've done it for two years."

"No, be a quasi-parental figure who doesn't screw up." Peter shook his head. "I don't even know what Common Sense Media is."

"It's dumb—that's what it is. Don't worry about it. You'll be a great pseudodad to Daniel."

"But I don't know how to do that. What am I going to do, teach him to fish?"

"Yes, maybe. If you want to. And you can keep being his Little League coach and his friend. You can treat his mom real nice and model how women deserve to be treated with respect. You can show up, Peter. You're good at that. You're not a bolter like Mom."

"Have you heard from her?" Peter asked.

"No, and I don't care either. We don't deserve what she did to us. Dammit, your phone is locked up." She handed it to him.

"This is the password." He showed her how to draw her finger across the screen.

"Are you ready, Coach?" Daniel called. "We're waiting."

Peter gulped. "You really think I can do this?" he asked Vanessa one more time. "I don't have any parenting skills."

She put her hands on his shoulders and looked straight into his eyes. "Of course you can do it. You're the guy who dragged me out of bed and got me to the bus on time every day in high school. You're the one who made sure there was a roof over my head when Milo was born and Ian and I were evicted. You're the guy my sons know they can turn to no matter what. Peter, you're great father material. I believe in you." She dropped her hands and swatted him on the butt. "Now get out there and coach."

"Sounds like you should be the coach. That was a great pep talk." Peter grinned. "Thanks."

"You're welcome."

Peter picked up the equipment bag and ran as fast as he could to the field. He was five minutes late for warm-up, but at least the game didn't start for another ten minutes. "Okay, T. Rexes," he hollered. "Circle up, and get ready to play ball."

SKAGITON MOMS FACEBOOK GROUP

Deirdre DeBoer
Wednesday, March 30

Admin
The annual Skagit Valley Tulip Festival is almost upon us. Every year 98% of our guests are wonderful but the 2% who aren't make me never want to open up DeBoer Tulip Farms to the public again. It breaks my heart to see visitors tromping through the fields, ruining our soil, or stealing from us. While farmers like me are excited to welcome you into our fields, we have rules that we'd like you to follow.
1) No picking tulips
2) No walking into the rows
3) No littering
4) No pets
5) No drones
6) No parking except in designated areas
Thank you!
COMMENTS CLOSED

Chapter Twenty-Three

"Why don't we start by introducing ourselves and explaining a little bit about the beliefs and backgrounds we bring to the table as volunteer moderators for Skagiton Moms." Deirdre sat on the whitest couch Noelle had ever seen. It was so white that it made her question if Deirdre was really a farmer. How did she keep it so clean? "I'll start, but first let me pour myself a cup of tea." Deirdre picked up her china teapot and added steaming liquid to a delicate cup.

"Your china is beautiful," said Anissa Solas, a woman in her mid-forties with salt-and-pepper hair. "I've always admired it."

"Yes," said Sabrina Kruger. "My wife would love your dishes and your slipcovered couches. Are they from Pottery Barn? She wanted to buy some like that, but they were too expensive."

"Heavens no." Deirdre blushed. "These are old couches from my parents that I recovered myself. They're at least thirty years old. I run the slipcovers through the wash a couple of times a month with bleach. Marty and our dogs get dirt all over them. Normally they'd be filthy, except I just took them out of the dryer last night."

"They're beautiful." Noelle sipped her tea and admired the relaxing decor. "But I like your view even better." She looked out the window to where the tulips were blooming at their peak for the festival.

"It *is* pretty, isn't it?" Deirdre gazed out the window, holding her teacup to her lips. "Until the tourists come, that is." Grimacing, she set the cup in the saucer. "I'm done; I'm just done. I have so many things stressing me out with our business and this next stage in Marty's and my life that I'm ready to offload my responsibilities with Skagiton Moms onto more capable shoulders. That's why I invited you."

"I haven't agreed to anything yet," said Sabrina.

Me either, Noelle thought to herself. What had she gotten into?

"We're only drinking tea and having a nice chat," said Deirdre. "That's it."

"After you promised us coffee." Anissa grinned. "I'm only kidding. Ladies, Deirdre is an angel. I've known her almost my whole life."

"Thanks, hon." Deirdre smiled and let out a deep breath. "Okay, here goes. I'm Deirdre DeBoer. I've lived in Skagiton for forty-eight years. My kids went through the public school system but are now finishing college. I started Skagiton Moms by accident. I didn't know anything about Facebook at the time, and it grew overnight like mushrooms. Politically, I'm conservative, and it's been hard for me to moderate a lot of the discussion since I know that Skagiton includes many liberals too. But above all, I value being a good neighbor. I hate it when women attack each other. Ideally, I'd like to create a team of three women from diverse backgrounds to take over for me so that you can herd these cats so I don't have to."

Anissa crossed herself. "Amen."

"Sabrina, how about you go next?" Deirdre asked.

"Okay. My name is Sabrina Kruger, and my wife, Aurora Lopez, and I have lived here twelve years. She's originally from Skagiton and actually went to high school with your late husband, Noelle."

"She knew Jeff?"

"Yeah, she did," Sabrina said in a soft voice. "She went to his memorial service but was in the overflow area since it was standing room only. I stayed home with our kids since they were little. Now they're three and a half and six, but back then they were even less portable."

"And how would you describe your political and spiritual background?" Deirdre asked.

"Does this answer your question?" Sabrina rolled up her sleeve and revealed a tattoo of Ruth Bader Ginsburg. "I'm as liberal as they come, and I haven't stepped foot in a church since my youth group leader told me I was going to hell for liking girls."

"Good," said Deirdre.

"Good?" Sabrina gasped.

"No, no!" Deirdre held out her palms. "I am so sorry. That came out wrong. I meant good that you're a liberal because Skagiton Moms needs one on the admin team for balance. Especially if Anissa joins, and I hope she does because she's one of my dearest friends and I trust her completely."

As the attention turned to Anissa, Noelle's mind raced. What would she say when it came to her? She'd had no idea that her political opinions would be grilled like this.

"I'm Anissa Solas, and I've lived in the valley ever since my parents moved here from Oregon when I was twelve years old. That's when I met Deirdre."

"Picking blueberries over summer break." Deirdre nodded.

"They paid by weight, and I don't think either of us earned more than fifty bucks that whole summer," said Anissa.

"But they fed us lunch," said Deirdre.

"That's right; they did. It was good honest labor. My papi worked at the community college assisting first-generation migrant workers attending college. My mami raised four children and volunteered for the women's shelter that the Catholic Community Services runs. I went to Mass a few times a week growing up. Now, I work as a domestic violence counselor with the shelter, and my two daughters attend Catholic school."

"And you vote conservative?" Sabrina asked.

"Usually, but it depends on who's running."

"Would anyone like a snack?" Deirdre asked. "I forgot to offer."

"Thank you," said Sabrina, helping herself.

"Everything looks delicious," said Anissa.

Noelle wasn't hungry. The tension in her stomach had built up so much that the thought of eating one of the tiny cucumber sandwiches on the tea tray made her feel ill. Not even the fresh strawberries could tempt her.

"What about you, Noelle?" Deirdre asked.

Noelle took a sharp breath. "Religion and politics?" Sweat dripped down the back of her neck. "You want me to talk about that?"

"No, I mean, would you like a sandwich?"

Noelle shook her head. "No thank you."

"But speaking of religion and politics," said Sabrina. "It seems like it's your turn to share."

Noelle closed her hands into fists. "Well . . . ," she began, stalling for time. Could she do this? Speak point blank about such difficult subjects? These were conversations she ran away from, not toward. Her avoidance had annoyed the heck out of Jeff, but back then she hadn't been ready to speak. Now, she felt different.

"Yes?" Deirdre leaned in attentively.

Noelle took a deep breath before continuing. "I grew up on a dairy farm in Hollenbeck. My dad hates the government and doesn't vote because he thinks elections are rigged. My mom doesn't vote either because she agrees with whatever my dad says and also because she lives with chronic pain." Noelle took another deep breath and let it out in a rush. "Growing up, I was always afraid that the government was going to come take us."

"Take you?" Sabrina raised her eyebrows. "What do you mean?"

"I don't know exactly. Take me, my sister, and my brother away from our parents. Take our land away. Take our cows. Take my father's guns. Take our money. Something. I grew up living in the shadows of my father's paranoia."

"That's horrible," said Deirdre. "I'm so sorry you went through that."

"Yes." Anissa squeezed Noelle's hand. "That sounds traumatizing."

Tears filled Noelle's eyes, but she blinked them away. "It was," she admitted, her voice breaking. "And then, after I met Jeff, they kicked me out because they didn't like him."

"How could they not like Jeff?" Sabrina asked. "Aurora said he was wonderful."

"He was wonderful. But my dad didn't like that Jeff worked for the public schools or held opinions that my dad didn't agree with. So my parents kicked me out when I was nineteen."

"So young," Anissa murmured.

"What did you do?" Deirdre offered Noelle a tissue.

Noelle took the tissue and blotted the tears on her cheeks. "I moved into a trailer in my sister's yard. She and her husband had four kids at the time, so there wasn't room for me in their house."

"No room at all?" Anissa asked. "Not even a couch for you to sleep on?"

"They had a couch." Noelle pulled a lock of hair behind her ear. "Two, actually."

"And you couldn't sleep on that?" Anissa asked. "In my family, we'd make room."

"Hold on—maybe the trailer was the better option," said Sabrina. "So that Noelle could have privacy. Was it a nice trailer? Like a fifth wheel or something?"

The sweat dripping down Noelle's neck turned icy. It felt like crystals of frost were breaking out down her back. "Um . . . it was an older trailer," Noelle said, trying to describe it in the most complimentary way possible. "It had electricity . . . um, a lot of the time. And I used flashlights." For barely two weeks, the electricity had worked.

"What about plumbing?" Anissa asked. "Sometimes women come into the shelter who've lived in vehicles that should have been condemned."

"Well . . . uh . . . this trailer might have been condemned, except it was cheaper for my brother-in-law to just leave it in the yard and let it fall apart."

"So no plumbing, then?" Sabrina's mouth gaped.

Noelle shook her head. "I had a bucket."

"What about showers?" Deirdre asked.

"Oh, I'd shower in the house. It wasn't like Kerry—that's my sister—didn't let me in the house to shower. But she and Hank didn't want me to be a bad influence on my nieces and nephews."

"Huh?" Sabrina rolled down her sleeve. "Why would they think that?"

"I'm saying this all wrong. Kerry and her husband are good people. If they hadn't taken me in, I don't know what I would have done. Besides, I'm supposed to be talking about politics and religion. Politically, I vote different ways each time. I only started voting a few years ago after Jeff talked me into it. To me it seems like politicians on both sides of the aisle lie, so I take things on a case-by-case basis." *There.* That wasn't so hard. She'd done it—talked politics. "As for religion, the private school I went to growing up was religious, and I went to my sister's church every Wednesday and Sunday for the whole time I lived with them."

"Wait. Wait. Wait." Sabrina gripped her forehead. "You're telling me the people who made you live in a broken-down trailer and kept you away from their children because you might, quote, 'be a bad influence' were Christians?"

"They might have called themselves that, but they most certainly weren't," said Deirdre in a soft voice.

"But they were," said Noelle loyally. "I mean, they are. Kerry and her family are very active in their church."

"That doesn't mean that they showed you God's love," said Anissa.

"No, sweetheart, it doesn't," said Deirdre.

Nobody said anything until Noelle wiped her eyes, blew her nose, and finally spoke. "I don't know what I believe, and sometimes I still struggle with what to think. So I'd probably be a horrible person to have on your team."

"I disagree," said Deirdre. "I think you'd be perfect. People who think they have it all figured out a hundred percent of the time, without stopping to ask questions, make me nervous."

"On that, I agree," said Sabrina.

"Yes." Anissa nodded. "But I hope you find peace. I will say the rosary for you tonight."

"Thank you." Noelle smiled fleetingly. Boy, would that make Kerry mad. She and Hank didn't consider Catholics to be true Christians.

Sabrina cleared her throat. "I have to say—I try to stay out of all the drama on Skagiton Moms because sometimes people make me nuts. But when I hear stories like yours, Noelle, it makes me remember that not everyone grew up like I did with two cats, two cars, and two parents who love me, my wife, and my kids. It's easy to stay in my own hobbit hole and not recognize what other people are dealing with."

"I've made so many friends through Skagiton Moms over the years." Deirdre smiled. "I can't even begin to list all of them. But I don't like to comment very much either. If threads become too heated, I close down comments, or else I delete them. Nobody's going to be able to agree on everything."

"Nor should they," said Sabrina.

"That's true," said Anissa. "And I also think that women need to talk with other women. I see that at the shelter every day. We spend so much of our lives rushing from one task to the next. Everyone relies on us. Our kids. Our spouses. Our bosses. Our parents. And then there's always another load of laundry waiting in the dryer for us to fold.

Women need women. Sometimes the best thing you could do for a person is to listen."

"Or share," Noelle whispered. When the other women looked at her, she spoke louder. "I've learned so much from Skagiton Moms. Things that maybe I should have learned when I was younger and didn't, like how to be brave and speak your mind. And also stupid stuff like how to clean grass stains out of white pants and where to buy a good bra."

"The outlet mall," said Anissa. "Knockers on Heaven's Door will set you up."

Noelle nodded. "If I did volunteer to help moderate Skagiton Moms, it would be because my life wouldn't be the same today without it. I might not have even stayed in Skagiton after Jeff died," she admitted. "I might have moved back to Hollenbeck because my dad told me to."

"No!" Sabrina drew in a sharp breath.

"Oh, poor girl." Anissa squeezed her eyes shut and bowed her head.

"I think my dear friend Anissa is right." Deirdre took Anissa's hand in her left one and Noelle's in her right. "Women need women. We weren't meant to walk this earth alone. And I think Skagiton Moms needs you three ladies to help it move forward. What do you say? Will you help?"

"I may regret this later," Sabrina muttered as she picked up Anissa's and Noelle's free hands. "But I'm willing to try if you are."

"Anissa." Deirdre looked at her expectantly.

"You know I'll say yes."

"And you, Noelle?"

Noelle felt like a spotlight was flooding down on her, but instead of avoiding the harsh glare like she usually did, this time she had allowed herself to be seen. "Yes," she said with a sense of power she hadn't known was possible. "I'm in."

On her drive home from Deirdre's house, Noelle thought about the future. Later . . . sooner than later . . . she would share her story with Peter. Her past was full of secrets, but talking about them helped. She didn't need to cover up for her family's bad behavior any longer. Noelle had stayed quiet because silence had helped her cope. But she was stronger now, strong enough to speak. Peter deserved to know all of it, and maybe while she was at it, she'd also tell him that she loved him, because that was true too. Noelle was in love with Peter Marshal, and so help her, she wanted the whole world to know.

SKAGITON MOMS FACEBOOK GROUP

Noelle Walters
Saturday, April 2

Admin
FYI: Peter Marshal and I are under contract together. We've signed a consensual relationship agreement with Windswept Realty. Peter and I would like Skagiton Moms to know that he is officially off the market.

Carol Durango
It's about time. Congratulations, you two!

Melissa James
Squeal! I am so excited! You two were so cute at the potluck.

Lexie Britt
See what a brand new haircut will get you? Ha! Love you, *Noelle Walters*. Glad you

got your man! And thanks for the warning about you-know-who. He can buy his own damn lobster.

Anissa Solas
I am thrilled for you! You deserve all the happiness in the world!

Sabrina Kruger
This is excellent news! Congratulations!!!

Courtney Nettles
Aw. Peter is such a sweetheart.

Deirdre DeBoer
See, I knew you could post. What happy news!

Tracey Fukui
Something was different about you when you showed me that house. You were glowing!

Jourdaine Bloomfield
Great news.

Olivia Doyle
Blessings to you both!

Corine Reeder
Congratulations!

Jessica Luoma
Yay!

Renee Schroth
Happy for you!

Rachel Glass
Peter is such a wonderful man. I hope that the two of you will be very happy.

Katie Alexander
I love a happy ending!

Vanessa Collins
Take care of him, *Noelle Walters*. He's my baby brother.

Noelle Walters
XOXO, *Vanessa Collins*.

Chapter Twenty-Four

One Month Later

The queen-size beds at Semiahmoo Resort were top notch, but the rollaway bed wasn't nearly as comfortable. It was too short by at least ten inches. Peter slept diagonally, and yet his feet still hung off the end. He woke up on Mother's Day with a crick in his neck and his right foot asleep. Wiggling his toes, Peter grimaced as the pins-and-needles sensation crept across his arches, and his foot slowly came back to life. He looked around the dark room to see any signs of movement. Greg and Daniel were in one bed, and Waylon and Milo were in the other.

Peter slipped out of the covers. If he were quiet, he could brew a cup of coffee without the boys stirring. Tiptoeing across the carpet, he almost tripped over a pair of shoes that one of the boys had left in the middle of the room. Then, as his eyes finally adjusted to the dim light, he narrowly avoided careening over one of their duffel bags. When Vanessa had poked her head in last night, she'd said it looked like a tornado had hit them. She and Ian were staying in the room next door, and Noelle and Joyce were on the other side. Peter being the responsible adult for all four boys was his Mother's Day gift to all of them.

Peter filled the Keurig machine with water and waited for it to heat up in the tiny alcove next to the bathroom. He removed his phone from the charger and checked his messages, right as the coffee began to drip.

Message from Evergreen Furniture. Your order is delayed. Expected arrival is June 1st-June 7th. We apologize for the inconvenience. Reply STOP to opt out of these messages.

Delayed again? What were they doing, sewing his new couch by hand? Peter rubbed his jawline. Maybe . . . he had no idea how couches were constructed. The coffee and end tables had at least been ready right away, but they made the recliner look ancient.

"Uncle Peter?" Waylon tugged his sleeve. "I'm hungry. When's breakfast?"

"Hey there, buddy. I didn't know you were up." Peter picked up his coffee. "There's some fruit snacks here to tide you over until everyone else wakes up. How about that?"

"We're already up!" Greg called from the bedroom.

"No, we're not," Milo moaned. "Go back to sleep."

"Daniel's awake too." Waylon looked over his shoulder. "Aren't you, Daniel?" he hollered.

"I am," called Daniel's small voice. "I've been up for a while. Milo snores."

"Do not," said Milo.

"Do too," Peter called back.

"At least he doesn't kick," said Greg. "Daniel karate kicked my back in the middle of the night."

"Well, it sounds like everyone got a delightful night of sleep, then." Peter chugged his coffee and flipped on the lights.

"So we can go get breakfast, then?" Waylon followed him back into the bedroom.

"Sure." Peter plucked his wallet and key card off the dresser. "But we shouldn't eat too much because brunch is at eleven."

"What time is it now?" Milo asked groggily.

"Seven." Peter sat on his rollaway to tie on his shoes. "We've got two hours until we need to drive to the farm."

Waylon sat on the carpet and pulled on his shoes. "I'm starving. Hurry up, people."

"Don't we need to get dressed first?" Daniel asked.

Peter indicated his sweatpants and T-shirt. "I *am* dressed."

"And I'm wearing my favorite pajamas," Greg said as he pulled the covers off of Daniel. "Freeze out!"

"Hey!" Daniel whacked him with a pillow.

"Come on," Greg said, laughing. "Let's go get Milo."

All three boys piled on Milo's bed, thumping him with pillows and generally harassing him.

"I'm up. I'm up. I'm up," he grumbled. "But I'm not going downstairs in my pajamas. Give me a minute to change."

Fifteen minutes later they were downstairs at the small grab-and-go café in the hotel lobby, and Peter was double-checking food labels as each boy brought his selection to the register. Milo couldn't have peanuts, and Daniel had to avoid dairy. It was a good thing Peter checked because Daniel picked out a muffin made with butter. "Why don't you try the granola bar instead?" he suggested. "It has blueberries in it. This muffin would make your stomach hurt."

Daniel heaved a sigh. "But that muffin looked really good."

"It was only so-so," said Milo. "I wish I could try the granola bar."

"You do?" Daniel asked, his eyes wide.

"Yup." Milo nodded. "If it ends up being delicious, don't tell me. I don't want to know."

"It's a deal." Daniel ripped open the granola bar.

"Put it on my tab," said Peter as he handed the cashier his room key card. Catching Milo's eye, he nodded his approval, proud of his oldest nephew for being such a good role model.

Loaded down with beverages and baked goods, Peter and the boys headed out to the beach to eat breakfast. Semiahmoo was a former salmon cannery and had been built on a spit. It was so close to Canada that they could see the Peace Arch, the iconic landmark on the

American side designating the entrance to the border. The tide was out, and the rocky shoreline extended so far that everywhere Peter looked, he saw crab shells, mussels, seaweed, or the squirts of water that signaled a geoduck lived below.

"Look at the harbor seal!" Daniel pointed at the water.

"Where?" Waylon asked. "I don't see it."

"It's over there, dummy," said Greg.

"No name-calling," Peter warned. He crouched down at Waylon's level and directed his gaze to where the harbor seal basked on a floating buoy. "There. See it now?"

"Wow." Waylon stared at the seal and then looked up at Peter. "This is so cool. Thank you for taking us on this vacation."

"Yeah," said Milo. "Thank you, Uncle Peter."

Daniel surprised him by holding his hand. "I'm having so much fun." He leaned his head against Peter's side, and Peter knew then and there that every penny he'd spent that weekend had been worth it.

"Well, Greg?" Milo asked. "Aren't you going to say thank you?"

"Oh." Greg stood up, holding a half-broken crab shell. "Yeah. Thanks, Uncle Pete. You wanna eat this for breakfast?"

Peter laughed. "Thanks, but I'll pass. I'm saving myself for pancakes."

"I'll eat it." Daniel dropped Peter's hand. "I love rotting crab." He charged forward at Greg. "I'm the Semiahmoo sea monster, and I'll eat anything!"

"You won't get this one," Greg half shouted, half laughed as he ran away.

All four boys joined in on an extremely loud game of tag.

"Careful on the rocks!" Peter called. He found a driftwood log to sit on as he supervised, wishing that he'd thought to bring a second mug of coffee. He looked back up at the yellow walls of the resort, knowing that his sister was in one room and his girlfriend in another. That thought comforted him. All his family was in one place, enjoying this weekend together. When Peter looked back at the boys, Daniel waved at him, like he was checking to make sure that Peter was watching.

Peter waved back, feeling proud to be needed.

Originally when he'd fallen for Noelle, it had been only about her. How beautiful, smart, and caring she was. But now Daniel had a hold on his heart too. "Go get 'em, Daniel!" Peter called. "Use your imaginary Nerf gun!"

"Great idea!" Daniel unholstered his weapon. "Bam! Bam! Bam!"

"Ah!" Greg cried. "You got me!" He pretended to collapse on the rocks.

"It sounds like I'm entering a war zone," said Noelle as she stepped carefully over the rocks. She wore leather boots, a tight jean skirt, and a light-blue flannel shirt over her Jansen Farms T-shirt. "I brought you coffee before I take off."

"I love you," Peter said.

"I know." Noelle smiled. "You've told me that on more than one occasion."

"I was talking to the coffee this time." He reached for the mug and grinned. "But I love you, too, now that you mention it." He slipped his free arm around her and nibbled her neck. "And I love this," he said, kissing her behind her ear. "And this," he said, grazing his lips across her jawline. "And especially this," he added, kissing her on the lips.

"Don't be gross!" Greg called. "There are children present."

"They kiss all the time," said Daniel. "Deal with it."

"Yeah," Noelle whispered to Peter. "Deal with it."

"Oh, I intend to." As much as he loved that mug of coffee, he wished that both hands were free to hold her tight. "Are you excited about today?"

"Nervous is more like it." She rested her head on his shoulder. "I haven't seen most of the Dairy Ambassador crowd in years—plus there will be so many people from Hollenbeck that I haven't seen in a long time."

"And your parents," Peter added. "That's got to be stressful."

"Exactly. My dad didn't flip out in the way I thought he would when I told him about you, but that doesn't mean he's okay with it either. I hope he's come to realize that he can't control me anymore, but who knows?"

"Well, whatever happens, I hope that you enjoy today." Peter kissed her cheek. "You look beautiful, by the way. I can't wait to finally see you wearing your crown."

"Ha! There are going to be a lot of women wearing crowns today, so I'll blend in."

"All hail the Dairy Ambassadors."

Noelle checked her watch. "I have to go help set up. Daniel has a new outfit to wear that he picked out all by himself. Can you help him with the tie?"

"Will do."

"Joyce is checking out of the room for me in a few hours."

"She's still not coming today?"

Noelle shook her head. "No, but that's just as well. My dad would definitely blow a gasket if Joyce showed up."

"You don't deserve family drama like that."

"Nobody does." Noelle frowned for a second before gazing back up into his eyes. "I love you, Peter. Each day with you gets better and better."

He set down his coffee mug and wrapped both arms around her. "I love you too."

Noelle parked her car by Sam and Shayla's house. It didn't look like the same home she'd grown up in anymore. They had sided it, painted it, and added a new roof. Shayla kept a clean yard. There wasn't an ounce of trash to be seen anywhere near the porch. Instead, flowers bloomed in pots by the front door. If Peter were here, he'd be able to identify them. All Noelle knew was that they were cheerful.

She left her purse in the car since nobody would steal it and grabbed the bag that had her apron and crown. Then she headed out for the short walk to the equipment barn.

"Hey there, prodigal sister!" Sam waved as soon as he saw her. He was staking signs in the ground to direct people where to park.

"Hay is for horses, didn't you know?" She smiled as Sam enveloped her in a bear hug.

"It's good to see you, sis. Thanks for coming."

"I wouldn't miss it."

Ending the hug, Sam held her at arm's length. "Something about you looks different."

"My hair is professionally cut, and I'm wearing clothes that fit."

"Ya don't say. Well, it looks good on you. Wait until Kerry sees you in that short skirt, though; she's going to think you're going straight to hell."

"It's not that short." Noelle held down her hand. "Look, it ends below my fingertips."

"Where's your boyfriend at? I can't wait to meet him."

"Peter and Daniel will be here soon. I came early to help set up."

"Which I'm sure Shayla will appreciate."

"Are Mom and Dad here yet?"

Sam shook his head. "No, I don't imagine they'll roll in until later. Kerry's still at church. She couldn't miss one service to help out her family."

"That's Kerry for you," Noelle said before she could stop herself. "I mean, ah . . . she's devoted."

"She's a sanctimonious prig, and you can tell her I said so."

"Oh, I would never—"

"By the way, Kerry's pregnant again. You didn't hear that from me, but . . ." He held out his hand in front of his stomach. "You'll notice."

Baby number seven. Was that what Kerry wanted? Or was that what Hank and their church wanted, and she felt powerless to say no?

"I'll pretend to be surprised when I see her." Noelle looked out at the field where the cars would park. "When you see the silver Mercedes roll in, that's Peter."

"Fancy." Sam whistled. "I'll keep my eyes peeled for it."

"See you in a bit." Noelle trudged off to the equipment barn. She was impressed as soon as she walked inside. Everything possible had been cleared out, and the tables and chairs were already in position. A red-and-white-checked cloth covered each table along with hurricane lanterns and flowers at the center. At the back of the barn, a buffet was set up with silver-covered dishes and butane lighters. A stack of plates and baskets of cutlery waited for guests to arrive, and a beverage station nearby had pitchers of orange juice and water.

"Noelle!" Shayla called from the corner. Her smile made Noelle feel welcome. "You're here!"

"Ready for duty. Well, I will be once I put on my apron." Noelle removed it from her bag and tied it on. "What can I do?"

"Could you light all the battery-operated candles in the lanterns? Then, after that, you can put the syrup on the table. Two bottles per table. And then you can set out the cream and sugar, and after that I need more napkins folded and—"

"Whoa, slow down. Deep breaths. We've got plenty of time."

"The Dairy Ambassadors come in thirty minutes, and I was hoping that more would be ready by then."

"It'll be okay. Once they arrive, they'll pitch in, and everything will get done in a hurry. Okay?"

Shayla sighed, pushing her wavy brown hair back from her face. "I just want this to work. Not only for saving the barn but also to see if I can handle event planning. If we could have weddings here, that would earn a lot of money."

"It sure would, and Jansen Farms is lucky to have you." Privately, Noelle realized that she was glad it was Sam and Shayla's responsibility and not hers. "I'll get right to work."

A half an hour later, once the other volunteers arrived, the whole barn transformed into a farmhouse-chic paradise. They strung up lights and set up the informational posters Shayla had printed about the history of Jansen Farms. They put out framed pictures of Jansen farmers through the decades. There was even a "Guess the milk" table ready to go, where guests could taste test milk from cows, sheep, and goats.

"Don't forget to put on your crown," one of the ambassadors reminded Noelle. "You did remember to bring it, right?"

"I sure did," said Noelle. "I'll go get it."

She had just retrieved it from her bag when she ran into Kerry.

"Slowpoke!" Kerry held out her arms. "You're here."

"I am." Noelle hugged her sister and couldn't help noticing the baby bump between them. She raised her eyebrows and smiled but didn't say anything.

Kerry patted her stomach. "I'm pregnant. Could you tell? This little one's due in November."

"Congratulations. That's exciting."

"It is, isn't it? I'm so happy that my kids are coming from a large family. It must be so difficult for Daniel being an only child. Where is he? I can't wait to see how much he's grown."

Noelle felt the jab from Kerry's only-child remark but refused to let it bother her. "Daniel's back at the hotel with Peter and his nephews. They'll be arriving shortly."

"Oh." Kerry wrinkled her forehead. "You all stayed at a hotel, did you?"

"At Semiahmoo. It was lovely."

"Wow. That place is expensive." Kerry frowned. "You didn't share a room, did you? To save on cost?"

"No," Noelle answered, even though it was none of Kerry's business. "Peter slept in one room, and I slept in the other."

"Phew. For a moment there I thought you might be setting a *really* bad example for Daniel."

"An example of what, two grown adults who love each other making their own decisions?" Noelle felt her blood pressure rise.

"No, I mean . . ."

"What were you implying? That Peter and I would have sex in a hotel room with Daniel there?"

"Of course not! But let's be realistic, Noelle; your track record with men isn't very good."

Noelle thought about bringing up Kerry's wild days in high school but chose not to. "I don't have a track record," she said instead. "I've only ever dated Jeff and Peter."

"Exactly. Look what happened when you dated Jeff. If Hank and I hadn't saved you, you would have been out on the street. But now you've got nobody to protect you from bad decisions."

"Loving Jeff was a wonderful decision," Noelle said with an edge to her voice. "And I don't need your help because I can protect myself. When I do make bad decisions, I learn from them." She planted her crown squarely on her head. "Like for instance, I can see looking back that when I paid rent to live in your trailer, I could have reported you and Hank for being slumlords."

"What!" Kerry gasped.

"You charged me market rate for substandard living conditions."

"Hank would never break the law."

"But he did." Noelle folded her arms over her chest. "You both did. No water, no electricity?"

"How dare you speak like that to me." Kerry grabbed her stomach protectively. "Especially when I'm pregnant."

"I don't wish any harm to you or your baby." Noelle lowered her voice. "But just because I don't go to the same church as you, it doesn't mean I'm trash."

"I don't think you're trash. I think you're a fallen woman who doesn't have a righteous man in her life to guide her."

"I'm sorry that you're stuck in a belief system that demeans women."

"Women are God's vessels."

"Yes, exactly. Ribs don't birth children; vaginas do. Women carry half the world." So what if she was quoting stickers from a water bottle? It felt good to speak the truth. "Women have human rights. We deserve education, health care, and fair wages."

"Keep your voice down," Kerry hissed. "All the Dairy Ambassadors are staring."

"I don't care. I'm not ashamed to be seen—or heard—sticking up for women. You deserve birth control, Kerry. Mom deserves a doctor. Shayla deserves for her whole community to see how smart and business savvy she is for arranging this thing. I deserve to be able to speak up for myself."

"You do. You sure do," said a soft voice. It was Shayla. "Why don't we get you a cup of tea before the guests arrive?"

Noelle nodded and let Shayla lead her away.

"That was quite a show you put on back there," Shayla said as she poured Noelle a cup of tea.

"Sorry about that. And this is nice, but you're busy. I get that. You don't have time for me."

"Don't be sorry." Shayla handed Noelle the tea. "And of course I have time for you. Come on; let's go sit in the catering tent for a sec. I could use a minibreak too—I'm going to have to get in better shape to handle this level of event activity."

Shayla waved to the staff as they entered the tent and found two chairs for them to sit in.

"I didn't mean to cause a scene." Noelle's hands shook as she held her tea, and she was too wound up to drink it.

"It's okay. You said things that you've been wanting to say for years. I'm sorry, Noelle, but your family is full of nutjobs. It's a wonder Sam's as normal as he is."

"College helped, I think." Noelle's jittery hands steadied.

"Education matters. So does leaving the nest and getting the chance to explore the world. Have you traveled much?"

Noelle shook her head. "Jeff and I went on a babymoon to Mexico, but that was it."

"Well, that's something, isn't it? Kerry's never left the state."

Was that true? Had Kerry been stuck in Washington her whole life? Noelle had never stopped to think about that. "It sounds like you know more about Kerry than I do."

"That's because I'm stuck seeing her all the time. I'm going to tell you the same thing I tell Sam. We can love people and have compassion for them without letting their crazy notions ruin our lives. Right?" Shayla held her hands up like they were a wall. "Boundaries. You deserve boundaries. The next time Kerry or Anika or Phil try to get into it with you, say: 'I'm not talking about this with you. Gotta go. Bye.' That's it. Boom. Conversation over."

"If only it were that simple."

"It *is* that simple. Boundaries. You're allowed to have them."

"Shayla!" a woman called from a giant griddle. "Can you take this batch out to the warming tray?"

"Sounds like you have to go," said Noelle. "Thanks for the advice."

"Thanks for coming today. You and Daniel are the only two in-laws I can stand." Shayla rushed off to help with the food.

Boundaries. Could she do that? Maybe . . .

Noelle removed her crown and polished it on her skirt. Then she put it back on, centering it so the largest rhinestone would be perfect, and walked back toward the barn.

Chapter Twenty-Five

"Hope you don't mind getting that shiny car of yours dirty in my pasture slash parking lot." A barrel-chested man wearing a Jansen Farms trucker hat stood by the gate. "You must be Peter," he said.

"Uncle Sam!" Daniel darted over to hug his uncle.

"Nice to meet you, Sam. I've heard a lot about you." Peter held out his hand to shake.

"I could say the same." Sam shook his hand with gusto.

"My sister's coming too," said Peter. "Vanessa was two minutes behind me."

"Well, thank you all for coming. It means a lot to me; my wife, Shayla; and our girls that you'd show up. Noelle too. She told me she was blown away to discover you'd sponsored a whole table."

"Where's my mom?" Daniel asked.

"Over there in the barn. You all can go in there and find your tables. Brunch starts soon."

"Sounds good to me." Peter started walking forward and felt Daniel's hand slip into his own a few seconds later.

"I need to warn you," Daniel said, speaking quietly. "My grandpa's mean. If he asks you to shovel compost, say you're busy and can't do it. Otherwise he'll make you work for him all day and then curse about how you can't shovel fast enough."

"That sounds horrible." Peter stopped walking and looked down at Daniel. "Did that happen to you?"

The small boy nodded. "In February, when Grandpa Phil brought down a load for our garden. It was raining, too, and I got a sinus infection right after."

"I remember how you kept getting sick before you realized you couldn't drink milk."

"That was right about then." Daniel repositioned his grip on Peter's hand, holding on tight. "I don't want to do farmwork today; I'm wearing my new outfit."

"And you look really spiffy too. I love the tie."

"Thanks." Daniel sighed. "I guess we have to go in there, huh?"

"We do, and it'll probably be lots of fun. Greg's coming, remember? Vanessa's family will be here any minute."

"And I'm sitting with you, not my cousins?"

"That's right. You're with me."

"Good. Aunt Shayla and Uncle Sam are all right, but the last time I visited with them, Aunt Kerry and Uncle Hank's kids were there too. They spent the whole time arguing about which was better, Christian radio or country radio, and I didn't know what to say."

"It sounds like you might have been out of your element for that conversation."

"What does that mean?"

"You didn't know enough about it to participate."

"But I *did* participate. When they asked me what type of music I listened to at home, I said showstoppers and smooth jazz because that's what Grandma Joyce always plays." He dug the toe of his shoe into the dirt. "That didn't go over so well."

"You can listen to whatever type of music you want to, even if it's Norwegian death metal."

"Ooh. That sounds scary. I'm going to tell them that the next time they ask."

"Okay, but then we'll have to ask Siri to play some on the drive home so it's the truth and not a lie."

"Aren't I riding with my mom?"

"Not if you're listening to Norwegian death metal."

"Good. I wanted to ride with you anyways."

"Why's that?" Peter asked, happy but curious.

"Because the windows in the back seat of our van don't roll down."

"Oh."

Daniel leaned his head against Peter. "And also because you're cool."

"That's the highest praise I'll probably ever get." Peter squeezed Daniel's hand. "The only thing that could make this day better is pancakes," he said, his heart full. "Are you ready?"

Daniel nodded, and together they walked into the barn and found their table. Vanessa's family arrived a few minutes later, and then the party really got started. All four boys sat in a row, blowing bubbles into their orange juice; Ian quietly drank coffee; and Vanessa told Peter all about her massage and facial the day before.

"It was so relaxing," she said, smiling peacefully. "I didn't get a chance to thank you at dinner last night, but this has been the best Mother's Day ever."

"I'm glad," said Peter. "You deserve it."

"Did you tell him your other news?" Ian asked.

"What's that?"

Vanessa clasped her hands together and leaned forward. "I've signed up for an online business course at the community college. I'm not sure what I'll do with it yet, but I'm going to start with my AA degree."

"That's awesome," said Peter. Nothing could stop his sister when she put her mind to something. "I've always been proud of you, but this is another reason why."

"Thanks." Vanessa settled back in her chair. "It was Noelle who gave me the idea. She brought over a course catalog and helped me look through it to figure out what I might want to do."

"Joyce did something similar for her. That's how Noelle ended up at Windswept."

"Joyce is a real good one. I like her a lot. How's she doing these days?"

"Great," said Peter. "Daniel started after-school care last week, Mondays through Wednesdays at the YMCA, and Noelle said that Joyce isn't as stressed now that she has more time to focus on her Etsy shop."

"Good." Vanessa nodded. "I like Joyce, and I think it's sweet how much you care about her too."

"Love is a package deal." Ian leaned back in his chair. "Otherwise there wouldn't be a sixth chair at my dinner table with Peter's name on it."

Vanessa swatted him gently on the shoulder. "We never see Peter at all anymore. Stop making me sad."

"You see me all the time," said Peter.

"Not like we used to." Vanessa's shoulders sagged for a moment before she sat up straight. "But that's okay. It's nice to finally have left-overs again."

"Is that my grandson I see?" called a scratchy voice.

"Oh boy." Daniel let go of his straw and stared at the popping bubbles in his orange juice.

Peter looked up and saw a wiry man wearing dusty jeans and an old flannel. Phil Jansen's skin hung along the jowl line, and his teeth were slightly yellow. Beside him stood his wife.

"Hi, Daniel," Anika said shyly. Her shin-length skirt hung shape-lessly, and she wore a white ruffled turtleneck underneath her sweater.

"Hi, Grandma." Daniel didn't move.

"Don't just sit there, boy. Give your grandma a hug," Phil commanded.

Peter leaped to his feet. "Why don't I say hello first. Peter Marshal. It's a pleasure to meet you, sir." Peter grabbed Phil's hand with a vise grip and shook. "And you, ma'am," Peter said, turning to Anika. "You are absolutely lovely, just like your daughter." He was gentler when he shook Anika's hand, but his eye contact was as strong as ever.

"So you're the boyfriend, eh?" Phil scowled. "Shows up wearing a polo shirt and khakis like he's never done a hard day's labor in his life."

"Whoa," said Vanessa. "That's not true."

"My husband is not a horse, missy," said Anika. "Don't *whoa* him."

"Okay, everyone. Let's take a step back," said Peter. *How has this gone so wrong so fast?*

"I will not take a step back." Phil glared. "Not until you stop interfering between me and my grandson. I told Daniel to give his grandmother a hug, and he hasn't done that yet."

"Daniel doesn't have to hug anyone he doesn't want to." Peter shifted his body weight to the right, shielding Daniel.

"It's okay, Peter. I'll do it." Daniel's chair scraped across the floor. He approached Anika solemnly. "Hello, Grandma." Holding out his arms, he gave her a quick hug.

"Hello to you too." She kissed him on the forehead. "My, how you've grown."

"What are you supposed to be dressed as, an IRS agent?" Phil pointed to Daniel's outfit. "Who wears a tie to a barn?"

"Oh, Phil, give the boy a break," said Anika. "Lots of people dress up for brunch. Shayla probably told them to. You know how she wants to turn this farm into a wedding factory."

"Which is a horrible idea," said Phil. "But nobody listens to me anymore."

"I wonder why not?" Vanessa asked.

Peter made scissors fingers at her to cut out her sarcasm, but it was too late.

"I'll tell you why not." Phil hitched up his jeans. "Because that know-it-all daughter-in-law of mine thinks she's smarter than everyone."

"It's true." Anika nodded. "My own son doesn't wear the pants in his family."

"Shayla tells him what to do." Phil shook his head in disgust.

"That must be difficult seeing your business pass to the hands of a different generation." Peter spoke in a neutral tone, still trying to smooth things over. He didn't want to make Noelle's relationship with her parents more difficult than it already was. "How do you like retirement?"

"He hates it," said Anika. "All he does is watch the news."

"Woman, I can speak for myself."

"Sorry, dear." Anika pressed the wrinkles on her skirt.

Phil stood ramrod straight and lifted his chin. "Since you ask, I am enjoying retirement. I subscribe to several periodicals, which I enjoy reading, and as my wife mentioned, I keep up on current events."

"That must be a nice transition for you after so many years of hard work," Peter said, relieved that the conversation was improving.

"It most certainly was," said Phil. "A man such as yourself wouldn't understand hard work."

"That's not true," said Vanessa. "Peter is an incredibly hard worker."

"Pushing papers around cannot be compared to farmwork," said Phil. "I'm talking about labor—hard physical labor."

"Peter's done that too." Vanessa picked up her coffee mug and flashed a chilly smile.

"I find that hard to believe. The man's wearing a polo shirt, for crying out loud." Phil looked at Peter. "What's she talking about?"

"Alaska." Peter squared his shoulders. *Here we go.* "I spent six summers working at a cannery near Bristol Bay." He pointed his thumb at Vanessa. "So did my sister. Sixteen-hour days sorting fish guts in plastic overalls, filleting with deadly knives, cutting patch to fit pieces into the top of the cans, working with the beach crew to offload boats with big vacuum hoses. Seven days a week and zero breaks in a town with one church and eight bars. Don't lecture us about hard work because we already know."

"Mom, did you do all that?" Greg asked, his eyes wide. "For real?"

"I sure did." Vanessa nodded. "I used the money to buy my first car and pay for my apartment in town."

"Well, Peter," said Phil. "Maybe you're not the idiot I thought you were." He turned to look at Ian. "And what do you do?"

"I work for the United States Postal Service."

That was when all hell broke loose.

◆ ◆ ◆

"Noelle!" someone called. "Come quick. Your dad's started a fight."

"What?" Noelle was just leaving the catering tent from her chat with Shayla. "Oh no!" She ran full throttle into the barn. There, in the corner of the room, she saw arms and legs flying. At first she couldn't tell what was going on. Peter held Vanessa by the back of her shirt, pulling her off of Phil, but not before Vanessa got a one-two punch into Phil's stomach.

"Don't you ever touch my husband again, you bastard," Vanessa hollered.

"Ian's okay now," Peter said. "Let's calm down."

Noelle glanced quickly at Ian and saw blood gushing out of his nose.

"He's not okay," Vanessa shouted. "That monster broke his damn nose."

"Bloodsucking government agent!" Phil groaned. "Get off my land!" He stumbled to his feet and lurched toward Ian. "I'll drag you out of this barn myself if I have to."

"Okay, then." Peter jumped between them. "There'll be no more of that, Mr. Jansen. My brother-in-law is not a violent man, and neither am I."

"I knew you were a pansy." Phil slipped his hand around Peter, grabbed a mug, and hurled it at Ian, narrowly missing his head.

"Dad!" Noelle shrieked. "Stop it!"

"Sam!" Shayla called. "Where are you?"

Noelle ran to the table. "Dad, why don't you go outside and calm down?"

"Great idea," said Shayla.

"*I* should go outside?" Phil whirled around to face Noelle, his eyes shooting fire. "This is my barn."

"No, it's not!" Shayla widened her stance. "It's my barn now."

"That's right," said Noelle. "And these are my guests."

"My guests too," said Shayla. "We've got a bunch more people arriving any minute now to raise money for property you let fall into disrepair."

"You bitch!" Phil spit at Shayla, and the spittle landed on Noelle's face too.

"Oh, hell no." Vanessa pulled back her elbow and punched Phil straight in the face. She knocked him so hard that he toppled back into the table, grabbing the cloth to try to break his fall. The hurricane lantern, the fake candles, and all the orange juice glasses fell down with him.

"Phil, darling!" Anika gingerly knelt down next to him. "Are you okay?" She felt his pulse. "He's out cold."

Vanessa shook out her hand. "Sorry, Noelle. You can take the girl off the cannery line, but . . ."

"Don't be sorry," said Shayla. "I've been wanting to do that since I met him."

Peter picked two napkins off the ground and gave them to Noelle. "We'll go," he said. "I'm sorry."

Adrenaline had rendered her speechless. Words wouldn't come. But then she found them. "Don't go." Noelle wiped her father's spit off her face. "And don't apologize." She looked at Vanessa. "Thank you for defending me."

"Technically I was defending Ian and her." Vanessa indicated Shayla. "I'm sorry; I didn't catch your name. I'm assuming it's not *bitch*."

"No," said Shayla. "It's Shayla, and I like you."

Just then Sam showed up. "Holy smokes. What happened here? I was walking Kerry to her car."

"It's about time you got here." Shayla put her hands on her hips. "Would you drag your dad out of here and check if he needs an ambulance or something?"

"Okay," said Sam. "But there's a huge line. We need to open this place up and get breakfast going."

Noelle sensed a pool of eyes behind them. Turning around, she saw a chorus of Dairy Ambassadors wondering what the heck they had gotten into. "Sorry for the drama," she called. "You just got an insider's view of why we need help restoring our old barn to begin with." She pointed to her father. "This one cheated on his taxes, made enemies at the co-op, refused to follow USDA regulations, and lost Jansen Farms a whole lot of money until my brother, Sam, and his brilliant wife, Shayla, took over. Now, if you could all put on your best Dairy Ambassador smiles and greet our guests while I get this table reset, I'd really appreciate it."

"You got it, Noelle!" said one of the youngest ambassadors.

"We've got a barn to save," called a woman from the back. "Let's do this!"

"I'm so glad we went with matching jean skirts," said another as they walked toward the door. "We all look so cute."

"Mom, are you okay?" Noelle crouched down next to Anika. Sam bent down, too, to pick up Phil and carry him outside. "That must have been hard to see." Noelle rested her hand lightly on her mother's shoulder.

"Don't touch me." Anika shrugged it off. "You always were a troublemaker."

"That's not true. I was an obedient child who fell in love with a good man." She thought of Peter and corrected herself. "Two good men."

Anika grimaced in pain as she struggled to her feet. Noelle heard her mother's knees pop and crack. "Have you been to the doctor yet?" she asked. "Kerry said she gave you the name and number of hers."

"I don't need a doctor. There's nothing wrong with me that oil of oregano can't fix."

"That's not true." Noelle stood up. "You're in pain. I can see that. Maybe if you weren't hurting all the time, then—"

"Don't pretend like you care. You haven't cared since the day you signed yourself over to the government."

"Mom."

"I need to be with my husband now. Goodbye."

Heart shattering, Noelle stood in place and watched Anika go.

"We don't have to stay," Peter whispered, putting his hand on her back. "We can go anytime you want."

"Maybe that would be for the best." Noelle felt jittery. "I don't know."

"Well, I know," said Vanessa. "This family's not going anywhere, and that includes you, Noelle. I saw how you ordered the Dairy Queens around. This is your big moment. You earned this, and I won't let that bastard steal it from you. Ian, get a napkin on that nose; you're bleeding all over the place. Milo and Greg, I want you to collect all the dishes and bring them to the back of the barn where dirty dishes go and then come back with new ones. Waylon, pick up that glass candleholder, and put it back in the center of the table."

"What should I do?" Daniel asked.

Vanessa's eyes softened. "You, my dapperly dressed friend, should give your mom a hug because I think you both have earned a good one."

"I can do that." Daniel rushed over and wrapped his arms around Noelle's waist. Peter held her on the other side. Supported between the both of them, she steadied her breathing and watched Vanessa get the table back in shape. Once new dishes covered the orange juice marks, nobody could tell that the tablecloth was stained.

The barn filled with the sound of happy people. Noelle wanted to be one of them. Then she realized that she *was* one of them. She was Noelle Walters, and she had everything she could need or wish for. She was a respected member of her community. Her voice carried weight. If Jeff were here, Noelle knew he'd be proud of the woman she'd become, the woman he'd always believed she could be.

"You look so pretty, Mom," said Daniel. "I love your crown."

Noelle looked down at her son. "Thanks. I do too."

SKAGITON MOMS FACEBOOK GROUP

Vanessa Collins
Saturday, October 22

In case you didn't notice, there's a new face on the Windswept Realty advertisement on the bus stop in front of the library. Congratulations to my soon-to-be sister-in-law, *Noelle Walters*!

Sabrina Kruger
Wait, what? You and Peter are getting married, *Noelle Walters*?

Corine Reeder
Congratulations, *Noelle Walters*! You and Peter are perfect for each other!

Anissa Solas
Have you set a date yet, *Noelle Walters*?

Jourdaine Bloomfield
This is wonderful news. Truly, *Noelle Walters.*

Tracey Fukui
I am not surprised by either bit of good news. Noelle did such a great job for my husband and I when she was our agent, and I've always thought she and Peter were perfect for each other. Congratulations, my friend, *Noelle Walters*!

Noelle Walters
Um . . . thanks for the shout-out about the bus stop ad, *Vanessa Collins.* But I don't know what you mean about me being your future sister-in-law.

Vanessa Collins
You told him no? Why the hell would you do that, *Noelle Walters*?

Noelle Walters
I didn't tell him no, *Vanessa Collins.* Peter hasn't asked me to marry him.

Vanessa Collins
Ooops. My bad. Yet . . . he hasn't asked you to marry him yet, *Noelle Walters.* I've seen the ring and it's GORGEOUS!

Epilogue

Friday, December 30

Skagiton United Methodist Church was packed. Noelle hadn't originally wanted a big wedding, but when she had seen how excited Peter was at the idea, she'd reconsidered. Then, when Daniel had discovered he could wear a tuxedo, that had cinched it; they'd booked the church. Vanessa had helped organize the guest list, and Joyce had created all the custom flower arrangements for the reception tables. Now, Noelle stood next to Peter at the altar, wearing a cream-colored dress and high heels. Daniel stood beside Peter, serving as his best man, and Joyce was Noelle's matron of honor.

Pastor Olivia held her hands up in a benediction. "Noelle and Peter, may your life be blessed with laughter, joy, hope, forgiveness, and honesty. May you go forth—with your son, Daniel—and embrace all the love that your family deserves." She lowered her hands. "It is my great pleasure to say the words that all of us have been waiting to hear: Peter and Noelle, you are husband and wife. Peter, you may kiss your bride."

Noelle caught her breath as Peter dipped her back into a Hollywood kiss. Laughing, she held on tight as he swooped her back up and faced the sanctuary. Friends and family cheered. The organist began playing "I Cross My Heart," by George Strait. It sounded strange on the organ, but since it had been Peter's request, Noelle thought it was perfect.

They'd walked only two steps up the aisle when Noelle realized it was going to be a long walk.

"Can you believe it?" Peter paused to talk with Carol, the first well-wisher they passed. "She actually married me!"

"I'm as stunned as you are," she replied. "Kidding! Come in here, you two." The diner owner tackled them in a bear hug that tugged Noelle's hairdo.

"Welcome to the family!" Sam exclaimed, hugging them next.

"I loved every bit of that ceremony," said Shayla. "What the pastor said about husbands and wives needing to be a team unit is spot on." Her daughters stood next to her in leggings and flowery tops.

"Pastor Olivia did a good job," Noelle agreed. "Are you all packed for the cruise?"

"We sure are," said Shayla. "Can't wait."

Noelle and Peter inched forward.

"You. Are. Gorgeous!" said Zara. "And might I say that your yoga arms look great in that dress."

"I agree with my sister on this one," said Jourdaine. "You don't look so bad yourself there, Peter—for a little brother."

"Hey!" Peter protested. "Little brothers have feelings too."

"Noelle, I am just thrilled for you," said Helen. "I've known Peter a long time, and I'm so happy to see him settled down with someone who loves him."

"Thank you," said Noelle. "I sure do love him a whole bunch."

"Where's your mom?" Helen asked. "I was hoping to meet her."

"Mom!" Jourdaine elbowed her. "What are you doing? Don't bring up a sensitive topic on their wedding day."

Noelle's smile faded ever so slightly. "I invited my mom, but she chose not to come since my dad wasn't included on the invitation."

"Her loss," said Carol, butting into the conversation.

"That's right," said Zara. "Her loss."

"It's okay," said Noelle. "Joyce is here." She looked over her shoulder and saw Joyce in animated conversation with Pastor Olivia, Deirdre, and Marty.

"My dad and his wife couldn't make it either," said Peter. "Their flight from Juneau got canceled due to a snowstorm, but they should be here tomorrow."

"Won't you be on your cruise by then?" Zara asked.

"Thankfully, no," said Noelle. "We leave on New Year's Day."

"I didn't know you were going on a cruise," said Helen.

"A Disney Cruise," said Peter. "We're bringing the whole family." He took a few steps forward and stopped when Rick held out his hand to shake.

"Have you given any more thought to teaming up to be a husband-and-wife real estate team?" Rick asked.

"Thanks for the suggestion," said Noelle. "But I'm happy with my focus on first-time home buyers and families in transition."

"And I'm happy to keep cashing her checks because she's so good at what she does," said Peter. "My wife is the number one real estate agent in Skagiton, after all."

Hearing Peter say that was a double thrill. First for being his wife and second for her booming business. "I've only been the top seller for one quarter," she said modestly. "Because of that new condominium building that's being built."

"And your face looks mighty good on that bus stop advertisement," said Rick. "People tell me that all the time. No offense to you, Peter. But a pretty face like Noelle's reels customers in."

"She's more than a pretty face," Peter shot back.

"Come on." Noelle pulled him forward. "We have more people to greet."

"Coming through!" Daniel called, zipping up the aisle in his tuxedo. Greg, Milo, and Waylon chased behind him.

"Boys, if you don't slow down, there will be no cake for you!" Vanessa picked up the hem of her bridesmaid gown and chased after them. "Sorry," she said as she hustled past Noelle and Peter.

"Yup, that Disney Cruise you all are going on promises to be loads of fun." Melissa laughed, standing next to the mayor.

Ryan chuckled too. "I hope you two have your own room."

"We sure do," said Peter. "We booked a cabin for Vanessa, Ian, and the boys; a cabin for Noelle's brother; one for Joyce; and one for my father and stepmom."

"That sounds expensive," said Melissa.

Peter shrugged. "We had a very good year."

"I'm not surprised," said Melissa. "You two work really hard."

"Thanks," said Noelle. "Hopefully the boys will float around the grandma and grandpa cabins to give Ian and Vanessa a break."

"They just can't come to *our* cabin." Peter slipped his hand around Noelle's waist. "It is our honeymoon, after all."

Noelle steered Peter forward to the next set of guests.

Former clients, neighbors, Little League families, friends from Peter's school days, and people Noelle had met at the YMCA mobbed them—greeting people was a joyful endeavor. Noelle was touched that so many of Jeff's friends had come too. Her heart was so full of joy that it was on the edge of bursting. It wasn't until she reached the end of the sanctuary that her joy mixed with flutters of anxiety. Kerry, Hank, and all seven of their kids sat in the end pew. Kerry wore a long, shapeless maternity shift that covered her latest baby bump, and the children wore stiff-looking suits and dresses.

"You came," said Noelle, unable to conceal her surprise. She hadn't spoken to Kerry since their Mother's Day argument in the barn. Noelle had sent Kerry a giant case of diapers when her baby had been born but hadn't heard anything beyond what Kerry had chosen to share on Facebook. "I wasn't sure you'd be here."

"I'll go take the kids outside," said Hank, a thin man with a stringy frame. Noelle noticed with a start just how much he resembled her own father. Kerry really was turning into their mother. "Congratulations on your nuptials." He nodded at Peter, without shaking hands, and led six of the kids away.

Kerry clasped the newborn to her chest. "Of course I'd come to see you wed."

"Thank you." Noelle held on to Peter's arm. "This is my husband, Peter Marshal." It was odd saying *Peter* and not *Jeff.* Noelle felt a pang in her chest, but she pushed it away, knowing Jeff would want this for her. He'd want it for Daniel and Joyce too.

"I'm glad to finally meet you," Kerry said, just as the baby started fussing. "Oh boy. Looks like this one wants to eat again."

"He's beautiful." Noelle gazed lovingly at her new nephew. "Congratulations to you too."

"Thank you." Kerry yawned. "Sorry. I didn't get much sleep last night." She stuck her finger in the baby's mouth, and it settled, suckling on the end of her fingertip. "I've been talking to Mom about going to the doctor. I wanted you to know that. I'm working on her."

"That's good," said Noelle. "Keep at it. She won't listen to me."

"I know; she told me. I'm all she has left. Dad's so crazy that he's cut off all of her friends."

"That's really sad," said Peter. "I'm sorry."

"I'm sorry too," Noelle said instinctively.

"You should be," said Kerry. "Mom needs you. You should call her every day like I do. Come up to visit on the weekends. Help out in the garden. She can barely bend down to plant seeds anymore, she's in so much pain."

"Maybe it's time for her to let her garden go and buy produce at the grocery store." Noelle glanced to her left, where the photographer was waiting to take more pictures. "Or maybe they could hire someone to help in their yard. Or maybe Mom could visit the doctor and deal with her health problems once and for all."

"You know they won't do that." Kerry frowned. "Besides, even if she would be willing, I'm not sure they'd have the money. Don't tell them I told you, but Dad owes forty-five thousand to the IRS. He asked Hank for a loan, but we didn't have the money to lend them."

"That's too bad," said Noelle.

"How much did that Disney Cruise cost that you booked for Sam's family and yourself? Shayla won't stop bragging about it."

"A lot," Noelle admitted, starting to feel guilty.

"But it was money well spent." Peter kissed the top of her hair.

"Is it? Because it sounds like a waste of money to me," said Kerry. "Especially when your parents are hurting. But then, you always did what you wanted without considering Mom and Dad."

Noelle blotted out the inky guilt she'd felt moments before. She refused to let Kerry or her parents ruin her wedding day. What was that Shayla had told her about boundaries? She'd given her something to say the next time she was drawn in. "Kerry," Noelle said in a firm voice. "I'm not talking about this with you. Gotta go. Bye."

"What?" Kerry's baby spit out her finger and fussed.

"I *said* I'm not talking about this with you. Not now, not ever. Bye." Noelle charged out the door into the vestibule, bringing Peter with her. Her heart beat like the wings of a startled dove.

"You were awesome," Peter said as they paused beside a table with a Wood You Be Mine? masterpiece. "Truly amazing. I am so proud to be married to you, Noelle Walters."

Tears misted her eyes. The confrontation with Kerry had rattled her more than she wanted to admit. "Thank you. And thank you also for understanding why I wanted to keep my name."

The name Jeff had given her. The name that was printed on her hard-won social security card, delayed certificate of birth, and driver's license. The name that was on her new marriage license too. Noelle looked down at the framed picture of Jeff that was displayed beside Joyce's flowers.

Peter brought both her hands up to his lips and kissed her fingertips. "Did I ever tell you how much I love your legs?"

"What?" Noelle laughed, her stress easing. "What are you talking about?"

"This." He ran his hands down the sides of her body, swooping over her curves, until they landed firmly on her hips. Then he took her hand and twirled her around to face all the crowd of onlookers spilling into the vestibule. "I'd like to announce," he called, "that I am the luckiest man in the entire world because Noelle Walters married me."

"And it was all thanks to your sister!" Vanessa hollered. "You are welcome."

Noelle's laughter turned to giggles as she looked up at Peter. "*And* thanks to Skagiton Moms."

Peter touched his forehead to hers. "And Skagiton Moms," he agreed with a groan.

A smile curled across Noelle's face. "Let's give those Facebook posters something to talk about," she said, tipping her head back. Peter pressed his lips to hers, and her heart filled all the way up, but it didn't burst. There was always room for more love.

SKAGITON MOMS FACEBOOK GROUP

Dorothy Caulfield
Saturday, December 31

Did you see that kiss at the Marshal-Walters wedding? Talk about a display! I saw someone post the video on Instagram.

Corine Reeder
I don't think Common Sense Media would approve that video for all viewers, LOL. Way to go! *Noelle Walters*, I'm happy for you!

Jourdaine Bloomfield
That kiss was hotter than hot yoga, which by the way, they are now teaching at the YMCA after that sleazy teacher was fired.

Alastrina Kelly
Hey, that teacher was my dad. He's not sleazy!

Lexie Britt
Your dad with the condoms, *Alastrina Kelly*? How's that going, by the way?

Maggie Swan
It's going well, *Lexie Britt*. Extremely well.

Carmen Swan
Mom! *Maggie Swan*, barf!

Sabrina Kruger
Admin here, coming in to say that my wife teaches the hot yoga class at the YMCA and I can vouch that it's . . . hot. Also, I'm turning off comments. Enjoy your honeymoon, *Noelle Walters*!

COMMENTS TURNED OFF.

ACKNOWLEDGMENTS

Years ago, I attended a fundraiser in a church basement and had the privilege of hearing women speak about what motherhood was like in my neighborhood fifty years ago. Back then, stopping by a friend's house for a cup of coffee after the kids left for school was common. That never happens now, in large part because women have career opportunities they didn't have in the 1900s. Another factor is that most moms don't have time to clean their homes to a standard where they'd feel comfortable with a surprise visit. But the camaraderie between women is still present; it's just moved online. I know because I've served as a volunteer administrator for my local moms' group for years.

In addition to being a moderator, I'm the woman who asks weird questions whenever I come to a sticky plot point in a book I'm writing. Over the years, the collective wisdom of local moms has helped me slay vampires, burn down a house, rescue a Sasquatch, steal money from an estranged spouse, and now can salmon. The next time you think scrolling through Facebook is a waste of time, remember that!

Speaking of salmon canneries, thank you to Dawn-Rene Becker, Alison Burke, Janet Determan, Heather Damron, Sharon Excell-Schierle, Kristin Gard, Amy Lyndon, and Erin Way for your input about what Peter and Vanessa would have experienced working in Alaska.

Thank you to Kia Alexander, Cindy Featherstone, Elaine Helm, Katherine Kidwell, Kristine Mantz, Erin Ones, Karissa Richards, and most especially Cymmie Knutsen for what you've taught me about community building.

A huge, massive thank-you goes to real estate agents Sarah Reece and Abby Rowe. They read an early draft of *Talk of the Town* in its entirety and provided valuable feedback. Any mistakes I made describing Noelle's and Peter's work are mine.

One of my best friends from high school, Jennifer Parmenter, beta read the entire book. I value her input as a reader, working mother, and person of faith.

Authors Eden Appiah-Kubi, Maan Gabriel, and Preslaysa Williams critiqued the first half of this book and helped cheer me on to completion. I am grateful for their contributions.

Journalist Gale Fiege came up with the cocktail names for the drinks served at the Western Cedar. Cheers to Tulip Tonics and Snow Geese Gimlets!

Author Julie Reece—grandmother, horsewoman, and devoted wife—surprised me by instantly brainstorming half a dozen naughty drinks that the Lumberjane Shack might serve. Her suggestions had me in stitches.

My friend Kassie Goforth helped me understand how a Catholic woman might offer support to a fellow Catholic who was grieving the loss of her mother. I appreciate the sensitivity Kassie offered.

Pacific Little League volunteer Rhienn Davis helped me figure out what would be a reasonable practice and game schedule for the T. Rexes. Thank you, Rhienn!

Authors Sara Goodman Confino, Elissa Grossell Dickey, Paulette Kennedy, Kate Myles, and Mansi Shah have championed me through the entire process of writing the book. I can't remember who came up with the name Knockers on Heaven's Door, but that brainstorm session was hilarious.

A few years ago, I won a year's supply of milk and butter from Darigold at a Girl Scouts auction. I've been reading their social media posts ever since because they are so informative. I also had the privilege of interviewing Erica the "Farmer Girl," who is a third-generation dairy farmer for my newspaper column. If you are interested in learning more about the Washington State dairy industry, you can follow them at @ darigoldNW and @erica.d.429 on Instagram.

Skagiton is a fictional place, but the Skagit Valley Tulip Festival is real. There is no Carol's Diner, but you can eat the best breakfast of your life at the Calico Cupboard Café and Bakery in Mount Vernon or La Conner. Thank you to Skagit Valley farmers, who grow over ninety crops, including flower bulbs and berries. I am grateful for all you do.

A huge debt of gratitude goes to my agent, Liza Fleissig, and my dream team at Montlake. Thank you to Alison Dasho for believing in me, to Krista Stroever for making my book better, and to copyeditor Mindi Machart and proofreader Megan Westberg for polishing every word.

My family—Doug, Bryce, and Brenna—was extremely patient with me while I wrote this book. At one point I packed up and moved to a hotel for two nights to finish it. Driving home, I remember thinking how lucky I was to have a husband who cooks me breakfast, a son who makes me laugh, and a daughter who loves to read.

Finally, thank you to you, my readers. I wouldn't be here without you. If you'd like to join my private readers' group, you can find "Jennifer Bardsley's Book Sneakers" on Facebook. It's not nearly as dramatic as Skagiton Moms, but it is a fun place to hang out.

ABOUT THE AUTHOR

Photo © 2021 Rachel Breakey

Jennifer Bardsley believes in friendship, true love, and the everlasting power of books. A graduate of Stanford University, she lives in Edmonds, Washington, with her husband and two children. Bardsley's column, I Brake for Moms, has appeared in the *Everett Herald* every week since 2012. She also writes young adult paranormal romance under the pen name Louise Cypress. When Bardsley is not writing books or camping with her Girl Scout troop, you can find her walking from her house to the beach every chance she gets.

To find out more, visit www.jenniferbardsley.com or join her Facebook reader group, Jennifer Bardsley's Book Sneakers.

Made in the USA
Middletown, DE
17 April 2023

28982999R00229